VIRGINIA

Hearts

VIRGINIA
Hearts

*Three Modern Couples Find Love
Along Unexpected Avenues*

TAMELA HANCOCK MURRAY

BARBOUR
PUBLISHING

Published by Barbour Publishing, Inc., P.O. Box 719, Uhrichsville, Ohio 44683, www.barbourbooks.com

Our mission is to publish and distribute inspirational products offering exceptional value and biblical encouragement to the masses.

Member of the
Evangelical Christian
Publishers Association

Printed in the United States of America.
5 4 3

Dear Reader,

Thank you for choosing to spend time with the stories in *Virginia Hearts*. I am a native of Virginia, and the state is indeed close to my heart.

My family has lived in Virginia for many generations. I grew up in a close-knit, God-fearing family in the Piedmont region of Southern Virginia. I graduated from Lynchburg College with honors in journalism.

Now my home is in Northern Virginia with my wonderful husband of over twenty years and two lovely daughters. The elder attends Lynchburg College and is the fifth generation of my family to do so. Our younger daughter hopes to matriculate there as well.

Daddy says I'm a Yankee since I live north of the James River. As far as I'm concerned, I'm still a Virginian, even though life so close to Washington, D.C., moves at a faster pace than the speed my relatives in the country enjoy.

When you read these stories, I hope Virginia will come alive for you. In noting scenery, I recall times of enjoying the smell of falling leaves, the sight of crystalline blue skies, and the warmth of Virginia sunshine. When a restaurant is mentioned, sometimes I have dined there myself. Perhaps you might try some of these places when you visit Virginia. If you haven't already traveled to my native state, I hope you will some day. In the meantime, sit back with a cup of coffee or herbal tea and enjoy your make-believe visit as you read *Virginia Hearts*.

May God bless you and the ones that are near to your heart!

Cordially in Christ,
Tamela

The Elusive Mr. Perfect

To my wonderful family and many friends in Virginia.
Y'all will always be close to my heart.

Chapter 1

An exhilarating night with the swinging singles—all six of us." Joelle Jamison's feet, clad in athletic shoes, dragged through the graveled area that served as the church parking lot. The time was 9:30, and the group had already broken up for the night.

Reaching to toss her hair over her shoulder in her favorite expression of disdain, Joelle was reminded she had recently traded her long mane for chin-length locks. Her straight blond hair had been mussed for an uncombed look. Contrary to its freewheeling appearance, though, the style was cemented with hair wax and a coat of ultimate-hold spray. After a week with the new do, she already entertained fantasies of growing it out into a controlled bob.

"Six people isn't so bad. At least we had an even number." Dean grinned, flashing straight, even teeth. Joelle couldn't help remembering four years of braces for him, and two for her. Both could thank Dr. Hart for their brilliant smiles.

Joelle smiled without exposing the orthodontist's handiwork. "Oh, I'm sure you and Zach were happy to be outnumbered by us women."

Dean arched an auburn eyebrow. "Sure gave us an advantage in the sports category of that trivia game."

"As if that were the only advantage," Joelle quipped.

He chuckled as he held open the passenger door of the silver hand-me-down family sedan for Joelle. "The balance at our meeting reminds me of that old Beach Boys song—'Two Girls for Every Boy.' Sounds ideal to me." He chuckled.

"You had the advantage this week, but we might have more women next week, and you'll be overwhelmed."

"I doubt it," Dean answered. "We're lucky even six people showed up."

"Really? You've got to be kidding!" Joelle wriggled into the blue seat. She felt pampered by Dean's gesture of opening the door, even though she didn't expect him to act the gentleman around her. Joelle had been best friends with Dean Nichols since they shared a bag of chocolate chip cookies the first day of preschool. Instead of acting as though he'd known her all his life, he remained gallant, as though he were still trying to impress her.

"I'm not kidding. There are usually only five of us, and I get the feeling Zach didn't mind you as an addition to our happy little group." With a muscular arm, Dean slammed the door shut. The old hinge objected with a creak. Joelle imagined herself a sardine, shut in a tin can for good. . .only instead of basking in mustard sauce or olive oil, she was enveloped in a musty odor emitted by moisture trapped in the cloth seats, typical of aged cars that had never been garaged.

Joelle waited until he jumped behind the wheel before she responded. "Zach and me? You've got to be kidding." She grimaced. "He's nice, but all he talks is sports. Just not my type. Anyway, didn't you see how Ashlynn was flirting with him?"

"Yeah," he admitted. "She brushed up on football all winter, and now she's trying to learn the ins and outs of baseball. Pun intended." Dean's lips curled into a smile of satisfaction as he pulled out of the lot.

"Oh, you're so brilliant." Joelle's tone indicated she didn't wish to be interpreted literally. "As much fun as I had, even you have to admit the group could use a few more people."

"You didn't really expect fifty singles when our church only has a hundred members, did you? It's not like we live in New York City."

She picked up on his disparaging tone. "You mean Gotham?"

"Some people call it that. And for good reason, I'm sure." Dean let down his window. "I'll take our little community anytime over hordes of people trying to beat each other in the rat race."

Following Dean's lead, Joelle pressed the button to lower her window. The spring day had turned into a cool night. The outdoors smelled of new blossoms and freshly cut grass.

"You won't get that kind of atmosphere in any city."

Joelle inhaled deeply. "True. Living in the mountains does have its merits, even if a large gene pool isn't one of them." She studied his profile, noting his familiar pointed nose. "Don't you get tired of the same people, week after week after week?"

"I never seem to get tired of you."

"But it's different with friends," she protested.

"Is it?" Dean wondered. Joelle was contemplating his point when he continued. "Who needs a lot of crazy people, when you can only marry one person?"

"One at any given time, anyway." Joelle kept her expression serious, just to see how Dean would react.

"If I didn't know you better. . ." Taking one hand off the wheel for a moment, Dean wagged his index finger at her in mock derision.

She couldn't hold back a rollicking laugh. Joelle could make light of such notions now. Before she responded to Pastor Brown's invitation to accept Jesus Christ as her personal Savior six months ago, she might have been a wee bit serious.

Jokes about Gotham aside, Joelle knew firsthand that one didn't have to live in a big city to find trouble.

"Speaking of crazy people, has that jerk ever stopped calling you?" Dean wanted to know.

"By 'that jerk,' do you mean Dustin?"

"Unless you have more than one jerk in your life."

"Thankfully not." She chuckled. "But I haven't seen Dustin lately."

"Good. You let me know if he bothers you again."

"You're so cute in your knight's shining armor, Sir Dean."

"How true. And don't you forget it."

Dean pulled into Mary's, an eatery the locals had affectionately dubbed "The Greasy Spoon." Mary's provided rickety cane chairs, kitchen noises that could be heard by every customer, and paneled walls covered with watercolor pictures bearing price tags, courtesy of a local artist. Out of habit more than interest, Joelle picked up two free copies of *Today's Southwest Virginian Christian Singles* from a rack at the entrance. Since the dinner rush was past, they quickly found seats. She handed Dean his paper as soon as they ordered a round of banana cream pie and coffee.

Dean glanced at the front-page headline. "Looks like the walk-a-thon was a success."

Joelle nodded. "It says here they raised almost two thousand dollars for the hospice." Her interest satisfied, she flipped through the circular, passing advertisements for religious bookstores and businesses owned and operated by Christians. Announcements of church-sponsored concerts and seminars were plentiful. She pointed to an ad. "Here's a seminar on Managing Finances According to Godly Principles." She looked up at her companion. "Maybe they can tell you how to save for that new car you've been wanting."

"New car? They'd probably tell me to keep old Vicky." Dean contradicted his words by leaning over to take a closer look at the page Joelle held open.

"I don't know. Looks like they have a lot of experts scheduled. May be worthwhile." She glanced into his hazel eyes. "What do you think?"

"I think I'll start practicing godly principles by staying home instead of wasting fuel driving to Raleigh."

"Suit yourself." She shrugged before flipping to the back of the paper. The word *Personals* jumped out at her. "When did they start carrying personal ads?"

Dean took a swig of coffee. "Who knows? I never saw them before. Then again, I wasn't looking." He picked up his copy and located the ads. "Listen to this: 'Wanted, Single Female, for days of hiking in the mountains, walks in the rain, and nights of gourmet meals accompanied by the strains of Mozart and Bach.'"

"What's so bad about that?"

"I'm just wondering who'll be cooking the gourmet meals."

"You've got a point."

Dean scanned the page and teased, "I found the ad you placed, Joelle. 'Beautiful single female with excellent build, variety of hobbies, interested in exploring her walk of faith. Looking for a godly man ready for a true commitment.'"

"Thanks for the compliment, but with such high demands, that ad seems to be courting disappointment." She scanned the page. "This one must be yours: 'Handsome single male with outstanding physique, ready for any challenge.

Godly, unafraid of commitment, light on baggage.' "

"You caught me." Picking up a white paper napkin, Dean waved it in surrender.

Joelle chuckled.

Dean balled up his napkin and tossed it on his dessert plate. "Just for the sake of argument, let's say that was my ad. Question is, if I'm so wonderful, then why do I need to advertise?"

"Because you only see five other unmarried people every week, and one of them is a guy? Like, duh!" She rolled her eyes. "Seriously, some of these singles don't seem so pitiful. A few might even be fun. Maybe answering one or two of these ads wouldn't be such a bad idea."

Dean placed his coffee cup on the table with a firm motion and leaned toward her. "Please say you're joking. You've got to know these people are losers. They're making up half of what they say, and the other half isn't true. It's a dangerous world out there."

"I know. But everyone in here is a Christian, right?"

"Or so they say," he answered.

"They're screened, right?"

Returning his attention to the paper, Dean studied the headings. "I don't see anything about that. All I see is a disclaimer saying the paper takes no responsibility for any contacts made."

"They've got to say that to keep out of court. There's always somebody ready to file a lawsuit in hopes of making a fast buck."

"Then don't take a chance by responding to these ads. Take my word for it, Joelle. You'll regret it."

Unwilling to argue further, Joelle shrugged. Dean might be her best friend, but he wasn't going to tell her what to do. Rolling up the paper, she slipped it into her denim shoulder bag. As soon as she got home, Joelle planned to comb the entries and select her next date.

Chapter 2

Two Saturdays later, Joelle waited for Prince Charming to arrive.

"What time is Lloyd supposed to get here?" her mother asked.

"Seven."

Eleanor Jamison looked toward the surrealistic clock on the kitchen wall. The words "Does It Matter?" and scrambled numbers decorated its face. "It's only six-thirty and you're set to go already? This guy must be something special. Is he from your singles' group at church?"

Joelle shook her head. "He lives two counties away."

"Oh." Eleanor's voice rose with inflection, but she continued wiping the breakfast nook table clean.

Joelle was relieved her mother's curiosity was satisfied. Since her job as a doctor's bookkeeper and billing clerk allowed Joelle to meet people from around the region, the explanation seemed logical. Joelle knew if a relationship developed, she could always give her mother more details about how she and Lloyd Newby really met. Later. Much later.

Joelle rose from the couch. "Can I help you with anything?"

Eleanor's gaze swept over her daughter. "I wouldn't think of asking you to do housework when you've got on such a nice outfit. Besides, I'm caught up. All I need to do is study."

Eleanor's schoolwork had been woven into the Jamisons' family life for the past couple of months. Joelle was proud that her mother was being tutored for her GED test. "Do you need me to call out questions or anything while I wait?"

"Nope. It's math. I'm just going to review some problems to make sure I understand them."

"I don't see how you do it, Mom. Working full time, then studying for your GED."

"It's not easy, but it's something I have to do. Just for myself. Besides, I'll earn my diploma soon enough." She let out a sigh. "I had no business dropping out of school to marry your father. Your grandparents tried to talk us out of it, but we were too much in love. Besides, I hated school and wanted to work."

"And then Benjamin came along and ruined your career." Joelle chuckled as she thought about her boisterous brother.

"Believe me, I was glad to exchange assembly line work for mounds of diapers. I was too naïve to realize how easy school was in comparison to working

13

every day of the week. Two years of sorting buttons at the factory was about all I could take."

"Harder than sorting out all the fights among the five of us, huh?"

Smiling, Eleanor shook her head. "I won't go that far, but I'm just glad none of you kids followed my poor example, at least as far as your education goes. You were smart to graduate from high school, and now you're smart to wait for marriage, Joelle." Eleanor took a seat at the table and flipped open her book. "Although, since you've seen your twenty-ninth birthday, I just hope you're not being too smart for your own good."

"I doubt I'll ever be that smart." Joelle tried not to flinch. Her mother's words hit too close to home.

Eleanor didn't seem to notice Joelle's discomfort. "Not that anything in life is easy, mind you. Back then, if not for the Lord's mercy, I wouldn't have made it. He sure must have been looking after me."

"I think He was. And He still is."

Joelle picked up the day's newspaper. Her eyes refused to focus on the print. Instead, she imagined what Lloyd Newby must be like in person. He had seemed nice enough on the telephone when he called to set up the date. He said he attended church almost every Sunday and was a Christian. Even so, if a relationship developed, she dreaded the day she'd have to admit she met Lloyd through a personal ad. The fact it appeared in a Christian paper would have comforted her parents about as much as it had Dean—which wasn't much at all.

Joelle's thoughts wandered to her best friend. When she had turned down his invitation to tonight's singles' meeting at church, Dean guessed the reason. Though he didn't express outright opposition, the crestfallen expression on his face revealed his disappointment so much, she almost relented. But she didn't. And now she fought pangs of guilt.

Dean knows I can see him anytime. He should understand.

Confident in that knowledge, Joelle put Dean out of her mind. Stealing a glance at her mother, Joelle could see the older woman was absorbed in her work. She sneaked the clipped ad out of her purse and studied it:

> *A rare combination in one package: charming, cosmopolitan, and Christian! Open-minded, handsome bachelor, 25, seeks fun-loving Christian bachelorette, 22–32. My favorite things are candlelight dinners, moonlit walks, and travel to exotic locales. Want to see London? Rome? Paris? Then I'm the man for you. Ooo—la la!*

He's perfect! Joelle felt a triumphant smile touch her lips. *Handsome, Christian, and with promises of travel, he must be rich, too. How could Dean possibly object? If anything, he should be happy for me.*

As if on cue, the unobjectionable Lloyd Newby rang the bell. Joelle heard her father's voice. He must have just returned from feeding the small herd of beef cattle that supplemented his income as a teacher. Joseph Jamison was speaking to Lloyd in a kind yet no-nonsense manner. Taking the opportunity to rush to the bathroom, Joelle indulged in one last check of her appearance.

Joelle always chose to avoid cosmetics. Her clear complexion and blushing pink lips required no enhancement. The only vanity she allowed herself was a pair of aqua-colored contact lenses to conceal light brown eyes she judged to be blah. Once the contacts were in place, the bolt of blue-green on her irises was so astounding that the artifice was evident even to the casual observer. Nevertheless, the lenses made Joelle feel beautiful enough to conquer any situation.

Lloyd hadn't told Joelle about his plans for the evening but to trust him that she would enjoy herself. Joelle knew her crisp white blouse, shaped by princess seams, and a slim pair of black pants with matching flats would take her in style to the restaurant and to most other places he might suggest. Classic pearl stud earrings and one strand of small pearls hanging an inch below the hollow of her throat added warm luster.

When she was convinced her father had had enough time to visit with Lloyd, Joelle set her shoulders back and strode into the living room for her entrance.

"Joelle?" A look of relief crossed Lloyd's face.

A quick glance at her father's furrowed brow revealed he wondered why Lloyd didn't recognize her. Joelle made a point of focusing on her date. She flashed him a smile. "That's me." Lloyd looked much as he promised during their one brief phone conversation—a tall blond his friends described as good-looking. "Dad and you are getting acquainted, I see."

"Sure are," Joseph chuckled, extending his hand to his daughter's date. "It was nice to meet you, Lloyd."

"You too, sir."

Cutting her glance to the den's entrance, Joelle noticed her mother peering into the room. Eleanor's reassuring smile comforted Joelle.

The door had barely shut behind the couple when Lloyd inquired, "Does your father interrogate everyone who comes to see you, or does he have something against me because of the way we met?"

Joelle felt her heart leap in fear. "You didn't tell him about that, did you?"

"About my ad? Of course not." His eyebrows shot up. "You mean to say, he doesn't already know?"

She shook her head with force, though not enough to disturb her waxed curls.

"In that case, I feel sorry for every guy that crosses your threshold." His lips twisted. "I wasn't expecting to meet parents. Aren't you a little old to still be living at home?"

She bristled. "I don't think so." Already on the defensive, she wasn't about to share her life story with Lloyd. Joelle made no further comment as she watched Lloyd stride to his side of his new car, a model she didn't recognize, without opening the door for her.

Dean would have opened the door for me.

Forcing the unwelcome thought from her mind, Joelle slid into the passenger seat, wondering what to say next. She needn't have worried.

"I must say, you look quite lovely. Even better than you described yourself."

His compliment caused Joelle to soften her stance. "I'm glad I didn't disappoint."

"You didn't. Trust me on that. But I had hoped you would appear in something a little more dressy, a little more upscale."

"Oh?" Joelle noticed he was wearing a black turtleneck under a blazer even though the warm spring weather hardly required a coat. A twinge of embarrassment turned to irritation, though she tried to keep her voice sweet. "Why didn't you say something? I would have changed."

He shrugged. "Never mind. I'm sure they'll let us in."

Before she could retort, he began chattering away about travel. Through a series of monologues, Lloyd relived every vacation he'd ever taken, down to the last detail. He expressed his sense of adventure in his plans to travel to Fiji, Australia, and Borneo. His enthusiasm lasted through the fifty-mile drive to Roanoke. Though she was used to more give-and-take in conversation, Joelle had to admit that hearing him talk about places she'd never been was riveting.

As Lloyd handed his car keys to the valet, he told her he had ordered Chateaubriand when he made the reservations. He explained, "The dish, filet mignon beef with béarnaise sauce, is usually shared by two people. Since the filet is large, the restaurant requires patrons to order Chateaubriand ahead to allow extra preparation time."

Joelle couldn't help but be impressed. Obviously, Lloyd was accustomed to eating well.

They were seated at an intimate table set with a linen tablecloth, gold-trimmed china, fine silverware, and several etched glasses. Large chandeliers hung from the ceiling. Each light bulb was covered by a small lampshade. Joelle had forgotten the month of May was prom season. High school students, dressed in colorful gowns and tuxedos, occupied several tables. Joelle wished she hadn't chosen to wear her black pants, dressy though they were.

Lloyd no longer seemed to mind how she was dressed. He relished taking charge, even placing her order along with his, from the first course to the last. Joelle thought perhaps she should object to Lloyd's presumptuousness. She was debating whether or not to speak up when she realized his willingness to tend to such details left her feeling relaxed.

Until the first course.

Six tiny phyllo dough pastries were placed before her. She guessed the filling inside wasn't chocolate.

Lloyd placed his napkin in his lap. "The escargot is especially good here."

"Escargot?" Joelle tried to remember the meaning of the French word. "You mean, snails?"

"Of course. The chef makes his own phyllo dough." He lifted his fork and used it to point to the pastries. "And see how moist it looks? That's butter. And, of course, it's seasoned with garlic."

Joelle tried not to grimace.

"What's the matter? You don't like escargot?" Furrowed brows signaled his disappointment.

"To tell you the truth, I've never tried it before."

"If you want to travel around the world, you'd better get used to sampling foods you don't normally eat."

"I suppose you have a point." With her fork, she prodded through several layers of thin pastry that reminded her of onionskin paper. Though the dough proved scrumptious, Joelle wasn't as pleased with the warm, chewy morsel inside.

"What do you think?"

She swallowed. "Not much taste. It's the same consistency as fried clams, only a little less rubbery."

"Fried clams? I'd expect to find that on a diner menu." He cringed as though she had confessed a penchant for feasting on dodo bird feathers while sitting in a pigsty. He pointed the tines of his fork at his plate. Placed decoratively upon it were thin slices of smoked salmon, trout, and pieces of pheasant on a few leaves of lettuce, sprinkled with capers and a dash of caviar. "Would you like to trade with me?"

Regarding her snails once more, Joelle knew she'd have trouble indulging in even a second pastry. She studied his plate of untouched food. "I'm not too sure about the pheasant." The bird looked like tuna showered with small peas.

He flashed an amused smile. "I'll take that, and you can have the fish."

"Sounds like a good deal. As long as you don't mind."

"Of course not. Escargot should be eaten by one who appreciates it."

Joelle was thankful the rest of the meal wasn't so daring. A house salad was followed by carrot soup seasoned with ginger, then the Chateaubriand. A smooth chocolate soufflé topped off the meal. Afterward, Joelle felt as though she had just dined at the table of King Louis XIV.

"I've never eaten so much yet not felt stuffed," Joelle observed as she placed her napkin beside her dessert plate. "The meal was excellent, Lloyd."

"Good." A self-satisfied smile flashed over his face as he handed his credit card to the waiter. "There will be more of the same with me, *mon cherie*."

Wanting the experience to last a few moments longer, Joelle savored each drop of rich coffee left in her cup. She had just finished the last sumptuous sip when the waiter returned to the table and mumbled something to Lloyd as he returned the card.

Lloyd crooked one eyebrow. "I can't believe it." As the waiter watched, Lloyd withdrew his wallet and fumbled through several credit cards before handing him a platinum-colored plate. "I'm so sorry. Try this one."

Joelle was grateful another waiter offered her more coffee, giving her a reason simply to nod rather than to speak.

"I do apologize to you, Joelle. How embarrassing."

"Oh, banks make mistakes all the time." Joelle hoped her assurances were more convincing to her date than they were to herself.

She had almost finished her second cup of coffee when the waiter returned, his lips tightened into a severe line. Joelle knew he would tell Lloyd the second card had failed to clear. She caught the words "credit limit exceeded" from their whispered discussion.

"I assure you, I am shocked and appalled." Lloyd's slack-jawed expression and shrill tone of voice matched his professed indignation. "We shall settle this. If you will give us a few moments, please."

Sending them a curt nod, the waiter left his side. Joelle noticed he kept a close watch on their table as he went about his other duties.

"Joelle, again, I apologize. I have no idea why both of my platinum cards were rejected."

She recalled a similar incident with her own cards, so Joelle wasn't about to judge Lloyd. "It can happen to the best of us."

A half-grin crossed his face. "Thank you for being so understanding. Let me assure you, those banks will be hearing from me first thing Monday morning." Folding his arms across his expanded chest, Lloyd nodded once for emphasis.

"So what do we do now?"

Releasing his arms, Lloyd clenched his teeth and raised his eyebrows. "You wouldn't happen to have any cash on you, would you?"

Joelle remembered she had tucked an extra twenty-dollar bill in her purse in case of an emergency. "Like, how much?"

He reviewed the bill. "It's one hundred, fifty-eight dollars and eighty cents."

She felt her jaw drop open in shock. "Come again?"

"I said, one hundred, fifty-eight dollars and eighty cents." His eyes met hers. "And, of course, a 20 percent tip is expected at a place like this. Always."

She wasn't able to contain her shock, though she was careful to keep her voice barely above a whisper. "How could two people have possibly racked up such a bill?"

Lloyd laid the receipt on the center of the table so she could see for herself:

1 Escargot	$ 9.95
1 Smoked Fish	$10.95
2 Soup	$13.90
2 Salad	$13.90
1 Chateaubriand	$90.00
1 Chocolate Soufflé	$10.95
1 Raspberry Soufflé	$10.95
2 Coffee	$ 5.90
Total	$166.50

Joelle swallowed. "And that doesn't even include tax."

"Thirty-five dollars should be a sufficient tip," he suggested. "Why don't we make it two hundred and ten dollars?"

"Why not make it two hundred and twenty-five dollars?" Joelle couldn't keep the sarcasm out of her tone.

"Look, I said I'm sorry. It's not like I forced you to eat here, you know—"

"Oh, yeah?"

Lloyd leaned closer. "Are you saying you didn't enjoy your meal?"

"No, but—"

"Besides, I'll pay you back. I promise." Lloyd let his spine touch his chair and folded his arms across his chest.

Reaching into her black satin purse, Joelle was thankful she was conservative enough that her own card wasn't maxed out. "I guess I have no other choice, unless I want to wash dishes."

"I said I'd pay you back." Lloyd didn't bother to hide his irritation. He extracted a black leather billfold from his pocket and handed her a twenty-dollar bill. "See? We haven't even left the restaurant yet, and I'm already paying the first installment."

His willingness to pay even that much made Joelle wish to give him the benefit of the doubt. "All right. Thanks."

The ride home was hardly as chatty as the trip to the restaurant had been. Joelle tried to keep the atmosphere pleasant. She forced herself to concentrate on Matthew 5:42: *"Give to him that asketh thee, and from him that would borrow of thee turn not thou away."*

The verse was still rolling in her brain when the car coasted to a stop. Reacting quickly, Lloyd managed to steer it onto the side of the road.

"What happened?"

"I'm not sure." He turned the ignition, but the engine didn't even turn over. Lloyd stared at the gauges. "Uh-oh. I must have run out of gas."

"Run out of gas?" Joelle felt a mixture of irritation and fear.

"I guess I wasn't paying attention. Sorry," he answered as though he really didn't mean the apology. "Do you know how far the next gas station is?"

"It should be a mile or two from here."

"Hope you enjoy walking." Lloyd pulled the door lever to let himself out.

"Do I have a choice?"

"Sure. You can stay here by yourself."

"No, thanks." Joelle looked down at her flat shoes and couldn't resist a dig. "Looks like I was right to dress casually after all."

As they walked in silence, Joelle thought about how the spring night, lit by a full moon, would have been enjoyed much more had she been with the right person. . .whomever that was.

Mr. Wrong broke the silence. "Um, I hate to impose on you further, but— well, would you mind all that much if I asked you for my twenty dollars back?"

"You've got to be kidding." Joelle hadn't meant to be uncharitable, but at the moment, her shock was greater than her tact. "Look, I'm sorry. Of course you can have the money."

He jerked the bill from her grasp. "Thanks."

More of Jesus' words struck her mind. *"And if any man will sue thee at the law, and take away thy coat, let him have thy cloak also. And whosoever shall compel thee to go a mile, go with him twain."*

"You're welcome," Joelle managed as the glare of headlamps lit their backs. Turning, she recognized Dean's car.

Oh, no! I can't let Dean see me like this! Bowing her head, Joelle stared at the ground just ahead of her feet. Maybe Dean wouldn't recognize her and would drive past.

Instead, the car slowed down and pulled over just ahead of them.

Lloyd halted in his tracks and grabbed Joelle's elbow, clutching it in a viselike grip. "I don't like this. Whoever's in that car could be some maniac, and we're easy prey."

"That's no maniac. That's my best friend."

Chapter 3

Dean squinted as his car approached a couple walking along the edge of the mountain road. He'd spotted an automobile abandoned about a half-mile back and wondered about its owners. They had to be strangers. Nobody he knew possessed such an exotic import. Dean figured the couple and the car belonged together.

Stopping for strangers on the roadside wasn't his habit, but the night sky threatened rain, and there was little chance they'd be able to walk to the next gas station before getting drenched. Dean knew he'd want someone to do him a similar kindness should he ever become stranded.

Slowing to a stop, Dean recognized the woman's lithe figure. His heart did a funny flip-flop. "Is that you, Joelle?"

The sweet voice he could have distinguished from thousands of others answered. "It's me." Joelle bowed her head and stared at the ground.

Her companion wasn't so shy, boring a hole into Dean with his eyes. Dean's lips tightened when he realized the tall, blond man was Joelle's reason for cutting out of Singles' Night. Meeting the stare of his competition, Dean didn't note anything special. Since his fancy car broke down, maybe Joelle wouldn't, either. He forced himself to smile as he exited his car.

After making introductions, Joelle took her place beside Dean. Lloyd, lips curled downward in a pout, plopped himself in the backseat.

"Did your car break down?" Dean asked.

"Of course not," Lloyd snapped. "It's just out of gas."

The solution was obvious to Dean. Ever since his fuel gauge became stuck on the halfway mark a couple of years ago, he had made a habit of keeping a can of gas in his trunk. "Not a problem. I've got a gallon—" He interrupted himself when he saw Joelle shaking her head in short, quick motions.

Lloyd's face brightened. "You've got some here in the car? Great!"

"That's okay, Dean," Joelle said. "Lloyd can pay for his own gas."

"I don't mind."

"He said he doesn't mind," Lloyd agreed.

Dean wondered why Joelle didn't want him to help her date out of the bind. Whatever her reasons, her protests were too late. Dean had made the offer, and he wasn't about to back down. After depositing the fuel into Lloyd's car, Dean made sure the car started before bidding them both good-bye. Lloyd didn't offer to pay, and Dean didn't ask. He didn't mind. It was the least he could do for Joelle.

As Dean pulled away, Joelle waved. To his satisfaction, she looked miserable.

As the following Monday, Dean was on his way home when his cell phone rang. He let out a sigh. *What else can go wrong today?*

He had already repaired two washing machines in one of the three Laundromats he owned. Counting today, that would make three repairs in the past month. He'd have to replace at least one machine soon, and two dryers were threatening to expire.

Despite the hassles, Dean was proud of the business he called his own. He had sunk every cent into buying the Laundromats when Mr. Chaney retired. Even then, the older man had given him a price break because he knew Dean well.

Dean had prayed about the purchase. He knew being an entrepreneur offered independence but carried a stiff price in responsibility. When Dean felt the Lord's leading to go forward with the purchase, he vowed to honor Him by being a good steward. One way was to offer his customers dependable machines. That meant not keeping those that were sputtering to a slow, lingering death, no matter how tempting the urge—or the need—to save money might be.

Dean made sure his facilities were clean. He was thankful his sister, Mandy, didn't mind the job. The small salary from Dean gave her a sense of freedom and his brother-in-law a couple of evenings a week to spend time with their two boys.

As he answered the phone, Dean expected to hear Mandy's voice, telling him about something gone awry at the site she was cleaning. If disaster was in the making, that would mean a round trip of eighty miles added to the end of an exhausting day. "Wash 'n Wear," he murmured, trying not to sound too depressed.

"Hi, Dean."

"Joelle!" His sigh of relief was audible. "Am I glad it's you."

She giggled. "You were expecting Mandy."

"How well you know." Dean remembered he was supposed to be mad at Joelle for dumping him on Singles' Night to go off with that snob she met through the personals, of all places. "I saw yesterday in church you got home all right from your date."

"I want to talk to you about that." Joelle's voice was a combination of mockery and teasing. "I tried to catch up with you after Sunday school, but you were off faster than I could shake a stick."

"An emergency at one of the stores. Water gushing all over the place." Dean cringed at the memory.

"Sorry. Well, at least it's fixed now." She paused a moment. "I want to thank you properly for stopping for Lloyd and me. How about dinner at Mary's tonight? My treat. Have you got time?"

Of course I have time for you, he wanted to say. Instead, he answered, "I think so."

"Good. Besides, isn't getting together what friends do?"

Friends. He had grown to hate that word. Sometimes Dean wondered if Joelle's lack of romantic feelings toward him was his own fault. After all, he hadn't said anything to lead Joelle to believe he loved her as more than a friend. He wanted to. Badly. But he couldn't. She was so vulnerable right now.

Dean had been at church with Joelle six months ago when she responded to the call to accept Christ as her personal Savior. Otherwise, he might not have believed it. Joelle had seemed perfectly content with her life. The youngest of five, she lived comfortably with her parents and never mentioned any desire to leave—except for once, a few years ago. After only a few months on her own, she returned, older and wiser.

And certainly now she was richer. He remembered the day Joelle pulled into his driveway in her new sports car. He'd been astounded that she had paid cash for it. As a child, Joelle had enjoyed few luxuries. When she became a young adult, Joelle developed a habit of splurging whenever she had money, and sometimes when she didn't. Pride in material possessions kept her on top of the world for awhile. But as debts piled high and her new possessions aged, Dean could see Joelle develop a longing for something deeper. She'd gone to school and grown responsible. She'd even told him about her yearning to meet a man she could settle down with, someone who wasn't afraid to commit.

Under other circumstances, Dean would have made it clear she'd already met that man. Only at that point, Joelle hadn't made the decision to accept the Lord. She was comfortable keeping Christ in the background, a benign figure who loved her and who would always be there.

Jesus was much more to Dean. He never made an important decision without consulting the Lord. That kind of prayer life wasn't something Joelle practiced. Even now, she would need time to develop a full relationship with the Savior. Dean didn't want to interfere with that.

He remembered 2 Corinthians 6:14: *"Be ye not unequally yoked together with unbelievers: for what fellowship hath righteousness with unrighteousness? and what communion hath light with darkness?"*

No way would he spend his life unequally yoked. Not even for Joelle.

But then she made the decision.

Joelle's voice brought him back to the present. "How about tonight?"

"Tonight?"

She must have noticed he seemed distracted. "If that's not good—"

"No, that's fine." He glanced at the clock on the dashboard. "I can be at your house at seven."

After they hung up, Dean found himself whistling a tuneless melody. The reason Joelle wanted to see him didn't matter. What mattered was, she wanted to be with him.

❧

"So what I want you to do, Dean, is help me find someone else."

Dean nearly dropped his cup of coffee. "Say what?"

"You heard me. I want you to help me find someone else."

He looked straight into her eyes. The teal contact lenses were a perfect match for the soft turquoise sweater she wore. After experimenting with hair flipped upward, on this day Joelle had styled her golden locks in a sleek fashion. He liked the effect. In fact, Dean was sure he was the only man who could appreciate Joelle. Why would she waste her time with anyone else? He didn't bother to hide his irritation. "After what you told me about that lousy date? Surely you can't mean you want to try again, Joelle."

"So?" She shrugged.

Dean snapped his fingers in front of her nose. "Joelle, time to wake up."

She laughed. "I'm perfectly awake, thank you."

"In that case, what planet are you from, and what did you do with Joelle?"

A chuckle was her only answer.

Dean shook his head. "Joelle, I know how much you value your money. It's not like you to throw away hundreds of dollars with such a cavalier attitude."

"But I've accepted Christ now. Like you always tell me, all earthly things belong to Him. Anyway, in the scheme of things, it was probably a good investment," she said. "I learned more about myself and what's really important."

"True," he admitted.

"Besides, Lloyd said he'd pay me back."

"Sort of like he paid you that first twenty dollars, huh?"

Joelle flinched. "Maybe he was just having a bad night. We'll see."

"Yes, we will. I'll tell you one thing. If I were a betting man, I'd gamble he won't pay you back. You'll never see him again." Dean took a sip of coffee. "Wonder how many other women he's taken advantage of like that?"

"Who knows? All I know is, I learned my lesson. I guess I was trying to be too greedy. Would you believe that verse we talked about in class a couple of Sundays ago kept popping into my head?"

" 'Give to him that asketh thee, and from him that would borrow of thee turn not thou away.' That one?"

She nodded.

"You wouldn't have been so nonchalant about this a year ago." He felt his eyes grow misty. "I can see the Lord really is starting to work in your life."

"He must have been there all along, to send me a friend like you."

Friend. There's that word again. Dean gazed into the face he loved, the one sending an angelic smile in his direction. He wished he were a painter so he could capture the rose flush of her cheeks, her lips the color of a strawberry milk shake, her lustrous golden hair. No photograph could portray such glory with any accuracy.

"What are you thinking?" she asked.

"You don't want to know."

She opened her mouth as if in protest, but something stopped her. Instead, she reached for the latest issue of *Today's Southwest Virginian Christian Singles*. He narrowed his eyes. He wished Joelle had never seen that paper. If only she had given him time. . .time to let her get used to the real presence of the Lord in her life.

Dean hadn't wanted to pursue Joelle when she was so vulnerable, at the point when she had approached the fork in the road and had chosen the right path. The narrow path. He had visualized himself helping her along the way, guiding her at times, walking beside her at other times, perhaps her even leading him on still other occasions. Now, because he had waited for her instead of pouncing, he was being asked to help her find someone else.

"No!" he blurted. His outburst was strong enough to elicit stares from the women at the adjacent table. Dean recognized one of them as a member of his mom's garden club. From the corner of his eye, he noticed they suddenly huddled together and whispered. He didn't even care.

A stricken expression flashed into Joelle's eyes. "No, what?"

He lowered his voice. "No, I'm not going to help you ruin your life. Wasn't one bad date enough?"

"Enough with him, yes, but I won't pick someone like that this time."

Seeing there was no use in trying to talk sense into Joelle, Dean extracted a twenty-dollar bill from his wallet and threw it on the table.

"Wait! I said it was my treat."

He was in no mood to take any gift from Joelle. "You can pay me back some other time." Slipping out of the booth, he headed for the exit without saying another word.

As he made his way to the car, he heard Joelle's footfalls crunching on the gravel behind him. Dean almost wished he could leave her standing there, but he opened the door on her side, catching a whiff of her floral perfume that saturated the inside of the car.

Dean sighed. It would be a long ride home.

❧

Joelle allowed silence to permeate the car. From time to time, she would steal a furtive look at Dean's profile, the straight nose, strong chin, and full lips she knew so well. He kept his eyes focused straight ahead. The road curved around in several hairpin turns, challenging even the best driver. Dean had navigated it so many times over his life, Joelle knew he hardly needed to concentrate. His anger filled the space between them. If she could draw a caricature of Dean at that moment, she would include a thundercloud over his head.

Just before they reached her driveway, Joelle knew she would have to be the one to break the oppressive stillness. "What's the matter with you, Dean? Don't you want me to be happy?"

"Of course I want you to be happy." His gruff tone would have put off a lesser friend.

"You don't seem like it."

"Things aren't always as they seem."

"What's that supposed to mean?"

He pulled the car up to the flagstone walk leading to her front door. "It means I won't go through that paper and pick your next date."

"All right. You don't have to." She stepped out of the car. "I can fend for myself."

He leaned toward her, his auburn hair catching the light from the porch. "Can you? Remember that the next time you're stranded."

Despite the edge in his voice, Joelle stood in place, waiting for him to kill the engine and walk her to the door, as was his custom. Instead, Dean drove off, leaving behind a cloud of red dust as he sped over the dirt road.

Her gray mutt ran up, leapt, and placed her front paws on the side of Joelle's leg, barking happily. Without taking her gaze from the departing car, Joelle gave Raindrop a pat on the head. "What could possibly be the matter with him?"

Chapter 4

NO FRILLS, JUST SIMPLE PLEASURES. Devout Sunday school teacher, 35, seeks Christian woman, 25–35, who enjoys quiet evenings at home reading fine books and listening to classical music. If you're cerebral and quality time with an equally cerebral, attractive man sounds good to you, I'm the one you've been seeking!

Scanning her latest copy of *Today's Southwest Virginian Christian Singles*, Joelle stopped at the ad. As she munched on a tuna salad sandwich, strawberry yogurt, and soda, she read in relative privacy behind the closed door of her office. Even better, her next date would likely be at work. She could quickly leave a message on his answering machine and get back to sending out the month's bills.

She read the ad one last time as she picked up the phone to dial the number listed. A Sunday school teacher! Even if the ad hadn't included the word "devout," the fact that this man was willing to teach a class every Sunday was good enough for her. Not even Dean could argue against a Sunday school teacher. Surely this new man was an unimpeachable Christian.

Joelle thought about the other specifications. Maybe "cerebral" wasn't the first adjective to describe her, but Joelle thought her grades in school had been good enough. Maybe classical music wasn't her first choice, but she could usually sit still through at least a couple of the unbearably lengthy compositions before turning the station to something more contemporary. Surely she wouldn't disappoint this brainiac. And surely he would prove a far cry from the world-class sponger she had chosen for her last date. Shuddering at the thought, Joelle had no time to dwell on her past failure before someone answered the ringing phone. "Hello?"

Joelle was taken aback by the fact that the voice belonged to a female, but she rebounded before her surprise became evident. "Is this the number where I might reach Dexter Smythe?"

"Who wants to know?" The voice sounded edgy, suspicious.

I hope this isn't his roommate!

Joelle's heart beat with anxiety. "Um, I'm calling in reference to the ad."

"Oh! The ad! The one in the Christian singles' magazine?" The voice sounded relieved, then became perky.

"Yes."

"Well, why didn't you say so?" She could hear the woman's smile.

"Um, I did—"

"You know, that ad hasn't gotten the number of responses I had hoped. I think that's because it takes a very special woman in this day and age to shun the glitz and glamour the world has to offer in exchange for an honest, down-to-earth boy like my son, Dexter."

Well, that explained why Joelle was talking to a female. She breathed a sigh of relief before uttering, "Thank you, ma'am."

"My Dexter is a good catch. He knows his way around computers, and everyone knows they're the wave of the future."

Joelle considered computers to be the wave of the present, but she refrained from making the observation.

"So many women are so pushy today. All they seem to want is a man who'll make plenty of money so they can laze about all day and have their nails done." She paused. "You do your own manicures, don't you?"

"Yes, ma'am." Joelle glanced at her unpolished nails that she had trimmed to an attractive length and buffed to a sheen.

"How charming that you keep calling me 'ma'am.' I can tell you were brought up right. But there's no need to 'ma'am' me. Just call me Bertha. And you are. . . ?"

"Joelle."

"Noelle? So you were born at Christmas?"

"No, ma'am. I mean, Bertha. It's Joelle with a J."

"Ah. That is a very unusual name, although it is quite lovely. I take it your father's name is Joe and he really wanted a boy?" Bertha managed to conjecture without sounding offensive.

"No, I have four older brothers. My name is a combination of my parents' names, Joseph and Eleanor." Having spilled so much information so quickly, Joelle realized she had let Bertha lure her into becoming much too chatty.

"Oh. How interesting. So your mom has five children, huh? It's so lovely to learn you come from a family that values tradition and old-fashioned ways. The world moves much too rapidly these days," Bertha opined. "So, Joelle, do you have a last name?"

Despite Bertha's obviously sincere attempts to be pleasant, Joelle was becoming annoyed. Calling a man she'd never met was difficult enough without having to undergo an inquisition from his mother. Nevertheless, she concentrated on making sure her voice revealed no negative feelings. "Jamison. Joelle Jamison."

"How darling! Does anyone call you J. J.?"

"Not as of yet." Joelle drew a breath. "I don't mean to be abrupt, but I really must keep this call short. I'm on my lunch break, and I need to get back to my work in a couple of minutes. If you want to know the truth, I figured an answering machine would take the call so I could just leave my name and number. Since I managed to contact a human"—she giggled in hopes her amusement would be contagious—"I may as well speak to Dexter."

"I'd be glad for you to speak to him, except Dexter's not in."

"Perhaps I could leave my number—"

"That won't be necessary. I know exactly what Dexter would say if he were here," Bertha assured. "He has tickets to Concert under the Stars at the community college. It's on Friday night. The symphony will be playing selections from Mozart and Debussy. You know their works quite well, yes?"

"Well enough, I'm sure."

"Good. And don't worry about dinner. Dexter can bring a picnic basket."

"Sounds like fun," Joelle had to admit.

"Oh, it will be!"

After firming up the details and giving directions to her house, Joelle asked, "Why don't I leave my number, just in case Dexter would like to talk to me before we meet?"

"You're welcome to leave your number, but I can tell just from your voice and how polite you are that Dexter will be as crazy about you as I already am."

❦

Friday night, Joelle's hands shook as she popped in her contact lenses as she readied herself for the date. She'd been the victim of friends' matchmaking efforts before, but never had she flown this blind. What had made her agree to go to a concert with a man she hadn't met, or even spoken to?

I wish I could talk to Dean before taking such a plunge. But why? All he'd do is say "I told you so" and add that I should cancel. He might even give me a lecture on going out with strangers, not to mention another reminder that I never should have tried to find someone in a personals ad—even if the magazine is published by and for Christians.

She sighed. Dean hadn't called all week, and she hadn't been able to manufacture a convincing excuse to phone him. She knew he wasn't pleased that she was trying the ads again, but she never dreamed he wouldn't even speak to her in the interim. For the hundredth time, she wished she could hear his voice. . .even if it was lecturing.

Joelle deliberately focused on the upcoming evening. She glanced at the daisy-shaped clock in her room, a relic from her teen years. Dexter was due in ten minutes. She wondered if he'd be on time. Maybe he'd be inconsiderate, showing up late and making them miss the first part of the concert. She shook her head at the reflection in the dresser mirror. Classical music fan. Cerebral. Sounded like someone who'd have his watch set with precision so he could be exactly on time.

Coaxing hair that hadn't quite reached her shoulders into a manageable bob, Joelle mused that Dexter was lucky her parents were at an annual awards banquet for her mom's work. That meant he wouldn't be subjected to Dad's standard pre-date interview. Not that Dexter didn't deserve it after the examination Bertha had conducted with her. Sighing as she remembered the grilling, Joelle slipped into a pair of denim sandals. They matched the indigo-washed jeans she wore, which in turn picked up the deep blue roses embroidered on a recent acquisition, a coral short-sleeved summer sweater. Going for cashmere had been a splurge, but the cloud-soft knit was so luxurious, she felt as though any evening would be a success when she was wearing such a garment. Remembering Bertha's comment about manicures, Joelle gave her nails one last swipe with the buffer before her date rang the bell.

"Here goes!" she said to no one in particular. After hurrying through the den and living room, she opened the heavy oak door.

Dexter's ad had promised someone attractive, but the description barely fit the man of slight build who was standing on the front porch. As if to compensate for a receding hairline, he had grown the hair on the back of his head almost to his shoulders. A full beard that hid most of his face looked as though it hadn't been subjected to a pair of scissors in a few months. She felt a sudden urge to braid it but held her face in rigid composure, lest she wrinkle her nose in distaste. Her gaze swept to a nondescript shirt and khaki pants before returning to his face and noting stylish, wire-rimmed eyeglasses. Joelle suspected their removal would not improve his appearance.

Well, he did say he's cerebral, and I remember reading somewhere that geniuses rarely care about their looks. Besides, if I learned nothing else from my date with Lloyd, it's that appearances aren't everything.

"You must be Joelle."

"Good guess." She grinned, but he didn't return her expression.

"Let's go."

Joelle expected Dexter to give her at least a cursory glance and perhaps compliment her appearance. Instead, the command was barely out of his mouth before he turned and led her to a dependable-looking blue car with four doors, its engine still running. She was puzzled by his nonchalance but excused it as shyness. Bertha had mentioned Dexter's love of computers. Perhaps he dealt with machines so much, he had trouble communicating well with people. Besides, there would be time to get to know each other over the course of the evening.

Dexter didn't bother to open the car door for her but hurried to his side and slid behind the wheel.

Is Dean the last man on Earth who still opens car doors for women? Shaking her head, Joelle willed thoughts of Dean out of her mind. This was no time to be thinking of anyone else. She had placed the call to Dexter's house. She owed him a fair chance.

Her thoughts were interrupted by a female voice from the backseat. "Hello, Joelle!"

Joelle's head snapped in the direction of Bertha's now-familiar voice.

Bertha looked nothing as Joelle had imagined. Based on their earlier telephone conversation, she had visualized Bertha in a no-nonsense business suit, probably black or navy blue. Joelle's Bertha wore precision-cut salt-and-pepper hair, blow-dried into a short and smooth ducktail. She used just enough neutral-toned makeup to remind her business colleagues that no matter how capable, she was still a woman.

The real Bertha was no comparison to the off-putting figure of Joelle's imaginings. In fact, this Bertha seemed to be a real human, if a bit colorful. Her hair had been dyed a brilliant orange, reminding Joelle of an October sunset of such an intense hue that one couldn't bear to stare at it for long. Bertha's hair was set in a short, wash-and-dry frizzy permanent. Thin but prominent eyebrows were drawn over hairless flesh in a shade of pencil that had probably been labeled "auburn" on the package, but had the effect of chestnut brown when applied. A generous coat of mint green eye shadow, along with thick false eyelashes, adorned the same hazel eyes that Dexter had apparently inherited from her. Neon pink frosted lipstick added even more color to the rainbow. Bertha's hefty frame was clad in a short-sleeved denim camp shirt with a playing card, lottery ticket, and dice motif on the front, buttoned by large red rhinestones. Plastic earrings that mimicked bingo cards hung from her ears, nearly touching her shoulders.

Shocked by such a contrast between the imagined and the real Bertha, Joelle thought only to utter, "Nice shirt."

"You like it?" Bertha looked down at it, smiling as she inspected the motif. "I got it on sale at Wal-Mart. Only seven dollars." She lifted her forefinger in the air as though she had just thought of the most marvelous idea. "You know, I think if I get there by early tomorrow, I might be able to get you one, too. They looked like they had some really tiny sizes like you'd wear. But I can't promise. The rack was pretty picked over yesterday."

"Thanks for such a kind offer, but I'd never want you to go to so much trouble."

"I don't mind—"

"It's so sweet of you to offer," Joelle said, and she meant it.

"It's no trouble."

She smiled and shook her head. "Thanks, anyway." Joelle turned her attention to the road. *Why am I not surprised to see Bertha?*

"Hope you don't mind that I came along for the ride," she said, as if she were able to read Joelle's thoughts.

"Not at all." Joelle's response was more a result of reflexive manners than sincerity. "I had no idea you're a fan of classical music."

"Oh, I usually listen to country, but I'm always up for something wild and adventurous."

Joelle couldn't help but chuckle. She looked over at Dexter and wondered why he hadn't spoken since he left her front porch. Perhaps saying something cute might bring him out of what seemed to be a sour mood. "So, Dexter," she ventured, "your ad says you're cerebral. Why don't you say something smart?"

Tilting her head, she threw him her best teasing grin.

"Something smart."

Bertha laughed and Joelle joined her. "I should have seen that one coming."

Dexter's lips refused to curl upward. "I take it Mother didn't tell you she was the one who wrote the ad."

Joelle froze. This wasn't good news.

"If you're looking to define 'cerebral' by me, I'd say it means 'hasn't played a sport since high school.'" He cut his gaze to her just long enough to measure her reaction. "So if you're a member of Mensa, then you might not be too happy with me."

"What's Mensa?" Bertha wanted to know.

"It's a society for people who do very well on IQ tests," Dexter explained. "Very, very well."

"Oh." Bertha tittered uneasily.

"I doubt Mensa would have me," Joelle assured. Not eager to continue their conversation in its present vein, she was thankful to see the exit for the concert site. That was one of the longest miles Joelle could remember traveling.

Tension eased as absorption in the tasks of securing a parking place and a spot of grass to place their lawn chairs brought them together in a team effort, at least for a time. Joelle soon found herself sitting between Dexter and Bertha. Bertha continued to chat, even through the music. Dexter seemed to sulk.

After a couple of numbers, Joelle leaned toward her male companion and said in a low voice, "Was your mother lying when she said you like classical music?"

He shook his head.

"Then why do you act like you're headed for the gas chamber?" she hissed.

Bertha interrupted before he could answer. "Are you two ready for supper? I sure am." Not waiting for a response, she placed the basket on her ample thighs and withdrew three lunch bags, passing two to Joelle and Dexter.

It wasn't until she had the brown paper bag in hand that Joelle realized her usual dinner hour was long past and she was more than ready to eat. Though unpromising on the outside, the package contained pleasant culinary surprises. Joelle discovered a roast beef sandwich. The oversized sesame seed bun was piled high with meat cooked rare and seasoned with lettuce, tomato, cheddar cheese, and horseradish sauce. As if that weren't enough, a large navel orange, a container of premium strawberry yogurt, a bag of chips, and a bar of imported chocolate followed.

"Wow, Bertha. This is more than I eat in two days."

"No wonder you're so tiny." Bertha waved a dismissive hand. "It won't hurt you to enjoy a decent meal now and then." Reaching again into the basket, Bertha handed each of them napkins, stainless steel spoons, and cans of soda.

"Mother," Dexter said, "'decent' is not always the same as 'large.'"

Joelle raised her eyebrows, surprised that Dexter had made an observation without prodding. All the same, she noticed he seemed to enjoy every last morsel of his supper, which was identical to hers.

During intermission, Joelle scraped the last of her yogurt out of its plastic container, deciding to save the orange, chips, and chocolate for another time. From the corner of her eye, she noticed a woman approach Dexter's chair and tap him on the shoulder.

From the other direction, Joelle heard Bertha say, "What is she doing here?"

Chapter 5

Dexter's eyes lit up for the first time that evening. "Anastasia! I thought you had to watch the kids tonight." He turned to one side and leaned toward the young woman. He rested his chin on his fist, obviously eager to hear her response.

"Genna didn't have to work after all. She and Jacob took the kids to a movie." Anastasia spoke with a thick accent. She squatted beside Dexter's chair, draping her left arm on top of its back.

Joelle couldn't help but notice Anastasia's fingernails were at least two inches in length. Each was lacquered sky blue. A tiny palm tree, leaves painted in green polish and trunk represented by bronze polish, had been meticulously painted on every nail. The effect was extraordinary, bringing to Joelle's mind tropical beaches. Though her reality was at present a cool night, Joelle could almost feel the sun's warmth mingling with a summer breeze. She wondered how long such artwork took to create.

At that moment, Bertha leaned over and said in a voice audible only to Joelle, "She's from one of those countries that used to be part of the Soviet Union. I don't know which one. I can't keep up with everything going on over there. Anyway, she's what they call an *au pair*. I think that's a fancy name for 'foreign baby-sitter for rich people.'"

"She seems awfully young for so much responsibility," Joelle whispered. "Barely out of her teens."

"I'd guess the same thing. Don't you think she's much too young for Dexter?"

Joelle hesitated. "I'm not sure that's for me to speculate."

"I know you're just being kind, dear, but you can feel free to speak your mind with me."

As much as Joelle wanted to console Bertha, she had a feeling anything she said would be repeated to Dexter, so she hesitated.

Bertha didn't wait for a response. "I must admit, I give you points for discretion. It's very ladylike of you not to badmouth your competition." Bertha patted Joelle on the knee. "You've been so good for Dexter."

Joelle's eyebrows shot up before she could contain her surprise. Dexter hadn't paid more than the most obligatory attention to her the whole evening. She couldn't imagine why Bertha would think she had had any effect on him at all.

"I hope you can encourage him to stay away from that little girl. If you want to know the truth, I'm afraid her main interest in my son is his American citizenship. What if she manages to get him to marry her so she can say she belongs here, too? And if he is fool enough to make it legal, how much do you want to bet she'll drop him like a hot potato? Probably before the ink dries on the wedding license. I'd hate to see him taken advantage of like that." Bertha tilted her head closer. "He needs a woman. Someone like you. I really mean it when I say I hope you'll see more of each other in the future."

Joelle stole a glance at Dexter and Anastasia. She was chattering in broken English about nothing, yet he never took his gaze away from her. Not that Joelle could blame him. With rich chestnut hair and smooth skin, Anastasia was attractive enough to entice any man. She had definitely bewitched Dexter.

Don't count on me seeing Dexter again anytime soon.

Joelle sighed. Even if Dexter had entertained an interest in her, there hadn't been enough sparks to encourage Joelle to cultivate anything further. Looking over at Bertha as the last musical notes of Debussy's *Le Mer* floated through the cool night air, Joelle couldn't help but feel sorry for her. Dexter's mother was kind and concerned, albeit interfering. Silently she lifted the older woman's name to the Lord, praying that Bertha could find it in her heart to love the woman He one day planned for Dexter to marry, whether that woman were Anastasia or someone else. She added a request for her date, praying that Anastasia's interest wasn't mercenary but sincere.

The concert ended, and Dexter bade farewell to Anastasia without so much as introducing her to Joelle. As they rode home in silence, Joelle wondered if his oversight was a natural extension of his awkward manners, an admission that he had no interest in Joelle, or fear that Anastasia would become jealous. Not that it mattered. After this night, Joelle knew she'd never see any of them again.

Dexter parked in front of Joelle's house, got out of the car, and walked her to the door. After his indifference, she was surprised he made the effort. Even as she paused to say good night, Joelle sensed Bertha peering from the car, no doubt reading more into the gesture than Dexter intended.

"Thanks for the concert and picnic dinner, Dexter," Joelle managed, though she was eager to escape into the security of her house.

"Sure. But I can't take credit for the dinner. Or even the date, for that matter. Mother was the one with the concert tickets. I just went along for the ride."

"Then thank your mom again for me." She extended a smile she knew was bittersweet.

"Wait."

Joelle paused, surprised that Dexter had anything more to say to her.

"About tonight." He looked down at the porch and shuffled his feet, reminding her of a maladroit adolescent.

She struggled to rescue him from embarrassment. "No need to explain anything. I enjoyed the concert."

"I know, but I'm sorry my mother dragged you into the middle of all this. I mean, you seem like a nice person. She had no right to involve you in all this, especially since she knows about Anastasia."

"So you really are more than friends?"

"I hope so. I just wish Mother liked her. She just doesn't see Anastasia the way I do," he muttered without looking up.

"She's only trying to do what's best for you."

"In her way, I guess that's so." Dexter's eyes met Joelle's, narrowed in determination. "But if she doesn't like my choice of women, that's her problem, not mine. Or yours."

Joelle leaned against the front door. "But do you know why she doesn't like Anastasia?"

"She thinks she's too young." He hesitated as though he were thinking of other possibilities. "That's all I know."

"She's also worried because Anastasia is a foreigner and she might want to use you to gain U.S. citizenship."

"That's ridiculous."

"Perhaps it is. If I were you, I'd make sure before I did anything drastic." She looked him squarely in the face. "Normally I wouldn't give advice to someone I just met; but like you said, I got dragged into this, and sometimes wise counsel is easier to take from a stranger."

"Maybe so." He took on a thoughtful expression. "I'll remember what you said. Thanks, Joelle."

As she watched Dexter walk back to the car, a thought suddenly occurred to her. *Lord, maybe this date was part of Your will after all.*

❧

Dean could hardly concentrate on the lesson Fiona was giving for Singles' Night. Not that he needed to. He'd already heard about Jesus' weeping over the death of Lazarus in many previous Bible lessons. The brother of Martha and Mary, Lazarus had obviously been special to Jesus. Dean wondered what Lazarus had done to endear himself so much to the Lord to cause Him to cry over his death. As far as he could see, the Bible offered no clues. But who can explain friendship? Not just a relationship forged over common interests and goals, but a life-sustaining connection that transcends circumstances. Dean had enjoyed only two such friendships. One was with a high school pal who had joined the military just after graduation. Through E-mail, the occasional phone call, and infrequent visits, Dean managed to keep in touch with him no matter where in the world he was stationed.

The other friendship was with Joelle. Even now, when he was determined to stay mad at her, he couldn't. He tried not to stare across the room at her, even though he knew she was sitting so far away only because she had been ten minutes late. If she'd been sitting beside him, avoiding eye contact would have been easy. He couldn't look her way. Otherwise, she'd know all was forgiven before she could even apologize. And he had made up his mind that she would apologize for going against his advice, even if the wretched date hadn't interfered with Singles' Night. Surely she had learned her lesson by now. She would admit it. He wouldn't forgive her until she did.

A catch formed in his throat at a disturbing thought. *What if she hasn't learned her lesson? What if the date was so fantastic she's made a second one? What if Joelle fell for this guy she met through a personal ad?* The thought was too chilling to contemplate. He stared at his Bible, determined to put such ideas out of his mind.

"Good lesson, huh, Dean?" Nicole asked as everyone's Bibles closed.

He didn't want to admit he'd tuned out the lesson long ago. "Um, sure."

Nicole's hand gently touched his shoulder. "This is such a great group of friends here. Aren't we all lucky to have each other?"

Dean nodded, wondering why she felt the need to make such an inane comment. He didn't have time to ponder her motives before Fiona, who was also in charge of the night's entertainment, announced the game.

"Is everybody up for Twister?" An enthusiastic smile covered her face.

A round of applause and a couple of whistles greeted the suggestion.

"At least this game doesn't involve sports questions." Dean hadn't expected Joelle to sneak up on him. He gasped in surprise. Her hot breath tickled his ear when she whispered. The breezy scent of her breath mints, mingled with her trademark perfume, wafted to his nostrils.

Dean's heart betrayed him by lurching. "Lucky for you," he managed.

She wrinkled her nose. "Although it does require one to be very agile." Joelle gave him a good-natured poke in the ribs.

Dean wasn't able to respond before he was summoned to help spread out the thin plastic sheet decorated with colored dots. He didn't relish the idea of contorting himself so he could place his hands and feet on the different dots at the whim of a spinning wheel. But to be a good sport, he had to go along.

After only a few spins of the wheel, the singles found themselves in a tangled mess. Dean was positioned with his left hand on the same spot as Joelle's. In turn, she had wiggled into a stance that placed her partially on top of him. He knew it wouldn't take much for him to lose his equilibrium, but Dean was determined to stay upright—or at least as upright as he could, considering he was balanced on all fours.

Despite his efforts, the next spin proved fatal. As Dean tried to move his right foot to a blue dot, he dropped to the floor, twisting and landing on his back. His flying limbs nudged Joelle, who fell on top of him.

For a split second, her face was inches away from his. Her teal green eyes were filled with astonishment, her pink lips parted. He had a sudden impulse to kiss her. He wondered what everyone else would think, should he make such a bold move. He imagined they would first stand and gawk. Then, Zach would start the applause. Fiona, Nicole, and Ashlynn would follow. Zach would whistle lewdly enough to embarrass Joelle, but all in good fun. As Dean fantasized about their reaction, a voice interrupted.

"You lose, Dean!" Nicole stood over him. Her eyes, rimmed heavily by black eyeliner, sparkled victoriously. Her mouth, glazed in a bold red, was contorted into a smirk.

The applause in Dean's imagination ceased.

"You lose, too, Joelle," Nicole added.

"Oh, all right," Joelle conceded, slipping away from Dean's grasp.

He hopped up in one fluid motion, hoping his nonchalant motion would belie his fantasies. "You okay, Joelle?"

As she nodded, he led her to a sofa that had been a castoff from a church member. "So are we still on for our coffee?" she asked as she sat beside him on the green-and-brown-plaid couch.

Suddenly he remembered once again that he was supposed to be mad. He decided to play it coy. "I had no idea you were still interested."

Her blond eyebrows shot up. "Who says I'm not interested?"

"I don't know." He shrugged. "I thought maybe I'd be old news after your hot date." Dean shot her a look from the corner of his eye. "You did go out on another date, didn't you?"

"Unfortunately, I did."

He brightened at the word "unfortunately," even though he was disappointed by the confirmation that she had disregarded his advice. "At least you didn't let it interfere with tonight. Everyone would have missed you," he hastened to add, lest she realize he was the one who would have missed her the most.

"I suppose." A series of hoots indicated that Fiona had fallen victim to an inability to wrench herself into an odd shape. After the momentary distraction, Joelle's hand rested on his knee. "So are we still on for coffee or not?"

"Sure, but only if you promise to tell me all about this awful date of yours."

"Promise."

The rest of the meeting flew by, with Dean even managing to emerge the winner of one of the games. After the closing prayer, everyone headed to the parking lot. Dean was sorry he hadn't arranged to pick Joelle up and take her to the meeting. He would miss her presence in his car. Dean let out a sigh as they made their way to separate vehicles. Without warning, someone touched his shoulder. He turned his head and spotted Nicole.

"Going home alone, Dean?"

"After coffee, yes."

Nicole tilted her head as though she were waiting for him to offer her an invitation to join him. When she saw none was forthcoming, she uttered, "Too bad." Flashing him a smile, she waved and headed toward her red Mustang Cobra.

Dean felt a moment of guilt. In an effort to be sure he and Joelle were alone for coffee, he had let his manners fly out the window. Well, maybe Nicole could tag along next time.

❦

As agreed, Joelle followed Dean's car to a favorite drive-in restaurant on Route 81. When Dean had suggested they take advantage of the comfortable spring night, she readily acquiesced. Lingering in the brisk night air at a picnic table sounded good, especially when dessert promised to be a large hot fudge brownie sundae with zebra ice cream, walnuts, whipped cream, and a cherry. The prospect was enough to justify a drive several miles over crooked rural roads past the county line.

Yet as she watched Dean's taillights, hot fudge sundaes were the last thing on Joelle's mind. She had seen Nicole talking to him as they left the church. Joelle hadn't liked the flirtatious look the other woman had cast Dean's way as she waved good-bye. In fact, Joelle hadn't liked anything Nicole had done all night. She had stayed by Dean constantly, talking to him every chance she got. Joelle didn't know Nicole well, but she was aware of Nicole's reputation as a vixen. After the evening's performance, she could see why. Even from across the room, Nicole's seductive body language was all too easy to read. So masterfully did she play the role that Joelle was surprised Nicole bothered to associate herself with any church. Even so, someone as sweet as Dean had no business anywhere near Nicole. Surely he had no experience with such a calculating temptress. She had to alert Dean. Doing so was only her duty.

She pulled in to the drive-in restaurant right behind Dean, gravel crackling in protest under tires. Jumping out of the car without bothering to lock the door, Joelle hurried across the sidewalk to Dean's side. She didn't bother with subtleties. "So what did Nicole have to say?"

The grin faded from his face as he continued to walk toward the substantial line of customers under the bright fluorescent lights. "Have to say about what?"

"Don't pull that innocent act with me. I saw her flirting with you all night, and then she was talking to you while we were leaving." Her voice took on an edge that astonished even her. Looking for a distraction, she swatted a few bugs that were flying near her face, attracted to the sweet smells of her perfume and hair spray.

"Maybe I'm acting innocent because I have nothing to hide," Dean protested. Lifting his head slightly, he arched one auburn eyebrow. "If I didn't know you better, Joelle, I'd think you were jealous."

"Jealous?" Joelle stopped in her tracks, right in front of the entrance. Her mouth dropped open in objection. "What a typical male you are, Dean Nichols! Conceited as all get-out." Balling her hand into a fist, she tapped him on his forearm just hard enough to emphasize her point.

"I'm surprised at you. I didn't think you were a female chauvinist, Joelle Jamison."

Joelle stepped to one side, allowing a couple of the other customers to leave the line without scraping cones of chocolate-dipped ice cream against her sleeve. However, she didn't let them stop her from making her point. She narrowed her eyes and set her lips in a straight line. "I don't have to be a female chauvinist to see a shark on the attack."

He flashed a wide, wolflike smile. "All the more reason for you to stay away from the male sharks you meet through the personals, my dear."

"Male sharks!" she hissed. Bowing her head, Joelle dug the toe of her ballet flat into dust-covered gravel.

This was not the moment to let Dean know she had already looked through the personals and chosen another date.

Chapter 6

Do you enjoy elegant evenings? Days at the ballpark? Afternoons at the theater? Walks in the rain? So do I! Are you 25–30 and believe variety is the spice of life? Do you want to share your spicy life with a devoted Christian man? Then give me a call today!

Intrigued, Joelle had done just that. A man named Wilbert Webster had answered the phone. After ascertaining that Wilbert had placed the ad himself and that he really wanted to meet Christian women, Joelle breathed an inward sigh of relief.

Wilbert wasn't shy about presenting his potential date with questions of his own. Not surprisingly, he asked about her Christian walk first. Nervous, Joelle had to admit she was still a new Christian. She was relieved when he answered that every Christian was new at the start, and he didn't mind. He seemed impressed by the physical description she offered upon his request, even though Joelle was careful not to exaggerate her best features. When they discovered a mutual fascination with old movies and travel, Joelle could feel his interest growing.

"I hope you don't mind spending an evening with a computer geek." Wilbert's smooth, mellow voice would have been at home on radio airwaves. Computer geek or not, Joelle thought she'd enjoy listening to him talk about anything *ad infinitum*, even if the term did force an image in her mind of a scrawny fellow with thick glasses and a pocket protector. "At least," Wilbert continued, "that's what my friends like to call me, since I repair computers for a living."

"Oh, they're just jealous," she answered.

"I'll have to tell them you said that." The tone of his voice told her he spoke in jest.

"Just don't give them my real name or address," she quipped.

"Don't worry. I'll protect you. None of them can bench press as much weight as I can."

The image of a scrawny guy faded, replaced in Joelle's mind by a heavyset man with bulging biceps and chest muscles. "I admit, I'm impressed."

"Don't be. I can't lift all that much. And just so you won't be disappointed when you meet me in person, I don't look anything like those guys on pro wrestling."

"Thank goodness!" She laughed.

"I don't have that much time to spend at the gym," he said without apology.

41

"But I do spend a lot of time at church, especially since we sponsor a Christian school. I maintain the church and school computers. I teach advanced computer courses."

"So you're a teacher, too?"

"Not professional. The course is an elective for juniors and seniors, and I teach on my lunch hour. If you're wondering how I manage that, I have to thank my company. They're pretty progressive. My boss lets me take a little extra time each day so I can be free to give back to the community." He let out a little chuckle. "I work more than enough hours to make up for the time, though."

Joelle couldn't help but be impressed. Not even Dean could argue against someone with such dedication to church and community. When the conversation wound down to a close, Joelle felt at ease planning a date for the following Friday night.

"Just one thing," she asked as they bid farewell.

"What's that?"

"Do you promise not to bring your mother along?"

"My mother?" His voice inflected with surprise. "What would she be doing on our date?"

"Trust me, you don't want to know the details."

He chuckled. "Sounds like you've been through this before."

"Just twice."

"Me, too. Maybe the third time's a charm."

❧

The appliance store was devoid of customers, a fact that surprised Dean since Friday afternoons were usually boons for retail businesses. Scanning the small showroom of thirty or so appliances displayed in tight formation, Dean didn't see the owner. He ventured to the back of the store, finding the cubbyhole that Earl used as a business office. Dean knocked on the door. "Earl? Are you there?"

A man in his midfifties emerged. "Dean! Good to see you...except I bet this means the old washer finally died?" Behind Earl's jovial demeanor was a note of sympathy.

Dean answered with a weak nod. Whenever events in his personal life and business tried his patience, Dean drew strength from the verses in scripture on pride. His favorite was 1 John 2:16: "For all that is in the world, the lust of the flesh, and the lust of the eyes, and the pride of life, is not of the Father, but is of the world."

Even with this verse in mind, Dean cringed as he followed Earl to the counter. The retailer didn't bother with a sales pitch or show Dean any new washer models. Earl already knew just the machine Dean would be purchasing. Dean always did business with Earl, and the appliance salesman was cognizant that Wash 'n Wear was barely turning a profit. He would have to ask Earl to extend more credit if the new machine was to be delivered anytime soon. Even then, "soon" was a relative concept when the time to order a commercial machine arrived. Since Earl didn't keep heavy-duty machines fitted with coin slots in stock, he would have to special order the washer. At least a month was sure to pass before the new machine would be delivered.

Dean tried not to let his discouragement show. With money a scarce commodity, he had delayed the purchase of a new washer as long as he could. Three times, he had repaired the old machine as it sputtered to the end of its useful life. After three strikes, Dean figured the point had come where sinking more cash into repairs would be folly.

Dean sighed. One day, after he had expanded his business to take in alterations and dry cleaning, he'd be able to pay cash on the barrel for any washer or dryer—even the top-of-the-line models. For now, he would have to swallow his worldly pride and beg Earl's indulgence.

He cleared his throat. "Earl, I hate to ask, but—"

The older man held up his hand, palm facing his customer. "Then don't." Earl put down his hand and began typing. Without looking away from the computer screen, he said, "Your credit's good with me."

Burden lifted, Dean felt so light he almost thought he could fly. "Thanks, Earl."

"No problem." He kept typing. "Besides, your account is paid up. I'd give you all the credit you need since you're a friend, not to mention you're on the finance committee at church. You're a good customer, too. I know you're as good as your word." He paused as a small machine beside the computer printed out a receipt.

Dean recalled the passage of scripture old Miss Williams had made her Sunday school class memorize when they were barely in high school. Her insistence on the verses in the fifth chapter of Matthew had been motivated partly by her belief in Bible memorization. It didn't help that she'd overheard Bobby Johnson taking the Lord's name in vain when he struck out at the church baseball game the previous Saturday.

Dean felt a smile tingle upon his lips. Miss Williams was certainly feasting with Jesus in heaven on this day. In the meantime, Bobby had long since relocated to New York City and become successful on Wall Street, the last Dean had heard.

No matter. The scriptural admonition had remained with him all these years:

But I say unto you, Swear not at all; neither by heaven; for it is God's throne: nor by the earth; for it is his footstool: neither by Jerusalem; for it is the city of the great King. Neither shalt thou swear by thy head, because thou canst not make one hair white or black. But let your communication be, Yea, yea; Nay, nay: for whatsoever is more than these cometh of evil.

Earl's easy voice, accented by his Southern upbringing, brought Dean back to the present. "Yep, you're one person whose word I'd trust any day. Can't say that about everybody these days, I'm afraid." He handed Dean the receipt. "Got anything to do tonight?"

"Not really. . .unless you think going home to microwave a hot dog and spend the night in front of the television is exciting."

"You've got something special to do now." Earl pulled a couple of tickets out of the pocket of his faded blue denim shirt and handed them to Dean. "My wife bought these a couple of months ago. Since then, her sister came down sick, and she had to go to Oklahoma to nurse her."

"I'm sorry."

"Thanks, but she'll be okay. So now I'm stuck with these tickets for a play I didn't want to see, nohow. I don't much hearken to theater stuff. Especially musicals." He wrinkled his nose. "To tell you the honest truth, I'm glad to get out of it."

Dean looked at the tickets. They granted entrance to the Bard Dinner Theater for a buffet and performance of *The Sound of Music.*

"Oh, and they feed you, too," Earl added.

"Are you sure you can't use these? You can always eat and run." Dean cracked a smile.

"Naw. I'd rather go bowling. Besides, who would I go with, an old married man like me? Now you go on and ask some pretty girl you know." Earl winked. "Women love them sappy stories, don't you think?"

"So I've heard." Dean grinned. "Thanks, Earl. I know just whom to ask."

⁓

On the night of the date, Joelle thought about how she was grateful Wilbert had suggested they take in a show at a dinner theater miles away. She had no desire to run into Dean while she was out with Wilbert. Even being seen by mutual friends would be risky. In their close-knit community, gossip traveled quickly. Not that she cared what Dean thought. Of course, he meant well to caution her against dating strange men. What else were friends for? But she just wasn't in the mood for any of his lectures or withering looks. Both were sure to be the result, should Dean discover she was out with Wilbert.

As Joelle searched her jewelry box for the pearl drop earrings she always wore with her little black dress, she recalled Dean's reaction to her story of her date with Dexter. Or rather, her date with Bertha. When Dean chuckled and pointed out how wise Joelle had been to win over Dexter's mother, she knew all was forgiven. Still, she wasn't sure he'd be so charitable, should he discover she had made yet another date with a stranger.

"Why can't I seem to stop worrying about Dean?" she asked her reflection as she struggled to slide the earring-back to the right place on the post. An angry-looking young woman stared back, hair deliberately mussed and sticking

44

out in a questionable fashion, eyebrows curved disagreeably, eyes narrowed into slits, and her mouth a pink slash. "Dean Nichols has no hold over me. He has no right to tell me who to see and who not to see."

So why am I hiding?

Frustrated, she dropped the earring back and heard it bounce and roll across the hardwood floor until it landed somewhere underneath her dresser. With an exclamation of distress, she knelt in front of the furniture, peering underneath until she eyed the little piece of gold lying in the far corner, amidst dust unreachable by even her best efforts with a vacuum. Wrinkling her nose, she lay on her stomach and stretched her arm and fingers to their fullest extent. The piece of metal was just within reach of her middle finger. With a little grunt, she slid it toward her. Successful in its retrieval, she blew off the dust it had accumulated on its journey and rose to her feet.

The abrupt motion made her realize she had developed a dull headache. Fighting pain was the last thing she needed to worry about tonight. After glancing one last time in the mirror to determine she was satisfied enough with her appearance, Joelle headed for the kitchen and the aspirin her mom kept on a spinning rack in the cabinet.

"You look absolutely lovely, Joelle," her mom noticed.

"Thanks." Joelle reached into the refrigerator for the milk. She poured herself a small glass and retrieved a little plastic bottle with a yellow label from the cabinet.

"What's the matter? Why are you taking aspirin?"

"Headache," she explained before swallowing the tablets.

"What are you doing with a headache? You're not that nervous about this date, are you?"

She shook her head. "I don't know why my head hurts."

"Maybe it's stress."

"I hadn't thought of that." Joelle's head pounded even more, and she noticed the pain had traveled to the back of her neck. With her left hand, she leaned against the kitchen counter. She clutched the throbbing muscle with her right hand and tried to massage away the ache.

Her mother came up behind her. With her fingers on Joelle's shoulders, she placed one thumb on each side of the base of her neck and pressed several times.

"Thanks. That feels better."

"No doubt. I can feel the tension in your muscles. Poor thing." She kept up the pressure on Joelle's neck. "You certainly have no reason to be nervous. Whoever this Wilbert guy is, he'd be crazy not to be thrilled with you, both inside and out."

"Thanks, Mom. You always know what to say."

"What else are mothers for?" She patted Joelle's back, ending the therapeutic rub. Leaning against the counter she had just wiped down, Mom folded her arms and took on a knowing expression that reminded Joelle of the Mona Lisa. "You've really been dining on a feast of men lately, haven't you?"

"A feast of men? Mom!" Joelle set her empty glass in the sink. "What's that supposed to mean?"

"Nothing." Eleanor's narrow shoulders rose in a shrug. "It's just that since you've been working at the doctor's office, you hadn't met all that many men. Now, all of a sudden, you seem to be going out with a different guy every week."

Joelle didn't remember a time when she was more grateful to hear the doorbell ring.

"Your dad's still out. Want me to get that?"

"That's okay, thanks." Joelle shook her head. "If he's worth meeting, I'll make sure to introduce you."

When Joelle opened the door, she was shocked to find a man standing on the porch wearing stained blue jeans and a faded gray T-shirt that looked as though it had seen a year of workouts at the gym. She felt her eyes widen, but soon composed her features into a poker face.

"Wow!" His mouth flew open.

"Uh, thanks, I guess." An idea occurred to Joelle as she remembered job seekers from the previous week. "Look, if you're canvassing the neighborhood looking to do chores, I'm sorry. We don't have anything for you."

He shook his head so hard, a few brown curls fell out of place. A quick runthrough with his hand replaced them well enough. "I'm Wilbert. I'm here for Joelle. I'm assuming that's you?"

"You assume right." Despite her best efforts, Joelle's eyes scanned the roughhewn man before her. Her tone of voice betrayed her disappointment. "But—"

"I know what you're going to say. Didn't I promise an elegant evening at the dinner theater?" He nodded. "That's right. I did, and I still plan to keep my promise. I even have my suit in the car." He cocked his head toward a late-model red sports car parked in front of the house. "It's just that I forgot I need to do something else first."

"Um, should I ask what that something else is?"

"I promised I'd clean up the churchyard after work today. It's got to look nice by Sunday."

"But it's only Friday."

"I know, but I have classes all day tomorrow. I'm working on my degree."

"Oh." Since her own mother was pursuing her education, Joelle understood all too well how lessons could interfere with someone's personal life.

"I wish I'd thought to call before you got dressed, but you wouldn't mind helping me, would you? The school has showers in the gym locker rooms. You can change there, and then we can go right to the show. The janitor and his wife will be there, so you don't need to worry."

She consulted her watch. "But won't we miss the play?"

"We can see the second show. The tickets are good for either one, as long as we go tonight."

Joelle shrugged. "All right. I guess a little hard work never hurt anybody."

His face lit up with a smile. "Thanks. I really appreciate it."

As she changed in her bedroom, Joelle wondered if Wilbert were putting her through some kind of test and what other women would have done in her place. Sighing, she thought about Dean. No way would he ever pull a stunt like that on any woman.

Dean. I wonder what he's doing tonight. Suddenly she became aware that her headache, which she thought had subsided, had returned to make her head pound. She resolved to take a second dose of aspirin as soon as she could.

Folding her dress, which was thankfully a knit that wouldn't wrinkle, she placed the garment in an overnight bag. Black hose, pearl earrings, bracelet, and necklace followed. Pulling a red T-shirt over her head, Joelle realized that getting dressed and redressed would result in her hair transforming from deliberately messy to really and truly messy. She decided to toss in the hair wax, a comb, and a can of super-hold spray. Then, remembering that a school locker room wouldn't necessarily provide soap, she added shampoo, soap, a towel, and a blow dryer. Last, but not least, followed the aspirin.

The overnight bag was bulging by the time she had finished packing. "Everything but the kitchen sink." She shook her head.

As she reemerged to the living room, Joelle cast her mom a grateful look for keeping Wilbert occupied while she changed. Her mom's response was to wink, a sure sign she wasn't too certain she liked hardworking Wilbert. Joelle sighed inwardly. She could count on a heart-to-heart when she returned home that night.

"See you later, Mom."

"When will you be home?"

"We should be home by midnight," Wilbert promised as the phone started to ring.

Joelle wondered if she should stay to see if the call was for her, but Eleanor shooed her out. "I'll get that. You don't have any time to lose. If it's for you, I'll take a message."

She could feel her mother's eyes on them as they walked to Wilbert's car. Wilbert did pause at the passenger side and open Joelle's door, a definite plus. *Maybe there are some men other than Dean who remember what chivalry is, after all!*

Chapter 7

By the way, Joelle, I need to stop by the dry cleaners," Wilbert said as they approached the next town. "I hope you don't mind."

"Sure. I understand." Joelle forced herself to smile. How many more delays did he plan to propose?

He pulled the car into a small parking lot in front of the cleaners and tilted his head toward the backseat. Following his direction, Joelle saw a large, lumpy duffel bag. "Mind taking those in for me?"

"Um, sure. As long as I don't have to pay the bill," she quipped.

"Maybe next time." Wilbert chuckled.

Although taken aback by his odd request, Joelle accomplished the errand quickly and soon slid back into the passenger seat.

"Thanks." He flashed a smile. "Oh, and by the way, I have to stop by my apartment. I just realized I forgot my good clothes. But before that, I need to stop at the gas station."

"We're getting a lot done this evening," she remarked, somehow managing to keep the edge of irritation off her voice. "You don't need to stop for a haircut, too, do you?"

"That won't happen until our second date." His serious expression made her wonder if he really was joking. "Although I just remembered I do need to pick up a quart of milk at the grocery store."

As hard as she tried to be patient, Joelle couldn't help but stew as she sat in the car, sweating from the heat, as he made one stop after another. "I'm beginning to wonder if you even have tickets for the play," she noted a half hour later as they parked in the lot of a six-unit apartment building. "Maybe you really don't and are just stalling until we run out of time." She let out a strained giggle.

He snapped his fingers. "Oh, I'm glad you reminded me. I've got to get those out of my sock drawer."

Joelle didn't answer. Her capacity to be amused by the absentminded professor type had surpassed its limit.

Wilbert hopped out of the car. Before he shut the door, he turned to Joelle and leaned his head inside. "Aren't you coming with me?"

"You mean, into your apartment? Alone?" She let her voice drift off so he could guess the source of her protests. Certainly she wouldn't need to spell them out.

Wilbert bristled so he stood fully upright. "I'm not going to attack you, if that's what you're afraid of. Anyway, both of my roommates are home. If I try anything, you can tell them to beat me up."

Upset that she had offended her date, Joelle acquiesced by exiting her side of the car. Wilbert had given her no indication he couldn't be trusted. Still, she made a mental note to bolt if she saw no evidence of his roommates.

Her anxiety proved unfounded. As soon as they entered, Joelle saw two young men who looked to be in their early twenties situated in front of the television. The sounds emanating from the oversized box were angry. Curious, Joelle turned her attention to the show. Overdeveloped men shouted each other down, vowing revenge against one another. A bikini-clad woman with long hair and muscular arms added screaming remarks. A slightly smaller man, dressed in a referee's uniform, acted as though he wanted the shouting to stop. Since his protests were weak, Joelle wasn't convinced.

"What's the matter?" one of the guys asked. "Haven't you seen pro wrestling before?"

"Apparently not," Joelle answered. She looked at her inquisitor, only to find his face was hidden by the brim of a Yankees' baseball cap.

The second roommate took a swig of beer from a brown bottle. "Have a seat and take a look, then."

"She doesn't have time," Wilbert answered. "Joelle, as you can see, this place is a mess. Bert and Josh don't seem to mind, but I'd sure appreciate it if you could pick up a little while I get my things together. You don't mind, do you?"

Joelle had been too absorbed by the television program to notice the room until Wilbert mentioned it. Looking around, she could see the place was, indeed, a mess. Five pizza cartons that appeared to be a week old were positioned in different places on the floor. Empty beer bottles and soda cans occupied various places on mismatched end tables, sofa arms, and the floor. Some had landed as though their consumers attempted to pitch them inside an overflowing black plastic trash can and missed their target by anywhere from a few inches to several feet. Balled-up wads of paper decorated the room like so much confetti. A stack of newspapers, magazines, and mail had become so large that the highest pieces had toppled out of position, resulting in a mishmash of paper. For Wilbert's sake, Joelle hoped no bills that needed to be paid anytime soon were hidden in the pile. Suddenly, she noticed the room was permeated with a stench that reminded her of how a dirty gym would smell if a pizza parlor were operating in the middle of it.

"Um—" was all she could manage before she realized Wilbert had left the room.

Baseball Cap laughed. "He's long gone, honey. You'd better get crackin' if you expect to go anywhere else tonight."

The other roommate let out a hearty burp. "Why don't you go in the kitchen and do the dishes? The dishwasher's broken, but there's plenty of detergent to do them by hand."

"I didn't come here to do the dishes." Joelle folded her arms.

"Suit yourself. But like I said, he'll stall until at least some of this work is done." Baseball Cap shrugged. "He does this to everybody he brings here."

"He does?"

"Yeah. See, we don't mind the mess. He does, but he doesn't want to pick up after us on principle."

"In that case, neither do I." Determined not to involve herself in their feud, Joelle plopped onto a chair. Only after she felt moisture on the side of her thigh did she jump back up. The culprit turned out to be a discarded half-eaten piece of pizza, with pepperoni and bits of cheese and ground beef still clinging to a sea of tomato sauce. The food had been wedged between the cushion and arm. Joelle didn't want to venture a guess as to how long ago.

"Sorry about that," Baseball Cap commented.

Without replying, Joelle headed into the small kitchen in search of a paper towel. Perhaps if she got a little water on the spot right away, there would be some hope of getting out the red paste and yellow grease in the laundry.

Not surprisingly, the kitchen table was piled with junk. Books and papers occupied the seats of the matching chairs. Sighing, Joelle headed for the counters. Behind a stack of open cookie containers and several boxes of cereal, she discovered a paper towel rack. To her amazement, the rack housed a clean, new roll. Noticing a pattern of blue and pink bears, she expected the bachelors hadn't noticed the motif was meant for a nursery. But she wasn't complaining. Finally she maneuvered the faucet around a sink of dirty dishes and dampened the towel. With a little scrubbing, Joelle cleared most of the spot from her jeans.

Task completed, she located another overflowing trash can. This one was surrounded by paper grocery bags filled with more garbage. Joelle tossed the crumpled towel in the general direction of the mess. Her reward was to see it land in one of the bags. Though her basketball skills were lacking, the sheer number of bags had guaranteed her two points. She returned to the living room, where she hoped to find Wilbert. He still hadn't emerged from his room.

"I know it's none of my business," she offered to Baseball Cap, "but cleaning up the old food you have lying around will do more to get rid of roaches than all that boric acid powder you have around the baseboards."

"Maybe. But they're permanent residents. They were part of the welcome wagon when we got here."

"Shh!" hissed the other guy. "I'm trying to hear the TV."

The program had switched from wrestling to a commercial featuring women wearing hot pants and halter tops. Between the disorder and the prurient programming, Joelle had had enough. "Tell Wilbert I've gone back to the car."

"Sure."

Joelle didn't believe they'd tell him anything, but at that point, being alone in a sweltering vehicle seemed better than enduring another moment in Wilbert's apartment.

"Too bad," she heard one of the men observe as she swung the door shut behind her. "She looked better than most of the others."

A grin touched Joelle's lips in spite of herself. No way was she returning to such a disaster. As she waited for Wilbert, Joelle opted to mill around the common area and enjoy what little breeze the day offered.

Her date snuck up on her moments later as she observed two young sisters playing in a small sandbox. "I thought I told you to help out in the house. What are you doing out here?"

"Waiting for you. Ready to go?" Joelle made sure her tone didn't invite further inquiry or criticism.

Without another word, he led her to the car. Joelle broke the silence as they pulled back into traffic. "What's the deal with your roommates? If you can't stand a mess, why don't you either hire a maid or throw them out?"

"One, I can't afford a maid. Two, they're my brothers. They're both still in school and don't have anywhere else to go. Don't ask for details. Besides, it looks to me like any nice girl wouldn't mind helping out a little. None of the others seemed to mind."

"Then where are they?" She regretted her retort as soon as it left her lips. "I'm sorry. Look, I can understand not wanting to leave your brothers in the lurch, but as long as it's your apartment, why can't you make them pick up?"

"I've tried. Believe me."

"You could at least put your foot down about the beer drinking."

"What they do is their business." His eyes narrowed. "I don't need criticism from you or anyone else."

Joelle and Wilbert rode in silence. Despite his defense of them, she wondered why Wilbert let his brothers get away with drinking beer all day and treating his home like a dump. And to think—he expected her to clean it! Just like he expected her to clean his churchyard. She started to confront him about that issue when she noticed his mouth was clamped shut. At that moment she decided to remain mute.

I agreed to help with the churchyard, and I won't go back on my promise now. If we see each other again, I can always bring up the subject later.

Joelle was glad when the church came into sight. The sanctuary building stood grandly in the center of a large plot of land, dominating the nearby landscape. A white steeple looked down upon huge oaks, sugar maples, and pines. The church building and the accompanying school, secluded among the trees, created a majestic picture.

Only the sign in front indicated strength and energy. It read:

KING'S ARMY CHURCH AND CHRISTIAN SCHOOL
DR. DILLON DOUGLAS, PASTOR
SUNDAY'S SERMON: HOW DOES GOD DEFINE VICTORY?

"This facility is really something, isn't it?" Wilbert asked as they exited his car.

Joelle continued her survey of the grounds. The colossal brick church building looked strong enough to withstand attacks. Rectangular sections protruding from the main portion of the building indicated at least ten classrooms. A well-maintained playground included a set of four swings, two slides, a tire swing, monkey bars, and a merry-go-round.

"This is quite nice," she readily agreed.

"We use the classrooms adjacent to the playground for Sunday school. During the week, they're used by the lower grades of the school."

Another building loomed to the left. "What's that?"

"The high school." Wilbert's pride was obvious. "We go from kindergarten all the way up through the twelfth grade. Almost five hundred students are enrolled here. Some drive fifty miles, one way, to go to this school."

"Wow!"

Still looking over the area, Joelle noticed a flat parcel of property with enough land to accommodate a soccer field and a baseball diamond. Two sets of bleachers were painted red and black. She could read "The King's Army" on the nearest scoreboard. The mascot—a knight in the armor of a Crusader—was painted on the board. He looked ready for battle.

"I'll say it again. You do have an impressive church and school facility." She gave Wilbert what she knew to be a hesitant look. "But there's only one thing. Do we have to finish working all this tonight?"

Wilbert chuckled. "Oh, no. I just promised to get the church grounds into shape. The high school is sending someone else over tomorrow to take care of the sports fields and the rest of their campus."

Placing her hand over her heart and exhaling, Joelle didn't bother to conceal her relief. For Wilbert to change their plans at the last minute was one thing—after all, he did make a promise, and anyone could be forgiven for being a little disorganized occasionally. But there was no way the two of them would be able to manicure the land surrounding both the church and the school and still be able to make the play. Now maybe they had a chance. "Why don't I do the mowing?"

"Sorry, but I don't think that's a good idea. For one thing, all we have is a standard mower, not a riding one like we really need. To make things worse, it doesn't work well. It tends to cut off without notice. I can barely handle it myself."

"What do you want me to do, then? I enjoy planting flowers, although I don't suppose you have anything like that in mind."

"Not today. Sorry." He surveyed the area, then inclined his head toward a far corner of the churchyard. "How about whacking a few weeds? That area over there needs tending. The tool's in the shed. I'll be right back."

Joelle looked at the area. She felt her mouth open in astonishment. Weeds at least three feet tall awaited. She turned back in his direction to protest, only to discover Wilbert had disappeared.

"Well, if that doesn't beat everything I've ever seen." Joelle placed her hands on her hips, not caring what strangers in passing cars might think. If she had brought her own car, Joelle would have been tempted to make a run for the vehicle, put the pedal to the metal, and make a fast getaway over winding roads to the calm of her house. But she was stuck.

Not seeing anything useful to do while she waited, Joelle sat in one of the swings. Slowly she rocked the swing back and forth, her feet barely leaving the ground. After a few minutes, Wilbert emerged from the tool shed. He was carrying a long wooden stick with a curved blade attached.

"Here you go." He held the instrument as if it were a prized possession.

She made a show of trying to locate an electrical cord. "Um, where do you plug this in?"

"You don't, silly. It runs on pure muscle." Wilbert observed what little portion of her biceps peered from under her short-sleeved shirt. "If you do this type of work often enough, your muscles will be hard as rocks." He handed her the outmoded instrument.

Joelle wanted to beg one more time to run the mower. Surely any gas-powered machine would be preferable to a blade and stick that looked like a nineteenth-century relic.

Before she could open her mouth, Wilbert wished her luck and headed for the waiting mower. Joelle knew argument would only delay the beginning of their real date. She refused to consider the work portion as part of the entertaining evening he had promised. Instead, she hoped to get the task done quickly and then make every effort to forget it. Whistling a series of tuneless notes, she headed for the corner. After assessing the best place to start, she whacked the far edge of the patch of prolific plants. On the third stroke, the blade flew off, sailing through the air as if it were a paper airplane instead of a piece of metal.

Grumbling, Joelle ventured into the overgrowth. Weeds scratched against her pants, making her glad she'd opted for jeans instead of shorts. After searching a few feet, she found the missing blade. She picked it up and pressed the sharp edged metal back onto the worn handle.

"There you go," she said to herself, pounding the metal an extra time for good measure. "Must not have been on very well to start with. Now I can get moving."

The next two strokes were successful, but to her frustration, the blade flew off again during the third swipe. Joelle could see this was a flaw that couldn't be corrected without attaching the blade to the handle with glue. Refusing to admit defeat, she established a pattern. Her best burst of energy went into the first whack, since the blade was properly in place at that point. On the second stroke, the edge would wiggle, allowing her to make less headway than with the first swipe. Before the third attempt, Joelle would reposition the blade before it had a chance to fall off. This process considerably inhibited her advancement.

She kept at it until Wilbert finally appeared behind her to say he was through mowing the churchyard. They were free to shower and go to the play.

"Nice job," Wilbert complimented her as he studied the corner. "I can't believe how much you've improved this area."

"Especially with a whacker that's falling apart." She studied the remaining weeds. "It still needs a lot of work."

He took the instrument from her willing hands. Motioning for her to follow, he began to walk to the shed. "That's all right. No one else wants to bother with that corner. Too many rats, you know."

"Rats?" Joelle shuddered. "I wish you had said something earlier."

He shrugged. "I see you made out okay." After vanishing into the shed, he emerged again to lock the door. Wilbert took as much care in securing the outbuilding as Joelle imagined he would have in locking up a valuable treasure. Considering the state of the tools inside, Joelle wondered why he bothered. She decided not to make her observation known to her date.

Joelle relished the light breeze that cooled her as they made their way across the campus to the high school. The gym was locked, so Wilbert summoned the janitor to let them in.

"Nice weather today, huh, Wilbert?" the older man asked as he jangled several keys, searching for the right one.

"Sure is." Wilbert sent him an apologetic smile. "Sorry I had to bother you, Al."

"That's okay. Had to unlock it for the wife, anyhow. She'll be here in a minute to mop the gym floor."

After bidding Al a good day, Joelle slipped past the gray door marked GIRLS. "I'll be out in a few minutes."

He checked his watch. "Don't worry. We've got time."

All the same, Joelle did her best not to delay. She quickly showered and shampooed her hair. As warm water covered her body, its soothing rivulets running down her head and neck, she suddenly realized her headache had disappeared. The exercise must have helped ease her tension. "At least one good thing came out of this adventure," she muttered as she dried herself.

After a few weeks of dealing with her new hairstyle, which had grown enough that she could curl it more, Joelle had mastered the best techniques for blow-drying and styling her hair in a hurry. After it was curled, she slipped on the faithful black dress that managed to be both elegant and comfortable. Once her accessories were in place and she had spritzed perfume on her wrists, she was ready. Pleased with her reflection, she noticed she looked as good as she had when Wilbert first knocked on her front door hours ago.

As expected, Wilbert was already waiting for her when she had completed her toilette, just like Dean would have been. Wilbert's dark, brooding looks had their appeal, yet Joelle couldn't help but form an image of boyish-looking, auburn-haired Dean. She imagined his crooked smile. "Joelle, you take forever to get ready to go anywhere, but why? You always look gorgeous," Dean would say.

And she would reply, "Men are so lucky. You always look fantastic with no effort at all."

"Why, thank you."

Joelle jumped when Wilbert's deep voice responded. She hadn't realized she'd voiced her last thought aloud.

"You don't look so bad yourself." Wilbert flashed a smile.

"Oh!" Joelle felt the heat rise to her cheeks. "Thanks," she managed to say before navigating the conversation to calmer verbal waters. "We'd better get going if we want to see the play."

"You're right." He began walking.

"By the way, you never mentioned the name of the show. Although whatever it is, I'm sure I'll enjoy it," she hastened to add.

He chuckled. "I'm sure you will. It's *The Sound of Music.*"

"I've never seen that play performed live. I've only seen the Julie Andrews movie." On impulse, she belted out a few lines of the title tune. Swirling and skipping, she moved her hands as if controlling a full skirt.

"Brava, brava!" Laughing, Wilbert clapped as they reached the car. Wilbert once again remembered to open her door. "I don't promise the lead in this cast will be as talented as Julie Andrews. They're just local players. Most of them like to act and sing as a hobby, but the play should be good enough."

As Wilbert walked around his car, Joelle leaned over to unlock his door. She happened into an angle that gave her a good view of the backseat. There was a paper bag on the seat she hadn't noticed before. Two or three inches of a thin, pink tail poured out of the top. She hoped it wasn't what she thought it was.

"What's that?" she asked Wilbert as he slid into his seat.

"It's a possum," he said as he started the car.

Joelle cringed as she buckled her seat belt. Wilbert had confirmed her worst fears. "A possum? What are you doing with that nasty thing in the car?"

"I found him while I was mowing. He was already dead. Don't worry." Wilbert pointed his index finger forward as he steered. "There's a dumpster along the side of the road just a couple of miles up. I'm going to leave him there."

Joelle wrinkled her nose. She wished Wilbert had let his friend rest in peace.

True to his word, Wilbert stopped and threw the bag in the dumpster.

Joelle felt better. "I must say, this evening has involved the oddest detours I've ever been on."

"Didn't my personal ad promise excitement?"

"Hmm." Joelle thought back to the ad. "I do seem to remember something about variety, but nothing about excitement."

"If you have variety, doesn't excitement naturally come with the territory? Maybe I'm just getting the ad you read mixed up with the one I put in *Swinging Christian Singles,* then." Wilbert shot his eyes to her. "Just kidding, of course."

"As if I'd think there really was any such magazine." Joelle chuckled. At least Wilbert possessed a sense of humor. Maybe he could turn out to be someone she could like.

She peered out the windshield, enjoying the summer greenery and smooth passage over curved roads. They hadn't been driving long when Joelle felt a tickling sensation on her leg. She looked down and spotted a small brown insect hurrying toward the hem of her knit dress. Picking it off of her hose, she was appalled to see it was a small tick. "Those weeds you had me chopping must be infested with more than rats." She held the bug between the nails of her forefinger and thumb.

"A sure sign of summer, though not my favorite," Wilbert agreed.

After rolling down the window, she evicted the offender. "No wonder you stuck me over in that corner." Her lips twisted before she spotted a bug on his sleeve. "Wait a minute. Looks like you managed to get a tick, too." She reached for the bug, retrieving it from his sleeve. Quickly, she tossed the second stowaway out of the window.

"Thanks. Looks like nobody's immune today."

No sooner had Joelle rolled up the window than she spotted two more ticks on her legs and another on her arm. Thankfully, none of them had laid claim to a place to bite, but Joelle was unsettled all the same. "I checked for ticks when I showered. I thought for sure I didn't have one on me anywhere."

Wilbert flicked one from his pants leg. "Same here. What could be going on?"

Joelle had a disturbing thought. "The possum. Wonder if that's where they're coming from?"

"But I didn't have him in the car anytime at all, and he's long gone now."

"He must have been in here long enough to leave us with a few souvenirs."

Wilbert rolled down his window as he spotted yet another offending insect. "Maybe you're right. It's not easy for me to concentrate on driving with all these ticks everywhere."

"And on my best dress, too." She tried not to sound too disagreeable.

Even though he kept his hands on the steering wheel, Wilbert's shoulders sank. "I hate to say this, Joelle, but I wonder if—"

"We should call it a night?"

He nodded slowly, demonstrating his reluctance.

"Maybe we'd better. I hate to agree since you've spent money on the tickets."

"The money will be wasted in any event, if we can't enjoy the show."

Joelle sighed. "You're right."

Without saying another word, Wilbert took advantage of the next driveway and used it to make a three-point turn. They were soon headed back in the direction of Joelle's house.

"I feel terrible about this, Joelle. I really wanted us to have a good time," Wilbert apologized.

"Don't worry about it."

"If only I hadn't picked up that possum."

"There's no point in beating yourself up. You can't turn the clock back now."

"Oh, the comfort of clichés." He chuckled.

Joelle giggled. "I guess that's why they're clichés."

He shot her a glance and returned his gaze to the road. "I'll make this up to you, Joelle. We'll do something special one night. I don't know yet what that will be, but I'll think of something."

"Don't worry. You don't owe me anything."

The rest of the drive was silent as Joelle watched for ticks and tried to keep Wilbert from being bitten, too. Of all the dates she'd had, this evening had to be the biggest bust of all.

Folding her arms, Joelle stared at the road. Though a native of the mountains, she still tended to get carsick if she didn't look up when taking a long drive over the deep curves. Not many cars met them on the remote road, so when she spotted a silver sedan, Joelle took notice.

That can't possibly be Dean. What would he be doing out here, especially this late in the evening? She gave herself a mental tap on the head. *Stop being so silly. Dean doesn't own the only silver sedan in the world. Or even in Virginia.*

Still, she looked closely at the couple as they approached. The driver looked too much like Dean for her to dismiss her suspicions. Though both cars were moving fast, she tried to get a good look at the passenger. The woman certainly wasn't Dean's carrot-topped sister, Mandy. Dark hair, overdone in a sexy feather cut looked like—no, it couldn't be. She gasped.

Nicole?

As the car passed, Joelle turned her head and watched until its taillights were out of view.

"Someone you know?" Wilbert asked.

"I'm afraid so." Turning back in her seat, Joelle pouted. She had a bone to pick with Mr. Dean Nichols.

Chapter 8

As soon as she hopped out of Wilbert's car, Joelle walked over the flagstone path to the porch, dropped her bag loaded with her dirty T-shirt and jeans, and rushed into the house. She hadn't cleared the living room before she heard her dad calling from the den, over the blare of a television news broadcast. "Is that you, Joelle?"

"It's me," she called back.

"Home already?"

By this time, she was halfway down the back hall. "Yes, sir."

"Everything okay?" he shouted.

She stuck her head in the door of the den on her way to her bedroom. "Fine. I'll tell you about it later."

After rushing through her room and into the bathroom, she hurried to shed her dress. Soon she had showered for a second time within the span of an hour. Joelle figured she was the cleanest woman in town. She grabbed a clean maroon T-shirt and an old pair of loose gray athletic shorts from the dresser drawer and put them on. After retrieving the formal outfit she had shed from the bathroom floor, Joelle dashed out of the front door and gathered her bag. Several more steps around the side of the dwelling took her to the backyard.

Now that the infested clothes were safely out of the house, Joelle moved a bit more slowly. After reaching the outdoor shed, she snatched a can of tick spray from one of the shelves. Then she hung her canvas tennis shoes, jeans, T-shirt, good black dress, hose, and underthings on the clothesline. Using the can of spray, Joelle saturated each garment to be sure no bug would survive.

Her mother came up behind her. "What in the world are you doing?"

"I'm getting rid of ticks. I got them all in my clothes."

"Of course you can expect a few bugs to be out this time of year, but aren't you overdoing it a bit? And on your good dress, too. That reminds me." She checked her watch. "Why are you home already? You couldn't possibly have had time to clean a churchyard and see a play, to boot."

Joelle rolled her eyes. "Wilbert put a dead possum in the car. He dumped it out, but not before the ticks that were on it got all over the car and us."

"A possum? *Ewww!*"

"Needless to say, we had to call the evening off."

"Too bad. He seemed nice enough."

"Who seemed nice enough? Wilbert, or the possum?" Joelle joked.

With an appreciative chuckle, her mother put her hands on still slim hips and watched the clothes sway in the mild summer breeze. "So will you and Wilbert be seeing each other again?"

Making plans for another date, especially with Wilbert, was the last thing Joelle wanted to consider at the moment. "I have no idea, Mom." She turned her attention to her clothes. Detecting a dry spot on her jeans, she misted it with the poison.

"After all that spray, I'm sure no insect in this world would dare come within a foot of the clothesline."

"Let's hope not," said Joelle.

"You know, I hate to mention this," Eleanor said, arms folded over her chest, "but you probably didn't need to put all that insecticide all over everything. You could have just run the clothes through the washer and then let them spin in the dryer for about a half hour."

She turned to her mother. "Oh." Still holding the can of poison, Joelle felt a bit foolish. "Really?"

"Really." Eleanor smiled her knowledgeable, yet comforting, smile—the one that must be taught at the secret school for mothers where universal knowledge is imparted sometime during every woman's first pregnancy. "But at least by spraying you'll be sure to kill them all."

"That's right." Joelle was glad her mother allowed her to save face.

"You must have gotten into a mess of ticks to be so hyper."

"You wouldn't believe it." Sighing, she looked at the garments hanging on the line. "I guess now the only thing to do is let these clothes hang out until tomorrow morning."

"While you're waiting, you can read your mail." Eleanor handed Joelle two envelopes and several mail-order clothing catalogs. "I forgot to give it to you earlier."

Joelle took the parcels. "That's all right. I didn't have time to read it before now, anyway."

After depositing the can back on its shelf in the shed, Joelle walked back toward her house. The path to the cement patio meandered through the expansive backyard. Carpeted with green grass, the yard had hosted many good times. Joelle remembered games of hide-and-seek, catching lightning bugs at dusk after long summer days, years of birthday parties, even one brother's wedding. At the far end of the plot was her mother's garden. The patch of land she called her own offered time alone to commune with God and to feel pride in watching her vegetables grow. Thanks to their mother, summer at the Jamisons' meant garden-fresh corn on the cob, green beans, and tomatoes.

Lifting her eyes to her bedroom window, Joelle watched the floral chintz curtains sway back and forth with the breeze sweeping through the screen. She thought about her happy years in that room. Joelle had never lived anywhere else for more than a few months. Her parents had bought the three-bedroom white frame house two years after they were wed. All their adult lives had been spent there. She imagined that no matter how old she grew, the Jamison residence would always feel like home. One day, Joelle hoped the house she and her husband—whoever he turned out to be—would have would be able to give their children the same sense of belonging and security.

Flipping through the mail as she walked, she noticed the return address on one letter was from the bank. Probably her savings account statement. That could wait until she was at her desk with her records nearby. Riffling past it, she noticed the second envelope was from a man who certainly would never be her husband. Lloyd Newby. "I don't believe it."

"Don't believe what?" Joelle's mother asked as she seated herself on the floral-patterned glider.

Joelle sat on the freestanding wooden swing and began moving back and forth. "This letter. It's from Lloyd Newby. You remember him."

She nodded. "The one who stuck you with the restaurant tab?"

"The one and only." Ripping open the envelope, Joelle was surprised to find a card. On the front was a photograph of a pouting baby. Inside was the word "Sorry." Lloyd had simply signed his name on the bottom. Even more surprising was Lloyd's check taped to the inside. It was written for $250, more than enough to cover the cost of their evening together.

What wasn't a surprise from a man so bent on keeping up appearances was the expensive lettering and fancy additions Lloyd had ordered to embellish his checks. His name and address were printed in an elegant blue script. The letter N, also in an elaborate script, appeared beside his name and address. The check itself appeared pale blue at first blush, but upon closer inspection, Joelle saw it pictured a sea and sky. The words "Ride the Wave of Success!" were emblazoned near the name of his bank.

Joelle held up the check for her mother to inspect. "Well, what do you know? He kept his word after all."

Eleanor's blond eyebrows rose. "I'll say. He certainly spared no expense on the check itself."

"That's Lloyd. Always showing off."

"Even so, I'm as surprised as you are that he paid you back." She folded her arms. "Especially since he's apparently fond of wasting money."

A grin tickled Joelle's lips. Her mother thought paying good money for embellished checks was foolish when her bank offered plain ones free of charge.

"That goes to show, you can't always tell about people," said Eleanor.

"I'll be telling Dean all right. He was sure I'd never get my money back." Joelle relished the thought of talking to Dean. She had to let him know he had been wrong about Lloyd. The check proved he was wrong. She wasn't such a poor judge of character.

"That reminds me. You remember how the phone was ringing when you were leaving the house? Well, it turned out to be Dean."

Joelle's heart skipped a beat. She let her hands fall to her lap. "Dean? Why didn't you tell me? I would have come back into the house and taken his call."

"What do you mean, you would have come back in the house? You were already out on your date."

"Such as it was," Joelle muttered.

"You didn't know at the time it would turn out to be a disaster. But anyways," Eleanor waved her hand as if swatting an annoying fly, "why would you stop everything just to talk to him? You always have said he's just a friend. Can't he talk to you anytime?"

"I—I guess. Um, you don't know what he wanted, do you?"

"He said something about having tickets to a show. I don't know what show it was."

The cogs in Joelle's brain began turning. She wondered if Dean had indeed been on his way to see the same play she and Wilbert had abandoned. If so, that would explain why their cars passed on the road. An unwelcome thought occurred to her. "You didn't tell him I was out on a date with someone else, did you?"

"I don't think so. I didn't see any need. I just said you were out for the evening, and I wasn't sure when you'd be home."

"What did he say then?"

"Nothing, really. Although, I could tell he was disappointed. He did say for you to call if you got back before eight." Eleanor gave her daughter a pat on the knee. "You know, you were better off not being home anyway. Even if Dean is just a friend, there's no need in you looking like you're not popular enough to be out on a Friday night."

It was Joelle's turn to roll her eyes. "Dean and I are close enough that we don't need to play games."

"Is that so?" Eleanor's lips pursed. "Can a man and a woman ever really be just friends?"

Joelle didn't want to answer. Her mother's oblique suggestion was too unsettling to contemplate, but so was the alternative. Now that she knew Dean had tickets to the play, she was certain of two facts. One, Dean was the one she and Wilbert had met on the road. Two, the woman with him had to be Nicole—not that it mattered. Whoever Dean saw was his business. But she wouldn't wish Nicole on her worst enemy, much less her best friend. If only she'd answered the phone before she left!

"And anyhow," her mother said, interrupting her thoughts, "if I had run out the door and hollered for you to come to the phone to speak to Dean, would that have changed anything?"

"Maybe."

"I don't see how. Unless you're trying to make me believe you would have left this Wilbert fellow standing out there on the front porch so you could go to the play with Dean instead."

"Well. . ."

"Well, nothing," Joelle's mother said with a wag of her finger. "Can't you see you're better off the way things turned out? If you'd answered the phone, you would have been forced to turn him down. You would have been cornered into telling him the whole truth. This way, he's just guessing."

"You have a point."

"Maybe you'll end up with Wilbert and Dean fighting over you." Eleanor chuckled.

"I doubt that." Joelle folded her arms. All that work, and she didn't even get to see the play. Not to mention her best black dress had become tick-infested. She wondered if she'd ever be able to get out the smell of insecticide. "After tonight, I have no intention of seeing Wilbert again. Ever." She nodded once to emphasize her determination. "Things wouldn't have been so bad if we had actually gotten to the theater, but I did all that work for nothing."

"Work done for the church is never for nothing. Even if it's not for your own church, what you did tonight helped others in the Christian community," Joelle's mother pointed out.

A sense of shame washed over her. "You're right. I do need an attitude adjustment."

"You've had a hard night. Tomorrow things will look better. Maybe then you can think about giving Wilbert another chance."

"You like him that much?"

Eleanor shrugged. "I don't know him. He's obviously involved in his church, so if I were you, I'd be willing to go out with him a second time if he calls."

"I don't know. Mom, even without the ticks, the evening was a disaster. I can tell all he really wants is a maid."

"I know the evening wasn't much fun, but it wasn't Wilbert's fault." After Joelle shot her a look, Eleanor added, "All right. Maybe it was his fault, but at least the incident with the possum wasn't intentional. I feel sorry for him. He'll be trying to get ticks out of his car from now until the first winter freeze." Eleanor covered her mouth to stifle a laugh.

Her comment brought to Joelle's mind an image of Wilbert attempting to get rid of the pests. In spite of herself, Joelle joined her mother's laughter. Funny, she wished Dean were there to share it with them.

Chapter 9

The next evening was Singles' Night. As members of the group filed in one by one and began conversations, they happily chatted without regard to the time. Just before the meeting was ready to kick off, Zach entered. With him were two teenagers he introduced as his twin cousins. Radical styles of clothing and accessories caused the adolescent boys to be noticeable among their working-age elders.

The group tried to greet them with open arms, but the boys were reticent. Spurning attempts at conversation, they turned away and talked between themselves.

"Looks like our guests are here under duress," Joelle whispered to Zach.

"I know," Zach answered. "I hated to put you guys out by bringing them, but since they're in town, my mom insisted. She even bribed me with a steak dinner so I'd drive to her house to pick them up." Zach studied his young charges. A worried look entered his eyes then sat upon his face. He shook his head and returned his gaze to Joelle. "I think she just might have wanted to get rid of them for an evening."

Joelle wondered if Zach didn't speak the truth. Raven took his name to heart. His long, straight hair was dyed an ebony that contrasted with his pale skin like coal buttons against a snowman's body. The goatee he was attempting to grow was dark brown. Joelle assumed he sported the facial hair to look older, but in actuality, the goatee made him appear younger. Raven's T-shirt was solid black, as were his pants. Black boots covered his feet in defiance of the warm weather.

The fact that Eagle's long, platinum blond hair didn't occur naturally was betrayed by deep brown roots that matched his long sideburns. A black leather vest partially concealed a white T-shirt with writing that Joelle couldn't decipher. Black leather pants and boots covered the lower half of his body. No jewelry was spared. Several gold hoops decorated the lobes of each ear. On his right wrist was a gold ID bracelet. The other, in a bow to practicality, bore a watch.

Joelle hated to judge by appearances, but their style of dress made it difficult to draw any conclusion other than that they were trouble. She tilted her head and set her own eyes on the ceiling as though she were in deep contemplation. "Hmm. Wonder why your mom would want an evening without the twins?"

"I wonder." Zach shook his head.

As she and Zach were exchanging quips, Joelle kept an eye on Dean. The time was almost ten minutes after the hour. Dean consulted his watch every few seconds. In the meantime, Joelle took a head count. On the green couch sat the twins. Dean, Fiona, and Ashlynn occupied the multisectional pit group seating that rounded one corner. Zach sat beside her in one of two wing chairs with matching but worn brown vinyl upholstery. Who was missing?

Nicole! Joelle's heart gave her a sinking feeling.

At that moment, Dean spoke to the group. "Where's Nicole?"

"Nicole? I don't know for sure," Fiona answered, "but remember last week how she said something about having other plans?"

"She did? I don't remember that," said Dean.

"I do," Ashlynn countered. "She said she wouldn't be here this week."

"I wish I'd heard her," Dean remarked.

Dean wasn't even bothering to conceal his interest in Nicole! Joelle felt her heart's rapid beating betray her.

"I thought sure she'd be here," Dean continued. "It was her turn to be in charge of the lesson and entertainment tonight."

Joelle didn't answer. The uncomfortable reality was, she didn't miss Nicole at all. If she were to admit the whole truth, Joelle was pleased that Nicole was absent.

"She's been really busy at work. I'm sure she forgot she promised to be in charge of the program." Zach's tone of voice indicated he didn't believe his own words.

Dean's mouth twisted into an unhappy curve. "I guess there's no other choice. I'll just have to wing it. We were supposed to talk about the Great Commission tonight. As for fun, you know me—I don't go anywhere without my guitar, so we can have some music later if anybody's interested."

A round of agreeable murmurs filled the room.

"You can practice your solo for tomorrow," Joelle observed. "We'll be your guinea pigs."

Dean winked. "Only if you promise to sing along."

Despite the teasing gesture, Joelle knew Dean wasn't joking. Joelle had developed her singing voice during high school with three years of lessons. At one time, she'd considered music as a career. After some contemplation, she decided she wasn't committed enough to the field to make it a profession. A steady job in accounting and bookkeeping seemed more appealing. Her associate degree in business management hadn't let her down. In the meantime, Joelle enjoyed singing as a hobby.

Joelle wondered why Nicole had skipped out on her commitment and left the group stranded. *At least now I look dependable, and she looks flighty.*

As soon as the thought entered Joelle's mind, a pang of guilt stabbed her. Allowing her own jealousy to get in the way was wrong. Nicole needed the church.

But I'm not jealous. I just know she's not right for Dean. That's all.

"You didn't know we had our own musical ensemble, did you, guys?" Zach told his cousins, Eagle and Raven.

"I can strum a few tunes," Dean said, "but I doubt I can compete with Hollywood."

"It's not like I'm up for a Dove Award or a Grammy, either," added Joelle.

"Don't worry about it. We're always on the listen out for new music," Eagle said. "We have our own band."

"Your own band? How exciting!" Ashlynn squealed, clasping her hands to her chest. "Have we heard of you?"

"We haven't gotten a deal with a major label yet," Eagle admitted.

"We haven't even gotten a deal with a minor label," Raven added. "We've sent our demo out to a lot of record companies, though. One day, somebody will notice us and give us a chance. Then, after we're stars, you'll be able to say you know the lead guitarist and vocalist—that's me—and the drummer—that's him over there," he said, pointing to his brother, "from PUG."

"Pug? Like the little dog?" Ashlynn wanted to know. "How cute!"

"Not really. It means Puked Up Garbage." Eagle's voice was filled with pride.

"Oh." A hint of a crestfallen expression crossed Ashlynn's face before she recovered and pasted on a smile. "I'd still be glad to listen to it sometime."

Still smiling, Ashlynn set her gaze on Zach. Though over the past few weeks he'd shown only vague signs of interest in the blue-eyed brunette, Ashlynn still tried to follow his interests and engage him in conversation whenever she could. Joelle was sure she knew the only reason Ashlynn offered to listen to the twins' music. Ashlynn hoped to parlay the experience into a chance to be near Zach.

"Don't pay any attention to them, Ashlynn," Zach said. "They like to get attention. A lot of what they say is for sheer shock value."

"Is not," Eagle protested.

"Don't think you're kidding anybody," Zach argued. "I know you love to say something shocking, just to see what people will do."

Dean tried to make peace. "It's a free country. You have the right to name your band whatever you want. Since you can read music, maybe you'd still like to play along with me. Did you bring your guitar, Raven?"

"I brought it out here, but I don't have it with me tonight."

"But you brought your vocal chords." Fiona smiled.

Eagle didn't respond to her lightheartedness with a smile of his own. "I don't know any hymns, and I don't want to learn any, either."

"We wouldn't be able to read the music, anyway. We don't write down our notes. We just remember them," Raven said. "Our music is alternative. We cover some songs by other groups, but mainly we write our own stuff. We don't play any religious songs."

"Sure we do." A reptilian smile covered Eagle's face.

"Not songs they'd like," Raven said. "You know that."

"What do you like to write about?" Dean inquired, keeping his facial expression and tone of voice friendly.

Raven shrugged. "Death. Suicide. How the world's an evil place, especially for teens like us."

"And how there is no God," Eagle added. Folding his arms, he offered them a daring look. The motion caused his shirt sleeve to move slightly. For the first time, Joelle noticed a tattoo on his forearm. The part she could see appeared to be the flat head and forked tongue of a cobra.

Joelle was all too aware of the popularity of tattoos. The body art came as no real surprise. Nevertheless, a warning from Leviticus 19 popped into Joelle's mind: *"Ye shall not make any cuttings in your flesh for the dead, nor print any marks upon you: I am the LORD."*

Zach's voice interrupted into her musings. "That's enough, guys." He looked around the room, briefly making eye contact with each single. "I'm sorry if my cousins offend you. As I said before, these guys like to play the role of agitators. It's part of their image. They don't mean most of what they say."

"Yes, we do," Eagle insisted. "The people who don't get it just aren't listening. Not to our music, and not to what we have to say."

"You'd be surprised by how people might listen if you'd drop the attitude." Though his words presented a challenge, the expression in Zach's eyes warned his cousins not to speak further.

Dean shot Joelle a look of unease. She knew he was wondering how Raven and Eagle would tolerate spending the evening amidst their group. She was about to find out.

Chapter 10

Putting on an optimistic expression, Dean turned to the teens. "I hope tonight's lesson will help change your minds."

"Don't count on it," Eagle said. "Everybody knows man invented God to explain where we came from, but modern science answered all those questions years ago. We don't need God anymore. Evolution explains it all."

"Is that what you think?" Dean asked without a trace of hostility. "Do you realize the theory of evolution is just that—a theory? It is not a proven fact."

"That's not what they say in biology class," Raven pointed out.

"Your teachers are trying their best to instruct you in what they believe to be the truth," Zach explained. "Unfortunately, some of them have been seriously misled."

"He's right," Dean agreed. "We were taught the same thing when we went to high school. Our teachers also looked exclusively to science for the answers, but all anyone needs is this." Holding up his book, Dean tapped his forefinger just under the words *Holy Bible*, imprinted in gold.

"That book does not have all the answers," Eagle argued. "If it did, we'd know why God lets evil happen."

"Just because God allows evil to happen doesn't mean He likes or approves of it," Joelle answered.

"True," Dean agreed. "Evil happens because we live in a fallen world. This is not the Garden of Eden."

"For once, something you say makes sense," said Raven.

"Eve made the mistake of listening to Satan and giving in to temptation. Today, all of us are just as human. We aren't perfect, either," Fiona elaborated.

Dean gazed unflinchingly into the teens' faces. "Some of us make a grave error. The error of not believing in Him."

"We have the privilege of not listening to Him." Eagle returned Dean's stare with a scowl.

"You're right," Dean conceded. "God gives us the free will to accept or reject Him."

"Really? Can you prove that?" Raven's eyes held a light of interest for the first time that evening.

"That fact is both written and implied all through the Bible. Let me see." Dean opened his Bible and turned toward the back. "I think I can find one especially good passage in the book of Revelation."

"The book of Revelation?" Raven's expression became intense, as though he was trying to recall something. Suddenly, his mouth opened into a slight smile of triumph. He snapped his fingers and then lifted his index finger. "Is that the part where some dude has a bunch of weird dreams?"

"Some might say that." Chuckles filled the room, along with the sound of pages turning in four other Bibles.

Raven's blue eyes lit up for the first time. "Wicked awesome!"

In contrast, Eagle's gray eyes narrowed. His arms remained folded. "Mom says that's the fire and brimstone book."

"Fire and brimstone. Cool, dude." Relaxing, Raven leaned back into the sofa cushion.

"Sounds more like it's hot to me," Ashlynn joked. A round of good-natured groans and a few giggles followed.

Joelle glanced at Dean. Apparently oblivious to the conversation around him, he kept his eyes on the page, scrolling down the words as he read. A few moments passed before he tapped his finger on the passage.

"Here it is," he said. "I'll start reading at Revelation 21:6. This is Jesus speaking to John at Patmos. 'And he said unto me, It is done. I am Alpha and Omega, the beginning and the end. I will give unto him that is athirst of the fountain of the water of life freely. He that overcometh shall inherit all things; and I will be his God, and he shall be my son. But the fearful, and unbelieving, and the abominable, and murderers, and whoremongers, and sorcerers, and idolaters, and all liars, shall have their part in the lake which burneth with fire and brimstone: which is the second death.'"

Raven nudged his twin. "Mom was right. There is fire and brimstone in that book!"

"See, I told you God tries to force you to believe in Him. It's saying we'll be burned to death if we don't," Eagle said. "Or at least I think that's what it's saying. It's hard to understand. Nobody talks like that anymore. No wonder nobody I know reads the Bible."

"Believe it or not, other people feel the same way," Dean said. "There are other versions of the Bible that are easier to understand."

"I have the New International Version," Fiona offered.

"That might help. Would you read it?" Dean asked.

Fiona nodded. "'He said to me: It is done. I am the Alpha and the Omega, the Beginning and the End. To him who is thirsty I will give to drink without cost from the spring of the water of life.'"

"That's a lie, man," Eagle interrupted. "There is a cost. They want you to go to church every Sunday and not have fun anymore."

"Church doesn't have to be boring. Services can be great, when you really want to worship the Lord," Zach pointed out. "And church isn't just for Sunday, either." He swept his hand over the room. "Being here tonight ought to show you that much. Look at how all of us here are friends."

Eagle surveyed the room. "I have more friends than this."

"Would they still be your friends if you started going to church?" Joelle wondered aloud.

The teenager's mouth opened with apparent surprise. He didn't respond right away. "I dunno," he said and dropped his gaze to the floor. His unwillingness to meet her eyes was answer enough for Joelle.

"Not so long ago, most of my friends were outside of the church, too," she explained. "But soon after I accepted Jesus as my personal Savior, a lot of them abandoned me."

Eagle looked up. "If that's true, then your friends weren't as loyal as mine."

His words cut too close. Without warning, an unwelcome tide of ill feeling engulfed Joelle. She remembered each of her old friends. In her mind, she revisited the pain of their departures from her life as if each event had happened yesterday. The realization that they could no longer accept her now that she had begun a true relationship with the Lord still caused her to flinch with grief.

She swallowed. "I don't know your friends. So maybe you're right," Joelle conceded. "But I do know why a few of the people I called my friends broke off with me."

"Let me guess," Eagle scoffed. "You're going to tell me whether I want to know or not."

Joelle ignored his loaded comment. "A year ago, instead of being here tonight, I probably would have been at a club."

"I sure wish that's where I was right about now." Eagle voiced his protest with enough volume for Joelle to hear him, but softly enough to stay out of trouble with Zach.

Hiding her frustration, Joelle sent up a silent prayer to be infused with the Holy Spirit. After taking in a strengthening breath, she continued. "But now I don't go to those places anymore."

"Just like that, huh?" Raven's eyes grew wide. "Don't you miss the clubs?"

She flinched. "Sometimes, as much as I hate to admit it. You have to realize, I always called myself a Christian, but it was only within the past few months that I really let Christ change my life. I don't pretend I didn't have any trouble shedding my old life. I still have to die to it every day."

"Die to it?" asked Raven.

"Yes. I mean, I have to remember I promised to serve Jesus. I can't let my desire to go back to my old habits get in the way of my walk with the Lord."

"How do you do that?" he asked.

"I pray for strength each morning."

"When do you have the most trouble?" asked Ashlynn.

Joelle was surprised by the source of the inquiry, but she answered. "When I start thinking about my old friends and my old habits, it's usually because I'm lonely or just feeling down for some reason. Memories come back if I have reason to drive by one of my old haunts."

"What keeps you from stopping the car and going in?" she asked.

"Concentrating on the Lord. Praying to Him." Joelle paused. "I think about how little I've lost and how much I've gained. I've traded a few small, fleeting pleasures for solid, meaningful relationships in the Christian community and the ultimate reward—eternal life."

"What does that have to do with your friends?" Eagle prompted.

"I did wander off the subject, didn't I? Sorry," she apologized. "I found out that the friends who really were interested in me as a person are still in touch. The ones who just looked at me as a buddy to fill out a table at a club and to gossip with are the ones who dumped me, so they weren't friends at all. Not really."

Her own words caused Joelle to remember one friend in particular. Actually, he had been much more than a friend. Dustin was the man Joelle thought she'd marry one day. She had been both surprised and heartbroken when he was the first to drop her after she responded to the life-changing gospel.

Ever since she'd known him in high school, Dustin had professed to be a Christian. Joelle knew neither she nor Dustin had been living a godly life, but she always assumed they'd get their frivolous ways out of their systems, settle down, and then begin walking the talk. When Joelle accepted Christ, however, Dustin wasn't ready for the change. He was happy going on as before, giving religion lip service and attending church once or twice a year. A larger commitment proved too much. When Dustin promptly dumped her for someone else, Joelle unhappily discovered that he'd never intended to live anything remotely resembling a righteous life. At least her acceptance of the Lord showed her Dustin wasn't right for her.

A ray of hope surged through her. *Surely God will help me find a man through the Christian personals. I've got to keep trying!*

Rising from her seat, she spoke again. "Sure, I was sad to lose my old friends; but as I said, I made new friends. And my best friend since childhood stayed with me." Joelle stopped behind Dean. Smiling, she patted him on the shoulder. She let her hand rest there for a moment, feeling his warmth.

He brought his hand to hers, touching it for an instant. "I'd say we're closer than ever. Joelle knows I'll always be here for her, no matter what."

"So it was worth it," Raven said, his voice barely above a whisper. He looked above Joelle's head, as though he were looking toward heaven and seeing God for the first time.

In a flash, she realized the embarrassment of confessing her struggles and imperfections in front of her friends and two strangers had happened for a reason. Her confession may have reached the adolescent. "Yes," she affirmed, her voice strong. "Accepting Christ was worth everything."

All eyes shifted to Eagle. Unrepentant, he glowered at them all.

Fiona finally broke the silence. "Shall I keep reading, Dean?"

He nodded. "Please do."

" 'He who overcomes will inherit all this, and I will be his God and he will be my son. But the cowardly, the unbelieving, the vile, the murderers, the sexually immoral, those who practice magic arts, the idolaters and all liars—their place will be in the fiery lake of burning sulfur. This is the second death.' "

"The second death? Ooooh, I'm so scared." Lifting his hands, Eagle shook them in feigned fright.

"You'd better be, dude!" Raven's laughter belied his words.

Dean sighed. Joelle watched his shoulders slump ever so slightly with discouragement. She wished she could think of something helpful to say, but no words fell on her lips. Raven, and especially Eagle, wouldn't be easy for anyone to reach. Their looks alone showed that much—but at least Dean had tried.

"If it's all right with everyone, what if we let Nicole pick up next week's lesson on the Great Commission?"

"Commission?" Raven asked. "Isn't that when you sell something and somebody pays you part of the profit?"

"In the business world, yes," Zach answered. "But when we speak of the Great Commission in the context of the New Testament, we mean Jesus' command that we should share the good news of His saving grace with everyone."

"Bo–ring," Eagle interjected. He let out an exaggerated yawn.

"Eagle, that's enough." Signaling his growing impatience, Zach's voice was firmer than it had been all night. "I don't expect you to like what you're hearing, but you're a guest here. There's no reason to be rude."

"That's all right, Zach," Dean said amidst nods of agreement. "We've hit on so many topics, all of us probably have enough to chew on for this week." He glanced at his watch. "It's time to move along to the entertainment anyway." After setting his Bible on the small table right beside the couch, he got up and retrieved the guitar from the corner where he'd left it. Propping it on his knee, he asked, "What song would everyone like to sing?"

Eagle suggested several offensive titles that Joelle assumed were hard rock or alternative tunes. She could feel Dean's embarrassment and distress.

Ashlynn and Fiona named a couple of bland secular songs, only to meet with blank looks from the twins. As titles were shouted out, only to be discarded, the tension became palpable. Everyone discerned that no song the regular group suggested would please, or even placate, the rebellious boys.

"How about something simple? Maybe 'Jesus Loves Me,' " suggested Dean. "Everyone knows that song, right?" He eyed the teens.

"That's it. I'm not singing a song for little kids. I'm outta here!" Eagle rose from his seat. He headed to the door. When he reached it, he pounded it open with the palm of his hand. He stomped down the hall, heavy boots causing his footfalls to echo on the tile floor in the hallway. They heard the door slam behind him as he escaped to the outdoors.

Zach made no move to follow his cousin. "Sorry, you guys." Letting out an audible sigh, he set his elbows on his knees and leaned his head in his hands.

"That's all right. You're doing the best you can," Ashlynn consoled him.

"Do you think you'd better go after him?" Joelle asked.

Zach lifted his head. "No need. He's just gone out to smoke a cigarette."

"Or maybe something else." Raven's voice was barely audible.

A fresh wave of unease washed over the group.

"Raven," Zach asked, "why don't you go and see what he's up to?"

Clearly relieved by the suggestion, Raven nodded and headed outside.

As soon as they heard the front door shut, Zach spoke. "I'm sorry I've ruined this meeting by bringing them. I thought they'd be on their best behavior. I should have known better."

"You haven't ruined anything," Dean assured. "Meeting them has given us a chance to practice what we preach."

"We've started out with pretty hard cases," Zach said. "They haven't had it easy. Their parents divorced a couple of years ago. They aren't saved, so how can anyone expect their boys to be any better?"

A collective intake of breath was followed by utterings of compassion and understanding from the group.

"I feel led to pray." Dean extended both hands to grasp Joelle's on one side and Fiona's on the other. He didn't have to ask twice. Everyone clasped hands and joined in a circle. "Since the guys might come back any moment, I suggest we keep our petitions silent."

The young adults bowed their heads, each immersed in private communication with the Lord. All too soon, they heard the front door creak open, followed by the sound of someone approaching the classroom, until Raven finally burst upon the circle. His eyes were wide and wild.

"I can't find Eagle. He's gone!"

Chapter 11

"What do you mean, he's gone?" Zach asked. "He just left a few minutes ago. He's got to be out there somewhere."

"I don't know where. I looked all over the place. In the front, in the back, in the parking lot. Everywhere." Raven's voice had become high-pitched with obvious fright.

"Don't worry," said Dean. "Zach's right. He couldn't have gone far. Unless—" He turned to Zach. "He couldn't have taken a car, could he?"

"I didn't hear a motor start," Joelle said.

"Thank goodness. Joelle, I'd like for you, Fiona, and Ashlynn to stay here," Dean instructed, pointing to each woman as he said her name, "just in case he decides to come back. If he does, one of you can stay with Eagle while the other two find us."

Joelle nodded. Secretly she hoped she wouldn't be the one who had to stay with Eagle. The prospect of handling a rebellious teen wasn't something she relished.

Unaware of Joelle's concerns, Dean turned to the other males. "Raven, you look through the forest in back of the church. Zach, why don't you and I take our cars and head off in both directions?"

Nodding, everyone began to put Dean's plan into place.

Joelle touched Dean on the shoulder. "Be careful," she whispered.

"I will." He gave her a sad smile. Joelle knew he blamed himself for Eagle's flight.

As soon as they left the church, Ashlynn said, "This night sure has been a disaster."

"It's not a disaster yet, and it only will be if they don't find Eagle," Joelle said.

Fiona smirked. "You say that as though finding Eagle would be a good thing."

"Fiona, you're so bad!" Ashlynn mocked.

She shrugged. "They might find him in jail. I'm sure he's got drugs on him."

Joelle sighed. "I feel sorry for him. For both of them."

"I don't," said Fiona, plopping herself into a comfortable chair. "They're troublemakers."

Though Ashlynn remained standing, Joelle sat on the adjacent couch. "But look where they come from. It can't be easy to conform when you don't have any support from your parents."

"Oh, stop blaming the parents, Joelle," Fiona sneered. "My parents divorced when I was in junior high. I didn't use that as an excuse to be a juvenile delinquent or to run away from God."

"But didn't your parents at least take you to church when you were little? Didn't you have a chance to learn about Jesus?"

Fiona's lips narrowed into a thin line. "Yes, they did. I have to admit that."

"From all appearances, these kids didn't have that chance. Can't you see they have no relationship with God at all? How can you run away from Someone you never knew?"

"I guess you're right."

"Good," Ashlynn interrupted. "Now instead of wasting time arguing, why don't we pray?"

"That's the second good suggestion we've had all night," Joelle said.

The three women joined together in good-natured chuckles before turning serious. Joining hands, they stood in a tight triangle and prayed aloud for the safe return of all involved.

⤛⤜

Dean hopped into his car and started the engine. He paused for a moment before pulling out of the gravel parking lot. "Dear Lord," he prayed, "please guide me as I search for Eagle. Keep him in Your care, that he doesn't run into any wild animals or anyone who will hurt him. Help me to find him, then be with me as I bring him back to Zach. In the holy name of Your Son, amen."

After exiting the lot, Dean felt led to make a left turn. The country road was so narrow, two cars passing could easily sideswipe each other. Hairpin curves didn't help matters. Even though Dean had driven over this road time and time again, he had no choice but to keep his speed down. "Eagle was on foot," Dean reasoned to himself. "He couldn't have gone far." He had a disturbing thought. "Unless someone picked him up."

The road was never heavily traveled, but since Saturdays were busy with people running errands, going out on dates, and getting together with family and friends, the probability that Eagle had encountered someone was high. He groaned. "He might have made it to town by now." If he had money with him, Eagle could have hitched a ride into town, found the bus station, and bought a ticket for who knew where.

Dean consulted the digital clock on the dash, noting that a half hour had passed since Raven told them his brother was missing. That meant Eagle had about a forty-five-minute head start. "If one of us doesn't find him soon, we could lose him altogether."

Nervousness caused his stomach to lurch. Zach was Dean's friend, and Dean would never do anything to hurt Zach. He felt responsible for Eagle's outburst. If any harm fell upon Eagle, how would he face Zach? How could they both tell

Zach's mother the awful news? No. Eagle had to stay safe. Dean had to find him. "Please, Lord, keep Eagle from going too far!"

Dean scanned the countryside. Night had fallen in full force, covering the earth with a blanket as black as Eagle's leather vest. Remembering Eagle's ebony boots, Dean held no hope that he'd be able to spot a thin glow-in-the-dark strip of light on athletic shoes meant to protect nighttime joggers. He'd just have to be vigilant in looking for movement and for any form that could be a human.

Realizing that Eagle might not be walking along the road, he peered into the surrounding forest. The trees had long since budded. Their branches were now laden with leaves that were impossible to see through. But he had to keep searching for Eagle.

Though he tried to investigate each side of the road while driving, Dean had a feeling Eagle wouldn't venture into the forest. Since he was used to concrete and city lights, the boy most likely would feel more comfortable staying with the road. Eagle put on a brave front, but Dean wasn't confident the scrawny teenager would want to go head-to-head with the occasional black bear that roamed these parts.

After driving several more minutes at a pace not unlike a tortoise, Dean gave up. "I'll just have to turn around in the Nelsons' driveway," he muttered, thinking aloud. "I guess then I'll go back by the church and try the other direction."

Rounding the next curve, Dean concentrated his gaze on the right side of the road. The Nelsons' driveway was marked by a black mailbox that tended to vanish into the night. If he wasn't careful, he'd miss it and would be forced to drive another mile or so before he could make a three-point turn in safety.

The headlights had just beamed on the mailbox when Dean detected movement a few feet beyond. His heart beat in rapid rhythm. "That looks like Eagle!"

Slowing down even more, Dean's headlamps illuminated the figure. Blond hair straggled midway over a black vest. White T-shirt sleeves extended over tattooed arms. In one hand was a lighted cigarette. "That's got to be him."

The object of Dean's attention stopped walking and spun on his heel. To Dean's relief, he stared into the expressionless face of Eagle. The boy placed the cigarette between unsmiling lips. His left hand tucked into his pants pocket, with his free hand he stuck out his thumb, waving it proudly in the night.

"Yeah!" Now Dean had every reason to stop. Passing Eagle by only a few feet, he eased his vehicle to the edge of the road, letting the tires on the passenger side glide onto the shoulder. Unable to pull his car completely off the road, Dean put the car in park and hoped no one else would choose that moment to speed by.

After reaching the car in haste, Eagle opened the passenger door, dropped his cigarette, and smashed it with his foot. "I need a ride to—" A look of recognition and horror crossed his face. "It's you!"

Seeing Eagle's fright, Dean leaned over and tried to grab him. Eagle proved too fast. Leaving the door open, the boy fled in the opposite direction.

Dean wasn't about to give up. He killed the engine, opened his door, and hopped out, quickly shutting it behind him. Eagle's dark clothes didn't keep Dean from spying the youth as he fled toward the Nelsons' driveway.

Dean soon overtook him. Eagle was at least thirteen years younger, but he wasn't fit enough to shake off Dean, who kept in shape by running three miles a day. At that moment, he was grateful that he had put in the time running each morning. As soon as he got within arm's reach of Eagle, he grabbed him by the vest.

Eagle tried to escape but didn't think quickly enough to shrug out of his vest. In a flash, Dean reached out and grabbed his arm. Eagle writhed and attempted to hit Dean with his other fist. Dean adroitly stepped out of the way of the swinging hand. Twisting Eagle's arm behind his back finally subdued the teenager. He became still.

"Okay. I give." Eagle's breathing was hard. "Will you let go of me?"

"I won't let go, but I will stop twisting your arm," Dean promised.

"Okay." His ragged breathing became slower.

Dean untwisted Eagle's arm, keeping both hands in a vise-like grip around his undeveloped biceps. For an instant, Eagle started writhing again, but Dean tightened his hold. Apparently seeing the futility of fighting further, Eagle stopped.

"Had enough?" Dean asked.

Eagle nodded, glowering all the while.

"As long as you don't fight me, we'll get along just fine."

Eagle scowled but acquiesced and kept pace with Dean as he led him back to the car. Suddenly, the youth looked at him with a surprised expression. "Hey, you're not even breathing hard. What's up with you? Are you a pro basketball player or something?"

"Hardly." Dean chuckled in spite of himself. At five feet, eight inches in height, he wouldn't have made third string on his high school team, much less have a shot for a place on a professional team.

"I thought I could outrun somebody as old as you, no problem."

"Well, for one thing," Dean answered, "I don't smoke."

"All right. I'll get more than enough lectures when I get home. I don't need another one now."

Dean had no doubt Eagle was right. Unwilling to antagonize him further, Dean remained quiet as they drove back to the church. To his relief, Eagle didn't pull any more stunts in an effort to escape.

Grateful the teenager had been found, Dean said a silent prayer of thanks to the Lord.

The women were still praying when Dean arrived at church later, holding Eagle by the wrist.

"They're praying for me, aren't they?" The teen was seething with anger. "Tell them I don't want their prayers."

"Where did you find him?" Joelle asked.

"He'd made pretty good progress on foot. He was near the Nelson place, trying to hitch a ride." Dean looked at his young charge. "You weren't too happy when you found out the guy in the car was me, were you?"

"I knew you were old, but I didn't think you'd have a car that bogus," Eagle countered.

Joelle grinned in spite of herself. "You must not have thought it was too bogus, or else you wouldn't have tried to thumb a ride in it, would you?"

"I would have taken anything with a running engine at that point. I might have known I'd end up with just another do-gooder in this hick place."

"Now what?" Fiona asked.

"Don't worry about it," Eagle answered. "As soon as I get out of here, I'm calling Dad and telling him we're flying back to L.A. on the next plane out."

"I wasn't talking to you," Fiona said. "Dean, we can't leave the others out there all night, searching for him."

Dean looked at Eagle, then sent the women a glance that said Eagle was tough enough for him to handle, let alone them. "Joelle, why don't you call Zach from my cell phone? As for Raven, let's just wait. He promised not to stay in the forest longer than a half hour." He looked at his watch. "And that's almost passed now."

Time seemed to move slowly as the group, including one sullen teenager, waited. Eventually Raven returned, followed several minutes later by Zach.

As soon as Zach expressed relief that his young charge had been found, he switched gears. "Eagle, what did you think you'd accomplish by pulling a stunt like that?"

For once, Eagle had no comeback.

Zach took Eagle by the bicep and began leading him to the door. The spindly teen didn't try to resist his buff cousin. "Let's go."

Chapter 12

An hour later, Joelle and Dean were seated at a table in Mary's eatery. All around them were other diners. Most, like Joelle and Dean, were indulging in late evening desserts.

They both ordered comfort food—generous slices of lemon meringue pie and two mugs of decaffeinated coffee. Dean made small talk until their desserts were set before them. Dean hadn't made a display of his feelings as long as he'd remained at the church. Once they were alone, however, he was honest with Joelle about what he was really thinking.

"I wish I'd done a better job of reaching those kids." Dean didn't look at her, but stirred his coffee more than necessary to dissolve two spoonfuls of sugar. "If only I could have said something to break through. I had the best of intentions, and even then I ended up losing Eagle." His mouth curved into a frown. "Literally."

Joelle reached across the table and patted the hand Dean had wrapped around his mug. "You can't go blaming yourself, Dean. I thought you were great, all things considered."

"Thanks." He began cutting into his pie. Joelle could see that the cheap fork easily slid through the crust, which flaked all over the unadorned, but serviceable, cream-colored dessert plate.

"Pulling off a lesson and entertainment without notice is no easy feat," Joelle added.

"I could have done a much better job if I'd been prepared." Dean lifted his overloaded fork halfway to his lips. "I wish Nicole had been more considerate. I can't believe how she left all of us hanging high and dry like that. Eagle and Raven must think we're the most disorganized group they've ever seen." He placed the pie in his mouth and chewed, although he looked too upset to enjoy the treat.

"I don't know about that. I doubt very seriously Nicole would have had a better lesson, even with prepared materials. She just doesn't have your experience, and she sure isn't anywhere near where you are in her faith walk." Copying her dining companion, Joelle indulged in a bite of her own pie.

"Thanks for the compliment, but comparing my behavior to others' isn't the way to go about deciding how to conduct myself." He sighed. "Not to mention it's obvious that Raven and Eagle think I'm a boring old adult with my mellow acoustic guitar. Wonder if they realized before tonight that not all guitars come with amplifiers."

"I doubt it." Joelle laughed. "They think we're all a bunch of Jesus freaks. And you know what? They would have thought that no matter what. You have nothing to be embarrassed about. Nothing that went wrong tonight was your fault."

Dean shook his head. "I let Zach down."

"No, you didn't. If Zach were here, he'd be the first to agree with me." Joelle set her fork on the edge of her plate. "If anything, he'd say he let you down by bringing the boys, and then by not keeping them in line once they got there."

Dean moved his mug in a series of circles, swirling the hot coffee. "Maybe Eagle would have stayed if I'd delivered a more effective lesson and played some songs he knew."

Joelle swallowed a tiny portion of pie. "What are you trying to say? That if you had known they were coming, you would have bought an electric guitar and learned a bunch of hard rock songs just to please them? Or maybe have even gotten a tattoo?" She shook one finger at him, letting it wave once with each word. "I don't think so."

"I assure you, the tattoo would have been one of those temporary ones that comes off the next day. Nothing too radical, either. Maybe just a heart." He flashed the endearing smile she had loved for so many years.

"What? You wouldn't have picked one that said 'Mother'? Your poor mom would be disappointed." She clicked her tongue in mock derision. He laughed along with her. "I'm just glad Ashlynn didn't find out Zach was bringing his cousins," Joelle observed. "If she'd known in advance they look like hard-core rockers, she probably would have worn leather clothes and covered her hair with a spiked wig. She might have even used henna tattoos on her arms and ankles." Joelle shook her head. "Anything to impress Zach."

"As if she would actually trade in her smooth Twila Paris and Rachael Lampa CDs for bone-jarring alternative music."

Joelle chuckled. "Maybe the boys would have been more comfortable the night we played Twister."

"I doubt it. My guess is they would have thought that game was silly, too."

"Probably," she admitted. "But there's no point in saying 'woulda, shoulda, coulda' now. We can't go back and change the meeting, and we shouldn't have to. We can't be expected to tailor our evenings to please everyone."

Dean thought for a moment. "You know something? You're right. I wouldn't have changed a thing. Even if I had tried, they would have been able to tell I was putting on an act. Secular folks can spot hypocrisy in Christians faster than we can see it in each other. Or ourselves." He drank a swallow of coffee and set the mug back down on the table. "But I feel bad that those boys didn't feel comfortable with us. I mean, when someone literally runs away and tries to hitch a ride somewhere else, that's saying a lot about your hospitality. . .and it's all negative."

"Eagle's problems didn't begin tonight, Dean. His running away like that is the result of many years of alienation."

A trace of a grin touched his lips. "Sounds like an accurate diagnosis, Ms. Psychologist. Too bad he couldn't have waited one more night before deciding to act upon his feelings."

"You would have blamed yourself, anyway." Joelle finished her coffee.

"True."

"I don't think we can count their boredom as our failure. You can't expect everyone who walks into our church—or any church—to become converted instantly. Raven and Eagle are very, very far from the Lord. They're living a totally different lifestyle. Although," she said thoughtfully, "I think I saw a glimmer of interest in Raven."

He nodded, his eyes alight with hope for the first time that evening. "I thought so, too. Let's just pray it's not short-lived."

"Just like the parable of the seeds?" she ventured. "You're afraid your words may have fallen on rock?"

"Precisely. Even if Raven's interest is piqued, he still hasn't made a commitment to Christ. At least, he didn't say so."

"It's too soon," she pointed out.

"You're right." He twisted his paper napkin around his fingers, although his faraway expression indicated he was too absorbed in contemplation to be conscious of his gestures. After a moment, he returned his full attention to Joelle. "Even if he tries to change, he has no motivation to alter his behavior once he gets back to L.A. He'll still be playing in the band with Eagle, and he won't have Zach bringing him to church."

"Are you sure Zach will bring him to church again after tonight?"

"He won't have a chance. The boys fly back to L.A. this week."

"Too bad. It would have been good to have another chance to reach them, although I don't know how far anyone can get with Eagle at this point. He seems set against the Lord." Joelle sighed. "I'm sure God has plans for Eagle and Raven. When the time is right, He will reveal them. In the meantime, we should just be glad we were able to plant some seeds."

Joelle watched as Dean took a few more bites of pie. He didn't speak for awhile but seemed to be concentrating on private thoughts rather than the taste of the dessert. She wondered if he'd even remember consuming the pie once he left the diner. Joelle didn't mind the silence. After years together, she and Dean were comfortable just being in each other's presence.

She had just finished her own dessert when Dean finally spoke. "How are things at home?"

"Wonderful. Mom finally took her GED test."

"That's great," Dean agreed. "She's been wanting to get her diploma for a long time now. I'm sure she's glad to get the test over with."

"You said it."

"How does she think she did?"

"She says she doesn't know, but of course she did fine." She leaned toward him. "After she gets her diploma, we're planning a surprise party for her. You'll be invited, but don't say anything about it."

"I wouldn't think of missing it." Dean glanced at his watch. "It's getting late. I'd better be hitting the road. I need to get some rest if I plan to sing that solo tomorrow in church." He snapped his fingers. "Oh, I almost forgot. The choir director wanted me to ask you if you'd sing a solo sometime."

Joelle moved her plate aside and propped her elbows on the table. She leaned closer to Dean. "She couldn't ask me herself?"

"Maybe she thinks I have some influence." He arched his eyebrows playfully.

She let her mouth curl into a coy grin. "Maybe you do."

"Does that mean you're willing to sing? I don't think she cares what the song is, as long as either Marla can play it on the organ or you can get a tape."

Joelle thought about the prospect of singing in front of the church. Mixed emotions of happiness, anticipation, and uncertainty reared their heads. She let out a sigh. "I don't know, Dean. I feel so unworthy, with my conversion so recent."

"No one else in the congregation thinks that way," he assured her. "If anything, now is the best time for you to sing His praises. Your outlook is fresh and new, unlike some of us who've been heavily involved in the work of the church all of our lives."

She was still unsure. Getting up in front of the whole church to sing by herself seemed daunting. An idea popped into her head. "You know, I like that Crystal Lewis song 'Beauty for Ashes.'"

"I know that song." He nodded. "That tune should work well with your voice."

"And your voice, too. Why don't you sing it with me?"

"A duet?"

"I think that's what they call it," she teased.

"I don't know. . . ."

She put on her best woeful face. "Please? I'd like having you there to help me sing. I know I'll have a lot more confidence that way."

"We do make beautiful music together," he noted.

Joelle wondered if he realized that statement could work on two levels. She decided she'd better head for safer verbal waters. "I like the words. All about how God gives us something for nothing."

"'For our ashes, He gives us beauty. Strength for fear.'"

"See? You already know the lyrics."

He stopped as if considering her offer. "All right. I'll do it."

"Great!" Joelle felt better already.

"When is the best time for you to practice? That is, if you can work a rehearsal into your busy schedule."

"What makes you say that?"

"I tried to call you last night. Your mom told me you were out."

"Speaking of being out, I just remembered something." Reaching into her white leather hobo bag, she grabbed her wallet. Inside was Lloyd's check. She held it open so Dean could read it for himself.

"Two hundred and fifty dollars, huh?" He kept reading. "Lloyd Newby."

"Remember him?"

Dean thought for a minute. "Is that the loser who stuck you with the tab at the French place?"

"One and the same." She pulled the check in each direction, resulting in a satisfying crackle of paper. "He paid me back, just like he promised." Joelle returned the check to its place in her red wallet.

Dean shrugged. "All right. You win. I'm happy for you. I know you're glad he finally repaid you. That's an awful lot of money to throw to the wind."

"It's all mine now. That check will be deposited in my bank account tomorrow." Joelle patted the outside of her bag as if putting the check to sleep for the night.

Dean tapped his fingers against his half-empty coffee mug. "Does this mean Mr. Lloyd Newby will be getting a second chance?"

Joelle couldn't believe her heart lurched when he asked. "Does it matter?"

"Just wondering. It's your life." He averted his eyes, and his voice took on a tone that convinced her he wasn't telling her the whole truth.

"If you really want to know, he hasn't asked me out again."

"Oh." He looked a little too pleased to suit Joelle. "If he did, would you go?"

She paused for effect but shook her head. "Not unless I had a lot of cash with me."

"Good. I think he was looking for a woman to foot his bills. From what you said, he seemed to enjoy the things money can buy." Dean drained his coffee cup. "Wonder what poor woman is paying his way now?"

"Woman? Why would you say that? It's his name on the check."

"So what? A girlfriend could have deposited the money in his account."

"I guess that's possible, but do you really think that's true?" The thought of taking another woman's money upset Joelle. She would rather not be paid back at all.

"I don't know, but if I were you, I'd deposit it as soon as possible." His voice took on an admonishing tone. "Just in case."

At that moment, the waitress interrupted them to offer refills on their coffee. After they both declined, she placed the check on the table.

"So," he said as he picked up the tab, "you never did tell me where you were last night."

"You never did tell me why you were calling."

He seemed as though he was about to say something when he thought better of it and changed his mind. "Tell you what. You leave the tip, and we'll call the whole thing even."

As they left, Dean promised to see her in church the next day. Only after Joelle got into her car did she realize that he hadn't offered her a lift to the worship service, as was his habit. For the first time in their long relationship, an uneasy emotion swept over her. She didn't like the feeling one bit.

Chapter 13

On Sunday afternoon, after the dishes from lunch were washed and the leftover chicken stashed in the refrigerator for sandwiches later, Joelle retreated to her room. The past weeks had proven to be such a whirlwind, she hadn't taken the time she needed to be alone with her thoughts and with the Lord.

As she changed out of her mint green cotton dress and pearl jewelry and into a comfortable pink terry cloth short set, Joelle thought about the day. During morning worship, Dean sat with Mandy and her family as was his custom, and Joelle sat with her parents and extended family who attended their church.

As expected, Dean's solo went over well. The poignant silence that followed his rendition of "Our God Is an Awesome God" told Joelle that the worshipers understood that modern music can be reverent. If Joelle had had her druthers, she would have led them in a standing ovation. She'd never heard the song performed as a solo. Dean's heartfelt, skillfully executed guitar arrangement, along with his rich tenor, made the words and tune seem especially worshipful.

After Sunday school, she congratulated him on a great performance. They agreed they needed to set up a time to rehearse for their duet. Then he was whisked away by some of the other church members who wanted to give their compliments, too. As she watched Dean shyly accept the praise, Joelle found herself looking forward to their rehearsals.

If only one of the men she'd met through the personals had been remotely like Dean!

She returned to the present with a sigh, remembering her resolution to answer one last ad. Surely the next person she called would be Mr. Right. Sitting on the bed, she drew the latest edition of *Today's Southwest Virginian Christian Singles* out of her nightstand drawer. Even though she hadn't fallen in love at first sight with any of her blind dates, she knew the little paper was the best place to find her next prospect.

Joelle flipped over the latest edition of the circular so she could study the front cover. A woman with frizzy permed hair and no makeup to hide crow's-feet wrinkles around her eyes stared back at her. The article about her was entitled "Living Single and Loving It!" Joelle noted the irony in the publication's running personal ads. The people they chose to interview each week weren't what the world would consider glamourous. Tricks of the secular magazines, such as windblown hair, soft lighting, and skimpy clothing, were never used to grab a reader's attention.

The paper she held had to be the safest venue to meet new men. With the word "Christian" in the title, she doubted anyone who wasn't a believer would even bother to read the newspaper. She nodded to herself. Any personal ads in this magazine were most definitely placed by Christians, she told herself again, particularly ones who were willing to look beyond the surface and into a person's heart. Even though the Christian men she'd met so far weren't as perfect as she'd first imagined, they'd been easier to cope with than nonbelievers such as Dustin, the boyfriend she had before her life-changing encounter with Christ. When she had still been enmeshed in that relationship, Joelle had kept her focus on the good times. Now that she had escaped, she saw that Dustin and his simmering rage had brought her more conflict than joy.

She turned to the back of the magazine. In the few weeks she'd been searching for someone, the ads, which appeared under the title "Solomon's Song," had doubled in size. Joelle wondered if the number of mateless people was increasing or if more people were finding out about the magazine and taking out ads. She couldn't help noticing that more men placed ads than women. She speculated men were more daring, or maybe they feared less for their safety than their female counterparts. Whatever the reason, she couldn't complain. More personals from them meant a wider selection for her.

Skimming the entries under "Single Men," she noticed Lloyd's ad was still running. His entry reminded her to say a word of thanks to the Lord for the check. Perhaps Lloyd hadn't been a perfect Christian, but over the course of their evening together, Joelle could see that he believed in Christ. He just hadn't given over his whole trust to the Lord. Otherwise, his interest in material gain wouldn't have been all-consuming. During her prayer, a surge of guilt shot through her, filling her with so much remorse that she stopped praying in midsentence. In that instant, she was convicted with the knowledge that money had motivated her to answer Lloyd's ad. He had promised candlelight gourmet dinners and travel to exotic places. Hadn't she wanted those things?

She had to admit, she still wanted to travel. She still liked to eat well. But she resolved not to let these carnal desires motivate other life decisions—particularly ones as critical as committing to the man she would one day marry.

After a moment, she resumed her prayer, confessing her weakness. Then she thanked the Lord that He had used her date with Lloyd to show her one area where she needed to change. She petitioned that she would stay on a path that led away from love of material possessions and the pleasures money can buy, and into His arms. She prayed that Lloyd would also find happiness in fewer possessions and seek fulfillment in the Lord's love. She closed her prayer without much hope that Lloyd would change or that she would hear from him again.

Joelle took a moment to marvel at those whose walk in the faith was such that they took comfort in all outcomes and lived as though they brooked no doubt. She knew she had a long way to go before she reached that point. In the meantime, Joelle was comforted by the knowledge that the Lord would be patient with her.

Quickly she added a prayer for the women who answered Lloyd's ad. The fact she didn't know their identities didn't matter. The Lord knew all.

Out of curiosity, she looked for Dexter's ad. She couldn't find it among the listings. Joelle mused that either Dexter had convinced Bertha to discontinue the ad, or he had finally become engaged to his Anastasia. Joelle sent up a prayer for the couple. If God's plan was for Anastasia and Dexter to make a match, she hoped the union would be blessed. No matter what woman Dexter eventually married, she prayed his mother would accept her new daughter-in-law.

She felt a nudging about Wilbert. She prayed he, too, would find the right woman. After she closed her prayer, Joelle wondered if Wilbert would ever find a woman whose goal in life was a sparkling kitchen floor—not that maintaining a clean apartment would be an easy task with his brothers around. Perhaps finding a woman would be the best thing Wilbert could do. If he married, his brothers would be forced to move and make their own way. Even so, Wilbert had given her the impression his main objective in a relationship was to gain an errand girl and housekeeper. Joelle wasn't afraid of work, yet she wanted the man she chose to see her as more than a way to accomplish his chores.

Sighing, Joelle picked up her beloved white teddy bear. She placed the bear, which she had improbably christened with the elaborate name Theodosia, next to her chest. Hugging Theodosia, she curled her legs until her knees touched the bear's ears. Joelle wished she could return to a simpler time, a time when she was a little girl and her main concern was whether she'd be getting the latest Barbie for Christmas. Hugging her teddy bear made her feel almost as though that dream were possible.

Joelle could indulge such a fantasy in her present surroundings. The bedroom had not been redecorated since she was twelve. On her birthday that November, her parents had presented Joelle with her very own bedroom suite. The desk, dresser, vanity, and canopy bed were made of knotted wood. She could tell because even the thick coat of white paint didn't conceal the round and oval shapes of the dark knobs. Pink flowers were strategically stickered onto each piece as decoration. They matched the medium shade of pink that Dad had painted on her walls while she was at a sleepover. She found out later the slumber party had been arranged just so they could surprise her. That day lived on in Joelle's memory as one of the happiest she could remember. As a result, the room remained almost untouched, a souvenir of that day.

Though she was no longer that preteen girl, taking refuge in that room was like turning back the clock to a simpler time, when the decisions she had to make seemed much more important than they were. Even now, she could lean her back against the pink pillow shams that rested on the headboard. She could turn on her CD player and let the soothing sounds of her favorite artists flood the room.

She could keep munching on the bag of cheese curls that she still wasn't supposed to be eating on her bed, despite the fact she was an adult and took care of her own laundry.

Retreating to her room, hugging Theodosia, listening to music, and feasting on forbidden cheese curls was what she'd always done whenever she had a problem or faced a dilemma. Usually, after contemplation, she could talk herself into doing what her parents wanted her to do, or what her friends thought she should do, or even what she thought was right.

She wondered what Dean would have thought of Wilbert.

Joelle let out a groan. Why did Dean always have to interfere with every decision? Could she ever get away from worrying about what he would think?

Maybe not. Maybe that's why she hadn't told him she'd been out with Wilbert. Maybe Wilbert was a threat, whether Joelle had acknowledged it at that point or not. But Dean had no reason to feel threatened, especially now that he was seeing Nicole.

Her treacherous heart reacted by sending forth a flood of anxiety. Why hadn't Dean told her about Nicole? He looked like he was about to, but something stopped him. What?

"He knows I don't approve of Nicole. That's what it is," she grumbled. "What in the world made him ask her out, of all people? They have nothing in common except the singles' group. And she doesn't even seem halfway committed to that."

An unbidden thought occurred to her. Dean didn't have to ask her approval. Sure, they were friends, but that didn't give her the right to dictate who he should and shouldn't see. She had to realize that.

"Besides, he sure wouldn't approve of me trying the personals again." With a motion of rebellion, she snapped the paper open and began reading. "I'll show Dean Nichols who's right."

Chapter 14

Still reclined on her bed, Joelle set her teddy bear by her side and started combing through the ads in earnest. With every man trying to make himself sound like Prince Charming, the ads differed little from each other. Joelle almost felt as though using the old childhood rhyme "Eeny meeny, miny, moe" would be as reliable as giving each great thought.

"Maybe you can tell me which one to call, Theodosia," she told her teddy bear. The stuffed animal's brown eyes remained unseeing, her mouth, with its pink tongue sticking out to one side, remained silent. "How does this one sound?" Joelle read aloud:

> *Handsome, physically fit male, 35, seeks attractive, physically fit female, 20–40, for fun and games. Must love to watch football, soccer, tennis, and baseball as much as I do. Must also be a worthy tennis opponent. If throwing a Super Bowl party for the gang is the highlight of your January, then I'm your man!*

"Whoever answers that will be running a mile a minute," Joelle told Theodosia. She scanned more ads.

"Here's one. 'I love the glamour of Old Hollywood and spend most Saturday afternoons with a bag of popcorn and a soda, staring at the silver screen. How about you?' " Joelle shook her head. "Not sure I want a couch potato. Wonder how much buttered popcorn he's consumed in his life?" After rolling her eyes at the bear, Joelle sighed and kept reading. Some of the ads had been running for weeks. She thought better than to take a chance on any of those. None of the new ads looked appealing. "Maybe I've gotten too cynical, or maybe the Lord is trying to tell me to wait. What do you think?" Ready to give up, she folded the paper. Suddenly, her gaze rested on a new ad:

> *Sensitive, spiritual man, 29, in quest of sensitive, spiritual woman, 22–32, who is willing to explore the love of God. Fellow seekers wishing to follow a path of inquiry and discovery with the desire to develop a committed relationship are most appealing. If you judge only by the outside of a person, not his heart, or if material gain, status, and power are what you desire, look elsewhere. But if you want to experience Freedom, true Freedom, then call me.*

She read the ad several times, concentrating on the meaning of each phrase. "Maybe that's it," she told her bear. "I've been saying I really wanted to focus on my spiritual growth. Since that's all this ad promises, maybe this man is worth meeting."

With hope in her heart, she reread the latest ad. Its author didn't reveal anything about his interests, other than the spiritual. Surely the Lord must be first and foremost in this man's life.

"That must have been my mistake," she mused. "I should have been looking for someone totally devoted to the Lord." She looked at the printed promises again. "He says he wants a fellow seeker. Hmm. I guess I qualify. What do you say, Theodosia? Do you think I should take the plunge?"

Speaking the words aloud gave her the courage she needed. Without thinking further, she picked up the phone and made the call. Expecting to wait through a few rings, Joelle was taken aback when a man answered almost before the first ring was complete.

"You must have been right beside the phone," she blurted.

"Yes, I was." The voice was guarded. "Do I know you?"

"No—"

"Look," the voice grew gruff, "if you're calling again about that newspaper subscription, I told you I'm not interested. Can't you people take no for an answer?"

"Don't hang up!" When she didn't hear the click of the receiver cutting off the connection, she continued. "I'm calling about the personals ad in *Today's Southwest Virginian Christian Singles*."

"Oh! The ad!" The voice became softer. "I'm sorry I was rude. You sound just like the woman who keeps begging me to take out a newspaper subscription."

"So I gathered."

He snickered. "Can we start over?"

"Sure. Can't hurt." She paused for effect. "I'm calling about a personals ad in the latest edition of *Today's Southwest Virginian Christian Singles*—the one that promises freedom. Am I speaking to the man who placed it?"

"As a matter of fact, you are. It's nice to meet you."

"Nice to meet you, too." She giggled in spite of herself.

"So," he asked, "out of all the ads you must have read, what made you decide to call me?"

As a variety of responses flashed through her mind, she decided honesty was the best tactic. "I'm looking for someone spiritual."

"Good. Are you a spiritual seeker?"

"I'm always looking to draw closer to the Lord, yes."

He paused. Joelle wondered if he didn't like what she had to say. "Hello?" she asked. "Are you still there?"

"Yes, I'm still here." He didn't say more, allowing silence to ease over the phone line.

She hadn't expected her future date to be so shy. An adventurer was what she had pictured, since he'd advertised himself as a seeker. Joelle tried to bring him out of his shell. "So, what else would you like to tell me about yourself?"

"I have good intuition. I can tell just from talking to you that you are a very good person."

"I'm working on it." She let out a nervous giggle. "So what's your name?"

"The name my parents gave me is Abe, but my real name is Freedom."

"Freedom." The name seemed strange, until she remembered the wording of his ad. "You sure were clever in your ad."

"I thought so."

"So why did you change your name?"

"I thought it suited me better than the name of a Jewish patriarch. When you meet me, I'm sure you'll agree."

Joelle found Freedom's objections confusing. "Are you Jewish?"

"Of course not," he scoffed. "If I were, I wouldn't have placed an ad in a magazine with 'Christian' in the title, would I?"

"I guess not." Joelle felt foolish—too foolish to ask him to confirm he was a Christian.

"So what's your name? I'm assuming you still use the one your parents chose for you."

"Of course. I'm Joelle."

"Joelle. Hmm." He paused.

"It's a combination of my parents' names," she found herself explaining.

"Charming. I'll bet you're a brunette."

Joelle smiled into the phone. "I'm afraid your intuition failed you this time. I'm a natural blond, although I do wear teal contacts to liven up the color of my eyes."

"Is that your only form of subterfuge?"

"I like to think so."

"Good. You sound like someone who's up for exploration," he said. "Meet me at the Towne Center Complex at seven o'clock this Friday night. You won't regret it."

"Wait! How will I know it's you?"

"You will. Trust me."

❧

"Who were you just talking to, dear?" Her mother was cutting up leftover meat for the night's roast beef hash. "Your father told me you were on the phone."

She shrugged. "A guy I know. It's no big deal."

Eleanor's face looked hopeful. "Wilbert?"

"No. Someone else. Sorry to disappoint you."

"Well, as long as you're having a good time. You're only young once, and the decision you make as to whom to spend the rest of your time on Earth with is the most important one of your life. Besides accepting the Lord, that is." She placed the chopped meat in a container and handed it to Joelle with a wordless motion for her to find a place for it in the refrigerator. She swept the floor as Joelle moved dishes aside and slid the container of beef in between canned sodas and Jell-O.

"Have a cup of tea?" her mother offered.

"Not right now, thanks."

Joelle's mother took a seat at the kitchen table. "Talk for a minute, then?"

Joelle smiled. "Of course." She sat beside Eleanor. "You have a serious look on your face. Am I in trouble?"

"Anything but." Her mom chuckled. "I don't know if we ever told you this, Joelle, but your father and I are so proud of you."

"Proud of me?"

"For accepting the altar call this past fall and for trying to live a better life ever since."

"Thanks. Is the change that obvious?"

Eleanor laughed. "You're a lot more relaxed and pleasant to be around. Plus, I know you've been reading your Bible a lot more." She bent an eyebrow. "Not to mention, we have been seeing a parade of different men lately. I'm happy to say that none of them seems to be the least bit like Dustin."

"They're not like him at all, Mom. They're Christians."

"Quite a difference, isn't it?" Eleanor didn't wait for Joelle to answer. A knowing smile crossed her features. "I might as well tell you this. Ever since you accepted the Lord and broke off with Dustin, I've been praying that you'd find someone. Specifically, the man the Lord has in mind for you."

"Mom! It's not like I'm desperate!"

"A beautiful girl like you? You could never be desperate. It's just that I know you miss Dustin, even if he was awful to you."

"He wasn't so awful, really." Joelle averted her eyes all the same.

"Don't try to fool me. I know better. I also know enough about the world to realize that most of us women miss any relationship with a man, even a bad one, once it's gone. I don't want you going back to that. It's high time the Lord showed you the man He wants you to be with."

She lifted her face. "I can't say we disagree on that." Joelle nodded. "I've been praying about the new directions my life is taking, and I keep getting the strong feeling it's time to connect with the man I'll eventually marry. You know, I'd think with all the changes I'm making, bringing romance into the mix is the last thing anyone would suggest. Isn't that ironic?"

"The Lord's plans don't always seem to follow logic," her mother counseled. "And they certainly don't go by what makes sense by the standards of the world. You're wise to stay with how you think He's guiding you. I'll keep praying."

Ready to turn the conversation to a lighter vein, Joelle shook her head in mock derision. "So what's the matter? Are you tired of having me around?"

"Never. I dread the day you leave this house, but I get a sense that it's time. Accepting the altar call was the first step of the rest of your life. I can't pretend I understand why you and I both get the feeling the Lord's plans for you involve a man, but He knows best. I realize you turned down a lot of dates when you were committed to Dustin. I'm glad that's no longer the case."

Joelle tried not to cringe. She still didn't have the courage to tell her mother she was meeting men through the personals, even if they were in a Christian magazine. "I have to admit, it's been an adventure. You know how it used to be. I'd just hang out with a bunch of friends, and we'd all do things as a group. Dustin and I just drifted together." Joelle remembered their long courtship. "Other than the junior and senior proms, I'm not sure we even had what you'd call a real date."

"I'm not even sure I'd call that a date." Joelle's mother shook her head. "All that money I spent on those evening dresses, just so you could go to the prom for a half hour and then go to Dustin's and watch TV the rest of the night. What a waste."

"I know. All that fanfare and not much fun." She patted her mom on the shoulder. "I promise the next time I go to a prom, I'll buy my own dress."

"Thanks a lot." Eleanor chuckled. "Of course, the last thing your father and I want for you is to get back together with Dustin, but don't you miss some of your old girlfriends? I liked Tory and Nina."

Joelle allowed her lips to curl into a thin smile. The girlfriends she spoke of were good at putting on virtuous fronts but were out for nothing but trouble when no one else was around. Too interested in having a good time to settle down, they hadn't changed much since high school.

"Maybe you could invite them over sometime?"

"No, Mom. But thanks for the offer." Joelle had no desire to renew those friendships. "I don't have much in common with them anymore. If I called them or suggested we get together, they'd only try to convince me I should go back to Dustin. There's no way I could ever consider that. He was never honest with me."

"Then you're smart for not trying. You can never have a good, solid relationship with a man who's less than honest with you. That's one of the secrets to your father's and my marriage. We're always honest with each other." She smiled. "Although we do try to be tactful and not hurt each other's feelings."

A surge of guilt shot through Joelle. She knew someone she hadn't been honest with lately. That was the one thing that held their friendship together when all else seemed to fall apart. "I just remembered, Mom. I have a phone call to make."

Ignoring her mother's quizzical look, Joelle made a beeline for the privacy of her room. She dialed Dean's number from memory, her heart beating rapidly all the while.

The line was busy.

Who could he be talking to?

Chapter 15

Running his fingers through still-wet hair, a newly showered Dean plopped into the easy chair in front of the TV. Years ago, his mother had bought the chair by redeeming a large number of S & H Green Stamps. He had affectionately dubbed the chair "The Throne." As far as Dean knew, Green Stamps were a relic of the past, much like the turquoise vinyl of The Throne's original upholstery. The vinyl, which had been chilly in winter and stuck to his legs in hot weather, was now covered by a heavy-duty, knotty brown fabric that reminded Dean of indoor-outdoor carpet, except that it was slightly less scratchy.

His parents had replaced their living room furniture with a matching couch and chair in medium blue with a floral pattern. Mandy had asked for their couch, and Dean had gladly taken the cast-off chair. So what if it didn't match the green sofa he'd bought on sale when a local furniture dealer went out of business? Later, he sprang for lamps with floral shades that had appeared as though they'd be perfect counterparts for the sofa. Only after he got home and discovered they looked too minty did he realize the lamps were a final sale and he couldn't take them back. No wonder they'd only cost forty dollars each, when they were originally marked two hundred dollars. Figuring that's what he got for being greedy, he set the lamps on two inexpensive end tables he'd spent a weekend assembling. As for the lamps, he resolved to be thankful for the light they cast.

At that moment, the sun broke through the clouds, shining unforgiving light through the picture window. His attention momentarily drawn to the window, Dean could almost count the squares in the loosely woven blue-and-green draperies, obviously a product of a discount store, that the landlord had left as part of the decor. The transparent curtains almost matched the teal blue walls.

In the meantime, Dean tried to ignore the fact that his living room looked like the revenge of a scorned interior decorator. He hoped one day his future wife would take pride in outfitting a house they could call their own. For now, the hodgepodge of furniture he owned was good enough for a bachelor.

Dean pulled up the footrest of the knotty brown chair and settled into comfort. He deserved to rest. His three-mile run had been a good one. No one else had been running or walking on the track today. Without distractions of other joggers, he was able to think of nothing for awhile, letting his mind go blank except for keeping count of how many laps he completed. Hiding behind thin cloud cover, the sun didn't beat down upon his back with any intensity. His moving legs stirred the air enough to keep him from overheating. Only after he stopped was Dean aware of how much he'd been sweating.

Now smelling of soap and deodorant and wearing athletic shorts and a T-shirt, Dean gulped a tall glass of cool water. He mindlessly pushed the buttons on the TV remote. Baseball season, a time when he pitched on Sunday afternoons for the church team, was over. Autumn's volleyball season had not yet begun. The Sunday night Bible study for young adults would resume soon, meaning Dean could fill empty Sunday afternoons preparing for the class.

In the meantime, the hours stretched out endlessly before him, an unwelcome break from his business. He knew it was wrong to feel that way. The Sabbath was a gift from the Lord. A time to renew and replenish oneself. A time to rest so facing the workweek would be less tiring. Dean somehow felt Sunday afternoons shouldn't be spent alone.

At least Zach had called and let him know how things were going with Eagle and Raven. As expected, Eagle had been sullen as he boarded the plane and made no secret of his desire to return to the West Coast.

Zach had been more optimistic about Raven. He had asked Zach a few questions about his own faith and how it affected his life. Dean was grateful to hear those encouraging words.

Dean was about to suggest to Zach that they get together for a pickup game of basketball at the school gym when his friend mentioned he had a full afternoon ahead of him catching up on work. After Zach hung up, Dean felt lonelier than ever.

If only he could make up some excuse to call Joelle. A year ago, he would have thought nothing of picking up the phone and asking her to share a malt with him at one of the local haunts. Though she'd usually be groggy from her Saturday night adventures, she never turned him down, but things had changed. She had made it clear she was looking for a man to share her life with. Why else would she persist in looking through the personals?

Dean had been keeping Joelle in his prayers all his life, but he had been especially vigilant since she accepted Christ. In his heart, he knew he had always loved her. When he first came to that realization, they were in high school. Dean remembered feeling jealous that Joelle was becoming too attached to Dustin. He tried to convince himself his concern was only that of a close friend. No one could deny Dustin was a bad influence, yet Dean knew he really wanted Joelle for himself.

He had spent time alone in his room, praying about whether or not to speak up and make his feelings known to her. No matter how much he argued with God, His answer had clearly been "no." Even Joelle's steady church attendance wasn't enough. She freely admitted to him that she went mainly to appease her parents. Otherwise, Joelle hadn't bothered to put on a show of living a life pleasing to the Lord. The pain in Dean's heart was great. Going against the Lord to pursue an unequally yoked relationship would have been wrong. At best, a brief romance would have cost their friendship. At worst, Joelle would have influenced him to take up some of her bad habits. Then they both would have been swimming upstream to get out of Satan's snare—if they ever could.

In the meantime, Dean was grateful that the Lord hadn't led him to dissolve their friendship. Sometimes being Joelle's friend was agonizing. Each time Dustin got in trouble with his parents, the law, or both, she came crying to him. Each time Dustin betrayed her, Joelle would ask Dean's advice, only to abandon it as soon as Dustin pleaded with her to forgive him. When people Joelle called "friends" abandoned her, Dean's shoulder was there for her to shed her tears. Not once did Dean let Joelle down. Not even now, when she had gotten it in her head that she should go off on a wild goose chase, looking through a circular for dates.

He felt just as helpless now as he did back in high school. Joelle said she felt led to find a Christian man to share her life with. Dean knew he could be that man. Yet he couldn't bring himself to admit it to Joelle. Not only was Dean reluctant to speak up because she was so new to the faith, the real, living faith just within her grasp, but the minute he declared his love for her, a perfectly wonderful friendship could be ruined. But if he didn't, he would never know how much more he—or, rather, both of them—could gain.

The thought of mentioning his feelings to Joelle left him with an inexplicable feeling of nervousness. He knew he just wasn't ready. At least not yet. His prayers didn't give him a strong leading to share his feelings, at least not for the time being. Dean knew the time would come when the Lord, not he, saw fit.

Clearly, Joelle wasn't ready. Dean wondered where she had been on Friday evening when he had wanted to take her to the play. He almost wished Earl hadn't given him those tickets. Then he never would have found out that Joelle wasn't sitting at home, as lonely and dateless as he was.

And he wouldn't have resorted to calling Nicole.

What had he been thinking? Dean mentally kicked himself for being so naïve. He thought she realized he made the offer as one Christian friend to another. That idea flew out the window from the moment he arrived at her apartment to pick her up. If he didn't get the message from her heavy makeup and teased hair, the skintight Lycra shirt and painted-on blue jeans she wore, she made sure he couldn't mistake the impact she was trying to make from the moment she got in his car. He remembered his nervousness when she slid toward him, positioning herself squarely in front of the radio. Warning her that they could be ticketed for her failure to wear a seat belt didn't work. She simply dug down into the cracks of the seat and retrieved the middle lap belt, a device that was really meant for use only when the car was fully loaded with six passengers.

During the drive, she leaned toward him, making sure her spicy cologne wafted his way. She would have been disappointed if she had known the scent only made him realize how much he preferred Joelle's perfume. Nicole's eagerness to carry on conversations and the light touches she'd place on his shoulders or wrists when she spoke to him weren't unusual. They were signaling she wanted to be closer friends.

Why hadn't he seen that?

In hindsight, Dean saw that Nicole flirted with everyone. She wasn't above doing almost anything to get Zach's attention, despite Ashlynn's obvious interest in him. Nicole's voice purred when she spoke to Dean, but it took on the same quality when she spoke to anyone of the male persuasion—from eighteen to eighty.

Dean should have known Nicole wasn't really interested in seeing the play. He wondered why she agreed to go out with him at all. She certainly hadn't been interested in serious conversation, at least, not about anything that mattered. As they drove the fifty miles to the theater, Dean found himself wishing the drive were quicker. Her conversation tended toward secular music groups, R-rated movies, and some of the more unsavory television programs on the air—shows on premium cable channels he didn't even subscribe to, precisely because he knew the type of lurid fare they ran.

Nicole had been surprised that Dean had no idea what she was talking about when she broached those subjects. He was lost when she tried to explain television soap opera plots, and the names of the bands she listened to left him blank. As soon as she ran out of subjects, her frustration was evident.

"I can't believe it when you say you don't know what I'm talking about," she had said.

"Sorry, but I don't." Dean had made a show of keeping his eyes on the road. He didn't want to face her icy stare.

"I don't know why you think it's such a big deal to watch TV. Everyone I know watches those shows, and everyone listens to the same music I do," she protested.

"Not everyone. I doubt anyone else at the singles' group does."

"Wanna bet?"

Dean wondered who among them she meant. He decided it best not to ask. "Now you know someone who doesn't." He smiled, hoping his levity would cheer her up.

"I don't believe it." Suddenly, she cast him an understanding look. Placing a delicate, manicured hand on his sleeve, she leaned close enough that he could smell the strong scent she wore. "Look, if you're afraid I'm going to tell anyone at the singles' group that you actually watch TV, don't worry. I won't. Besides, I've already told you I do, so we'd both be in trouble, wouldn't we?" She sent him a sly little smile, as if they shared an intimate secret.

Dean wasn't sure what to say. If he protested that his lifestyle wasn't an act that he turned off and on to please different audiences, she'd probably accuse him of being a goody-two-shoes. If he pretended to agree, he'd be a liar. The more he thought, the longer the silence in the car lasted. Nicole had obviously figured out his answer without his saying a word. Moving toward her side of the car, she folded her arms across her chest and looked out her window.

"You think I'm immune to temptation, don't you?"

She turned her face in his direction. She was wearing a sneer. "You act like it."

"Well, I'm not. I'll give you one example. Not a month goes by that I don't get offers in the mail for cable television. Not just for the good stations, but for the ones that show what they call 'adult' programs, too. I have a confession to make. I should throw the ads away without even reading them, but sometimes I look at them anyway. I have to say, some of the pictures they show and the plot lines they describe are enough to make the pages sizzle."

Nicole let out a throaty laugh. "Then why don't you subscribe, just to see the programs you like? You're a big boy. It's your right to watch whatever you want. Besides, if you don't like a program, you can always switch the channel or discontinue the service. Since you live alone, no one will ever know."

"That's where you're wrong. I'll know, and God will know."

She arched a doubtful eyebrow. "Do you really think God will send down a bolt of lightning to punish you for hearing a cuss word?"

"No, but I don't think Jesus would want me to live my life that way."

"Your conscience is overactive. It's keeping you from living in the real world."

"Thank the good Lord for that!" he couldn't resist replying.

Nicole's expression didn't become more friendly, nor did she share his amusement. They spent the rest of the car ride in silence.

True to Nicole's observation, his conscience did become overwrought. Once again, he'd had a chance to witness. . .and once again, he had failed.

As he thought back to that night, the telephone rang.

"Dean?" The sexy purr was unmistakable.

"Nicole?"

"Surprised to hear from me, aren't you?" She let out a melodic chuckle.

"I must say, I am."

"First of all, I hope you can forgive me for last night. I didn't mean to skip out on my promise to do the lesson."

"That's okay. I muddled through. Although I must say, you missed out on some excitement with Zach's cousins." He went on to fill her in on the previous night's events.

"I wouldn't worry if I were you," she consoled. "I'm sure they'll both benefit from your influence. Speaking of influence, I have a favor to ask. Can I come over?"

Chapter 16

Several days later, Joelle sat at the computer in Dad's home office. She typed Dean's e-mail address and couldn't help but think of the irony of contacting him by computer when they lived only two miles apart. There seemed to be no other choice. After several unsuccessful attempts to reach him by phone on Sunday, she had given up and driven by his house, hoping he wouldn't notice. Worry was needless. His car was gone.

After work on Monday, she drove by his house again, only to see that the driveway was still empty. Phone calls to his home led to nothing but listening to his answering machine. His cell phone had been turned off. This afternoon was Tuesday, and the same pattern prevailed. E-mail seemed to be the only answer. After dashing off a quick note for him to contact her, Joelle pressed SEND and hoped for the best.

She hadn't even gotten up from her seat at the desk when the telephone rang.

She chuckled to herself. "That was quick!" Smiling, she picked up the receiver, ready to talk to Dean. "Hello?"

"Yes, hello." To Joelle's disappointment, her telephone caller was a female. "Is this Joelle?"

The voice was familiar, but she couldn't pinpoint the caller's identity. "Yes? This is she." The hesitation in her own voice was evident.

"This is Bertha."

For a split second, the name didn't register. Then she remembered. "Bertha!" Joelle wondered what possible reason Dexter's mother could have for calling. She only hoped it wasn't to arrange another date with her son. Unable to think of anything better to say, she uttered, "Good to hear from you."

"Good to talk to you again, too." Bertha's voice sounded as chipper as she remembered. "Is this a good time? You've already eaten supper, haven't you?"

"Yes." She consulted the clock. The time was 5:56. "Your timing is perfect. I got up from the table not ten minutes ago," Joelle assured her caller. Unenthusiastic about continuing with mindless chitchat, Joelle let silence permeate the line, hoping Bertha would get to the point. She didn't mind that Bertha had called. The older woman was charming enough. Still, considering Dexter's and Bertha's opposite opinions about his girlfriend, Joelle knew any further involvement on her part would only place her in the middle of a family war.

"So how are you doing?"

"Fine, thanks." Joelle tapped her foot.

"Any luck with the personal ads?"

Joelle decided on a truthful answer that she hoped gave enough information to deter Bertha's plans for her to see Dexter again, assuming that was the reason for her call. "I met someone else."

"Oh." Joelle could visualize Bertha's crestfallen expression.

Feeling a rush of guilt, Joelle added, "But I can't say I've been swept off my feet by any of the other men I've met through the personals."

"Oh!" Her voice sounded hopeful. "In that case, I'm calling to invite you on a fabulous trip!" Bertha was saying her words at a fast clip, her excitement unmistakable. "How does Las Vegas sound?"

"Las Vegas?" No way could Bertha have an inkling as to how significant Las Vegas was to Joelle.

She and Dustin had talked many times of eloping to Sin City. How many times had they seen its lights on television and in the movies? Blinking and running lights that looked so fascinating on film had to be even better up close and in person. Fabulous hotels, all meant to recreate the wealthy lifestyles of times past, looked bigger and better than any place Joelle had ever seen, much less stayed at as a guest. Spinning black and red wheels, men and women card dealers dressed in black-and-white tuxedos, a sea of machines, all ready to take—and give back—money; all looked appealing to a young woman who'd seldom had reason to leave her home in the mountains.

If the prospect of seeing such man-made wonder wasn't enough to lure the adventurous young couple, the city's reputedly lax attitude and promise of a wedding chapel on every corner sealed the deal. Their shared secret plans, usually whispered when Dustin knew Joelle was miffed with him, seemed at the time to draw them closer. Only recently had Joelle come to the realization that Dustin had merely dangled the prospect in front of her, stringing her along. His failure to keep his vow made Joelle feel as though she were the one who had failed. Only now could she be thankful that Dustin had never kept his promise to marry her in Las Vegas or anywhere else.

Joelle no longer had any desire to visit the city. Especially not with Dexter and his mother.

Bertha broke into her thoughts. "I guess you're wondering how I could afford to offer you such a wonderful vacation. Can you believe I won it? I never win anything. I just filled out a sweepstakes form on impulse. You know, one of those solicitations that comes in the mail? I seem to have gotten on all the lists of people who like to try for prizes. Guess a little birdie at Bingo must have tipped them off." She giggled. "Anyway, the trip is for two! Isn't that exciting?"

Unwilling to obligate herself to Bertha, Joelle searched for something graceful to say. "I'm flattered that you thought of me, but I would have assumed Dexter would be your first choice as a traveling companion."

"Oh, he's going, too!"

"I thought you said the trip is for two."

"It is! But since we will be going for free, I can pay your way. What do you say?"

Joelle didn't answer right away.

"I can't believe you're not jumping at a chance for a free trip to somewhere so exotic." Bertha sounded hurt.

"I know. It sounds lovely, but—" Joelle searched for an excuse. "I might not have the vacation time, and I don't gamble. That's the main attraction at Vegas, isn't it?"

Bertha chuckled. "For an old lady like me, maybe. But there are a lot of other things to do. You can see Hoover Dam, and there are lots of shows." Bertha took in a breath. "Oh, I almost forgot. They included tickets to a rock concert. I've forgotten the names of the people who are scheduled to play. I haven't kept up with that sort of thing since the Beatles broke up. Let me get my glasses so I can read the tickets. Hold on."

The receiver clunked, presumably on a table, while Bertha searched for her eyewear. Joelle heard rustling noises, then the sound of footsteps clacking this way, then that. Bertha seemed to be having trouble finding her glasses. Still sitting at the computer, Joelle was tempted to begin a game of Freecell. She had just begun to call up the program when Bertha returned to the phone.

"Here they are. Do you know any of these groups?" Bertha named three rock groups that had been Joelle's favorites when her relationship with Dustin was hitting its stride.

"Yes, I know them," she admitted.

"Great! Wouldn't you like to go to the concert?"

Joelle swallowed. She didn't want to admit she'd always wanted to see every group Bertha named but had never gotten a chance.

"You don't have to tell me. I know you'd love to go."

"But—"

"You don't have to give me a firm answer right away. Why don't you sleep on it and give me a call later in the week? It'll be so much fun! That much I can promise." Bertha's delight was such that Joelle could almost hear her smile. Painful as the situation was, Joelle knew she had to be firm. "I can tell you right now, Bertha. My answer is no. I'm really sorry, but I just can't go."

"Are you sure?"

"Positive."

Bertha mumbled something polite and quickly excused herself. Joelle felt sorry for her. As she hung up, Joelle wondered if perhaps seeing some of the shows would be nice, and to go somewhere touted in the movies would be a novelty. Most likely, she would never have another chance to visit Las Vegas, at least not in the foreseeable future. Yet even if she were an avid gambler, going on the trip would unfairly encourage Bertha, and it certainly wouldn't be fair to keep stringing along Dexter.

Why did the wrong men always chase her? Or at least, the wrong man's mother? At the thought, she laughed in spite of herself. Being courted by a man's mother on her son's behalf was a first.

Not that being with Dexter was worse than death itself. He seemed decent enough. Maybe he'd liven up and actually enjoy a rock concert.

A rock concert. She sighed. A year ago, she would have packed her bags as soon as Bertha mentioned the concert. The prospect of hearing and seeing the performers extol one-night stands, whiskey, even drugs, to catchy tunes would have been too hard to resist. Self-indulgent lyrics encouraged listeners to look out for their own interests and pleasures, to credit themselves with any success they had in life, and to grab every carnal opportunity. Joelle knew the lifestyle they espoused wasn't moral. It certainly wasn't the one her parents would have chosen for her. Yet only a few months ago she would have argued that there was no harm in enjoying the tunes as long as she didn't try to follow their suggestions too closely. The desire to stay healthy had kept Joelle from indulging as the singers suggested. So did the casual, intellectual relationship she had with the Lord at the time.

Now she realized she had to go beyond simply not acting upon every suggestion. Now that she sought a personal relationship with Christ, Joelle realized how wrong it would be to attend a concert that did nothing to honor the Lord.

Okay, maybe it is wrong, a voice inside her head argued, *but no one will ever know. Well, no one except Dexter and Bertha. And who'd ask them?*

Dean would find out, her conscience argued.

Not if you don't tell him, the voice insisted. *Besides, who cares what he thinks? He left town and didn't even bother to leave a number with you.*

The more she considered how Dean was neglecting her, the more her ire rose. Joelle let out a ragged breath and narrowed her eyes. Unwilling to debate with herself any longer, Joelle scanned the nearby bookshelf. A few of her old compact discs were still in the place where she had abandoned them months ago. Pulling out one of her former favorites, she slipped it into the computer tower and set the audio function to play the best song. Pounding drums and wailing guitars were her reward.

Joelle signed back on to the World Wide Web. She had to see if Dean had returned her e-mail. By the time she discovered there was still no message, the singer was boasting about his latest conquest. Somehow, the songs didn't seem fun anymore.

Chapter 17

"I can't believe how out of shape I am!" Joelle groaned as she stepped into the shower a few nights later. Every muscle in her legs felt tight from doing over a hundred walking lunges during class. Both arms were limp from a heavy-duty session of lifting free weights. Even five pounds felt like too much by the third set. Joelle shuddered at the memory.

She had stopped by the high school gym on the way home from work. Fawn, an old classmate, had just become a certified aerobics instructor and was offering new classes. The previous week, Fawn had dropped by the doctor's office where Joelle worked, class list in hand. She prodded Joelle to take a class. Joelle had agreed, wanting to help out an old acquaintance and feeling confident that an hour-long class would prove effortless.

After the first twenty minutes, Joelle had barely broken a sweat and her breathing wasn't labored. As the class progressed, however, the exercises and dance moves increased in complexity and intensity. Forty minutes into the hour, she was huffing and puffing. The neck of her athletic shirt was drenched. Joelle's glance fell on the clock every few seconds. She hoped the next twenty minutes would move fast. If they didn't, Joelle was tempted to quit. Mercifully, after fifteen more minutes of agony, the class moved into the five-minute stretch and cool down. She hadn't remembered a time in the recent past when she'd been so glad to see the end of an hour.

Once in the shower, Joelle was grateful to feel streams of water pounding all over her body. As steam rose into her nostrils, her thoughts returned to Dean. At least the class had taken her mind off of him and why he still hadn't called. She couldn't recollect the last time four days had passed without them speaking to each other. Over the past week, Joelle realized for the first time how much she depended on his companionship, and how much she missed him when he wasn't there.

Sweat washed away by moisturizing soap and warm water, Joelle jumped out of the shower, toweled dry, and applied scented lotion. After retrieving her comfy, white terry cloth robe from the hook, she wrapped it around herself. Never mind that the weather outside was hot. In her air-conditioned bedroom, she enjoyed the comfortable feeling of being safe and snug inside the cozy garment.

Sitting at her vanity dresser, Joelle had just plugged in her hair dryer when the buzzing telephone demanded to be answered. She ran to the nightstand and picked up the receiver, hoping to hear a familiar baritone. "Hello?"

"Joelle?"

Her shoulders sagged with relief. "Dean! Where were you? I've been trying to get you all week."

"So I saw on my caller ID."

"Oh." Joelle felt her cheeks flush. She'd forgotten he could tell the number of attempts a caller had made, even if the person didn't leave a message. How many times had she tried to reach him during the past week? Chagrined, she didn't even want to think about it. "I guess I thought if I tried enough times, I'd eventually get an answer."

"Apparently." He chuckled, as though he were accommodating a precocious young girl rather than being cruel or teasing. "I was at the men's prayer and fasting retreat, remember? I told you about it at least a month ago."

Groaning, she tapped her hand against her forehead. "Now I remember."

"So you were worried about me?" He sounded pleased.

"Okay, I admit it. I would have been really concerned, except I got an away notice in response to my e-mail message. You better be glad I did. Otherwise, I might have called the police." She tried to keep her tone light, but she was only half-joking.

"I'm glad you didn't resort to that. I'm sure the police have better things to do."

"I don't know. There's so little crime around here, they might like a little excitement." Joelle plopped down on her bed. "The main thing is, you're home now. So how was the retreat?"

"Great. Men from all over the mid-Atlantic region attended. I saw a couple of people from last year. Remember I told you about Brock? His wife had a baby."

"Good. You had said he was concerned about the pregnancy. I'm glad everything turned out all right."

"So am I."

Even though Joelle couldn't have picked Brock out of a lineup of two men, the idea of a new life held genuine appeal. "So what was it?"

"What was what?" Dean paused, presumably to think. "Oh, you mean the baby? I don't know. Hopefully it was either a boy or a girl." He let out a little laugh.

"Oh, I get it. You couldn't tell by the name, and you were too embarrassed to ask. What was it? Let me guess." Joelle pursed her lips as she thought. "Sam? Alex? Lee?"

Dean hesitated. "Uh, I don't know what they named it."

"You were with him the whole week, and you don't even know if he had a boy or a girl, or what its name is, or anything?" Joelle's mouth was hanging open. "How can that be possible?"

"Um, I don't know."

"Men! They never find out anything." Joelle grimaced, even though Dean couldn't see her mock disgust. Giving up hope, she changed the subject. "So have you been home long?"

"Not too long. I would have called as soon as I got here, but I knew you were traveling in between work and home."

"Not to mention I stopped by the gym and took a new cardio class. Remember Fawn, from high school? She's teaching them now."

"Fawn Fields?"

"Fawn Johnson now. She married somebody from Maryland."

"She was in algebra with me, but other than that, I didn't know her. But you and I must be on the same wavelength. I got back from my run a few minutes ago and took a quick shower before I called. I'm willing to bet we both have wet hair." He chuckled.

"You'd be right." Joelle twisted a lock of dripping hair around her finger. "You're a bundle of energy. I can't imagine driving two hundred miles, then immediately going to the track."

"To tell the truth, I missed running. They didn't budget any time for exercise, and I was ready to get my legs moving again."

"Even on an empty stomach?"

"We broke the fast with a simple dinner, so I can't really say I was starving when I left the retreat. I'd be lying if I didn't confess that I stopped at the first fast-food place I saw and ordered a double cheeseburger and large bag of fries." Joelle could imagine him grinning into the phone. "Fasting was definitely my least favorite part of the retreat."

"I don't think I'd be enthusiastic about it, either," she admitted.

"So now you know what I've been up to. What about you? I know you must have had some reason for calling a hundred times. What did you want to talk about?"

"Nothing. And everything." She let out a sigh. "I have something to tell you. It's about these guys I've been meeting through the personals."

"Oh." His utterance was devoid of expression, and he didn't elaborate. The silence was heavy with anticipation.

Though Joelle had set out to tell him everything right then, suddenly spilling over the telephone didn't feel right. "Dean," she asked aloud, "can I come over?"

"Umm—"

"Oh, I know what it is. You want to dry your hair." Her tone was teasing. "Don't worry, I'll give you plenty of lead time to get all gussied up. Even if it is just little ol' me."

He chuckled, but it sounded forced. "Uh, this isn't exactly the best time."

"It's not? Are you okay?"

"Yeah. Yeah, I'm fine. It's just that—" he interrupted himself. "It's just that,

I promised I'd meet someone at the diner, that's all."

Joelle felt her heart leap into her throat. Her stomach did a funny backflip. It wasn't a nice backflip, the kind she got when she was about to open a long-anticipated gift, or even the daredevil feeling of fright just as the hydraulic safety latches tied her into the seat right before a roller coaster ride. Instead, the feeling was one of disappointment, unwelcome surprise, and—

No. It couldn't be.

Taking a mental breath, Joelle decided to keep her voice as light and coquettish as she could. "I don't suppose you're going to tell me who your mysterious compadre is, are you?"

He hesitated. She could visualize the wheels turning in his mind, debating whether or not to tell her. That wasn't a good sign. If he had dinner plans with Zach or any of his other male friends, the name would have instantly zipped off of Dean's lips. His meeting had to be with a female. Maybe a female who was more than a friend. . .or wanted to be more than a friend.

Joelle became conscious that her heart was beating faster than usual. She didn't speak. She waited for him to answer.

"It's Nicole."

Nicole. The very name she didn't want to hear.

"I see." A familiar rush of feeling swept over her, the kind of feeling she used to have whenever Dustin had been out without her and wouldn't tell her where, why, or with whom. She recognized that feeling.

It was jealousy.

"Just hope you enjoy your little visit." If she didn't end the call at once, Joelle knew she'd say something she'd later regret—probably for the rest of her life. She was just about to send him off with an abrupt farewell and hang up when he answered.

"What's that supposed to mean?" His voice was testy.

"Nothing. I'm sorry. As soon as I said that, I regretted it." A shocking realization came to her at that moment. One she did not embrace.

"That's okay, Joelle."

Dean was always so understanding. Too understanding, sometimes. Too willing to let her treat him like a favorite pair of blue jeans. Always reliable. Always dependable. Always the right fit. Always there. Always convenient.

But it looked like all that was about to change.

"Look, Dean," she said, "you don't owe me anything. You have your own life, and I understand that. I should have realized that long ago. You're entitled to see whoever you want, whenever you want. It's really none of my business. It's not like I have a claim on you. I'm sorry."

"No problem. Thanks for the apology."

Joelle hung up the receiver slowly, letting it barely touch the cradle before gently releasing it to its proper place. She ran her finger up and down the receiver, but she wasn't thinking about the object. She was thinking of Dean. For a man who'd just gotten her to apologize, he hadn't sounded happy. Not happy at all.

⁓

"I was wondering where you were," her mom called as Joelle passed the master bedroom some time later.

Responding, Joelle detoured into the room. Eleanor was standing in front of the full-length mirror, spritzing her blond hair with spray. "I wanted to let you know, your dad and I are going out with the Martins for dinner. You're on your own tonight, kiddo."

Joelle let out a low whistle. "I could have guessed. That dress looks great on you, Mom."

Casting her gaze downward, Eleanor appraised herself, then twirled 360 degrees for Joelle to see. "You think?"

"Sure do. Royal blue has always been your color."

"I hope so. We're trying that French place Lloyd took you to. I know it's pretty nice. The Martins said they wanted to treat us because I finally got up enough courage to take the GED test." Her mother's face took on a pink hue, a sure sign she was embarrassed to mention her accomplishment.

Joelle remembered the party that was being planned to celebrate. She couldn't let on, since she'd been sworn to secrecy. "You deserve to go out to a fancy place and much more."

"I don't know." She smiled shyly, reminding Joelle of how she looked in pictures taken decades before. "So how was the exercise class? Will you be going back?"

"Probably." Joelle grinned. "I always was a glutton for punishment."

Eleanor chuckled. "Oh, before I forget, you got some mail today. I have no idea why your father brought it in here. I just happened to see it, thankfully, or else we might not have paid the electric bill. He never bothers to sort it." Shaking her head, she picked up a stack from a tray on top of their television and handed it to Joelle.

"Thanks." Absently, she riffled through catalogs, charge card offers, advertisements, and letters. Stopping at her bank statement, she opened it, even though she had no intention of balancing her checkbook until after dinner.

"Who was that on the phone?"

"Dean."

"Oh, good. So where was he? I know you were wondering."

"The men's retreat. I'd forgotten all about it."

"So had I," said Eleanor, before launching into a story of a mishap that had occurred to Joelle's father and his friends on a golf retreat.

Joelle wasn't listening to her mother. She was too astounded by what her bank statement revealed. "I can't believe this."

"Can't believe what?" Eleanor interrupted herself. She placed her hands on her hips. "You weren't listening to a thing I said, were you?"

"I'm sorry. I guess I wasn't. It's just that, well, you won't believe this." Joelle wasn't sure she believed it herself. "Lloyd's check bounced. His bank returned it because of insufficient funds. And if that's not bad enough, our bank charged me twenty-five dollars."

"That's awful, Joelle. That bad check didn't cause you to overdraw your account, did it?"

"No, though that's no thanks to Lloyd." She sighed. "I just can't believe it. All this time, I thought he really was trying to make things up to me. I just ended up looking like a fool again. How stupid am I?" Her mouth drooped. "Don't answer that."

Eleanor chuckled. "You're not stupid. He fooled me, too."

Joelle grimaced. She had rubbed what she thought was a victory in Dean's face. He'd been right about Lloyd all along. "I guess I owe Dean another apology."

"You seem like you have a lot to talk to him about lately." Eleanor's eyes took on a knowing look. She seemed to be ready to make another comment but shut her mouth in a tight line, as though she thought better of it.

"Have a good time tonight, Mom," Joelle said. She hoped her voice showed the proper measure of enthusiasm.

Exiting the bedroom, she retreated to the kitchen to scrounge around in the refrigerator for supper. Not that she looked forward to eating.

All she could think about was Dean. And what he was doing with Nicole.

Chapter 18

Joelle was nervous as she drove to the next town. Consisting of two large department stores and a few small retailers, the shopping area where she and Freedom had agreed to meet was hardly what could be called a regional mall, yet the variety of merchandise offered was enough to satisfy the basic needs of most people in the surrounding communities. The theater and food court provided places for teens to meet and greet, and for families to get away for a relatively inexpensive evening out. Although he had made no such promise, Joelle assumed Freedom planned for the two of them to take in a movie after a light supper.

Finding a convenient parking place in the crowded lot wasn't easy. The cinema ran four movies at once, so the lot tended to fill up and stay full. Since it was Friday night, Joelle didn't bother to circle her car around the lot containing the closest spaces. The search would no doubt prove futile.

Anticipating her presence at the Silver Screen Matinee within the hour, Joelle didn't begrudge her fellow movie lovers their spaces. She didn't even care what movies were showing. Joelle was content to watch any of them. Against her will, she remembered several occasions when she and Dean had shared an afternoon and a bag of popcorn as they watched flickering black-and-white images. She hoped Freedom liked old movies, too.

Joelle pulled into a space in the far lot meant for an anchor store, making sure she parked beneath a light pole. Since darkness would be upon her by the time she left, she wanted to be sure her car was located in the safest place possible.

Unsure as to how her date would be dressed, Joelle had opted for the same outfit that had taken her to the French restaurant—casual slacks and a blouse, with flat shoes she knew would be comfortable. Being able to wear the same outfit several times had proven the only advantage to a series of blind dates. One change was evident—she had styled her grown-out hair into a flip that managed to look updated while sparing her the messy look.

As her steps took her closer to the entrance, she looked for Freedom. He had promised he'd be easy to spot. She wondered what he meant until she saw a tall, carrot-topped man in his twenties. He reminded her of Howdy Doody except that he was dressed in solid white. White shirt, white pants, white socks, white shoes. Since he was the most distinctive figure in the crowd, he had to be Freedom. She drew closer, still nervous.

He made eye contact. "You must be Joelle."

"I am. But how could you tell?"

He arched red eyebrows. "We just made a rhyme." Freedom cleared his throat and lifted his hand, pointing his forefinger skyward as though he were a professor. "You must be Joelle. But how could you tell? Because you look like a belle I'd like to know well."

Joelle laughed out loud at his corny humor. "I don't think I've heard a poem that bad since kindergarten."

"What?" His tone was mocking. "Are you implying my poetry isn't good enough for Public Television?"

"It's not even good enough for cable access. Sorry." She chuckled, shaking her head all the while. "So how did you know it was me? What really tipped you off?"

"You were scoping out the place like you were looking for somebody, so I took a guess."

"Well, you guessed right." She smiled. Though he was dressed in a somewhat unorthodox fashion, Freedom seemed harmless enough. "So what are your plans?"

"Hungry?"

"As a matter of fact, I could use a bite to eat." She hoped he'd suggest eating at the mall's midpriced restaurant since it offered a bit of atmosphere and a degree of privacy in comparison to the open layout of the food court.

Instead, he tilted his head toward one of the nearby booths, Very Veggie. "I like their organic pita sandwiches. Don't you?"

Since Joelle preferred to indulge in hamburgers and fries, Very Veggie was one of the places in the food court Joelle made every effort to avoid. "Uh, I've never tried one."

He seemed surprised. "As they say, there's a first time for everything. How does a BLT sound?"

Bacon, lettuce, and tomato sandwiches were a rare indulgence for Joelle. Yet at that moment, the prospect of salt and fat seemed comforting. "Sounds good."

"Why don't you go grab us a table, and I'll bring you back a treat?"

Joelle wasn't sure she liked this idea, but she decided to acquiesce. Watching him walk toward the booth, she noticed he was carrying a tan leather briefcase. She wondered about its contents. Had he come straight from work to the date? If he had, he could have left the briefcase in his car. Unless he took a bus from his office to the mall.

But what makes you sure he works in an office? He never told you what he does for a living.

Joelle wished she'd asked more questions when they first spoke on the phone. Still, she brushed her worries aside. At least they were in a very public place. And, she reasoned, if the briefcase contained something sinister, he wouldn't be so open about carrying it.

Her thoughts running wild, she was thankful his order was filled quickly and he returned to the table as promised. She was considering whether to ask about the briefcase when he began the dinner.

"Here you go!" He handed her a sandwich. "I hope you like this. My wallet sure didn't." A nervous chuckle escaped his lips.

Joelle wondered if he was going to ask her to chip in, but since she had no say in the choice of restaurant or food, she decided not to extend her generosity. "I'm sure I'll like it."

"Very Veggie is a bit pricey, especially by food court standards, but I assure you, it's worth every penny."

"I'm sure." The smell the sandwich emitted was noxious. Trying not to make a face, at that moment she decided for certain there was no way she would pay for whatever it was he'd ordered for her. "What is it?"

"It's a BLT."

Joelle looked again. "This may have lettuce, but I don't see any tomatoes or bacon."

"That's right. This is a Beets, Lettuce, and Tofu sandwich. You'll see by its green color that the pita is spinach. They also use a scrumptious mustard-and-cider vinegar dressing. They're the only people who make this sandwich, and I make sure to get one every time I come here. Delicious! You'll be pleased to learn that all the vegetables are grown without harmful chemicals or any other artificial enhancements. They even make their own pitas and dressing." Beaming, he seemed pleased to present her with such a treat.

Organic or not, Joelle didn't think the combination sounded appealing. With an expectant glance at his sandwich, she inquired, "How about a trade?"

Freedom stared at the glass ceiling that loomed high above them. "Hmm. Let me think about that." After a moment he shrugged his shoulders and gave her a nod. "Okay. This is a sacrifice, but I'll trade just to show you I'm quite the gentleman." He handed her his sandwich.

"Thanks." She knew her relief was obvious, until a strangely familiar odor wafted to her nostrils. A quick look at her new sandwich confirmed her worst suspicions. "This is exactly the same."

"Precisely." A sheepish expression crossed his face. "Sorry you don't think you'll like it. Try it. You might be surprised." He placed a large drink next to her. "I got us both a banana sesame yogurt shake. I even splurged and bought us dessert." Freedom reached into a small bag and extracted a container with a transparent plastic lid. The cup contained an icy dessert that appeared to be orange sherbet.

"Looks yummy," she observed. This time she didn't have to control a grimace.

"It is! One of my favorites. Cantaloupe sorbet."

Joelle hoped she heard wrong. "What kind of sorbet?"

"Cantaloupe." Freedom looked at her as though she had just disembarked from a Venusian ship. "Never tried it?" He tapped his unopened straw on the lid. "You're in for a treat."

Joelle stared at the unappetizing meal. "Yum." She knew her expression and tone belied her approval.

Instead of noticing her facial cues, Freedom looked for the invisible. "I have a special talent for seeing auras. You know, very few people do." He bit into his pita.

Joelle was no longer accustomed to eating without pausing for a word of thanks. "You don't say a blessing before meals?" she asked. If any meal needed a blessing, it was this one.

He shook his head. "No. God is everywhere, in all of us. But if you feel the need to pray, I can respect that. I'll wait." Setting down his sandwich, he looked down at his lap.

Joelle bowed her head. "Lord, we gather to thank You for Your provision once again. Please be with us tonight, and bless our time together. In the holy name of Your Son, Jesus Christ, our Lord and Savior, amen."

Obviously untouched by her gesture, he picked up his food before the "amen" had left her lips. "Back to auras," he said. "I can tell by yours that you and I would make good companions."

"You can tell that just from seeing me for a few minutes?"

"Unequivocally. Through my spiritual exploration, I have gained the keys of knowledge." After taking a sip of his drink, he leaned forward. "Take, for example, your name. Joelle is not the name you were meant to have." He set down his sandwich and touched his fingers to his temples. "Give me a moment to release the energy in my mind and connect to your soul. Then I will see what you really should be called."

"I don't know. I like Joelle—"

He held up his hand. "Shh! I can't communicate without absolute silence."

Unable to think of a reason not to accommodate his request, offbeat though it was, Joelle decided to obey. She was glad for the excuse to stop nibbling on the portion of the spinach pita that had managed to escape a soaking from beet juice.

As Freedom closed his eyes and kept them closed for some time, she cast shy glances at those around her. They were ignored by most of the people milling about the mall, but others looked at them in wonderment. They even attracted a couple of snickers. Joelle tried to ignore them by sipping on the oddly flavored shake.

Finally, Freedom came out of his trance. "I just received a message about your new name." He opened his blue eyes. "It's Discover."

"Discover?" She wasn't sure she could get used to such an eccentric name. "You mean, like the credit card?"

"So you are overly concerned about wealth. If you weren't, you wouldn't have thought of a credit card when you heard that name. But don't worry," he consoled her. "Soon the name Discover will come to mean much more to you than a piece of plastic. You have so much to learn, so much to explore, so much to discover."

"I don't know—"

"Today's women are more free than they have been in any other time in history. I don't believe in keeping women in the shackles of old myths and ideas. That keeps me at liberty, too. I am free from all jealousy and can easily give you as much space as you give me. That way, we both can share our liberty." He leaned closer. "Are you free from the bonds of the world? Can you pick up and move anytime you like?"

"I don't know. My parents might be disappointed if I were to move out, except to get married, of course."

"You live with your parents?" His eyes widened. "You're not still in high school, are you?"

"Of course not. I work full time in a doctor's office."

"I hope she practices alternative medicine."

"It's a he, and no, he doesn't practice alternative medicine." This was not going well. Joelle began to wonder how she could finagle her way out of the rest of the evening.

Instead of delivering her the expected lecture on women's equality and the merits of alternative medicine, Freedom went off on another tangent. "Speaking of alternatives, I'm sure you've been speculating as to what I have in my briefcase."

Joelle was stunned. Just as she was about to cut him off, Freedom always managed to come up with something to intrigue her enough to stay put. "I'll have to admit, I was wondering."

Leaning over, he pulled the briefcase onto his lap, snapped it open, and drew out some pamphlets that appeared to be professionally printed. He smiled endearingly. "You never asked me where I live or about my career."

"I assumed you live within striking distance of here. As for what you do, I figured you'd tell me sooner or later."

"You are a very unusual woman, Joelle. Normally that's the first thing a woman wants to know. I'll let you in on something. The fact you didn't ask is one reason I knew you're special. You look beyond the money issue," he grinned, "even if you do think your new name is like a credit card."

"I've been working on my attitude about money. I guess what you said proves I still have a ways to go." She let out a sigh. "I only recently accepted Jesus Christ. He has a lot of molding left to do."

"Ah, Jesus Christ. A fine teacher much like Buddha. If you choose to embrace Jesus why not let Him mold you where you can truly be free? Where you can live out the potential of your new name?"

"I'm making plenty of discoveries where I am, thanks."

"Maybe. But look at how much better this place is." He handed her a pamphlet.

Joelle studied the picture depicting a quiet valley in full summer bloom. Mountains touched an azure sky. Just looking at it had a calming effect.

"How would you like to live there?"

"I already live in the mountains. I love it here. Maybe that's why I find this picture so appealing." She tried to return the pamphlet, but he refused to accept it.

"Read the inside."

The leaflet expanded into more full-color photos. Some showed smiling people working together at a pottery wheel. A crowd of happy children played in another. Two large, rustic-looking cabins were shown in a third picture. She read aloud the snippets of text. " 'Tired of offices, computers, traffic, and all the other trials of life? Would you like to live free of these burdens? Does getting away from disagreeable, disgruntled people sound good to you? Then come and enjoy true harmony with our family at Wisdom's Design.' "

"Believe me, it's as wonderful as it sounds. Wisdom—she's our leader—allows each of us to be who we were meant to be." Freedom exhaled a contented sigh.

"So you make your living selling what you make at the commune?"

He bristled. "We don't use the term 'commune.' The world has sullied that word so it has negative energy. And anyway," Freedom continued, "I've already contributed my trust fund to Wisdom's Design."

"Your trust fund?" Joelle could only imagine Freedom's background and how heartbroken his parents must have been to see their son taken in by a cult leader.

He shrugged. "I don't need the money. I'd rather spend my time making other seekers aware of Wisdom's Design than working myself into the cardiac unit at the hospital like my father did." Anger clouded his features.

"I'm sorry."

"Don't be. He created his own destiny." Freedom pasted on a smile. "Now why don't you create yours by helping me hand out these brochures? We only have five hundred. It shouldn't take long to distribute them."

"You're here to hand out materials about your co—whatever it is?"

"And to meet you, of course."

"Even if I were willing, this mall doesn't attract that many people. Getting rid of that many pamphlets will take all night," she protested. "Besides, when you suggested we meet here, I thought maybe you had plans for a movie. The Silver Screen Matinee is in progress, you know."

"Silver Screen Matinee?" His look was blank. "No, I had no plans to go to a movie. I don't care to see what the world has to offer." Freedom's look changed to one of genuine puzzlement. "I can't believe you're suggesting we waste time in a theater. You seem so spiritual. I thought you agreed with me."

"I do agree that some of the things the world offers aren't good, but they're not all bad, either." She remembered something Dean told her once. "As Christians, we are to be in the world, but not of it."

He held up a leaflet and tapped it with his forefinger. "That describes Wisdom's Design exactly."

Joelle found herself praying to the Holy Spirit. She needed to be shown what words to say. Within a split second, she answered. "Not exactly. Wisdom is not a person, but God the Father. The only way we can find God the Father is through the Lord, His Son, Jesus Christ."

Freedom shook his head. "There are many paths to God."

"Not according to the Bible. Jesus said He is the way, the truth, and the life. No one comes to God the Father except by Him."

"I disagree. That viewpoint is too narrow for my mind."

Joelle rose from her metal seat. "I'm sorry, Freedom, but I just don't think this is working. If you change your mind and want to learn more about the Lord—the true Savior—you can call me. I work for Dr. Mulligan. You can reach me there every weekday."

Joelle saw Freedom open his mouth to protest, but she turned before he could make his next point. Bailing out on an evening wasn't easy for Joelle. She had been brought up to be polite, even to the point of putting up with boredom, inconvenience, and expense, but she could see talking further to Freedom was useless. He was lost, and she wasn't about to hand out materials urging others to take the wrong path. She sent up a silent petition that Freedom would one day come to Christ. In the meantime, she prayed that she had planted a seed.

Discouraged, she was in no mood to shop and certainly in no frame of mind to sit alone in a theater. She decided to leave the mall, go home, microwave a bag of popcorn, and watch one of her dad's old movies on the VCR. Maybe becoming engrossed in a story with a happy ending was the answer.

Joelle was just about to step onto the crosswalk when she spotted a brunette with a fussy hairdo and an auburn-haired male form she instantly recognized. Disinclined to being caught on her way back from a bombed evening, Joelle looked at her black flats.

"Joelle!"

Too late. Dean had already seen her.

Chapter 19

Nicole nudged Dean, sending a sharp pain through his ribs. "Do you have to speak to Joelle? She didn't see us," she hissed.

"Of course I want to speak to Joelle. She's my best friend." Dean didn't add that he'd been thinking about Joelle all evening. In fact, he'd been thinking about Joelle often as the weeks passed. He'd spent considerable time at the retreat praying about whether or not the Lord wanted him to pursue a romantic relationship with her. The more time passed, the more Dean became convinced it was the right thing to do. Otherwise, why would he feel such a sense of peace after praying about her, and why else would Joelle continue to weigh on his mind?

In the meantime, Dean wasn't surprised by Nicole's objection. He'd made a huge mistake in asking Nicole to see *The Sound of Music* with him after his attempts to reach Joelle failed. Ever since, Nicole had clung to him like static electricity. He'd never seen such a chameleon in action.

After their first disastrous night together, Dean never expected to hear from Nicole again. To his surprise, she later begged his forgiveness. When he accepted her apology on the condition she cool off, she molted into a student in search of a spiritual mentor. Over the past weeks, she'd seemed eager to learn more about the Lord. So when she invited him to the Silver Screen Matinee, Dean saw no reason not to tag along.

This night had turned out no differently from the first. Over dinner, he realized Nicole's spiritual quest was a ruse to launch a hoped-for romance. The proverbial last straw broke when Dean handed her a list of suggested religious books.

"What is it with you and religion?" Nicole asked over veal parmesan. Her voice revealed her disgust. "Don't you ever talk about anything else?"

Dean's surprise was genuine. "I thought you wanted a book list. You asked me what you could read in addition to scripture."

"Of course I want to read, but I can't stay focused on religion every minute of the day. There are other things in life, you know. Things like—" she drummed her fingers on the table, "fun."

"Fun? But I have lots of fun," he protested.

"I mean real fun." Fork midway in the air, she leaned toward him, her voice becoming husky. "You seem to forget I'm a woman and you're a man."

His consciousness returning to the present, Dean shuddered. He wasn't fond of hurting people, especially when they were as wobbly in their spiritual walk as Nicole, but he could see she wasn't going to give up on a romantic relationship. That was something he couldn't offer her. Better to hurt Nicole now than to give her false hope.

Dean made a deal with himself. He would keep his promise to watch the movie with her. Then he would make sure he was never alone with Nicole again. Ever.

Thankfully, Joelle was only steps away, but she seemed to be concentrating on the pavement. As soon as they reached her at the end of the crosswalk, he said, "Find any loose change?"

Joelle stopped and looked up. "Not yet, but I'm feeling lucky." Her flat voice and sour expression told another tale.

"If I believed in luck, I'd say you are fortunate," Dean said.

"I do believe in chance. So keep looking," Nicole advised, "and maybe your luck will pay off."

Dean hoped Joelle would ignore Nicole's snide remark. "We're lucky because we ran into you. Unless you're in too much of a hurry to talk."

"I'll bet she is." Nicole looked at her with a steady gaze. "I'm sure Joelle is on her way to somewhere important."

"Not really," Joelle answered, shaking her head. "I was just on my way home."

Dean couldn't resist seizing the opportunity. "Then why don't you join Nicole and me? We're on our way to the Silver Screen Matinee. They're featuring Jimmy Stewart movies. 'It's a Wonderful Life' starts at seven forty-five."

"And it's almost that time now." Nicole tugged on Dean's arm. "We'd better hurry, Dean. I'd hate to miss the beginning."

"I think that's the only Christmas movie I don't mind seeing in June." Joelle smiled warmly until her gaze shot to Nicole. Dean could feel her stewing in fury. Apparently, Joelle could sense her anger, too. "But I think I'll take a pass this time. I don't want to impose on your evening."

Nicole let out a breath. "Some other time, then—"

"Nonsense, Joelle. You won't be imposing," Dean rushed to argue. "We'd love to have you join us."

Joelle's lips tightened as though she were uncertain, but he could tell even underneath her teal contacts that her eyes were sparkling. "I don't know—"

Dean interlocked his elbow with Nicole's, then stepped forward and did the same with Joelle. "Aw, have pity on a guy. How often do I have the chance to escort a beautiful blond and a gorgeous brunette to a movie at the same time?"

To his relief, both women tittered at his compliments. Dean smiled to himself. Already he was keeping his resolution not to be alone with Nicole.

⁓

In the theater, Joelle sat on one side of Dean, and Nicole sat on the other. Joelle tried to ignore Nicole's obvious flirtations. She watched as Dean remained polite but indifferent. She had a feeling her presence wasn't holding him back from responding with enthusiasm to his date. Joelle couldn't help but shake her head. If Nicole had any perception about Dean's personality, she would know he'd never react well to such blatant ploys, at least not for long.

But who was she to criticize Nicole? Joelle hadn't been thinking about the movie as they sat together. All she could contemplate were the events of the past months. Why hadn't she seen the obvious? Why hadn't she considered Sir Dean as her knight in shining armor all along, instead of foolishly chasing a dream? He was already her best friend. He knew her better than anyone else did. What better basis for a lasting love?

At that moment, Nicole placed a bold hand on Dean's. She whispered something in his ear, causing them both to giggle. Despite her brave thoughts from before, Joelle's heart betrayed her confidence with a fearful lurch. What if she was already too late? Unbidden tears filled her eyes. Joelle placed her fingers on the inside corner of each eye, hoping she could pass off her upset as seasonal allergy symptoms. But as they began to fall in earnest, she realized that excuse would never work. She sniffled.

Dean's arm wrapped around her in response. He whispered in her ear, "Happy endings always did make you cry."

A nod of the head was all the answer Joelle could muster at the moment. She wasn't so sure this ending would be a happy one.

∽

The following Sunday after church, Joelle was surprised when Dean dropped by the house. He hadn't sat anywhere near her throughout worship or Sunday school. Even though Dean never missed Singles' Night, he had been absent the previous evening. Phone calls to his house yielded busy signals. Since he had avoided any chance to talk to her for the past two days, Joelle couldn't help but wonder if he was miffed or maybe confused. At least now she would find out.

After his assurances to Eleanor that he'd already eaten and didn't require a slice of pie or a cup of coffee, Dean followed Joelle onto the back porch. The day was mild and sunny, perfect for sitting together on the glider.

She got right to the point. "Where were you last night? I missed you at the meeting. I tried to call later to be sure you were okay, but the line was busy."

"Sorry. I—I just couldn't make it."

"Neither could Nicole." Joelle's voice was heavy with meaning. "I feel like it's my fault. I shouldn't have horned in on your date Friday night."

"It's not your fault. If anyone needs to be blamed, it's me." He placed his hand on hers. "I told Nicole when I took her home that I couldn't see her again outside of church."

Emotions—a mixture of triumph, happiness, and wonder—churned through her. "But I thought she liked you" was all she could manage.

He looked at his athletic shoes. "I think she did, but the feeling just wasn't mutual."

After witnessing Dean's lack of enthusiasm toward Nicole at the movie theater, she couldn't say she was surprised. Curious, but not surprised. "So what happened between you two?"

He shook his head. "Nothing major, but it's nothing I want to discuss."

"Oh." Tight-lipped, Dean was obviously not going to reveal more. She decided the best course was for her to respect his wishes to remain silent, and to confess her own feelings. "About those guys I met through the personal ads—"

Turning his face toward Joelle, Dean held up his palm as a signal for her to stop talking. "You don't have to explain anything to me." He placed his hand back in his lap, a distressed look shadowing his boyish face. "Unless you need to tell me you've found someone you're planning to see a lot more of."

"No." Shaking her head rapidly to emphasize her point, Joelle let out a sigh. "I guess you're right. It's probably better if we don't share each other's misery. At least not about other dates. Especially since I've come to realize. . ." She couldn't finish, choosing instead to stare at her sandaled feet.

"Come to realize what?"

Joelle looked up and saw his hazel eyes opening wide. She swallowed and returned her gaze to her feet. "That no one compares to you," she said softly. She waited for his response, conscious all the while of her beating heart.

"I could have told you that."

She looked into his face. Discovering a broad grin was no surprise. "Oh, you!" She tapped him playfully on the shoulder. Unwilling to let go of the opportunity to tell him her true feelings, Joelle turned serious. "From the moment I met the first guy, I found myself comparing him to you. It was the same with the others. They always came up short." She smiled. "But it was really at the theater on Friday night that everything came together."

"That night, huh?" Dean looked back at her, gazing into her eyes.

Suddenly she knew she could look into those eyes forever. She became engrossed in his face, the straight nose, the fine features that had become so familiar. Joelle found herself looking at his lips, wondering if he might—

"Joelle, I don't think we should see each other again."

She bolted up in her seat, her torso moving away from him. Her eyes widened so much that her lashes seemed to touch the skin underneath her eyebrow. "Say what?"

Joelle hoped she'd misunderstood. Surely she hadn't just spilled out her feelings, only to be rejected! She folded her arms over her chest, each hand clutching the opposite elbow. The motion, she knew, was a subconscious attempt to protect herself. Only it was too late. She'd made herself vulnerable.

Fool!

Her voice shook as she uttered the next question. "What do you mean?"

"Let me finish." His voice dropped to a whisper. "I don't think we should see each other until your mom's surprise party."

Her fingers tightened their grip. His words were of some comfort, but it felt like a hollow victory. "But that's two whole weeks from now. What about our rehearsals? We're supposed to sing our duet soon, aren't we?" Her voice was shrill.

He pressed his finger to his rounded lips. "Shh! I know. I already called and arranged to have it postponed until next month. Mandy's been wanting to sing her solo, anyway."

Joelle remained silent.

"What's the matter?" He smiled a boyish smile. "Don't think you can do without me that long?"

She didn't know whether to laugh or strangle Dean for his attempt at humor. She resisted both urges. Dean's usual way of coping with unexpected emotions was to employ wit. Best to respond in kind. Deliberately she arched an eyebrow. "I didn't think you could do without me for that long."

"Maybe I can't." His smile turned bittersweet. "But I think this will be good for us—not easy for me, but good for us." Gently, he took her hands from her elbows and guided them into his. Her small hands protected in his larger ones, Joelle felt as though her entire being was secure. "While I was at the retreat, I invested a lot of prayer time in us," Dean told her. "I think I know what the Lord wants us to do. But now I want to give you time to confer with Him. I'll keep praying, too." The longing in his eyes was unmistakable. "If I pray when you're anywhere in the vicinity, I won't be able to hear God."

Though the enormity of his words didn't escape her, Joelle couldn't help but protest. "But can't we just follow our feelings? I mean, you must be thinking the same thing I am—that we were meant to be together."

"True." He nodded once more. "But I don't want to pursue a deeper relation-ship with you based entirely on feelings. Emotions are fickle and can't always be trusted. If I'd gone with my feelings, I'd have made a major play for you a long time ago." His mouth curved into a sheepish grin.

"Really?" Joelle wondered. Dean had always been the gentleman, never even hinting he'd like to be more than friends.

"Really. I know I've hidden my feelings well all this time."

"Why?" she asked. "What stopped you from telling me how you feel?"

"The day you accepted the altar call, it was like a part of me was there with you. I thought it would be unfair to make my feelings about you known then. You were at a high point in your life, having accepted Christ, really and truly accepted His saving grace. You didn't need those complications."

"Says who? If you'd let me decide that for myself, you'd have saved me the trouble of going through a lot of bad dates," she pointed out only half-jokingly.

"Maybe so, but have you considered that it could have been the Lord's plan for you to meet those other guys? Now if He wants us to be together, you could really appreciate me." Dean flashed her a charming smile, letting her know his observation wasn't motivated by bloated ego. "And maybe I needed to spend some time with Nicole as part of the process of confirming my feelings."

"Makes sense," she agreed. "But since we've both gone through this process, we should be all set."

"Not yet. Not until we both know the Lord's answer for certain." Breaking his earnest expression, Dean grinned. "Besides, if I'm going to ruin a perfectly good friendship, I want to be sure I'm exchanging it for something even better."

❧

Two weeks later, Joelle was nervous as she and her mother walked up to the front porch of the Jamison home. Joelle was grateful her dad had chosen her to provide distraction so her mom wouldn't be tipped off about the surprise party. Joelle was so excited that the thought of preparing to greet a houseful of party guests was more than she could handle. She was glad her visiting sisters-in-law were up for the job.

Dean had made himself scarce for fourteen days. As he asked, she'd been in prayer about their relationship. Each time she prayed, she was assured that her feelings about Dean were right. She thanked the Lord for the ability to acknowledge them. Then, selfishly, she prayed Dean would decide to court her. Today she would know if her prayers, both selfish and unselfish, would be answered.

In the meantime, she couldn't wait to see the look on her mom's face when she saw that all four of her sons and their families had come to the celebration—two only a few minutes by car, and two by plane. They could all be thankful Mom had given up her last year of high school to marry and start her family. For the first time in her young life, Joelle understood how her mom could feel a love so powerful that she gave up her education.

"That was fun, Joelle," Mom said as she stepped onto the porch. "We should go out for coffee more often."

"I'd like that," Joelle answered loudly enough for those inside to hear. She didn't want to take a chance the partygoers inside would miss her mom's entrance.

"Good. I don't need a hearing aid, you know." The older woman chuckled as she unlocked the front door. She stepped into the living room.

A chorus of voices rang out. "SURPRISE!"

"Surpize, Gam!" two-year-old Todd added belatedly.

Good-humored laughter flooded the house. Todd clapped his hands, congratulating himself that his greeting had been so well received.

Eleanor was speechless. The look of amazement mixed with pleasure on her mother's face was one Joelle would never forget. Flashes from several cameras blinked brightly as Eleanor gawked at the room full of family and friends, surrounded by lots of streamers and balloons. Dad had even made a banner on the computer. It read "Congratulations to Our Graduate."

Dad stepped forward and gave his wife a big bear hug. "Congratulations, honey. After all these years, you did it!"

She nodded, and tears suddenly began to flow down her cheeks. The crowd murmured their approval and broke out into applause. Joelle knew this was one of the happiest days of her mother's life.

After she gave her mother a hug and endured a loving lecture about her part in the charade, Joelle turned and faced Dean. Eyes alight, he nodded to her before greeting the guest of honor. Joelle felt her own face brighten upon seeing him again. She wished she could take his hand and get away from everyone at that moment, but etiquette demanded otherwise. Joelle wished Dean hadn't chosen the day of the party to see her again. Disinclined to look too eager, Joelle made the rounds among the other guests and caught up with her four brothers and gave their wives and their children a round of hugs before she allowed herself anywhere near Dean.

As the party progressed, Joelle kept looking for an opening so she and Dean could talk. Over and over, she could see no hope for any privacy. Giving up, she decided to wait until the party wound down and only her family remained. Since she was occupied by the duties expected of her as daughter of the house, Joelle managed to keep her mind off her nervousness as the hours passed. She could only hope Dean's prayers had confirmed his earlier feelings.

By the time the party was over, night had fallen. Joelle was in the kitchen, putting up the last bit of leftover cake, when she felt a warm hand on her shoulder. "Did you miss me?" Dean's whispered voice flowed into her ear.

His warm breath sent a shiver down her spine. "Why don't you come with me and find out?" She sealed the cake box, then led him outdoors to the empty floral-patterned glider on the back porch. Her heart was beating rapidly as Dean sat close beside her.

"Don't tell your mom this, but I didn't think the party would ever end."

"Me, either." She giggled. "Your secret's safe with me."

"I hope so. You've been avoiding me all day."

"I wouldn't have if I thought there was a shred of hope we could have some privacy. I couldn't run away from the party."

"You've got a point." He took her hands in his. He held them firmly but not too tightly. "So did you pray?"

"Yes. I prayed every day. How about you?"

"The same. And I got the same answer. I know this is what the Lord wants for my life, and the time is right." He looked deeply into her eyes. "But if you got a different answer, I'll wait."

"No, I'm certain. I don't want to wait."

"Neither do I." Leaning closer, he wrapped her in his embrace. When his lips touched hers, she knew she was where she belonged.

Epilogue

Months later

Joelle and her father watched as her sister-in-law, Susan, as matron of honor, walked down the aisle. Her rust-colored chiffon dress looked good with her flowing blond hair. Autumn flowers filled the sanctuary of the small country church.

Joelle had awakened that morning to blue skies that suggested a summer day, yet brisk mountain air revealed that October had arrived.

Joelle remembered returning from her hair appointment around lunchtime. The familiar smell of her neighbor burning leaves filled the air. Happily, she hummed a few lines of "Beauty for Ashes." Ever since she and Dean sang the song together in church, everyone they knew associated the tune with them.

The bride searched the side of the altar and spotted auburn-haired Mandy. She had sung the song beautifully as part of the ceremony. Joelle resisted the urge to hum it once more.

Aware that in just a moment all eyes would be upon her, Joelle self-consciously smoothed her dress by extending the fingers of the hand that held her tiny white Bible. In the other hand, she held a bouquet of white roses that complemented her lace-covered white silk gown. Joelle had chosen long sleeves with a mandarin-style collar, a full, flowing skirt, and modest train. Her veil was simple and added no height.

"You've never looked more beautiful, Joelle," Dad said.

She looked into his eyes. "I've never felt more beautiful." Joelle meant it. Over the past months, she had grown in her relationships—with Dean, with the friends they shared, and with their families. Most importantly, the time had given them a chance to grow together in their faith. For the first time in her life, Joelle felt worthy to walk down the church aisle to meet her groom. Once joined, together they would walk side by side in love, in faith, in life.

The wait had been long but well worth every minute.

She took the last seconds before Susan took her place beside the other bridesmaids to say a silent prayer. *Lord, please walk with Dean and me as we marry today, and for the rest of our lives. We pray that, as we marry in Your will, we will please You in every aspect of our marriage. In Your Son Jesus' name, amen.*

Her stomach leapt with anticipation at the first strains of the "Bridal

March." On cue, all two hundred wedding guests stood, turning their heads to see her veiled form. Dean waited at the altar, a look of anticipation covering his face. The elusive Mr. Perfect was no longer out of reach. After this day, he would be hers.

Forever.

More Than
Friends

Prologue

"Mommy, don't go!" Tears spilled from four-year-old Piper's brown eyes. "I wish I didn't have to, honey." Lexie Zoltan bent down and hugged her daughter.

As Piper's face burrowed into her shoulder, Lexie gazed beyond the columns of her childhood home and noted the irony of the idyllic day. A cloudless blue sky and light breeze carried with it the scent of freshly mown grass. Any other time, she would have relished the chance to relax on the porch swing. She could imagine herself sipping a glass of iced tea flavored with a sprig of fresh mint, watching Piper jump rope and run around the expansive yard where she herself had played as a little girl. But not today. She had never felt worse—except on the day Curt died.

Squeezing Piper, Lexie struggled to keep from shedding her own tears, but to no avail. A tear hit the corner of her mouth, leaving a salty taste. Burying her face in Piper's hair, the same blond as Curt's, Lexie refused to worry about whether her dark mascara and pink blush would rub off on her daughter's hair.

"Why do you have to go, Mommy? Can't I go with you?" Piper uttered between sniffles.

Lexie held on to her daughter, her face pressing against Piper's T-shirt. She didn't dare look at Piper, lest her heart shatter beyond repair. "Not this time," she murmured.

"When can I come with you?"

"Soon. I promise." Lexie forced herself to break the embrace. She took Piper's soft little chin in her hand and met her trusting but inquisitive eyes. She swallowed. How could she leave her preschooler? Would she still see the same trust in those eyes when she returned?

Heavenly Father, keep us in Your tender loving care while we are apart.

"When?" Piper persisted. "Tomorrow?" Hope lit up her face.

Lexie shook her head. "I'm afraid it will be longer than that. I have to get settled in Richmond."

"But I want to come with you. I want to live in our house there."

"I know. But we don't have a house there, at least not yet," Lexie explained. "I'll be staying with Miss Kassia. You remember her, don't you? My friend from school?"

Piper shook her head.

Lexie stroked Piper's head. Of course the child wouldn't remember Kassia.

127

"As soon as I find us a nice place to live, I'll come back for you. It won't take long."

The bang of the screen door turned Lexie's attention to her parents. Mom and Dad had given Lexie a few moments to say good-bye to Piper. Their entrance signaled the time to leave had come—too soon.

Her mother's lips formed a tight line, and her eyes held a look of sadness. Her father's arms were folded tightly across his chest, resting over his ample stomach. Lexie knew both parents were ambivalent about her decision to start a new life in another state, but she had to leave North Carolina, her childhood home, with its problems—and its memories.

They didn't understand, but they supported her by promising to care for Piper for a short time. Maybe they never would understand why she had to move or why this step toward newfound independence was so important to her. She had to succeed. She just had to.

She turned back to Piper. "Just think of all the fun you'll have with Grammy and Pops while I'm away."

Piper barely smiled. "I know."

"I'll be back as soon as I can." Lexie gave her daughter one last squeeze. Tears filled her eyes when she had to let her go.

"You can still change your mind. You'll always have a home here with us," her father reassured her.

The urge to take him up on his offer was almost too much to resist. Lexie glanced at the window of her room, unchanged since her teen years. That room would always represent warmth, security, and comfort—feelings she didn't want to relinquish. But what she needed to accomplish took precedence.

She drew in a breath and squared her shoulders. "I know. But I have to try."

"I guess this is good-bye then," her mother said.

"Oh, Mom. I'm not going so far away. Only a few hours."

"That's too far for me, but you have to do what you have to do."

"Drive defensively," Dad cautioned.

"Okay, now I can leave." Lexie winked at her father and hugged him.

"If your dad didn't tell you to drive defensively, you'd think something was wrong, wouldn't you?" her mother said as she embraced Lexie.

Then Lexie bent over and gave Piper one last hug and kiss. "Be good now."

"I will."

Lexie slid behind the wheel of her modest decade-old car and backed out of her parents' driveway. Unable to resist one last look, she waved and blew kisses to her little girl. Piper sent kisses back and waved with both arms in return. Her parents and daughter stood in front of the brick rambler. White shutters framed the windows, and their old calico cat was slinking away from its hiding place behind a boxwood shrub. She put the car in drive and pressed on the gas pedal.

At the end of the dirt road, the right-hand turn she took seemed to signal a departure from everything she had ever known and loved. She had driven this country road a thousand times. She knew each dip and bend. The interstate, with its open space and unspoken promises, would soon stretch before her.

She took a tissue from the box on the seat beside her and wiped away the last of her tears. "This is it. No more crying. I'm on my way. It's now or never. With God's help, I will succeed."

Chapter 1

Lexie set her suitcases down on the bed in the small second bedroom Kassia showed her in the rear of the apartment. Several pictures that weren't to her taste adorned beige walls, and she could tell the dresser was too small to hold the clothes she usually kept folded at home. Still, Kassia was being generous to let her share the apartment for less than half the rent until she could find a place where she could afford to live on her own. Far be it for Lexie to complain.

"Thanks for the room." Lexie hoped her repeated expressions of gratitude would spur Kassia to leave her, so she could unpack in privacy.

Kassia didn't budge. "I hope you brought some good clothes."

Lexie shrugged and opened the smaller of her two suitcases. "Just clothes for work. No evening gowns or anything. Why? Did you enter me in the Miss America pageant?"

"If I did, you'd win. But I have a good consolation prize." She paused. "Theo Powers."

Lexie's stomach seemed to jump into her throat. "Theo. Oh. Well, that's nice of him to think of me. I guess he has a wife by now. I'm sure she's pretty, too."

Kassia shook her head. "I have good news for you. He's not married."

So Theo had stayed single. An image of his striking face and toned physique flashed into her mind. "I don't believe it."

"He's probably been waiting for you all these years." Kassia sat on the foot of Lexie's bed. "I think he's still holding a torch for you, Lexie."

"Don't be ridiculous. I wouldn't flatter myself to think such a thing." A warm feeling rushed over her, though, just imagining he still cared in the least.

"You'll think differently once you see him again. I know he wants to see you."

"You told him I was moving back to town?"

"Of course. I remember how tight the two of you were back in school."

Lexie remembered, too. She and Theo had been inseparable until Curt entered the picture. Feeling abandoned, Theo hadn't taken well to her marriage. But Lexie had her reasons. And she didn't need new problems now. "I wish you hadn't said anything, Kassia."

"This town may look big, but it really isn't. Whether I said anything or not, you'd run into him sooner or later."

"Later would have been better. Or not at all." She busied herself transferring blue jeans, T-shirts, blouses, and church dresses from the suitcase to hangers, hoping they would fit in the small closet. Lexie refused to let her gaze meet her roommate's.

"Why won't you even consider it?"

Why not? She and Theo had once been close, but there was a deal breaker. He'd always said he never wanted children.

Lexie had been away from her daughter for only a few hours, and she already missed her. She yearned to touch Piper's face. . .but instead returned to unpacking.

"I didn't come back to Richmond after all this time to find a husband," Lexie said. "I came here because of my job promotion."

A promotion I pray will help me clear my debts. A job in another state, away from the painful memories. And the guilt. Curt died, and it's all my fault. Maybe if I can make a go of it here, away from the town where he died, I can forgive myself.

"Besides," Lexie added, "it was high time for me to grow up."

Kassia shrugged. "I guess we all come to that place in our lives. Or at least we should."

"Once I get settled in my own place," Lexie continued, "I'll send for Piper and get out of your hair."

"You're not in my hair. I'm glad for the company." The brunette's smile conveyed genuine emotion.

Lexie gave her old college roommate a hug. "Thanks, Kassia. I really do appreciate you."

"You know you can always count on me." Kassia returned her light squeeze. "I love having you as a roommate again. It'll be like old times."

"You mean pizza and popcorn at midnight? Studying for midterms and finals?" Lexie scrunched her nose. "I'll take the pizza, but skip the tests—thank you very much. And I definitely wouldn't want to go through Dr. Stein's macro-economics class again."

"But wasn't all the trouble worth it, to graduate with an economics degree? Try hitting the job market with liberal arts and a minor in Renaissance history."

"You're doing great! What are you complaining about?"

"Only because my uncle found a place for me in his office. Look at Morgan," Kassia said, referring to another classmate. "She was laid off from her job three months ago and still hasn't found anything else."

"As if she has to worry. It's not like Gary doesn't have a good job." Lexie regretted the tinge of envy in her voice. She and Curt had never enjoyed job security.

"I guess. But I think she's worried since they just moved into their new house." Kassia grinned. "You know, Theo has a good consulting job and a nice place on a cul-de-sac. I've seen it. That house is bigger than Morgan's. All new, with spotless beige carpets and everything painted off-white."

"Sounds inspired."

"Oh, it is." A laugh escaped Kassia's lips. "He managed to get some shades on the windows, but that's about it. There's stuff from college thrown around as if he just moved in yesterday. I don't think he's bought a stick of furniture in ten years. Believe me, Theo's place is ready for a woman's touch."

"Good for him. I hope he finds the right woman to decorate it in grand style. Maybe someone like you," she teased.

"Me?" Kassia chuckled. "Theo's a great guy, but we couldn't ignite enough sparks between us to start a fire with a box of kitchen matches and the biggest pile of dry brush in the world." She pointed a finger at Lexie. "But the two of you could rub two sticks together in a torrential downpour and start a bonfire."

Lexie turned away from Kassia and occupied herself by folding several pairs of socks. Unbidden, a picture of Theo flitted across her mind. Brown hair, streaked from summers as a lifeguard, deeply tanned skin, and eyes the color of melted semisweet chocolate. All those looks and a brain, too. "That was a long time ago," she forced herself to admit.

"He had a lot of promise back then, and as far as I can see, he's lived up to his potential."

"You do realize I'd never pursue a man because of his job, don't you?" Lexie knew her voice sounded artificially bright.

"I have to agree 'gold-digger' doesn't describe you, Lexie. Besides, I can't imagine you as anything but independent. Even as Curt's wife, you kept your own identity." Kassia stopped herself. Her face flushed pink.

"It's okay. You don't have to act as if it's taboo to mention his name." She stopped folding her socks and looked at Kassia.

"Yeah. But I know you're still hurting."

Kassia spoke the truth. How could Lexie not be hurting? Curt's accident on the construction site would always be with her. He'd gone home to the Lord much too soon. Lexie never quit blaming herself for his death. If only she hadn't been so greedy, he would still be alive today. "I always will hurt."

"Maybe seeing Theo will make you feel better."

"Feel better? No way." Lexie resumed folding with more vengeance than necessary. "I can't see anyone else. I can't do that to Curt."

"It's been two years," Kassia pointed out. "No one will think you're being unfaithful to Curt after all this time."

Lexie looked directly into Kassia's eyes. "No, Kassia. I won't see Theo. And that's final."

❧

Theo Powers swallowed the lump in his throat as he walked toward the two-story, red-brick apartment building. He hadn't remembered being this nervous in a long while.

Looking for a distraction, he noted the care professional landscapers had taken to keep the grounds pristine. Some garden spots were filled with strategically planted bushes—some with red leaves, others with green—and bordered by blue-faced pansies. Each plant looked robust and in full flower, evidence that any wilted specimen was yanked and replaced without hesitation to keep a uniform appearance at the upscale complex. Along sidewalks and the edge of the common areas were what looked like every type of flowering plant known to thrive in Virginia. Pink and white dogwood trees, apple trees, Asian pear trees, azaleas, and other flowers burst with color. They made a beautiful picture. He could only imagine their lovely scent. Too bad his stuffy nose prohibited him from taking in the sweet fragrance.

Observing the blooms, Theo wondered how anyone could doubt God's existence and His intelligent design. He had only one question. Why did the Creator choose to afflict him with allergies to pollen?

He sneezed.

Theo paused on the sidewalk. At that moment, a group of young men in a 1970s muscle car sped past. The drumbeat and wail of guitars from rock music pulsated from open windows. In such a presence, he felt wimpy extracting one of the ever-present white tissues from his pocket. As Theo sneezed into it twice more, he imagined the young men inside the car were laughing at him. When he ventured a look, he saw them staring back but not laughing. Those workouts had paid off.

He sneezed once more. Why didn't the pills the doctor prescribed work or, at least, work better? For the thousandth time, he considered allergy shots.

Naturally he and Lexie were reuniting on a day when his allergies were at their worst. How could she enjoy being with someone who was constantly sneezing and coughing and watery-eyed? Then again, if he delayed their meeting until his symptoms subsided, they'd likely not see each other until months from now. He didn't want to wait.

Theo stuffed the tissue back into the pocket of his chino pants and tightened the grip on the dozen red roses he had picked up for Lexie at the grocery store. At least he didn't sneeze around roses. Not that he'd had much contact with roses lately. He hadn't bought flowers for a woman in years.

Theo groaned before straightening himself to his full height of just over six feet. He put on the confident expression he always wore when he felt jittery and climbed the two flights of stairs to Kassia's apartment.

Kassia had called a week ago to let Theo know that Lexie planned to move back to town, and long suppressed feelings had emerged. He'd missed Lexie and the easy friendship they'd once shared. When she'd moved back to North Carolina after graduation, disappointment had flooded him. The feelings were compounded when, a few months later, he watched her walk down the aisle of a little country church, dressed in flowing white, to marry Curt.

He preferred to think of a more distant time, when Lexie was a carefree coed. Burnished golden hair flowed almost down to her slender waist. Eyes as luminous as sapphires sparkled with ready laughter. Lexie had been pretty and popular in school. So popular that Theo hadn't been alarmed when Curt Zoltan, a jock known more for brawn than brains, joined their study group to cram for a history exam. Before he knew what had happened, study sessions turned to romance for Lexie and Curt. If only Theo hadn't taken her for granted. If only he hadn't misinterpreted Curt's attention toward Lexie. If only he'd spoken up in time to let Lexie know his true feelings—that he wanted to be more than friends. If he had, perhaps Curt wouldn't have stolen her away.

Theo delayed his steps as he walked down the hall, in keeping with his resolution to take things slowly with Lexie. Kassia had told him Curt had died tragically in a construction accident. From what little he'd heard over the years, Theo gathered that Curt had been an ideal Christian husband. Theo sighed. Who wanted to compete with a ghost?

I probably don't stand a chance after all these years. But I have to see her. I have to try. There's no other way I can get her out of my mind.

He stopped in front of Kassia's apartment. His heart beating rapidly, Theo fought the temptation to call her on his cell phone and tell her he wouldn't be visiting after all. He stood there a moment and adjusted the bouquet in his left hand.

The door opened. Too late. The decision had been made.

Chapter 2

Hi, Theo." Kassia's broad smile covered her face, an expression he didn't see on her often. She stood in the doorway and twisted a dark curl around her finger.

"Hi." Theo had hoped Lexie would answer the door.

"Nice roses."

He looked at them. "I thought so." He felt awkward standing in the hallway. "Uh, aren't you going to invite me in?"

"Oh. Yeah. Sure." Kassia lurched as though she had just been awakened from a deep sleep. She stepped aside. "Come on in."

"She's here, isn't she?" he said in a low voice.

Kassia nodded. "She got here a couple of hours ago," she answered in a stage whisper. "She's hardly had time to settle in yet."

Just then Lexie called from the next room. "Who's that, Kassia?"

Lexie! He'd forgotten the sweetness of her voice. Without warning, emotions he thought he would never again experience rose to the surface.

"Is it the delivery man?" Light footfalls approached the living area, bringing the sound of her voice closer. "I'm still expecting a few things—" In an instant, she stood at the entrance to the kitchen. The woman he loved! He took in a breath. Theo knew his love for her had never died.

As soon as her blue gaze met Theo's stare, she stopped.

"Lexie!" The voice coming out of his mouth sounded eager. Too eager.

He fought the impulse to run toward her. His hand, still holding the roses, jerked in an awkward motion. First he held them out toward her, then pressed them back against his chest. Their freshman psychology professor would have said the gesture reflected Theo's inner debate.

"Theo." Instead of the look of pleasure he longed to see, Lexie's face revealed a combination of surprise, discomfort and—could it be—fear?

"Hello." Theo snapped out of his dream state. His second greeting sounded much more restrained than his initial outburst. He swooshed the flowers behind his back.

Lexie turned her attention to Kassia. "What is he doing here?" Her tone seemed almost accusatory.

A sheepish expression covered Kassia's face. "I, uh, I invited him."

"As soon as Kassia told me you'd be coming in today, I decided I'd like to take you both out to dinner. Sort of like a 'welcome home' celebration," Theo added.

135

"You did?" Kassia asked. "Oh, how nice of you, Theo." She turned to Lexie. "Isn't that nice of Theo?"

He wished he hadn't let his emotions carry him away, but he tried to make the best of the situation. "I thought we could go to that seafood place on Cary Street where we always wanted to eat but could never afford. Remember that?"

"Oh, I remember." A nervous titter sprang from Kassia's lips.

Theo took a moment to drink in Lexie's appearance. He wouldn't have thought it possible, but she looked even more beautiful now than she had in college. Her hair had grown a few shades darker, just enough to accentuate her creamy skin. Her hair no longer fell to her waist, a fact he noted with regret. Instead she wore it in a shoulder-length flip that somehow managed to look both retro and up-to-date all at one time. The style became her, he realized. Framing her face, it drew more attention to her blue eyes and pert nose. The bone structure of her heart-shaped face looked more prominent than before, but the soft sleeveless turtleneck and blue jeans she wore revealed she hadn't lost so much weight as to appear gaunt. In fact, she epitomized perfection. Just perfect. But then, maybe she always had been.

"I'll even treat you both to the most expensive dinner on the menu. Won't it be great, after all this time? We won't have to pinch pennies or argue over how to split the bill," Theo said.

"I don't know if I have to eat the most expensive thing on the menu, but I sure could go for some surf and turf," Kassia said. "How about you, Lexie?"

Instead of brightening into an anticipated smile, Lexie's face darkened, and her mouth set itself in a thin line. "Thanks for thinking of me, but I really can't go."

Why not? Theo waited for her to offer a valid excuse, but instead she folded her arms across her chest, raising a silent but visible barrier.

"That's the first time I've known you to turn down a free dinner," Theo joked.

His jesting did nothing to lighten Lexie's countenance or mood.

"That's just it, Theo. You don't know me anymore." He didn't like her edgy tone.

"That doesn't mean—"

Her face and expression softened with apology. "I'm sorry, but I can't go with you to dinner. Thanks for the offer." She tilted her head toward her roommate. "Why don't you go ahead with Kassia and have a nice time?" Before Theo could protest, Lexie retreated into the bedroom and shut the door behind her with a thud.

"What's the matter with her?" Theo asked.

"I don't know. I have no idea why she's acting like this. Maybe she's just tired." Kassia shook her head so hard her curls moved back and forth.

"Or maybe I moved too fast," Theo wondered aloud. "Maybe I should have waited for her to settle in before trying to meet again. Or inviting her anyplace." He brightened at a thought. "Should I try again in a couple of days? Maybe this coming Saturday?"

Kassia shook her head. "I'm not so sure even that would help."

Theo dropped his arm to his side, leaving the roses facing the floor. They looked as dejected as he felt. "Oh."

"Look—it's not you," Kassia explained. "It's Lexie. For some reason, she has this idea she can't see you because of Curt. As if she's being unfaithful or something."

"Unfaithful? That's ridiculous."

"I think so, too. I'd hoped that seeing you would change her mind."

"Maybe she's disappointed with how I've changed since she last saw me."

Kassia looked him up and down in an exaggerated manner. "I don't think so."

Theo grinned. He and Kassia had been friends too long for them to entertain any romantic notions toward each other. "Thanks for the boost. I needed that."

"You're welcome." She sighed. "Maybe I overreacted when I told you not to try later. Why don't you? She's been through a lot. I'm sure she'll be in a better frame of mind once she settles in."

"Yeah." Theo had his doubts. He handed Kassia the roses. "Here. Why don't you enjoy these at least? There's no point in letting them go to waste."

"They're beautiful. I wish they really were for me." Kassia sniffed one of the blooms. "These just might be your ticket."

"Really? If she turns down a free dinner that easily, she must be a pretty hard nut to crack these days."

"You'd be surprised how far a few roses can take you, even with independent, modern women." Kassia disappeared into the kitchen with the flowers.

In her absence, he studied the familiar living room. Kassia hadn't acquired much in the way of décor since school days. She had upgraded the old nineteen-inch television set that had been in her dorm room to a larger screen, and the computer looked new. Other than that she had the same furniture, a mixture of castoffs and cheap bookshelves he had helped her cart in when she first rented the place after graduation. The sameness offered a bit of comfortable familiarity in an ever changing world.

"Are you still up for that surf and turf?" Theo called.

Kassia reappeared with the roses, which she had placed in a cut-glass vase with water. "You don't have to do that. You came to see Lexie, not me." She held the roses toward him. "Don't these look even more beautiful arranged in the vase?" She smiled and set them on the end table beside the sofa.

"Yes, if I do say so myself. And just to compliment you on your fine talent as a florist, I'll take you to dinner as I promised."

She looked toward the kitchen. "Well, I hadn't made any other dinner plans, so a good meal out sounds like a plan. Are you sure?"

"Sure, I'm sure. Hey, I'm not as nice as you'd like to think. I have a motive," he confessed. "I have to eat, too."

Kassia laughed. "You convinced me. Surf and turf it is."

⤳

Loneliness wrapped itself around Lexie when she heard the door shut behind Theo and Kassia. She had overheard enough of their conversation to realize they had gone to the restaurant without her.

Why did she have to be so stubborn and turn down a perfectly good meal and let Kassia go out alone with Theo? And why did a feeling of discomfort tug at the pit of her stomach? She'd told them to go without her. They had every right to take her up on her suggestion.

She grimaced. Who cared about the meal? She'd missed Theo's company. Seeing him again brought forth unexpected feelings—feelings she had long forgotten. She wished she hadn't passed up the chance to spend time with him again, to renew their friendship, or maybe—

She shook such unwelcome thoughts out of her head.

Well, fine. If they wanted to go out and have a good time together and leave her alone, fine. Fine with her. She felt in no mood to put on a good face and engage in idle chitchat in a public place. Not tonight.

She made her way into the small kitchen and inspected Kassia's refrigerator. Only a half head of lettuce, a few carrots, and a carton of skim milk occupied the shelves. Maybe she should have gone out for seafood after all.

She opened the freezer and counted six frozen burritos. Bingo! She popped an extra spicy beef and bean burrito in the microwave. While she waited, Lexie stared at the apartment door.

Inviting Theo to visit on the first day she arrived in town? How could she forgive Kassia for ambushing her like that?

Better yet, how could she forgive herself for her silent reaction to seeing him again? Her heart betrayed her with its rapid beating and its sudden yearning.

The years had barely touched Theo. Sun streaks from summers as a lifeguard had given way to a natural brown. She realized she liked the way Theo's hair looked with his eyes, the color of fine mahogany. And from the way his orange polo shirt draped across his chest, Theo hadn't missed too many days at the gym. If only—

The phone rang. Lexie rushed to answer, hoping it was Piper. "Hello?"

"Mommy?" The voice removed all doubts about her decision to stay home instead of going out with Kassia and Theo.

"Piper!" Lexie smiled into the phone. "Yes, honey, it's me! Have you had a good day with Grammy and Pops?"

"Yep!" Piper began a long story about her day with her grandparents. Apparently she had made friends with the other little girls in the park and had seen someone from Sunday school.

"Did you play on the swings?"

"Yeah! Grammy doesn't push me as high as you do, though."

Lexie imagined her little girl, blond hair flying in the breeze, begging her grandma to push her higher. "I know you had a good time all the same."

"Yeah! Grammy let me have money for the gum machine. I got a bracelet."

"That sounds like fun. I miss you. Do you miss me?"

She hesitated. "A little bit."

"I miss you a lot bit." Lexie chuckled. "I know you're having fun with Grammy and Pops. I don't get to have fun the way you do."

"When are you coming home, Mommy?"

"Soon." Her heart lurched. They would be together in a matter of weeks. The time could not pass quickly enough for Lexie.

"Grammy wants to talk," Piper said. "I'm gonna hand her the phone now. Don't hang up, okay?"

"All right, honey. I love you! Here's a big smooch." Lexie made a kissing sound into the phone.

"I love you, too, Mommy." Piper smacked her lips back. "Here's Grammy."

She assured her mother that everything in her life was humming along at a smooth pace, then hung up a few moments later. She remained fixed in the chair. Piper's feelings came first.

Then why did Lexie feel so confused?

Chapter 3

The next afternoon, Lexie was humming the chorus of a melody as she sorted laundry in her room.

"I'm home," Kassia called.

Lexie heard the door shut behind her friend. "I'm in here," she responded, knowing Kassia could follow her voice in the small apartment. "I'm doing a load of reds so a dress I want to wear to work will be clean. I'll be glad to throw in anything of yours. Well, except maybe whites. Unless you want them to turn out pink."

"Cute," Kassia replied from the hallway. "I'll look and see." Moments later, she entered Lexie's room, a few red items in her hand. She threw them in the small pile. "Thanks." She smiled. "You seem to be in a better mood today."

"You said it." Lexie threw a scratchy red broadcloth blouse on the pile of red, orange, and magenta clothing.

"So you're not mad at me?"

"Mad at you? What for?"

"You know what for. For going without you last night. I would have apologized to you after I got home, but you were already asleep."

"I went to bed early." Lexie turned to Kassia. "I admit I was a little annoyed, but then I realized I have no right to be mad. You and Theo invited me to dinner. I was the one who wouldn't go."

"You may as well have been there," Kassia said. "Theo couldn't stop talking about you all night."

"He couldn't?" The unsettling emotions she had felt the previous night returned.

"No. I could tell that seeing you again had an effect on him."

"Really?" Lexie blurted out. "He's not hoping for—?" How could she express herself without sounding like a total egomaniac?

"You mean," Kassia asked, smiling, "he's not hoping for a romance?"

Her face flushed hot. "Or anything else, I guess."

"I don't know," Kassia answered. "But I think he was pretty disappointed you didn't go out with us. You know, it wouldn't have hurt to give him a chance."

"I might seem harsh to you, but there are things you don't know."

"Like what?"

Lexie felt no desire to elaborate. Besides, if she argued with her friend, Kassia would defend Theo. Then she would insist that Lexie spend time with him. She refused to consider any relationships based on guilt. She harbored enough remorse over her husband's death to last a thousand lifetimes.

"Well?"

"Let's just say it's a good thing I didn't go," Lexie said. "Mom and Dad called while you were gone. I got to talk to Piper."

"I know you wouldn't have missed that for the world." Kassia smiled. "She's probably having a great time being spoiled by her grandparents."

"You're not kidding." Reviewing the hamper's contents, Lexie decided her orange capri pants were bright enough not to be affected by the dyes in the rest of the load. She scooped them out of the ivory-colored wicker container.

"Are you sure about those pants?"

Lexie studied them, then nodded. "I've washed them a couple of times. And I'll be using cold water."

"Decisions, decisions." Kassia chuckled. "Not quite as glamorous as our real jobs, huh?"

"I don't know if you'd call my job glamorous, but it's the best one I've ever had. Ms. Smith has given me an interesting project. Plus, she doesn't breathe down my neck all day. I really enjoy the work."

"That must be novel for a technical writer," Kassia observed. The corners of her mouth turned up.

"Very cute," Lexie noted. "I know technical writing seems dry, especially for people who'd rather read novels."

"Like me." Kassia raised her hand.

"I know." Lexie grinned. "But you'd be surprised at how rewarding my job can be."

"Oh, sure." Kassia glanced upward. "So many instruction manuals, so little time. How many creative ways can you say, 'Press the red button'?"

"Technical writing actually is very creative," Lexie said. "I look at it as helping people understand what they've just bought. If it weren't for people like me, owner's manuals would be written by design engineers, heavy on the technical jargon. If people who buy our products read the manual I write and follow the directions, they'll be getting the most out of whatever they buy, since I work the technical terms into everyday phrases."

"Assuming anyone actually reads the manual." Kassia shook her head. "I hate to tell you this, but very few people get as excited about instruction manuals as you do."

Lexie scrunched her nose. "I know. Well, if they don't read the directions, then it's their own fault if they don't understand how to use what they buy. And if they don't learn, they're not being the best stewards they can of the money the Lord gives them."

Kassia let out an exaggerated sigh. "You haven't changed a bit, Lexie. Everything's a sermon with you, isn't it? I don't see why you don't go to seminary."

Lexie tossed a red-and-black patterned blouse onto a pile of similar colors. "No, thanks. Teaching Sunday school is challenging enough for me."

"Doesn't sound half as exciting as what I have planned for this evening." Kassia cocked her head to one side and looked at Lexie from the corners of her eyes.

Lexie made a mental list of Kassia's favorite ways to spend a night out. "Let me guess. You're going to use the gift certificate your mom gave you for your birthday and splurge on a massage."

"That sounds heavenly." Kassia closed her eyes and let out a deep sigh.

"May I join you?"

"Yes and no."

"Huh?"

"Yes, you can join me, but, no, it's not for a massage."

Lexie couldn't hide her curiosity. "What then?"

"I have a date."

"A real date, eh? Not just a get-together with the women at work?"

"Nope." She tilted her head. "I"—she placed a forefinger on her chest—"have a real date. Dinner out with a man."

"Great!" Lexie said with genuine happiness. "Then what do you want me along for? I doubt you want a chaperone. Besides, I believe in 'two's company, but three's a crowd.' "

"But four works out pretty well."

"Four!" Lexie groaned and placed her hands on her hips. "No, not again. You just tried to set me up last night. Don't tell me you were on the phone all day at work, making plans for tonight, too."

"No way. My job's too important to me. I allow very little time for social planning," Kassia assured her. "It's just that Brad called and, well. . ." She hesitated.

"Brad? The one you told me about, the one who works down the hall from you?" Lexie's voice rose with excitement.

Kassia nodded. "The same one."

"Good for you. I know you've had your eye on him for some time. And that's exactly why I shouldn't barge in." Lexie wagged her forefinger at Kassia. "I don't want to ruin things for you."

"You won't," Kassia assured her.

Lexie shook her head. "Just call whoever my date is and tell him it's off."

"I can't do that. It's already planned. Just consider the free dinner a payback for my running out on you last night."

"You didn't run out on me." Lexie felt tempted, though. Seeing Theo again had stirred her heartstrings in a way she liked. And didn't like. Reigniting a long lost relationship held no appeal for her, especially with Theo. He had always been adamant about never wanting children. How could he accept Piper?

"Okay," Kassia said. "Maybe Theo and I didn't exactly run out on you. But I'd like to show you a good time while we're roomies all the same. You won't have the freedom to come and go as you please once Piper gets here, you know."

"But I don't want freedom. At least, not complete freedom like you have. If I did, I'd just leave Piper with Mom and Dad indefinitely."

Kassia placed a sympathetic hand on Lexie's shoulder. "Lexie, if I could have picked any mom but my own, I would have picked you. You have to be one of the most unselfish women I know. But you're a woman, too. Need I remind you that you're still in your twenties? You're not an old lady. I think you forget that sometimes."

Lexie swallowed. How could she argue? "You're not setting me up with Jake, are you?"

"Jake? No way. Even I can't stand listening to him brag. Nope, it's someone you'll like very much."

"Well. . ." Doubts tugged at her. "I know you have the best of intentions, and I love you to death for it; but I've already told you I did not come here to find a husband. I just want to get established in a great job and get settled so Piper can have a good life. The kind of life she deserves."

"And she will. But you owe it to yourself to be happy, too, don't you?"

Lexie twitched her mouth into a playful grin. "What are you selling—cars, soda, or hair color?"

Kassia laughed. "I'm selling life. A good life. One you can't buy. Come on, Lexie. If you don't go for the guy, at least look at it as a free meal."

Lexie folded her arms. "Isn't that kind of mercenary?"

"Only if you let yourself think of it that way," Kassia added. "Okay, I'll make a deal with you. If you really don't like the guy, you can pay for your own dinner. Or you can pay for your own dinner, anyway. How's that?"

Lexie weighed Kassia's suggestion. "I appreciate the offer, but I honestly don't want to go. I was planning to stay in tonight." She tilted her head toward the mound of clothing on the floor. "Wouldn't you say I have a few things to do? Besides, I have a good book I've been saving for this occasion." To prove her point, she grabbed her book from the night table and held it up for Kassia to see.

"How to Be a Success in Twenty-One Days?" Kassia's eyes widened. "Don't you think you're already a success?"

Lexie shrugged. "Good advice is worth reading."

"Good advice or not, success can wait until tomorrow night." Kassia viewed the laundry. "On second thought, I think I'll take this out." She retrieved a skirt with red flowers on a white background.

"That's probably a good idea. Maybe you should wash it by hand."

Kassia grimaced. "Maybe I'll just take it in to the dry cleaners."

"I know!" Lexie exclaimed. "I can do that for you instead of going out."

"You're not getting out of this dinner that easily." Kassia's voice took on a pleading tone. "You really have to go with me."

"I do?" Lexie looked at her friend suspiciously.

"Yeah." Kassia paused. "I sort of, uh, promised you'd be there."

"Kassia!" Lexie moaned. "Oh, all right. But don't tie up any more evenings for me without asking, okay? I can take care of my own social calendar."

Kassia rewarded Lexie with a big smile. If spending an evening out meant that much to her, she would make the sacrifice. Lexie relied on Kassia's friendship. Without her generous offer to share the apartment until she could gain financial security, Lexie'd be living in lesser accommodations with a stranger. Lexie knew she owed Kassia a lot.

She looked down at her faded blue T-shirt and gray gym shorts. "I'd better put on something that's a little nicer than this. How much time do I have?"

Kassia glanced at her watch. "It's already a quarter to six. You have exactly one hour. Think you can make yourself look good enough for Le Bistro in that amount of time?"

"Le Bistro?" She recalled reading a review that had raved over the restaurant's high-priced entrees. "I'll be sure to bring my credit card."

"Trust me—you won't be paying for dinner," Kassia assured her. "You'll like this guy, remember?"

Lexie shrugged. "So you say."

Almost an hour later, Lexie emerged from her room looking like a different woman. She had freshened her hair with hot rollers. Touches of light color on her eyes and face brought out her natural beauty without calling attention to the fact that she wore makeup.

She had chosen an Irish linen shift for the occasion. Its fresh peach color complimented her complexion. A few extra minutes spent applying peach polish to her nails paid off in colorful dividends. A gold necklace, earrings, and bracelet in a matching set went well with low-heeled sandals decorated with gold accents.

When Kassia saw her roommate, she let out a whistle. "I thought you were prepared not to like your date."

"I'm not dressing for him. I'm dressing for myself." She looked directly at Kassia as she spoke.

As a young widow caring for a daughter and holding a job that didn't require a suit, Lexie found few opportunities to dress the way she liked to as a woman. She felt no qualms about her dress. The linen shift had been bought for church, not to attract a man.

The apostle Peter's words from his first epistle passed through her mind: *Your beauty should not come from outward adornment, such as braided hair and the wearing of gold jewelry and fine clothes. Instead, it should be that of your inner self, the unfading beauty of a gentle and quiet spirit, which is of great worth in God's sight.*

Kassia's teasing brought her back to the present. "You're dressing for yourself, huh? Who are you trying to kid?" She surveyed Lexie's appearance. "Looks to me like you've been saving that dress in your closet in hopes of snagging a guy."

"No, I haven't." Realizing she sounded testy, Lexie softened her tone. "At least, I didn't think I was." Lexie glanced at her outfit. "Is it really that daring?"

"Not daring. Just flattering." Kassia winked. "He'll like it."

Lexie raised her hands in frustration. "Forget it. I'm changing." She turned back toward the hall.

"Wait!" Kassia called. "I was just joking. Besides, we don't have time. We have to leave right now."

"Aren't they coming to pick us up?" Lexie asked.

"No. We're meeting them there."

Lexie ran her hands over the shift. "It won't take me a minute to put on something else."

"You'd better not! Trust me—you look fine."

Lexie took note of Kassia's dress. A skimpy black number with spaghetti straps and V-neck, its short length complimented Kassia's thin legs that seemed to melt into strappy sandals with high heels. By comparison, Lexie seemed to be playing the part of a school marm.

"All right. I'll take your word for it," she conceded. "Let's go."

The ride in Kassia's small car passed all too quickly. Lexie's hands felt clammy, and her foot tapped to an unheard tune on the floorboard. She wished they could ride around all night so she wouldn't have to meet Mr. Mystery Man. Unless—

No. Kassia wouldn't do that. She wouldn't think of asking Theo to be her date. Not after last night. Lexie hoped her date would be someone new. Someone she didn't know. Someone who didn't remember her the way she once was, before her life fell apart.

She didn't want to face Theo. Not after the way she had treated him, when really he was only trying to show her a little hospitality as a welcome-back gesture. How could she ever make it up to him for being so rude?

Maybe she could call him sometime. Sure, that was it. Times had changed. Lexie wasn't her grandmother. She didn't have to wait by the telephone, hoping against hope a man would call. Then again, if she called, Theo might misread her gesture as a ploy for romantic attention. And she couldn't have that.

"Here we are." Kassia pulled the car into an underground parking lot and handed the attendant a few dollars to cover the flat fee for the evening's parking privileges.

Lexie reached for her purse. "Here. Let me help with that."

Kassia eschewed the offer with a wave of her hand, then pressed the gas pedal. "You can cover us next time."

At one time Lexie would have objected, but money was too tight for her to display the generosity she felt in her heart.

"Are you excited?" Kassia whispered a few moments later as they approached the restaurant.

If Kassia could feel Lexie's beating heart, she would know the answer. "I–I guess so."

Kassia lifted her empty hand in a pretend toast. "Here's to a new adventure."

Lexie returned the favor as they entered. "To a new adventure."

"You girls don't have to toast now. I'll buy you a drink," a teasing voice greeted them.

"Hi, Brad," Kassia answered, giving him a big smile.

Consistent with Kassia's taste in men, Brad possessed smoldering good looks. A tan made him appear as though he spent hours in the sun, and his build indicated he might have played football in school. Lexie sent Brad a shy but pleasant smile and searched with her eyes for the man Kassia had chosen for her.

When Brad stepped aside, Lexie learned her worst fears had been confirmed. Kassia had managed to hoodwink her again.

Chapter 4

Lexie caught her breath. Theo appeared even more handsome than he had the previous night.

"I see she tricked us both again," Lexie whispered to him while Brad was telling the hostess they had reservations in his name.

Theo's brow furrowed. "Tricked us?"

Seeing his apparent innocence, Lexie regretted her observation. "Isn't that just like her?" She chuckled in hopes he would know she wasn't upset. "I guess I should thank you for being such a good sport."

"Kassia didn't tell you?" He let out a breath. "I didn't want her to bring you here against your will."

Lexie cringed. She wished she hadn't made such a lame attempt at humor. Now she'd let him know she didn't want to be on this date. Even though she had no intention of finding romance at this time, if ever, Lexie knew hurting Theo's feelings wouldn't accomplish anything good. "I'm not here against my will. I agreed to the date. I even dressed up. See?" She motioned to her dress.

"I noticed." His smile confirmed the truth. Theo extracted a tissue from his pocket and wiped his nose. "Sorry."

Suddenly she remembered his allergies. In the past, he would take out a tissue when he was nervous. "Poor thing. I'm sorry your allergies are acting up."

"That's okay." He shrugged then stuffed the tissue quickly in his pocket, as if to hide his embarrassment. "I can't imagine life without them anymore."

She understood what he meant. As inconvenient as they were, his allergies somehow endeared him to her. They made him human when otherwise he seemed nearly perfect.

"You could have worse problems." Lexie smiled at him. "She told me I had a blind date, but I didn't know I'd be so lucky."

"Thanks for the thought, even though I know you don't mean it."

Lexie opened her mouth to object but was interrupted.

"Will this table be all right?" The hostess indicated the cozy booth in a corner of the restaurant. A mauve-colored cloth decorated the table. Silver forks rested on matching napkins. Several glasses were set for each person, along with gold-rimmed plates. The elegant table would have been ideal—on any other night.

Lexie hesitated. Trapped or not, she realized she didn't mind being in Theo's company after all. But the thought of spending an evening with him, sitting in such an intimate, dimly lit part of the restaurant, left her with mixed emotions.

"This is perfect!" Brad and Kassia spoke in unison then broke into laughter at their mutual agreement.

Theo and Lexie rolled their eyes at each other. Their nonverbal communication sent them into chuckles as well.

Perhaps I shouldn't be so hard on Kassia. I'm being just as silly as she is.

Theo's arm bumped against Lexie's for an instant. Nonverbal communication or an accident? Either way, the slight contact sent a wave of emotion through Lexie that both surprised and confused her. She immediately stepped away from him.

At the same time she realized she wanted more of his touch, however casual. She found herself imagining him taking her hand in his. How she missed being in love!

But love wasn't in the picture for her. Not now. Not yet. Even though she and Theo could build on a foundation of friendship, the memories they shared happened a long time ago. They would have to start over. Yet being with him still felt so comfortable, so right.

A male voice interrupted her musings. "You should have been at the meeting yesterday." Brad's crowing was too loud for anyone sitting at their table—or those nearby—to ignore.

"I wish I could sit in on all the big meetings," Kassia cooed. She rested her elbows on the table and propped her face in her cupped palms.

"One day you'll be in on all the action," Brad assured her.

Kassia looked at Lexie. "Brad goes to all the meetings for the bigwigs. Little ol' me just has to sit in the office by the phone all day."

"Sometimes I think I'd like to change places with you," Brad said. "You wouldn't believe the incompetent morons I have to deal with every day." He winked at Kassia. "Present company excluded, of course."

Kassia giggled.

"The Goen presentation was a mess before I showed Bob how to use the computer presentation program. He didn't even know how to put together a pie chart. Can you believe that?"

"Really? What a scream!" Kassia laughed.

"If it weren't for me," Brad said, "the whole place would shut down tomorrow."

"You're so right!" Kassia agreed.

Lexie tilted her head toward Theo and sent him an amused look. He returned the gesture.

With Kassia hanging on Brad's every word, Lexie and Theo could ignore him for the most part, particularly since his talk continued to focus on his job. Lexie was much more interested in Theo and how he'd spent the past few years—mainly making his way up his own corporate ladder. Somehow, when Theo talked shop, he wasn't boring at all. She found her attention centered on his conversation. Perhaps he was so fascinating to her because he didn't seem to boast about his accomplishments, unlike Brad. Or perhaps it was because she and Theo had a shared history. Lexie didn't want to contemplate feelings beyond that.

As the meal progressed, Lexie not only forgot about Brad and Kassia, but she hardly noticed the food that normally she would have savored without distraction. Salmon baked in dill, lemon, and butter, accompanied by a sautéed mixture of zucchini and yellow squash, seemed to melt in her mouth. Yet Theo's company offered far more satisfaction.

Lexie knew from Kassia's glowing reports that Theo's job occupied a significant place in his life. She halfway expected him to spend most of the night talking shop while she nodded blankly or otherwise feigned both knowledge and interest. To her delight, once Theo gave her a brief rundown on his career, he didn't dwell on it. Instead, he spoke about the dreams he still held—dreams she remembered he'd shared with her years ago when final exams worried them more than anything else. Despite having worked in the real world, he still possessed the charm of an idealistic student. His longings—to write a volume of poetry, to travel to exotic places, to own a vacation home—had never changed. He had lots of dreams. But none of them included what was most important to her.

She waited for him to talk about a desire to have his own family one day. After all, college was past, and Theo was now closer in age to thirty than twenty. Her waiting proved in vain. Not once did he mention marriage or the hope of one day being a father. Desperately she wanted to throw him hints. She couldn't. What would he think? Nothing would make a man run away faster than a woman who seemed marriage-minded too soon. Besides, hadn't she just told herself that nothing was farther from her mind?

"Lexie," he said over his dessert, a slice of chocolate mousse cake drizzled with raspberry sauce, "I just realized I've been a lousy dinner companion. You've let me drone on and on all night, and you haven't said a thing about yourself."

"But didn't you like having an audience?" She wrinkled her nose at him.

"Sure! Especially one as beautiful as you are." His voice caressed the words.

Where was a quick quip when she needed one? Her mouth went suddenly dry. Speaking seemed impossible. She took a drink of water.

It didn't help. Unnerved by her reaction to his compliment, Lexie set down the glass, then crushed her napkin in her fist. She became conscious of the cloth fibers and how rumpled they would become.

Not knowing what else to do, Lexie stared at her empty plate as though it were an exhibit at the Smithsonian. She felt Theo's presence draw nearer. He still wore the same citrus cologne he always had. Her memory flashed back to the one occasion they exchanged Christmas gifts, during their junior year. A phase when they were growing closer. So close, she thought they might become a couple. She had bought him a bottle of aftershave. The purchase seemed extravagant at a time when her only income came from her summer job in her dad's office. But the splurge had pleased him.

Lexie inhaled softly. She had forgotten how good the fragrance smelled on him. She wanted to draw closer to him, too. She forced herself to resist.

"I know life hasn't been everything you wanted. You didn't deserve to lose your husband so young." Theo's voice conveyed genuine sympathy. He placed his hand on the table as if he would take hers.

Lexie couldn't bring herself to respond to the gesture. Instead she nodded without speaking.

Theo quickly picked up his glass and took a swallow of iced tea. "Tell me about what you've been doing lately." The intimacy had left his voice.

"Oh, there's nothing to say. Nothing nearly as exciting as the things you've been telling me." Guilt prodded Lexie. Except for the Lord, Piper occupied the center of Lexie's universe. Yet she hadn't uttered the first word about her. Usually eager to pull out Piper's photos from her wallet, Lexie kept them hidden.

Piper is part of me. Why am I so reluctant to talk about her? What is wrong with me? When she looked into Theo's eyes, she knew exactly what bothered her. *I don't care how I feel; any man who wants to get anywhere near me must know about Piper. He must accept my daughter. Even love her.*

Lexie reached into her purse. She had to find her wallet, to show Theo a picture of Piper.

At that moment Theo cleared his throat and nodded toward their companions. Lexie's eyes widened. She had noticed Brad taking Kassia's hand during the meal, but now, nestled in the corner of the booth, they had progressed to kissing and seemed no longer concerned about where they were—or who was watching.

❧

All night, a vague feeling of drowsiness threatened to overcome Theo in spite of Lexie's charms, a side effect of taking two antihistamine pills a half hour before dinner. All that changed when Kassia and Brad chose to display their affection so openly.

Theo knew he shouldn't watch them and, after a moment, finally tore his gaze away from them. He glanced sideways at Lexie. She shifted in her seat, crossing and uncrossing her legs, tugging at her dress. Seeing Lexie's beauty only reinforced in Theo's mind how much *he* wanted to kiss *her*.

Why can't I be like Kassia and Brad? What would it be like not to be saved—or at least to act that way—not to care what the Lord or anyone else thinks? What would it be like to indulge my feelings, the feelings I have for Lexie, the ones that have never died, even after all these years?

No! He wouldn't trade his relationship with Christ for all the kisses in the world. Waiting for the right woman hadn't proved easy, but Theo knew that once the Lord did lead him to his future wife, she would be worth everything. Sure, Brad and Kassia were obviously enjoying themselves, but how long would their feelings last? Theo suspected they wouldn't last long at all.

Theo stole another glance at Lexie. The napkin in her lap held her attention. Why did she avoid looking at him? He sighed inwardly. Lexie showed no sign of welcoming any expression of emotion from him, a man she had been friends with for years. Otherwise she wouldn't have been so careful to avoid even the slightest touch. Although she hadn't made an issue of the fact, Theo could tell by the way she conducted herself—with the reserve of a lady—and by the fact she still wore the gold cross he remembered from her student days that they agreed on spiritual matters. Life without the Lord would be nothing. Though she looked as stunning as ever, her faith made the attraction even more compelling.

❧

She waited for Theo to say or do something—anything—to keep the other couple from embarrassing them so much they could never patronize the restaurant again. But he didn't.

She cleared her throat. "Kassia," she managed to say, "why don't you and Brad get some fresh air?"

Theo chuckled a little too loudly at her chiding. She could tell by the strained look on his face that their friend's public display of affection with a man she barely knew was making him uncomfortable as well.

For an instant a picture flashed in her mind of Theo taking her in his arms and kissing her. Lexie pursed her lips and blinked, willing the picture away.

Kassia and Brad broke their embrace. "Hey," Kassia said, "it isn't as if you two don't have lips, you know."

Lexie groaned.

"Don't worry." Brad winked at Kassia. "We can catch up later."

Kassia's giggle only served to make Lexie more anxious. Had her friend lost her mind? How could she let this strange man speak to her that way, as though she were little more than a conquest?

"I don't know," Kassia said. "Lexie is living with me for awhile. I'll have a chaperone for at least a few weeks." Kassia winked at Lexie.

Brad cast Lexie a sly look. "You say that like it's a bad thing."

Lexie crushed her napkin in her fist again.

"Apparently, Brad," Theo said, "you must not be used to hanging out with women who are ladies."

Brad raised his eyebrows. "Is that what you think?" He placed a possessive arm over Kassia's shoulders. "The women I hang out with don't need a guy to speak for them. Isn't that so, Kassia?"

"Oh, I don't know. I think Theo's being kind of cute." Kassia sent a sideways, heavy-lidded look Brad's way. "You'd defend me if I needed it, wouldn't you, Brad?"

"I'm assuming you can defend yourself. It looks to me like your mouth is working pretty well."

Lexie laughed even though Brad's humor was hardly in good taste. She was simply eager to ease the tension around the table. Kassia took the hint and joined her laughter. Theo's expression remained dark, but his jaw seemed to loosen a bit. The waiter didn't delay in presenting them with the check.

"Let me pay for my dinner," Lexie whispered to Theo.

"No way," he answered. "I invited you. Well, sort of." He grinned in the way she had seen a million times back in school. Once again, the years seemed to dissolve into oblivion.

"Are you sure?"

"Sure, I'm sure." He took out his wallet and extracted a credit card.

"Thanks." Lexie hoped her expression didn't reveal her secret relief. She needed to save every dime she could. She sent a silent prayer of thanks to the Lord that Theo still treated her like a precious jewel.

A gentleman. The word described Theo through and through. He hadn't changed a bit since college. Yet her fascination with him felt fresher than ever.

Stop it! You are not here to find a husband!

If only her feelings didn't betray her.

As did Kassia's, apparently. How could she have given everyone in the restaurant such a display, embarrassing Theo and her and surely herself by attracting the attention of nearby diners?

A few minutes later, on the drive home, Kassia broke the silence in the car. "So. How did things go with you and Theo?"

"I'm sure you wouldn't know, since you were so busy."

"Sure was." Kassia giggled. "Too bad you couldn't follow our example with Theo. He's neater than ever, isn't he?" Kassia glanced at her.

Lexie felt herself blush as she nodded.

"Admit it. You're glad I set you up with him tonight."

"Well, it wasn't the worst evening of my life," Lexie said.

Except when you made a fool of yourself.

"That's what I thought." Kassia smiled. Her display of affection with Brad had been inappropriate by almost anyone's standards. But if she felt the least bit of embarrassment, she didn't reveal it to Lexie.

Lexie sighed. Kassia had been decent—even a little on the shy side—in school. Tonight showed she must have fallen—hard and long. If Kassia jumped on every man she met, Lexie knew she should reconsider living with her. She would have to confront her friend.

She looked over at Kassia. The smile from earlier in the evening lingered on her face. Even though her happiness resulted from a shallow type of physical love, Lexie could tell Kassia was still too enthralled to listen to reason. The confrontation would have to wait until tomorrow.

Chapter 5

The next morning, Lexie tried to swallow past the knot in her throat. She dreaded the idea of challenging Kassia about her behavior the previous night. How could she fall all over a man she barely knew? At least Lexie could only conclude she hadn't known Brad well before last night. He worked in another department of her company, but she had admired him from afar. Kassia hadn't told Lexie how she managed to get her crush's attention—but she should have known to exercise more self-control.

She could hear the swishing of Kassia's nightshirt and padding of her bare feet on the kitchen linoleum. Thoughts of Kassia's generosity popped into her mind. She didn't expect much of Lexie—only that she share in the cooking and cleaning and contribute to the rent.

And how did Lexie plan to repay her friend? By passing judgment. By acting like a parent instead of a peer, ignoring the fact that Kassia was well past her twenty-first birthday.

Maybe I shouldn't say anything. Or maybe I should. Father in heaven, please guide me!

"Good morning!" Kassia's voice exuded cheerfulness.

The lilt could only be the result of last evening. Lexie wondered if Kassia might break into song.

"Good morning." Lexie's voice didn't match her friend's tone. "Are you always this happy in the morning?"

Okay, I know I'm grasping at straws, but—

"You know better than that!" Kassia laughed, grabbing a mug out of the cabinet and cocking her head toward the half-filled, four-cup coffeemaker. "Does that coffee have my name on it? Not that I need it today. I'm already flying."

Lexie peered into her empty cup. She had been saving the coffee for herself, but she could wait. "You're welcome to it."

"Thanks!" Kassia poured a cup of the brew. She leaned against the counter and took a generous sip. "Mmm. You've turned me on to espresso. I never thought it would be good in a regular drip coffeepot."

Lexie shrugged. "I don't know. It really doesn't taste the same."

She remembered how much she enjoyed the espresso her mom made. On special occasions, and even on some rainy Saturday afternoons, she'd brought out her collection of tiny Turkish coffee cups a friend on the mission field had given her as a Christmas gift. Lexie's favorite cup was decorated with red enamel paint that served as a background for filigreed gold leaves. Her mom liked the white cup with a single yellow rose best.

Lexie took a sip of her beverage. "It'll have to do." She chuckled. "At least until I have several hundred dollars to blow on an espresso machine."

"An espresso machine? Have you ever seen one of those things? They're huge. I hope if you manage to save up that much money, you'll have plenty of counter space."

Lexie noted Kassia's overburdened countertops. The European kitchen—a euphemism for "tiny" in Lexie's book—was a far cry from Mom's generous surface area that held her espresso machine with ease. "Good point."

Kassia sat down at the square pine table and reached for a box of low-fat cereal. Lexie tried not to grimace. She preferred her sugary childhood favorite. She couldn't see the merit of eating cardboard flakes, no matter how few calories they contained. Besides, light flakes left her stomach growling with hunger well before lunch.

"Care for some?" Kassia teased. They had discussed cereal choices several times. Neither one would change her mind.

"No, thanks." She tapped on the red box that remained on the table. "I'll stick with this, thank you."

"These aren't so bad once you get used to them." She lifted her spoon then brought it to her mouth as if she were trying out for a part in a commercial.

Lexie decided to ignore Kassia's jesting. "So what's on your agenda for the day?"

"Grocery shopping and errands. I'm keeping my cell phone with me all day. Brad promised to call."

"Oh. He promised, huh?"

"Yeah, I know what you're thinking," Kassia said. "You remember all about those guys who say they'll call but never do. You can spare me the lecture. I've heard it before." She wrinkled her nose. "And I've lived it a few more times than I'd like to admit."

"But you think Brad's different."

"I know he is."

Lexie was certain Kassia was deluding herself. Despite her resolve not to pass judgment, she realized she couldn't keep her feelings quiet. She braced herself for an argument. "Is he different because you work with him or because he thinks there's more where last night's actions came from. . . ?" Her voice trailed off. Lexie knew her convictions. Why did she suddenly sound so weak?

Kassia's eyes narrowed at her, and Lexie remembered why. When confronted, Kassia tended to react like a threatened viper—recoiling then striking with venom.

"What is that supposed to mean?" Kassia set her spoon down in her cereal bowl with a thump. Milk splashed on the table.

Lexie wished she hadn't started the conversation. Now that she had confronted Kassia, she couldn't back away. "I–I guess you don't realize how you and Brad looked last night. Theo and I aren't used to seeing couples kiss so openly."

There. She'd said it. Adding Theo's name made her feel more confident. Telling Kassia he shared Lexie's revulsion made her feel more justified in mentioning it.

Kassia sneered. "I should have known."

"Should have known what?"

"That if I let you stay here, you wouldn't be able to keep your opinions to yourself."

"I'm sorry."

"Sure," Kassia spat out. "Sorry I don't agree with you. I'm an adult, and I can do what I want. I did nothing wrong. You're as self-righteous as ever. I'm not Piper, and you're not my mother."

"I know—"

Kassia's eyebrows shot up. "And speaking of your daughter, what did Theo say when you told him about her?"

Lexie wished she could fall through the floor. She pressed her lips together and balled the hem of her robe in her fist.

"Well?" Kassia prodded. "Did he mind?"

"I, uh, I–I didn't tell him."

"What?" Kassia's voice rose. "What do you mean, you didn't tell him? How can you spend a whole evening with somebody and not even mention you have a daughter?"

Lexie looked down at her empty cereal bowl. "I–I just didn't."

Kassia's raised eyebrows were all the condemnation Lexie needed. Instead of retorting as Lexie expected, she ate a fresh spoonful of cereal. In her silence, she expressed more graciousness than Lexie had in her criticism. Lexie slumped in her chair, feeling like a hypocrite.

"Look—I know I seem like a poor excuse for a mother and a sorry example as a friend." Lexie faced Kassia's stare. "You're right. I have no business making comments on your life. But you're more than a roommate to me. You're my friend. I don't want to see some insensitive guy hurt you."

"You let me worry about insensitive guys." Kassia's icy tone demonstrated no forgiveness.

"Don't worry," Lexie said. "I'll be out of here soon. I'll be looking for my own apartment next week."

Kassia swept her hand toward the front door. "Why wait? It's Saturday. The apartment rental offices are open."

Lexie felt the sharpness of her remark. Had Kassia fallen so far that the slightest discussion about her life could dissolve their friendship?

"Brad is coming over with some DVDs tonight," Kassia added. "I doubt you'll want to be here."

Stunned, Lexie could scarcely nod. "I won't be able to rent an apartment today, I'm sure, but I'll be out of the way tonight."

Before Kassia could answer, Lexie retreated to her room. She looked around at the small room, which barely held her double bed and dresser. Hunting for an apartment when a foul mood and troubled thoughts occupied her mind would only spell trouble.

A jog. That's it. She needed a run for mental and physical therapy. She threw on a pair of black leggings, a T-shirt, and her running shoes. As she bound her hair into a ponytail, she felt better. A jog guaranteed she would forget her argument with Kassia, for a little while anyway. At least it would get her out of the apartment and away from Kassia's ill temper.

Her roommate surveyed Lexie from head to toe. "You're not apartment hunting in that getup, are you?"

"No," Lexie assured her as she headed for the door. "Maybe I'll try after my run. See you later."

"Don't take too long," Kassia said as Lexie closed the door behind her. "Some of the apartment rental offices close at noon."

"Thanks," Lexie muttered. "I'll remember that."

As soon as her feet hit the sidewalk, she reveled in her freedom. The brisk spring air felt good against her skin, and she picked up speed. She traveled swiftly through the apartment complex parking lot and headed into the adjoining neighborhoods. Though her exercise regimen kept the weight off, the sense of well-being from strenuous movement offered its own reward.

Deep in thought, Lexie jogged through one street after another. The foliage and flowers along the sidewalks varied according to whatever development, complex, or subdivision she passed through. Whether the plantings were red maples, ornamental pear trees, pines, pansies, or a combination, their expression of God's creation contrasted with the constant drone of one car after another whizzing by her. Did everyone go out on Saturdays?

Before she realized what had happened, Lexie saw that she had ventured into a different neighborhood. A stoplight forced her to jog in place as cars passed through an intersection.

"Where is this?" She looked at the street sign and realized she'd run to the entrance of Theo's development. Waiting for the light to turn, she contemplated the rooftops. Gray and black proved the most popular colors, but an occasional red roof brightened the scene. She wondered whether Theo had chosen a red roof to express his individuality, a basic black roof, or gray for the ultimate in conformity. She ventured black as a guess. The word "maverick" never described the Theo she knew.

The light turned.

"Should I, or shouldn't I?" she muttered to herself as she crossed the street. "I know I shouldn't, but I'm going to. I'm going to see if Theo's home."

Chapter 6

W ho can that be?" Theo wondered when he heard a knock on the door. He looked at his watch. Who would come knocking this early on a Saturday morning?

In a housing development filled with families, he guessed his caller might be a child selling cookies, magazines, or trinkets. Nothing he needed to buy. If he answered the door, he'd feel too guilty to turn down a waiflike little girl or boy in a Scout uniform. He often ended up with a box of candy or a magazine subscription he didn't need. But, if he could ignore the knocking, the young salesperson would go away.

He hoped.

Theo stared at his computer screen. He'd been at the game since he'd finished his workout earlier that morning. After putting in extra hours the previous week, he'd finally gotten caught up at work. His reward was a Saturday to himself and the rare opportunity to play his computer game. No unexpected visitor would keep him from winning.

Theo sent his character down a dark path, searching for a lost treasure. Just as the dwarf was about to enter a virtual cave sure to harbor a virtual dragon, the knocking on his real-life door became urgent and punctuated by the ringing doorbell.

What could be so important? He sighed as he remembered someone even more sinister.

I hope it's not the president of the homeowners' association bugging me again.

Jack would have no qualms about using this Saturday morning to convince Theo to install a privacy fence to match his neighbors'. Something about presenting a uniform appearance. Theo continued to resist. His reasons were hard for Jack to understand.

Each day before work Theo indulged in a cup of coffee. Often he would carry it to the deck he'd built onto the back of his house and sit in one of the green chairs he'd bought on sale at a drugstore. Watching the birds feeding and the squirrels scurrying through the yard offered him a bit of pleasure to start his day. Erecting a privacy fence would mar his view of the open space, however small. Now Jack wanted to deprive him of this pleasure. He believed uniformity would maintain property values. Theo wasn't so sure. The two of them would never agree.

How can I get out of this one?

Theo sighed as he allowed his character to be defeated by a laser blast. The punitive and powerful dwarf evaporated into a puff of white smoke. He had been so close to winning. Now Theo would be forced to start the level all over again. He paused the game.

As Theo made his way to the front door, he thought of every possible excuse not to erect a fence. Proclaiming his desire to blaze his own trail in the suburban jungle wouldn't do. He sighed. He would just have to face Jack and stand his ground.

He looked through the peephole. When he saw his visitor, he took in a breath.

Lexie!

Letting out a big sigh of relief, Theo opened the door. "What are you doing here?"

"Thanks for such a warm greeting." She smiled wryly. "I was about ready to leave. I knocked and knocked before I finally found the doorbell. I wouldn't have been so persistent except I saw your car."

"I'm sorry I took so long. It's just that, well, I wasn't expecting you."

"I know." She looked away. "If this is a bad time—"

"No. It's fine." He opened the door wider. "I wasn't doing anything much."

So much for playing the cool, disinterested bachelor.

She stepped inside. "I guess I'm not following what they call *The Rules* by dropping in on you like this."

"The rules?"

"Yes. Don't you remember the book that came out with that name some time ago? Two women wrote about the things their mothers and grandmothers told them to do and not do to get a man."

Theo made a show of rubbing his fingers against his chin in mock contemplation. "Considering I'm not trying to get a man, I guess I let that one pass me by."

She grinned. "Good point."

"Oh, so you're trying to get a man, eh?" He folded his arms and puffed out his chest.

"Don't flatter yourself," she told him. "Besides, you know me too well for any rules to work on you."

"Oh, really? Maybe you'd better tell me what they are so I can be on the lookout for some other sly female."

Lexie's eyes widened for a second before she composed herself.

Could she be just the least bit jealous? The thought was not an unhappy one.

"All right, then. I wouldn't want you to get bamboozled by a viper." She arched her eyebrow. "Let's say I just read that book and was trying to follow it. Then I'm supposed to be mysterious and unavailable most of the time."

"And you're breaking the rules how—?"

"Because here I am, dropping in the day after we had dinner out. Which I enjoyed, by the way. Oops. Just broke another rule." She chuckled. "So much for being mysterious."

"Sounds to me like those rules are worth breaking. I'd rather you be yourself than pretend to be a mystery woman." Theo cleared his throat. "Besides, I can't get too much of a good thing. So what brings you here?"

"My feet. Literally." She chuckled and pointed to her running shoes. "I was out for a jog and ended up here. Somehow."

He noticed that sweat stood on her face and arms and her T-shirt proclaimed the message "God Loves You." An image of the two of them jogging together formed in his mind. If only—

"That's why I don't look as nice as I'd like to," she explained. "I guess I should have realized I'm too sweaty to visit anybody. Maybe I'll stop by another time, when I'm more presentable." She stepped toward the door.

"No!" he nearly shouted. Then he added softly, "I mean, you don't have to go."

"Are you sure?" She seemed relieved.

"Sure, I'm sure. Besides, I think you look just fine. Even better than you did last night."

She gave him a comical look.

"I didn't mean that," he added. "I mean, you looked great last night, too. Beautiful, in fact. Even more beautiful than you do today." No, that didn't sound right, either. "I mean, well—I'm not doing well with this, am I? No wonder I'm stuck playing computer games on a Saturday morning."

She laughed. "Is that what you were doing? Playing a game? No wonder you didn't want to answer the door. I like computer games, too. I can start on a Tuesday night, and the next thing I know, it's Thursday afternoon!"

"You, too? Hey, that reminds me. I'd better cut off the game. I left it on pause." He motioned for her to follow him into his office, which was bare except for the desk, a lamp, some papers, and the computer.

Lexie didn't enter but hovered in the doorway. "I don't get to play much, though."

Theo swallowed. No doubt Lexie had far too many dates to worry herself with computer games. "Well, I did work out this morning. And I plan to mow the lawn this afternoon as soon as the grass dries out. So I hope that lowers my nerd quotient." He smiled nervously.

She looked at him. "No one would call you a nerd."

He smiled at her compliment and headed for the kitchen. "In that case, may I get you a soda?"

She shook her head. "Water would be fine."

"I have some sports drinks here if you'd rather have something with a little flavor."

She didn't answer right away. "Sounds tempting, but I think I'll go with plain water. Thanks."

Theo noted she was about to follow him into the kitchen. He remembered the dishes he'd left in the sink. "Uh, why don't you make yourself comfortable in the family room? I'll be right back."

He hurried to pour her water, then entered the family room. "So, besides your feet, what brings you here?" He handed her the water and sat beside her. "To be honest, I didn't know you had my exact address. Not that I mind."

"Kassia told me. She's quite impressed with how well you've done for yourself." Lexie surveyed the room from the floor to the cathedral ceiling. "I have to say, she was right."

Theo didn't think Lexie was visiting to inspect his house and thus gauge his success. Money had never been the highest priority in her life. Otherwise, she wouldn't have married Curt after he dropped out of college his sophomore year.

"I'd show you around the house, but it's a mess." He wouldn't let anyone into the unfinished basement he used for storage. He rarely made his bed; the guest room hadn't been dusted since one of his fraternity brothers last visited; the third bedroom was piled with books. He still needed to buy a bookshelf for his collection. Why he held on to his political science and biology textbooks, he didn't know; but he couldn't bear to part with them.

And the bathrooms. Did he remember to put hand soap in the powder room? He could keep her out of the upstairs, but he couldn't deny her entrance into the hallway powder room. Uh oh.

"That's okay," she was saying. "I didn't come to see the house. I came to see you."

"Good. I hope you're not embarrassed to visit the smallest model in the development."

She glanced around the room again. "This is the smallest model? You're kidding, right? Seems pretty big to me."

"Especially for a bachelor? I bought it as more of an investment than anything else. Real estate is usually a pretty safe place to put your money."

"Nice place. Even if it is nearly empty." She laughed.

"I'm just waiting for a nice woman to come along and decorate it for me."

Theo stopped. He refused to look at Lexie. *Did I just say that?*

"Nice yard, too, I noticed."

"I hope you're not too upset that I don't live in a swinging bachelor pad."

"Why would I be upset by that?"

He shrugged. "I don't have a pool or Jacuzzi for us to lounge around in. And the neighborhood kids are always running through my yard."

"I noticed." She gulped. "You don't mind that?"

Kids. How could he answer that question without sounding like an ogre? "Funny you should say that. I thought you were a kid selling things for school or

Scouts just now. That's why I didn't answer the door right away."

"You mean you can't spare a few dollars to help out the schools?" Lexie's voice was teasing.

"The first three or four aren't bad, but it seems every kid in the development stops by here. I hate to turn any of them down."

"So you're a softy after all. And a gentleman, too."

"A softy and a gentleman who could go broke buying all that stuff." He heard youthful voices shrieking in the adjacent yard. "As you can hear, they can be noisy. I'm getting used to it, but I wish they'd hold it down. You'd think they'd drive their own parents crazy after awhile."

"I like how the black roof and black shutters contrast with the white vinyl siding." She finished her water.

Huh? How did she jump from kids to siding?

"Uh, yeah," he answered. "I thought going with the basic colors was the best bet. I guess you saw some of the red roofs. I'm still not too sure about those."

Lexie chuckled. She started to set her glass on the end table, then stopped.

"Here. You can use this for a coaster." Theo handed her an old envelope. "Do you think that's what I should have gotten?"

"An envelope?" she shrugged. "Sometimes I use a CD case if I'm too lazy to get up and get a coaster. So far be it from me to criticize."

"Oh, not the coasters. I don't have a set of those yet. They're on my 'to buy someday' list. I mean should I have gotten black shutters and white siding on the house? I couldn't have gotten a red roof and red shutters anyway." He answered his own question. "The house beside me has those, and they wouldn't allow two houses in a row to have the same color."

"Makes sense, even if it does hamper individuality. And now I also understand why they have three different shades of gray roofs here."

"It makes black seem pretty distinctive, doesn't it?" He held up his hand. "Don't answer that. I prefer to talk about last evening." His stomach tightened. This was Lexie, his friend, so why did he suddenly feel like a tongue-tied junior asking the most popular cheerleader to the prom? He swallowed and forced himself to go on. "I—I hope we can do that again soon—without Kassia and Brad."

"If we do ever go out again, it will have to be without them," Lexie said. "May I be honest with you?"

He wondered if she was about to reveal the real reason for her visit. He wished she could bring herself to say something more—romantic.

"I'm being honest with you," he managed.

"I know, but it's been awhile since we were close friends—really close friends—and I don't want to impose."

"You could never impose." He was disappointed by her aloofness. Maybe if she could get whatever it was out in the open, she'd be able to move on. "It's Kassia, isn't it?" he guessed.

She nodded. "We had an argument."

"I can imagine what happened. You said something to her about the way she acted with Brad last night, and now she's mad."

"You're right."

"Sounds like Kassia," he said. "At least she's consistent."

"Consistent?"

"Yes. I'd expect her to act that way."

"Really? I didn't know she had gone so far away from the Lord."

"Was she ever that close to Him?"

Lexie rested her chin on her hand. "I don't know. I never thought she took her commitment to Him as seriously as we did, but I also didn't think I'd see her act like that with someone she hardly knows."

As committed to Him as we were. She's talking to me as if we're on the same team. And I guess we are. Theo felt a wave of pleasure course through his veins. *Yes, we are on the same team, and she's sitting right here in my house, acknowledging that.*

"Did you?" Lexie interrupted.

"Did I what?"

"Theo? Are you listening to me at all?" Lexie asked.

"Oh. Um, yes. You were talking about Kassia."

"Yes." She dragged out the word as though she were talking to a disobedient pet. "I was saying I didn't think I'd ever see her behave as she did last night. Did you?"

"No. No, I didn't." He tried to find some way to defend Kassia. "Unless, well, she knew him better than we think."

"No. She told me she's had a crush on Brad for some time, but it's as if she's been watching him from afar, you know?"

"I know." With Lexie so close but treating him as just a friend, Theo suddenly sympathized with Kassia. "I guess they didn't do anything that goes against the world's standards."

Lexie ran her finger over the rim of her glass several times, observing the motion. "I wish I could disagree with you, but I can't. In fact, they probably showed a lot of restraint in comparison to how other couples might have acted."

"You're right. Some of the guys at my work probably would have taken her to a hotel room."

"That's what I'm afraid of. Except they won't need one," she said. "Kassia said he's coming over tonight."

"Maybe if you're a good enough chaperone, you can stop them," Theo suggested.

"I don't think so."

"I'm sorry Kassia's apparently changed since school," Theo said. "I'm not sure what happened. She's never responded well to criticism. Even constructive comments from a friend who cares about her."

"I'm not so sure she thinks I care that much. She told me to find another place to live," Lexie said.

"You're kidding!"

"No. I'm going to start looking soon."

"Too bad. I don't think she realizes what a good friend you are to her," he said. "How many of us have stayed in close contact since college? And I don't count attending the occasional homecoming."

"Not many—that's for sure," Lexie said. "It's not as if you and I even stayed in touch."

"Do you have to keep reminding me?" he asked. "But I'm hoping that can change now."

"I'm sure it will."

He smiled.

"We're in the same town."

So much for making any progress. Why is she so standoffish? Did I do something to offend her? Maybe I should ask.

Lexie was holding her cheek in her palm while she ran the finger of her other hand over the rim of her empty glass. No, this wasn't the time.

He cleared his throat. "You know, if you go back home, I'm positive Kassia will have forgotten the whole thing. She never was one to hold a grudge."

"If you were a betting man, you'd lose. I don't think she'll forgive me too soon. When I tried to talk to her about Brad, she told me to start looking for another apartment today."

"Today? That's awful!"

"I feel rotten about it. Kassia and I have been friends for a long time. I never thought a little disagreement would lead to this."

"That doesn't sound like Kassia," Theo agreed. "What will you do? Do you have any other places in mind?"

Lexie shrugged. "I don't know what to do. I have no idea what kind of place I can afford on my own."

"I thought you had a good job."

"I do. But—" She closed her mouth and shook her head. "You don't know the half of it."

Theo didn't know what to say. "Is this where I'm supposed to ask you to crash here with me?" He chuckled.

Instead of laughing, Lexie exhaled sharply. "How can you even think of that?" She rose from her seat. "I thought you were different, Theodore Evan Powers, but you're not. You're just like every other man I've ever known—except Curt."

He stood. "Now wait a minute—"

"No, you wait a minute. Here I am, trying to share a serious problem with you, trying to tell you how worried I am that this Brad guy is taking advantage of our friend, and all you can do is answer with an insult you try to pass off as a joke."

He didn't answer. Judging from her hostile reaction, he had overestimated Lexie's trust in him and the bond of their friendship.

"I'm sorry," he managed to say.

"Not sorry enough." Lexie swiveled on her heel and headed for the front door.

Theo ran behind her. "I'm not the problem here, Lexie. Your trouble is Curt's ghost. You can't expect a living, breathing man to compete with your sainted husband."

"Is that so? Well, you're wrong. Just plain wrong." Lexie turned and jogged down the porch steps.

"Wait!" Theo started out after her, but his bare feet were no match for her feet clad in running shoes. After less than a block he stopped, winded and discouraged.

What did Lexie mean? If Curt wasn't the problem, then what was?

⁓

As she jogged back home, Lexie took the quickest route. For the first time in her memory, the joy of running, gliding along in her shoes, sweating, the breeze offering a cooling effect, didn't melt away her problems. Rays from the sun felt hot on her hair. She became conscious of the bandage she had wrapped around her blistered middle toe. Neither the sun nor the bandage would have bothered her at any other time, but today was different. Each step brought her closer to the realization that she had argued with her only two trusted allies in her newly adopted city. How could she have made such a mistake? She could blame no one but herself for her loneliness.

Loneliness. After Curt's death, loneliness was too familiar. But was Theo right? Had she really been shutting out her chances of a new love because of his ghost?

No, no one was competing with Curt's ghost. Least of all, Theo. But how could she convince him?

You'll never convince anyone with that judgmental attitude of yours, she chastised herself.

As she often did while jogging, Lexie prayed. *Lord, is Kassia right? Am I being too judgmental? Why can't she see beyond her perceived criticism and realize I talked to her only as a friend out of love?*

She felt a sense of peace after she spoke to the Lord, but not a complete sense of well being that her prayers so often brought. This would take more time to resolve. But how much time did she have? Kassia had just told her to leave, and now she had argued with Theo.

Theo. What about him?

Time.

166

Time. Why was that word the only answer she got? Lexie exhaled, both from exertion and frustration.

She noticed an ice cream shop a short distance away. The pink-and-white sign promised a different kind of comfort. She dug into her waist pack and found her emergency five-dollar bill. Well, this constituted an emergency, didn't it? Okay, maybe just a pseudo-emergency.

As she entered the ice-cream parlor, then took her place at the end of the long line, she suddenly felt guilty about indulging in such a sugary treat. She fought it. So what if it would replace every calorie she had worked so hard to burn? She would run again tomorrow. Besides, the body burns more calories after exercise, right?

Large tubs of ice cream offered an array of colors and flavors—everything from rich, dark chocolate to unreal colors of blue and pink with shapes meant to draw the attention of children. No matter how interesting or tempting new concoctions could be, Lexie never changed her mind about her favorite flavor.

An image of the United Nations delegation in New York popped into her head. If they would just sit down together and share big bowls of peanut butter brickle ice cream, perhaps they would be agreeable enough to solve the world's problems.

Lexie chuckled quietly at her silly thought.

"Lexie?"

The male voice sounded familiar, yet strange. She searched her brain to place a face with the pleasant tenor. Finally she spun around to see who had recognized her.

"Brad!"

Lexie had no desire to talk to anyone, but she couldn't dodge him now. She noticed he looked as good in shorts and a shirt with an athletic logo as he had the night before in a knit shirt and dress slacks for dinner. No one could deny Brad's handsomeness.

"So what brings you here on a Saturday morning?"

First Theo and now Brad. This question had become too popular. "Ice cream."

He looked down at her athletic shoes. "Really? I thought you came here by foot."

Lexie groaned at his corny joke, similar to the one she had used earlier with Theo.

"Makes sense, doesn't it?" His smile could have melted all the tubs behind the glass counter. "It isn't every day I run into a pretty jogger in an ice-cream store. I didn't think a woman as fit as you would eat anything but celery sticks."

"Celery sticks!" She thought about the sugarcoated cereal she had eaten that morning for breakfast. "Why do you think I have to jog?"

He laughed, somehow adding an alluring purr. Lexie could see why Kassia had been attracted to Brad so quickly. She debated whether to remind him he had promised to call Kassia but decided against it. Why encourage him?

Brad motioned to a small table that had just been vacated. "Since we're both here, why don't we eat together?"

"Makes sense, doesn't it?"

"Hey, that's my line." His eyes sparkled as he smiled. "I see you pay attention. I like that in a woman."

Could Brad make the telephone directory sound like an invitation?

They were inches from the table. In a second her chance to escape would evaporate. Yet after such an unpleasant morning, Lexie wanted to linger with Brad and share conversation over ice cream. She was even willing to endure his bragging, simply to get her mind off her troubles.

Yet Brad seemed different. He had nothing to say about his work or his possessions. He didn't even complain about the exorbitant prices of skiing in Aspen or how he'd run into various celebrities on his last jaunt to the mountains. Lexie wondered if he sensed that status, possessions, and travel didn't impress her. Too committed to Piper, Lexie had no desire to claw her way to the top of a large corporation, and with her financial life in near shambles, luxury items and travel were out of the question. In the few moments they waited in line, bantering about nothing, her mood lifted. Yet she sensed an overwhelming need to flee.

"Come to think of it, I'd better be getting out of here." She made a show of consulting the wall clock. "I didn't realize it was getting so late." How convenient the truth had become!

"You plan to run and eat ice cream at the same time?"

"What better way to burn a few more calories?" she quipped. "Besides, I'll be seeing you again this evening."

"Oh?"

"When you see Kassia."

"Oh, yeah. That's right." He pointed to her playfully. "I'll be bringing over some DVDs. Tell me what you'd like to see, and I'll pick it up at the store."

Lexie could only imagine how Kassia would react if she took Brad up on his offer. "That's okay. I'm caught up on movie viewing for the time being. I'll be out anyway."

Brad's smile disappeared. "Oh. You already have plans."

This time she pointed at Brad. "And so do you."

"Just for tonight. Maybe we can get together some other time?"

Lexie waved as though she were a beauty queen riding in a parade. "See you later." She bounced out of the store, ice-cream cone in hand, and her change rattling in her waist pack.

Since she did indeed have to eat her ice cream while she walked home, Lexie didn't enjoy the indulgence as much as she would have if she hadn't run into Brad.

How could he act as though he had fallen hard for Kassia one night, then turn around and ask Lexie out the next day? She could only conclude that Brad had no intention of developing a deep relationship with Kassia.

Lexie returned to the apartment in time to see Kassia hang up the phone. She didn't dare ask Kassia to identify her caller. She hoped it wasn't Brad.

Kassia sent Lexie a half smile. "That was a long jog. Too long. Don't you know it's already past lunchtime?"

Lexie consulted the clock on top of Kassia's television set. "Oh. It sure is."

Kassia spotted the paper napkin Lexie held. "You had lunch on the go?"

"Not really. Just some ice cream."

"You must have broken even in calories then." Kassia's mouth formed a hard line. "I wish you had called. I was getting a little worried."

"Really?"

"Sure. I don't care if this is a good neighborhood. Jogging still isn't the safest activity for a woman alone, even in broad daylight."

"I know. But I'm careful." Lexie held her tongue from further comment. Kassia knew that Lexie couldn't afford a gym membership, and the complex didn't offer a workout room. What else did she expect her to do?

Kassia folded her arms and tilted her head toward the phone. "I called Theo to see if you'd jogged by his house."

"Oh." She prayed Theo didn't reveal the details of their conversation.

"He said you stopped by for a glass of water." Kassia winked. "Sly girl."

Lexie let out a nervous chuckle. "That's all he said?"

"Sure. Is there something else I should know?" Her voice held an edge of suspicion.

"I—I did tell him I'd be leaving the apartment soon."

"Oh." Kassia looked at her feet. "I'm sorry about that. Stay as long as you want."

"You really mean that?"

"Sure. Or else I wouldn't have said so."

"Before you make any more promises, you'd better hear what happened later. I ran into Brad at the ice-cream parlor."

She gasped. "You saw Brad? Did he ask about me?"

"We mentioned you. At least I did. He wanted me to join you both tonight watching DVDs. I told him I wouldn't be here," she hastened to add.

"Sure—you can watch with us." Her flat voice held no sign she meant what she said. "It was nice of him to invite you. I'm glad he did." A weak smile lit her features. "What else did he have to say?"

Lexie didn't have the heart to tell her more. "Not much. I left as soon as I bought my ice cream. But, Kassia, if I were you, I'd proceed with caution if you decide to pursue this relationship with Brad. There's something about Brad I don't trust."

Kassia's eyes narrowed. "You're just telling me that. You wanted to accept his invitation to watch movies with us."

"No," she blurted.

"You tell me not to trust Brad, but I think you're the one I shouldn't believe."

"Wait! I didn't mean to run into Brad. I had no idea he was at the ice-cream place. He saw me while we were standing in line."

"That I believe. But you're a smart girl, all alone in the city. You saw a chance to make a play for Brad, and you took it."

"Now look—I'll admit I enjoyed joking with Brad for a few minutes while we were waiting in line, but that was it. I promise you—I have no romantic interest in Brad whatsoever."

Kassia's lips tightened. "Then I suppose you were there talking to him about how wonderful I am, huh?"

"Forget it, Kassia. I don't need to hang out here and upset you even more. No man is worth our friendship." Lexie ventured an idea. "Look—how about if I spend the evening on my own and stay out late? Then you and Brad can enjoy your DVDs and have some peace and quiet without me here."

"That would be great, Lexie. Thanks for the offer."

Chapter 7

Lexie felt no relief as she sat in the restaurant and tried to read the book she'd brought with her, the one she'd been so eager to read. She'd hoped it would help her forget she was sitting there alone, with nothing to look forward to the rest of the evening. But she couldn't concentrate on the words in front of her. It wasn't the book; it was simply that she couldn't stop thinking about her day. It seemed as if no matter whom she had run into that day, the encounter resulted in a fight.

She'd found little reprieve in the phone call to her mother. Mom expressed her displeasure. How could Lexie have argued with a friend who had been so generous to her?

Lexie sighed. Of course she couldn't share with her the details that led to the argument. Humiliating Kassia would do no good.

A smile tickled her lips when she remembered her brief conversation with Piper. Lexie could listen to her little voice twitter about her day, how she found a cricket in the garage and wanted to adopt him, how Grammy had promised she could catch fireflies at twilight the next night, how Pops said they could go to the new kids' movie that weekend.

"I miss her so much," Lexie muttered. "I have to get my life together."

She closed her book.

I need to pray for Kassia. And, Lord, please guide me in my scripture reading.

She picked up her Bible and turned to the seventh chapter of Matthew.

"Why do you look at the speck of sawdust in your brother's eye and pay no attention to the plank in your own eye? How can you say to your brother, 'Let me take the speck out of your eye,' when all the time there is a plank in your own eye? You hypocrite, first take the plank out of your own eye, and then you will see clearly to remove the speck from your brother's eye."

Okay, Lord. You don't have to tell me twice. Lexie meditated on the words, reading them again and again. She hated to admit, even to herself, that she enjoyed how attractive Brad's attention made her feel. When she appeared in public with Piper, men looked upon her as a mother—and unavailable. Without Piper beside her, men saw her as an intriguing, complex woman. But they didn't see her in her true light; she was, in fact, her whole self when she was with Piper.

Her thoughts drifted to Curt and the times they shared as husband and wife. He valued her role as a mother but made her feel loved as a woman at the same time. Curt had never been the type of man to shower her with flowers and candy, but he'd always been there for her. She could share everything with him, from daily frustrations and victories to long-held dreams of a distant future.

Lord, I miss him so much! I miss how Curt made me feel. Lord, will You send me someone who will love me as a woman?

Not an instant passed before a name flew into her mind.

Theo!

No.

Lexie felt the blood drain from her face. *But, Lord, Theo can't possibly be that man. He doesn't want children. My husband must love Piper, too.*

Lexie glanced around the restaurant and noticed she was the last patron. She looked at her watch and saw how late it was. *Surely I can go home now, and I won't be disturbing them.*

She pulled into the parking lot and didn't see Brad's car. She let out a sigh of relief. *Maybe he went home early and left Kassia here.* She tiptoed into the apartment and slipped down the hall to her room. She noticed the door to Kassia's room was closed, but it usually was when she went out or was sleeping. *I just pray she didn't do anything she'll regret later.*

The next day when Lexie woke, she momentarily forgot about the argument the previous day. Then she remembered. She had made a shambles of her life, and she could lay the blame at no one's feet but her own. Sighing, she slipped on a summer dress, poured a cup of juice and left the apartment as quietly as she could. Maybe going to church would help clear her mind. Even if it didn't, she could depend on being uplifted spiritually.

Later, as she drove through town, she harbored no fear of running into anyone she knew during worship. Her knowledge of local congregations was limited. A coworker had mentioned a new church. The congregation met in a rented school auditorium and hoped to raise the money for a new building within five years. Lexie had not yet moved her membership from her home church, but for now, being part of the vibrant congregation filled her longing for a stable place to worship with other brothers and sisters in Christ but for now, she wanted a vibrant place to worship. Originally she'd planned to attend church with Kassia but soon discovered her friend no longer went to church. The past Friday night, Theo mentioned he attended a large church that televised its services. He invited her to join him there, but Lexie declined. She wasn't sure she was ready for such a large church—or to see Theo every Sunday.

Once she arrived, she settled into a padded seat in the auditorium. In no mood to talk to anyone, Lexie read a few passages from the Psalms and Proverbs while the four-piece band played contemporary Christian music. The service featured lively singing and a stirring sermon titled "Showing the Love of Jesus in the Workplace." It left her feeling encouraged and ready to face the week—at work anyway.

Being ready to face her life at home was another matter.

Lexie turned the key in the lock and entered the living room of the apartment. Kassia was sitting on the couch. An open bag of potato chips lay beside her on the end table. The television blared with the voice of a woman trying to convince viewers to buy a laboratory-created ruby and cubic zirconia ring. Kassia wasn't watching but instead was reading the newspaper. "Good, Kassia. You're home."

"Oh! It's you!" Kassia jumped, then waved the newspaper at Lexie. "I was wondering what happened to you."

"I went to a restaurant and had a book with me. I ended up staying really late. In fact I was the last customer to leave. And this morning I attended a service." Lexie walked toward her and picked up the remote control. "Do you mind if I turn this down a little bit?"

"Go right ahead." Kassia put the paper in her lap, then folded it in half. "I guess I should thank you for staying out late last night. Are you going out again tonight?"

"Do you want me to?" Lexie knew her voice sounded weak.

"No." Kassia paused. "I know what you're thinking. You're dying to ask, so I'll just tell you. No, I didn't do anything with Brad that you wouldn't have done in my place."

After the display in the restaurant, Lexie wondered. "Really?"

"Really. Not that Brad didn't try. But you're right. I made sure I didn't let myself get carried away."

"I'm glad to hear that."

"So you see, you could have stayed in, after all." Kassia averted her gaze to her feet. "I'm sorry you felt as if you needed to stay out so late last night. I shouldn't have done that to you. I let you down."

Lexie sat beside Kassia. "No, you didn't. I'm the one who should be apologizing to you. I have no business making any comments about your life. You can make your own decisions, without interference from me. And I really and truly have no interest in Brad. I don't know how many times I have to say it. Maybe I can never say it enough. I didn't mean to hurt you. It was all a misunderstanding." She ventured a smile. "I promise I won't interfere again. Girl Scout's honor." She held up three fingers as a sign of her pledge.

"Are you sure you were a Girl Scout?"

Lexie could hear the challenge in Kassia's remark but decided to overlook it. "I was a Scout for five years. Is that long enough?"

"I win then. I was in for six years." Kassia winked.

Lexie chuckled. Kassia had apparently forgiven her.

"Well, I guess I deserved your trying to tell me what to do," Kassia confessed. "I was the one who set you up on a blind date without even asking if it was okay. Payback is fair play."

"But I knew you only wanted me to be happy. You know, only true friends would care about each other so much."

"Yeah."

Lexie moved closer to Kassia, arms outstretched. Kassia leaned toward her and accepted her embrace.

"I'm here for you if you want to talk," Lexie added.

"Okay." Kassia's mouth narrowed. She studied the television. This time the woman wanted them to buy a pair of hoop earrings set with small stones of cubic zirconia.

Why won't she confide in me?

Lexie held back a sigh and excused herself. Even after she had retreated to the safety of her room, she didn't feel better.

Lexie's thoughts jumbled together as she threw some of her clothes in the hamper and folded others. *No matter what Kassia says, I can't stay here much longer. We're just too different. I have to find a new place. And soon. It's time for Piper and me to be reunited.*

Piper. The daughter she couldn't live without. But what about her growing feelings for Theo? No matter how hard she tried to deny them, she couldn't. She wished she hadn't pushed Theo away, yelling and overreacting because of a joke. She realized now that her response was nothing more than a defense mechanism, a way to keep him from getting reacquainted with her—this time as more than a friend.

I don't want to lose him.

A sense of dread filled her. What would Theo say when he met her daughter?

Chapter 8

The following Friday, Lexie sat in her cubicle at work, staring at a picture of Piper she had pinned to the gray panel facing her desk. She wished she could call her little girl, but a stack of paperwork demanded her attention.

A week had passed since her disputes with Theo and Kassia. Sharing an apartment with Kassia was only just starting to feel more comfortable, although Lexie feared her relationship with her roommate would never be the same.

Theo was another matter. Why hadn't she tried to make amends with him? She knew the answer. She stared at Piper's photo, taken on her last birthday. Piper held up a blond baby doll dressed in pink. The toy, which Piper named Cinda after her favorite heroine, Cinderella, had become her constant companion.

I wonder if Piper is playing with Cinda now. I wonder if she's holding a tea party with her little pink plastic cups and saucers, pretending to serve Cinda tea and pastries.

Musky perfume wafted her way. Lexie didn't have to look to know that Jennifer, wearing her trademark scent, stood by her desk.

"Hey, what's up?" Lexie asked.

"Not much." Jennifer placed some papers on top of the pile in her In box. "Mr. Haynes needs these by noon on Monday."

"Noon on Monday?" Lexie sighed. "I'll do my best." She looked at her ever-growing pile. "Maybe I'd better take some of this work home. It's not as if I have anything else to do."

"Sure you have other things to do," Jennifer offered. "You can go out with us girls after work, you know."

"I know. Thanks. Maybe next time."

Lexie didn't mention the real reason she avoided going out with the single women from the office. Every Monday Jennifer would share stories with Lexie about the wild times her group enjoyed as they visited local bars. She seemed to believe she and her friends were having fun, but Lexie wasn't so sure. The conflict of being in such a situation was certain to lead to arguments. After her fight with Kassia, Lexie had decided to be more careful about expressing the truths of the Bible in relation to how others chose to live. Better to be thought a snob or a loner than to be called self-righteous. When she flinched at the thought, Lexie realized how much Kassia's words still hurt.

"Are you positive? We always have a lot of fun. You're missing out," Jennifer added.

Lexie searched for a truthful excuse and found one. "Mom and Dad might call. For Piper's sake, I'd hate to miss them."

Jennifer looked at Piper's photo. "I can understand that. But that's what a cell phone is for."

"I'll join the twenty-first century eventually." Lexie hoped her pleasant smile hid her real thoughts. She could just imagine her parents calling her on a cell phone, only to hear the ruckus of a bar in the background. Not to mention she couldn't swing another monthly fee on her already strained budget.

Just then Jennifer's eyes widened, and she drew in her breath, leaned toward Lexie, and whispered, "Who's that?"

Lexie looked toward the entrance and saw Theo heading for her desk.

Theo!

His rapid steps mirrored the beating of her heart. "What's he doing here?"

Jennifer's eyes widened even more. "You know him?"

"Yes. He's a—a friend." Lexie's gaze flew to the picture of her daughter. She hoped Theo would notice it. That would be the perfect opening for her to tell him about Piper. On the other hand, she hoped he wouldn't see it.

Coward!

Jennifer interrupted Lexie's inner monologue. "Does he have a name?"

"Huh? Oh, yes. It's Theo."

"He's just a friend? Then maybe you wouldn't mind setting us up."

"No!" Lexie said quickly. Her office mate's apparent interest sent a pang of jealousy through her. "I mean—he's an old friend from college."

"Oh. So that's how it is."

Lexie shushed Jennifer and hoped she'd take the hint to leave her desk. But she didn't budge.

"Hi, Lexie," Theo greeted her, his gaze directed only at her. "I'm glad I caught you. The receptionist told me you might still be in a meeting."

"I'm out now," Lexie said.

Wow. Any more brilliance and some honor society will be calling me to join.

"So what brings you here?"

Oh, yeah. They'll be calling any minute.

"I was wondering if you'd like to go to the Tobacco Company restaurant after work. You remember that place, don't you—the one they converted from an old tobacco warehouse?"

"Yes, I do." She hesitated. "The name used to bother me until someone explained its history." She paused again. "Do you mean after work today?"

"Yes, I mean today. Unless you have other plans."

She looked down at her simple summer dress. Yes, it would do.

"If this is a peace offering, I'm the one who should be making amends with you." Lexie heard Jennifer shift her weight from one foot to another and remembered they weren't alone. She didn't want to have this conversation in front of her coworker. Now it was too late. Jennifer was sure to ask about their argument at the first opportunity.

Theo seemed to sense Lexie's discomfort. He grinned. "I know this is short notice. I hope you don't mind."

"A lady's not supposed to accept a date for Friday that she's not invited to by Tuesday," Jennifer interrupted.

"Is that so?" Theo turned to her. "Did you read *The Rules*, too?"

"*The Rules*? What's that?" Jennifer asked.

"Never mind now. I'll explain later." Lexie sighed. "Theo Powers, meet Jennifer Newman."

"Hello, Theo," Jennifer said sweetly.

"Hello, Jennifer." He extended his hand. "Nice to meet you."

Jennifer shot Lexie a look. "If you don't go out to dinner with him tonight, I will."

"But I thought you said a lady shouldn't accept a date on such short notice."

"Never mind what I said." Jennifer waved her hand.

"Lucky me," Theo said. "Either way, I have a date."

Lexie almost quipped that maybe Theo would be happier with the carefree, never married, childless Jennifer than he would her, a widow with a child in tow. Then she remembered the Holy Spirit's prodding and decided to accept Theo's invitation, especially after he had visited her in person to extend it. "In that case I'll take you up on your offer."

"Great!" He smiled warmly.

She looked at the clock. "I have a few more minutes here; then I'm free."

"Forget the clock," Jennifer piped up. "Go on. I'll make sure everything's set for the weekend."

"I don't know—"

"Hey," Jennifer said. "I saw you work through lunch. They owe you fifteen minutes and then some."

Lexie often worked through lunch and put in extra hours after closing time. "Oh, all right. Thanks."

"Any time."

An hour later, Theo and Lexie were still waiting to be seated at a table. Since Friday nights were always busy, the wait came as no surprise.

"Want to walk around a little while? Maybe some of the shops are still open," Theo suggested.

Lexie couldn't think of anything she wanted to buy, but just being with Theo, doing nothing, still sounded like fun. "Sure." Her stomach rumbled. "I'm getting hungry. I wish they took reservations so we wouldn't have to wait."

"Can't stand being with me that long, eh?" He didn't wait for Lexie to answer. "Watch the cobblestones," he warned.

"I will." Lexie glanced down at the uneven stone street and hoped she could manage in her heels. "Wonder why they never fixed this?"

"I guess whoever's in charge thinks this is part of the area's charm."

"I guess," she agreed.

Theo took her arm. "Or maybe a bunch of guys thought the rough street would be a good excuse for holding their dates closer."

Lexie giggled, partly from his observation and partly because his touch made her feel suddenly giddy.

"You know," he remarked as they passed several stores and restaurants, "I recently read a newspaper article about restaurants and their reservation policies."

"Sounds thrilling."

He chuckled. "Maybe not thrilling, but it was interesting. It said that twenty percent of the people who make reservations don't show up, even if they call to confirm a few minutes ahead."

"Wow! That's hard to believe."

"The restaurants run on such a slim profit margin that some of them don't like to take reservations. The lines and the wait just add to their cachet," Theo explained.

Lexie thought for a moment. "I can see that. If people think everyone wants to get in, the place seems more desirable."

"Right. Plus they can fill tables as soon as they are vacant, instead of having to wait for the reservations to show up."

"I hadn't thought of it that way." Lexie glanced up and down the street. "Looks as if they have plenty of turnover at the restaurants on this street."

"And we were willing to wait."

Lexie didn't want to admit how little she minded, as long as she could enjoy Theo's company. She peered into the window of an antique shop. "Look at that pincushion."

"Interesting." He nodded. "Too bad they're already closed. I might have picked up a trinket for Mom."

"She likes antiques?"

"Yes, but she has her limits. Anything she has to dust has to be pretty special."

"I'm sure anything you pick out is special to her."

"I try." He grinned. "Her birthday is next month. Maybe we can come back sometime, and you can help me pick out something."

The idea that Theo thought of them together in the future gave her a pleasant feeling. "Are you sure you want me to? I mean, after last Saturday. I'm sorry I flew off the handle."

"I know. You've been under a lot of pressure, starting a new life. I'm just glad you agreed to come out with me tonight. Especially on such short notice."

Lexie didn't want to answer with more than a smile. With Theo's arm around her, she knew she didn't care when or where they were or how long in advance he asked. As long as they could be together. She didn't want the moment to end. All she wanted to do was think about the present. The future, and its complications, could wait.

Later, Lexie looked around the busy restaurant. White linen tablecloths and napkins and elegant place settings awaited customers who looked forward to fine food. A large group of people who seemed to be members of a wedding party occupied several long tables in a more secluded section of the restaurant. Their presence added a festive air. The atmosphere was just what she needed.

After they prayed over their meal, Lexie kept looking for a chance to talk about Piper. She knew she had to tell Theo about her daughter. Why was she so fearful? Theo may have thought he didn't want children at one time, but surely he would change his mind once he met Piper. Surely he could find love in his heart for her little girl. She just knew it.

Yet, as dinner progressed, Lexie realized why she'd felt so much fear.

"Of course, I don't want to take off much time from work now, not with the new house and everything," Theo said as he cut into his steak. "But I'm working on building up enough leave so I can take a sabbatical one day."

"A sabbatical? Do they let you do that?"

"I don't know if they call it that. Maybe a leave of absence." Theo shrugged. "But they let you accumulate some time off to use as you like."

"That sounds good. I guess you'd use the time to travel and write poetry?"

"Sure would." He smiled.

Lexie thought about what she would do with a sabbatical. Spending unlimited time with her daughter at home sounded wonderful to her. "Or maybe you could write a travel book." She took a sip of coffee.

"A travel book." Theo laughed. "Makes sense."

Lexie smiled. Theo always laughed at her lame humor, something she cherished.

He reached over and took her hand in his. The warmth of his hand connecting with hers made Lexie tingle. She wondered if perhaps Theo could occupy a special place in her life.

He looked at her. "How would you like to be my secretary?"

She let out a nervous chuckle. "Oh, I don't know."

"You'd be a good one. Didn't you tell me you type eighty-five words a minute?"

"Just you, me, and the laptop computer, all alone in the wilderness?"

"Sounds good."

"Can we bring anyone else along?"

He seemed surprised. "Why would we want to?"

Lexie looked down at her empty plate and withdrew her hand. No way would Piper or any other child ever fit into Theo's dreams.

"What's wrong, Lexie?" Theo asked.

She shook her head. Why did Theo always sense her changing moods? Every time they talked, she felt as though they had picked up where they'd left off the previous time.

"What's the matter? Are you homesick?"

Lexie nodded. "You could say that."

"You'll feel great after dessert. A good dose of chocolate cures everything. Even homesickness."

His comment enabled her to skirt the issue. She did miss her home, but she missed Piper more. "How do you know about being homesick?" she asked. "Your family lives less than a hundred miles from you. You can see them any time you want."

"Yeah, we're still pretty close. But I'll take plenty of chocolate with us on our trip anyway." He grinned. "In the meantime, I wonder what the waiter will tell us they have for dessert tonight."

"I don't care for dessert. May we just go home?" She knew politeness dictated she offer to wait for him to eat dessert if he wished, but she had passed the point of caring about etiquette.

Why am I such a coward? I should have said something about Piper in the first few minutes I saw Theo again. Now it's too late. He won't understand why I haven't mentioned her. He'll think I'm a horrible mother. Maybe I should just forget this whole thing. Theo would be better off without me. Then he can live out his dream, unencumbered. Let some other lucky woman share his life.

"Lexie? Are you okay?" Theo asked.

"I'm all right. Let's go home."

Heavy silence filled the car on the way home. Lexie knew Theo thought the food hadn't agreed with her and that illness kept her from speaking. She decided to take advantage of his inaccurate conclusion. She didn't feel like talking.

Once home, Lexie was turning her key in the lock when suddenly Kassia opened the door. Horror mixed with relief covered her features.

"Lexie! I'm so glad you finally got here!" A look of fear crossed Kassia's face.

Lexie's words tumbled out. "What is it, Kassia?"

"Your parents called. They just took Piper to the hospital."

Chapter 9

Theo didn't say a word. He could only stand there and wonder what had transpired.

Piper? Who was Piper? Whoever she was, her significance in Lexie's life was obvious by the way Lexie ran to the phone in the kitchen.

With both women in a frantic state, Theo could see no point in waiting to be invited in. He stepped inside the door and shut it behind him.

Kassia was looking toward the kitchen, even though neither of them could hear Lexie's conversation from where they stood. "I hope Piper's okay." She seemed to be talking to the air rather than to Theo. "I don't know what would happen to Lexie if she got seriously hurt." She paced back and forth.

He drew in a breath. "Uh, this might sound strange, but who is Piper? And why is she in the emergency room?"

Kassia turned toward him. Her mouth dropped open. "You mean she didn't tell you tonight, either? She hasn't said anything after all this time?"

Kassia's remarks made Theo even more uneasy. Why would Lexie feel the need to hide someone from him? "Uh, no."

"Sorry. I just thought Lexie would have told you at dinner tonight." Kassia pointed to the couch. "You'd better sit down."

Theo felt a knot form in his throat. At the moment his feet didn't feel like moving. "I'll stand—thanks."

"I'll be glad to sit." Kassia dropped onto the couch, then looked up at Theo. "I can't believe she didn't say anything. Maybe I shouldn't, either." Kassia stared at her feet.

"You might as well tell me. I'm going to find out sooner or later." He glanced toward the kitchen. "From the looks of things, Lexie is in no condition to tell me herself."

Kassia nodded. "All right then. I'll tell you." She took in a deep breath but kept her gaze on her feet. "Piper is Lexie's little girl."

Theo didn't speak for a moment. He wished he'd taken Kassia's advice. He looked about for a seat, then sat on the chair beside the couch. He stayed at the edge of the chair and leaned toward Kassia. "Little girl? Lexie has a little girl?" His voice was strained.

"Yes."

Theo performed a few mental calculations and decided Lexie's daughter couldn't be more than six years old. How could he ever cope with a young child?

He gulped. "How old is she?"

"She's four."

Four. Was that better or worse? He didn't know. Theo was the youngest in his family and the only boy at that. He didn't know enough about children to have any idea other than Piper was somewhere between diapers and talking back to her elders.

A child? He hadn't counted on Lexie's bringing a child into the picture. And a girl at that. Theo could imagine connecting on an emotional level with a boy, but a little girl? His sisters had been older by the time Theo was aware of their existence. Now that two of them were married and had presented their parents with three grandsons so far, Theo's role as a fun-loving uncle consisted of giving his young nephews the latest expensive toys at Christmas and mailing a U.S. savings bond to mark the passing of each birthday. He felt ill equipped to deal with a little girl.

Embarrassment and anger soon replaced his fear. How could Lexie have let him talk on and on about the adventurous life he wanted and not say the first word to him about someone so important to her? He knew Lexie's days as a carefree coed had passed when she moved back to town. He was well aware that losing her husband at such a young age would change her forever. He had already thought about how Lexie's recent past would affect their renewed relationship, and he had come to terms with the fact that he could—and would need to—take Lexie as she now was if he wanted to be in her life.

But a little girl! He had no idea Lexie brought with her a child who would need years of intense parenting. Theo tried to imagine himself as a father. He hadn't given much thought to having children. How could he, with no romantic prospects on the horizon? Ever since he lost Lexie to Curt all those years ago, Theo had neglected his romantic life, throwing himself into his job. The monotony was relieved only by his dreams. Dreams of exotic travel and adventure. He would fictionalize his travels in a great novel that would sell millions of copies. Then he would be rich and live out his well-earned freedom.

With Lexie back in his life, old feelings had resurfaced. He realized what an emptiness he felt after losing her. An emptiness he wanted to fill. But to overflowing with a child, too? His plans for travel and adventure didn't include kids—certainly not now, perhaps never. And being a dad to someone else's child? Especially Curt's child—his nemesis from college—the man who stole Lexie from him in the first place. The thought had never occurred to him. At this point the idea seemed inconceivable.

How could I possibly manage such a thing? Reuniting with Lexie and now having to get acquainted with a child. It's too much. Piper's situation isn't ideal, since she's lost her father. What if Lexie, in misguided compassion, overcompensated and spoiled her rotten?

Theo, as insecure as he felt, couldn't stop thinking about the negative side.

What if Piper doesn't like me? What if I don't like her? Aren't relationships hard enough with just two adults? But a child, and a girl at that. . .

Camping trips, being a Scoutmaster, playing catch, teaching his son how to fish—the images that passed through Theo's mind didn't include activities a girl would likely enjoy. He pictured himself failing in trying to raise a girl. The word "failure" was not a welcome addition to Theo's vocabulary.

Not to mention Lexie's own failure to tell him the truth. How could she let him go all this time without the first peep that she had a child? How could he ever trust her again? And if he could not, how could they hope to build a lasting relationship?

The urge to walk out of the door at that moment and leave Lexie overcame him.

"Theo!" Kassia snapped her fingers in front of his face. "Yoo-hoo! Are you still in there?" Her cockeyed look told him she was only half joking.

He nodded as he awoke to the present.

"I know this is a shock."

"That's an understatement."

Kassia settled back onto the couch. "Try to look at this from Lexie's viewpoint. She didn't want to scare you off. I'm sure that's why she didn't say anything."

"Then when did she plan to say something? On our wedding day? Or on the honeymoon?"

"Huh?" Kassia's eyes widened. "Are you saying you're thinking about marriage?"

"I don't know. Did I say that?" He couldn't believe he'd uttered such words out loud. Had he indeed been thinking of Lexie in such permanent terms? His rapidly beating heart told him he had, whether or not he admitted it to himself.

"It sure sounded like it."

"Don't hold me to anything I might say tonight. I'm too upset to think straight. Maybe I should just leave." He searched his pocket for his car keys.

"No, don't do that. That's the last thing Lexie needs right now. She's upset enough as it is."

At that moment, Lexie entered the room. "If you're talking about me, you're right." Theo turned to Lexie and saw that her face held no color. Fear filled her eyes. Even though he was still angry, Theo had to resist the impulse to cross the room and take her in his arms and tell her everything would be all right.

"What happened?" Kassia asked.

"Well, you know how curious Piper is." Lexie stopped herself. "Theo. You don't know who Piper is, do you?"

"I do now," he said evenly. "Kassia just told me."

"I'm so sorry. I should have told you. I wanted to. It's just that the time never seemed right."

A number of retorts flickered through his mind, but Theo knew he would regret voicing any of them.

"I'm sorry, Theo. I shouldn't have been such a coward. I–I just didn't want to spoil—" She shook her head. "Never mind."

Spoil the moment? Is that what she was thinking?

Theo remembered how he had talked nonstop on every occasion they had been together. Even though Lexie's failure to tell him about her daughter still left him disturbed, his own emotions could be dealt with at another time. Now they needed to focus on Piper and her safety.

"You two can work out whatever is going on between you later," Kassia interrupted, expressing Theo's thoughts. "I want to know what happened to Piper."

"She got into Mom's purse and swallowed some of her headache pills. As soon as they found out, they called poison control, then took her to the emergency room."

"Did she lose consciousness?" Theo asked.

"No, praise the Lord," Lexie said.

"Is she going to be all right?" Kassia and Theo asked in unison.

"I think so. They induced vomiting, and now she's in the hospital. They're keeping her overnight for observation."

"I'm sure your parents will call as soon as they know something more," Kassia said.

"No. I don't want to wait. I want to go home." Lexie reached for her purse, which she had dropped on the floor beside the couch in her haste to call. "In fact, I'm leaving right now."

"You're in no condition to make such a long trip alone," Theo said, watching her. "What is it, three hours from here?"

"Yes, that's about right."

Compassion filled Theo. Clearly Lexie shouldn't make such an anxiety-ridden journey without someone by her side. "No way am I going to let you drive such a long way alone. I'll take you home myself."

She looked at him and straightened her shoulders. "No. Thank you, Theo, but Piper is my problem, not yours."

"She's not a problem." Theo's words defied his most recent thoughts, but he had to help Lexie, whether she wanted him to or not. "I insist."

"He's right," Kassia urged. "You should let Theo drive you. I'd offer, but I promised to go in to the office tomorrow to help Mandie prepare for her big meeting on Monday. She'll kill me if I renege on her."

"That's okay, Kassia," Lexie said.

"Then there's no reason why I shouldn't go," Theo said.

Lexie's lips were trembling and her eyes moist as she looked back at him. "You don't have plans, Theo?"

"I didn't promise my boss I'd be at work tomorrow. And I don't have much of a life outside work." He smiled at her. "Sure, I'd be glad to take you home."

"Well, all right." Her voice was soft. "My nerves are shot. And I sure would like the company."

❧

Theo exited onto Interstate 85 at Petersburg, grateful that light traffic enabled him to travel at a reasonable clip. The tires made hypnotic bumping sounds as the car hit pavement gaps. The trip offered little in the way of scenery except for an unbroken highway and dark stands of trees that were scarcely visible at night. Green and white signs promised a town at the next exit, and more signs announced the inevitable fast food restaurants at each stop. He wished he could have a conversation with Lexie, but she barely said a word.

He thought about confronting her, but he knew questioning her now would be a mistake. Initial feelings of anger and betrayal had dissolved to the lesser emotion of hurt, but he still couldn't rely on himself not to say something he might regret. A question nagged at him. Why hadn't Lexie trusted him enough to tell him about Piper?

Maybe the problem isn't her, but you.

The thought didn't make Theo feel any better. But what if he was the problem? Did Lexie see him as selfish, in both his dreams and the way he dominated their time together?

Whenever he faced fear and doubt, Theo knew he needed to pray. He decided to invite Lexie to join him. "Lexie?"

"I don't need to stop, thanks." She didn't turn her gaze from the passing trees.

Theo remembered they'd just passed a sign for a rest area. "That's not what I was asking. I thought you might like to pray."

"Oh." She nodded. "Okay."

Together they sent up their petitions to the Lord, for a safe trip to and from North Carolina, for Piper's recovery, for Lexie's parents, and for Lexie. As they prayed, Lexie placed her hand on his right shoulder. He felt strength in her light touch. Her faith had deepened since they had been school friends. The college coed had apparently matured into a woman. A woman of God.

Theo hoped the prayer would lead to a discussion, but he was disappointed. Instead Lexie leaned back away from him and continued to stare out the window.

He concentrated on the road for another hour until she finally spoke.

"Theo, I don't deserve you. I'm the worst mother in the world and a poor excuse for a friend. I should have told you about Piper right away."

"I've been thinking, Lexie. I admit I was hurt that you didn't trust me enough to tell me about her from the start." Theo glanced her way and noticed she opened her mouth to speak. He rushed on. "But there probably never was a good time, or at least not an ideal time. I know I've talked a lot since we've been seeing each other again."

"I wouldn't say that." Her voice seemed weak.

"Thanks for the thought, but we both know it's true. I've been talking a lot about my future plans, and you probably thought they couldn't include a little girl."

"It wouldn't be easy to traipse around the world to all sorts of exotic places with a preschooler."

"Wow! I guess I did sound self-centered."

"Why shouldn't you be?"

Lexie's answer surprised him. "What do you mean?"

"You're a single man with no ties. You have a right to enjoy your freedom now, before you take on a wife and family."

She spoke softly, as if to console and forgive, but her words only made him feel guilty. Yet her gentle ways were part of why he had been so eager to see her again when she returned to Richmond. And she had just made him realize he didn't want to think of himself, and only himself, forever.

He decided to talk about something else.

"I have something to ask, if you don't mind," Theo said gently.

"As if I have a choice," Lexie said and glanced at him, a slight smile on her lips. "I don't think I have the energy to jump out of the car."

Theo laughed. "I was wondering why you didn't bring Piper with you to Richmond. Don't you miss her?"

"You have no idea how much I miss her!" Lexie sighed and fell silent for a time.

After a few moments, Theo looked over at her. A tear fell down her cheek. "I'm sorry. I didn't mean to upset you."

"No, you didn't. It's been an upsetting day for all of us."

"You don't have to answer me now."

"No. I want to." Her voice strengthened with determination. "You need to know if you're going to be with me and my family." She paused. "Mom and Dad agreed to take Piper for a couple of months while I established myself in Richmond. We all thought it was a good idea, especially since I'm sharing an apartment with Kassia. She's not used to kids."

Theo snorted. "I know. If Piper was around, Kassia couldn't have any more dates with Brad—that's for sure."

"Don't even mention his name."

Her voice held an edge that piqued his curiosity, but he decided not to press for more information. "Okay. I won't."

"Tonight made me realize something. I'm more than ready for Piper to come and live with me," she said. "Even if it means losing you."

Chapter 10

Lexie sank deeper into the bucket seat of Theo's sports car. She glanced sideways at him. His eyes were wide and his body tense. Her admission had made an impact. She groaned inwardly and fixed her gaze on the trees alongside the road as if they were the most fascinating she had ever seen.

What's the matter with me? How could I have been so careless?

She had all but admitted to Theo that she loved him! With the commotion of leaving Piper, moving to a new location, living with Kassia, and renewing her friendship with Theo, Lexie hadn't thought through the repercussions of a new romantic relationship. Yet no matter how hard she tried to resist, she seemed to be chasing Theo full throttle.

Her thoughts turned to Piper. What kind of mother would she be if she weren't fully committed to her daughter, especially since she had been responsible for her father's death? No way would she commit to any man who didn't love Piper.

But you haven't given Theo a chance to love her, have you?

Lexie swallowed. She couldn't tell how Theo was handling the news. Always the gentleman, he would naturally offer to drive her to the hospital. She couldn't read through his tight expression as he concentrated on the road or figure out what his feelings were—toward her or the idea of Piper.

The knot grew in her throat. But what was she afraid of? Maybe she wasn't fearful for herself, but for Curt and his memory?

Will Theo try to take Curt's place in Piper's life? Or am I jealous of anyone who might take part of Piper away from me?

Now you're being as self-centered as Theo!

She let out a groan.

"Is my driving that bad?" Theo asked.

She felt embarrassed he had heard her. "Not so far."

"So far so good then." Theo pointed to the exit sign for Route 1 to Raleigh. "Is this it?"

"Yes. This is the one."

Lexie thanked the Lord silently for Theo's graciousness—and for their imminent arrival at the hospital.

Only forty miles now.

The hospital. She knew her job offered some type of health insurance, but Lexie hadn't studied the policy enough to know the details. Besides, had she been working there long enough for her benefits to start?

A picture of the pile of bills on her desk passed, unwanted, through her mind. She shook her head to dismiss the image as she shut the car door behind her and walked toward the hospital's pediatric unit.

Lexie swallowed hard to fight the dryness in her throat. She wished she had the courage to take Theo's hand. She longed for his supportive touch, but reaching out for his comfort seemed too much to ask at the moment.

Lord in heaven, please let Piper be okay.

She stepped quietly into the room. Her mother was reading the newspaper in the only chair. Even though the hour was late, Piper sat up in bed, watching television. She held a stuffed bear Lexie didn't recognize. She guessed the toy was a gift from her parents. To Lexie's relief, Piper looked like the happy little girl she was, full of energy. Only the beeping monitor beside her bed indicated anything was amiss.

"Piper!" Lexie hurried across the room.

"Mommy!" Piper exclaimed, reaching out for her mother.

Lexie swept her daughter into her arms. How she had missed Piper! Tears flowed down her cheeks, but she did not care.

Finally she released Piper and looked into her face. "How are you feeling, sweetie?"

The little girl nodded. "Okay now. They made me drink some yucky stuff, and I threw up." Piper scrunched up her nose and rubbed her tummy.

"A charcoal shake." Mom folded the paper, set it on the table beside Piper's bed, and stood. "I'm so sorry this happened, Lexie." She crossed the room and hugged her daughter. "I feel it's all my fault. I shouldn't have left my headache medicine out where Piper could get to it."

"Never mind that, Mom. I'm just glad Piper seems to be okay?" She ended with a question in hopes her mom would reassure her.

"She's going to be fine, I'm sure. As I told you earlier, they're just keeping her overnight for observation." Mom stroked Piper's head. "Isn't that right, sweetie?"

"Right, Grammy. When can I get up?"

"Not yet." Mom chuckled and looked at Lexie. "That's a good sign."

"It sure is," Lexie agreed.

Her mother took her aside, although they didn't leave the room. She lowered her voice. "The medicine she took affects the heart, and they want to be sure Piper's is okay before they release her."

"Her heart?" Lexie's own heart started pounding.

"I really don't think the doctor's worried about it. Nothing dramatic has happened since you called. I'm sure she'll be fine. It's just a precaution." Mom put her hand on Lexie's shoulder. "I'm worried about you now, Lexie. You look so tired. How are you doing, honey?"

"Better—now that I'm finally here." The two women embraced again. "Where's Dad?"

"He's gone to the vending machines for a soda. He'll be back soon. How was the trip?"

The trip! Lexie had forgotten about poor Theo. Unwilling to overwhelm Piper, he had volunteered to stand in the hallway until they exchanged their greetings.

"I was so worried about you," Mom continued, "driving all that distance by yourself and in a car that's not so reliable. I prayed for you the whole time."

"Thanks, Mom. But I wasn't by myself."

Her mother's features softened. "Good. Kassia came with you. Where is she?"

"Not Kassia, Mom. Theo."

Her eyebrows raised. "Theo?"

"Theo Powers. You remember him. He was one of my friends from college."

She was quiet for a moment. "Yes, I think I do remember. You know, I think he liked you, but Curt stole your heart."

Lexie felt heat rise to her cheeks. "Mom!"

"Well, it's the truth, isn't it?"

Sure, Theo had always been there for her in college, but she hadn't thought of him romantically. When she met Curt in an informal study group, though, his boyish ways and handsome face captivated her. Soon they were a couple. In her self-absorption she hadn't taken Theo's feelings into consideration. Could Theo still harbor disappointment after all these years?

"What?" Piper interrupted. "Did Daddy steal something?"

Lexie's mother laughed. "No, sweetie. It's just us grown-ups talking. Don't pay any attention to Grammy."

Piper folded her little arms across her chest. "I never get to know about any of the good stuff."

Lexie and her mother laughed, but Lexie's thoughts soon turned serious. The little girl said she didn't remember her father, but through family conversations, photographs, and videotape, he remained in memory. Though the Lord chose to take Curt home early, Lexie made sure Piper knew that both of her fathers—earthly and heavenly—loved her very much.

She choked back a lump in her throat. "Speaking of paying attention, I'd better let Theo know he can come in now."

"Yes," Mom agreed. "Let's not leave the poor boy standing out there all night."

"Is Theo the friend you and Grammy were talking about?" Piper asked.

Lexie nodded. Sometimes she wished her daughter didn't have a talent for hearing every word not meant for her ears. "Do you mind if I bring him in to see you? He drove Mommy all the way here from Virginia."

"Did he bring me a toy?"

"Piper!" Lexie and her mother admonished in unison.

"You can't expect people to bring you gifts all the time. Your mommy should be gift enough for you," Mom added.

Piper looked down. "I'm sorry."

Lexie patted Piper's hand. A small twinge of guilt pricked her. "I wish I could have brought you a gift myself, honey; but it's late, and we didn't want to take the time to stop. We wanted to be here with you."

"That's okay."

Children. How easily they forgive.

Lexie smiled uncomfortably. This meeting wasn't happening the way she had hoped, but hiding Theo and Piper from each other any longer didn't feel right.

Lord, I know this is selfish, but I pray it's Your will for them to like each other.

Lexie crossed to the door, stuck her head outside, and looked down the corridor for Theo. She recognized him by the reddish-orange hue of the camp shirt he had changed into before the drive. The color contrasted with the blue wall he leaned against as he absently watched nurses coming and going about their business.

"Theo," she said in a stage whisper, motioning for him to come closer.

His face lit up on seeing her. She smiled in return. As she watched him approach, she couldn't help but reflect on how he always conducted himself as a gentleman. He easily could have listened in on the conversation she had just shared with her mother. Remembering what Mom had said about him, Lexie felt grateful he didn't overhear.

"How is she?" he whispered as soon as he came within earshot.

"She seems pretty happy. Are you ready to meet her?"

"Sure, I guess." He swallowed.

Lexie took his hand and gave it a squeeze. "She'll like you. I just know it." She didn't want to let go of his clasp but decided that entering while holding hands with a strange man might be too much for Piper. She kept a smile on her face as she walked into the room with Theo.

Piper looked up at Theo when he came in but had no particular expression on her face. Lexie thought she would reintroduce him to her mother first so Piper wouldn't look upon him as an intruder. "Mom, you remember Theo Powers."

A warm smile lit her face. "Yes, I do. How are you, Theo?"

"Mrs. Downey." He gave her a polite nod and a shy smile.

Ignoring the butterflies in her stomach, Lexie motioned toward her daughter. "Piper, I have someone I'd like for you to meet. This is Mr. Powers. He drove me here tonight."

"You mean Theo?"

Lexie felt her face flush, but Theo chuckled. "So they've been talking about me, eh? Did they say all good things?"

Piper thought for an instant, then shrugged. "I dunno."

The adults laughed. Lexie noticed Theo was smiling warmly while he watched Piper. She felt a sense of relief.

Piper held up the brown teddy bear Lexie had seen earlier. "How do you like my new bear?"

"He's cute. Did they give him to you here at the hospital?" Theo asked.

"It's not a him. She's a her," Piper corrected him.

"Oh. I'm sorry. Did they give her to you here at the hospital?"

Piper nodded. "I named her Peanut Butter."

"How about that? She *is* the color of peanut butter," Lexie noted.

"Peanut butter is one of her favorites," Mom explained to Theo. "I think she'd eat it every meal if we'd let her."

"Yeah!" Piper agreed. "They gave me a really bad drink. It was dark and yucky. They said I had to drink it. Then I threw up." She gave her mother a pleading look. "You won't let them make me drink that anymore, will you, Mommy?"

"I don't think you'll be needing it anymore."

"Good. It was awful." She grimaced. "But I feel better now," she told Theo.

"Good," he said.

Piper turned to Lexie. "I'm sorry, Mommy."

"Sorry? Sorry for what?"

"For makin' Grammy have to take me to the hospital. And for makin' you come back."

Lexie hugged her daughter. "I'm sorry you feel bad, but I'm not sorry I came back. I missed you."

"Every minute?"

"Every minute." Lexie hugged Piper again. "You know, I was so busy making sure you're doing okay that I never asked—why did you swallow Grammy's pills, honey? I thought I had taught you better than to go in her things and eat something without permission."

"I know." Piper looked down at the blanket covering her. "But they were pink, and I thought they'd taste like strawberries. Or maybe watermelon." She glanced up and wrinkled her nose. "I sure wish they had. They were awful! How can you eat those, Grammy?"

"When you're in pain, you'd be surprised what you might be willing to swallow. But I only take one at a time, and I don't chew them," Mom answered.

"I know you upset Grammy very much," Lexie told Piper.

"I already told her I didn't mean to upset her," Piper said.

"She did," Mom agreed. "I know you didn't, honey. The main thing is, I hope you learned your lesson."

"I did. When can I go home?"

Lexie sat on the bed beside Piper and took her hands in her own. How small they felt! The difference in Piper's hands and her own emphasized how much Piper depended on her. She made a silent promise never to leave her little girl again.

"You can't go home tonight."

"I can't? Why not?"

"The doctors and nurses want to make sure you're okay now."

"But I feel fine!" Piper protested.

"And I'm so glad you do. But they just have to make sure. That's their job. I know you don't understand all about it now, but you will someday." She squeezed Piper's hand. "I'm sure you'll be going home first thing tomorrow morning."

"Are you gonna stay with me?"

"Of course I am. I wouldn't think of leaving."

"Yay!" Piper wiggled up and down, causing the EKG cables to pull against the heart monitor. "Can we stay up late and watch television?"

"You're already up way later than you should be." She stroked her daughter's forehead.

"I let her stay up since I knew you were coming," Mom explained.

"Can I still stay up?" Piper asked.

"We'll see."

Piper pouted. "That means no."

"No, it means I'll have to think about it."

"That still means no." Piper folded her arms. "Is that my punishment for takin' Grammy's pills?"

Lexie thought for a moment. "No, I'm not going to punish you. I think you've learned your lesson. All of us have been through enough."

"Yay!" Piper leaned over and hugged her tightly.

Lexie stroked her hair. Touching her soft curls made her realize how much she missed being home.

A familiar male voice interrupted. "Here's my little girl!"

Lexie turned to face her father. "Dad!" She rose from the bed and gave him a hug.

"How's my big girl by now?" he asked Piper.

"Fine!" She beamed.

"Good." He tilted his head toward Lexie, then toward the door.

"We'll be right back," Lexie assured Piper as she followed her father.

Mom waited for them both in the hall. "Are you all right?"

"Fine, now that I've seen Piper."

Mom placed a hand on her shoulder. "I'm so sorry about what happened. I couldn't believe it. I was in such a panic."

"Piper told us her stomach hurt," Dad said. "It took us awhile to get her to admit she'd taken some of your mother's pills."

"I feel so guilty. I had no idea Piper would be interested in my pills. I know

now I should have kept them better secured." Tears moistened Mom's eyes. "The bottle had a childproof cap. I just don't understand it."

"I know, Mom. She's a curious little bird. If anyone is to blame, it's me. I should have remembered to tell you she learned how to open the caps early. Don't ask me how. I've always known to keep all medicines out of her sight." Lexie shook her head. "Apparently when she saw the color of the pills, the temptation was too great."

"She's a smart girl, that one is." Her dad puffed out his chest. "Takes after her old grandpa."

"Maybe so." Lexie giggled. She jumped slightly when she sensed someone's arm slip around her shoulder. She turned and saw it was Theo's. How wonderful it made her feel, so secure and protected. She had forgotten how such a touch felt. Lexie reached for his hand, touching his strong fingers, and smiled at him. The tiredness in his eyes disappeared, and he grinned in return.

She peeked at her mother. Her arched eyebrow indicated the gesture hadn't gone unnoticed.

After a few moments of easy conversation during which Theo became reacquainted with them, Mom pulled Lexie aside.

"Do you need any help getting your things to the room?"

"No, thanks. Theo brought my overnight bag in for me. The rest is in the car."

"Speaking of Theo, I couldn't help but notice the two of you seem to be more than friends."

Lexie felt her cheeks grow warm. "I wouldn't say that."

"Are you sure? What are your feelings for him?"

"At this point I'm not sure I can talk about my feelings about anything. So much has happened." Lexie realized she meant not only the evening's events with Piper, but also how fast events had occurred since her move. "Try not to worry about me. I want to be a blessing to you, not a burden."

"You never have to worry about that. I think of you and Piper every time I read Proverbs. 'Children's children are a crown to the aged, and parents are the pride of their children.'" She looked into Lexie's eyes. "But that doesn't mean I don't worry." Her gaze rested on Theo. Still engrossed in conversation with Dad, he didn't look her way. "Curt was so good to you. He worked so hard to give you and Piper everything he could, and then there was the accident. . . ." Her voice trailed off, leaving any other thoughts unspoken.

"I know, Mom."

"Then how can you even think of another man? It seems like, well, like a—sin."

"A sin?"

"Yes."

Lexie brought to mind each verse of scripture she could recall concerning marriage. "I don't know of any admonition in the Bible that forbids widows to remarry."

"I can't say that I do, either." She shuddered. "But I'm still not sure it's right for you even to be thinking about it." She placed her hand on Lexie's shoulder. "I know things are tough for you right now and that you haven't recovered from the expenses. I wish your father and I were in a better position ourselves, so we could offer you more help. Maybe I could talk to him—"

"No, that's okay. The reason I moved in the first place was to gain more independence."

"I know, but I don't think that means you should strike up a romance with the first old friend you run into."

"Theo just did me a favor, Mom. Kassia said she would have brought me if she hadn't needed to go in to her office tomorrow."

"On a Saturday?"

"She's dedicated to her job. You have to be nowadays."

"I suppose so. I'm not sure the changes the world has seen since I was a young woman have been for the better."

"There's not much we can do about it." Lexie shrugged and smiled at her mother, grateful she'd been distracted by another subject.

"Take your father's mother, for instance," Mom continued. "She lost her husband in World War II, leaving her alone to raise your father and your two aunts by herself. And she never remarried. She stuck it out and did a fine job with all her kids."

Lexie nodded at the familiar story. As much as she admired her grandmother, she wanted to be her own person instead of patterning her life after someone else's. But arguing with her mother wouldn't help. "I know, Mom. And I know you want what's best for Piper and me. I promise I'll keep the whole situation in prayer."

"That's a good idea."

Lexie wished she could forget her mother's guilt-inducing words about Curt, but she knew it was impossible. She had to think of her daughter now. And of Theo.

"Do you have everything?" Theo asked as Lexie approached.

"Enough to see me through the night."

"I'll be back tomorrow morning, if you like."

"Yes, that would be nice."

"I told Theo he could spend the night with us," Dad said, "but he had already reserved a hotel room."

"I knew you'd offer. I tried to keep him from calling ahead in the car, but he wouldn't listen," Lexie explained. But she understood Theo's—and her parents'—need to be alone after such a stressful evening.

"Maybe next time. I appreciate the offer all the same," Theo said.

"Good night. See you in the morning."

Lexie wasn't surprised when Theo gave her a longing look, but she was both surprised and pleased when he gave Piper a similar look of warmth and concern. She was just as delighted when her daughter smiled back.

Could Theo love Piper already?

Chapter 11

Lexie made herself a temporary bed out of a chair and hospital linens. Just to sleep beside Piper was worth the discomfort.

"Mommy?"

"Yes?"

"Is Theo like Mr. Mathis?"

Lexie searched her mind and decided Piper must have been referring to the dad of a friend from preschool. "Mr. Mathis? You mean, Jessica's father?"

"Uh huh."

"What do you mean?"

"Well, one day her real dad just left, and then her mommy got married to somebody else."

"Are you afraid of that? That I might marry someone else?"

"I don't know." She shrugged. "I guess not, if he's nice. Is Theo nice, Mommy?"

Lexie stroked her daughter's hair. "I think he's nice. He's just my friend, though."

"Oh." The smile disappeared from her face.

Lexie swallowed. Surely Piper wanted a father in her life. Maybe more than Lexie realized. "You don't need to worry about anything right now. It's just you and me tonight. I want you to get some sleep so you can leave the hospital bright and early tomorrow, okay?"

Piper yawned. "Okay."

The last sound she heard was the EKG monitor beeping at regular intervals. With Piper by her side, Lexie slept more soundly than she expected. More soundly than she had in a long time.

❧

"I think she'll be fine," the doctor informed Lexie the next morning after unhooking Piper from the monitor. "We didn't see any irregularities in her heartbeat or any other abnormalities. She can go home today."

Lexie sighed with relief. "Thank you."

"Can I get out of bed now?" Piper asked.

"You sure can," the doctor said. "Mrs. Zoltan, since you've learned your daughter likes to raid the medicine cabinet, you need to be more careful with how you store medications."

Lexie fought the urge to defend herself and her mother. "I know. I don't think this will be happening again."

"Let's hope not." The doctor turned her attention to Piper. "You won't be eating any more pills without an adult saying it's okay, will you?"

"No!"

"I think we've all learned our lesson," Lexie agreed.

"Good. Just keep a close watch on her for the next few days, and call me if you have any concerns."

Piper was dressed in a pair of black jeans and a T-shirt when Theo entered a few minutes later. "Everybody sleep well?"

"Better than ever," Lexie answered. With the scare of Piper's visit to the hospital behind them, seeing Theo made her feel even more reassured.

"Hi, Mr. Powers," Piper greeted him.

"Hey, there!" Theo waved. "I brought you a present." He handed her a bag decorated with a picture of Winnie the Pooh. A rectangular box peeked out from underneath yellow tissue paper.

Piper squealed and clapped her hands, then reached for the box. "I know what this is, Mr. Powers. It's a doll."

"Well, you'll just have to see."

Piper tore through the paper in a flash. She drew in her breath when she saw the blue-eyed, blond doll wearing a long blue dress. "She's pretty! She can go home and live with all my other dolls. I think they'll like her." Piper brought the doll up to her neck and embraced it, swaying back and forth.

"Watch out, or she'll smother in your hair," Lexie cautioned.

"Oh!" Piper released her embrace and started to walk the doll, although the result looked more like hopping. She held up the doll for her new bear to see. "What do you think, Peanut Butter? Do you like her?" Piper moved the bear's head up and down. "She likes her!"

"Good!" Theo said amid Lexie's chuckles. "I wasn't sure what to get you. I just have nephews."

"What's nephews?"

"He's an uncle to boys," Lexie explained.

"Boys!" Piper scrunched her nose. "Yuck. I don't like boys."

"You will one day," Lexie said, laughing, then turned to Theo. "You didn't have to bring her anything, but she surely does like the doll you picked out." Lexie tapped Piper on the shoulder. "What do you say, Piper?"

"Umm." Piper's eyes looked upward.

"The magic word."

"Please?"

"No."

"Oh. Thank you, Mr. Powers."

"You're welcome," he answered.

"As you can see, we're still polishing our manners," Lexie apologized.

"I think she's doing very well. But if you don't mind, can she call me Theo? I feel so old with her calling me Mr. Powers. Not that I want to undermine what you're trying to teach her," he added quickly.

"That's all right. Part of etiquette is making the other person comfortable. She can call you Theo if you like."

"She seems to know how to respect her elders. Don't you, Piper?"

"Sure do!" She twisted her mouth. "Hey, does this present and me callin' you Theo and stuff mean you're my new daddy?"

"Piper!" Lexie's cheeks warmed. "What—what made you think such a thing?"

She shrugged. "Grammy was saying stuff."

Lexie groaned. "Kids overhear—and misinterpret—everything," she said to Theo.

"That's okay. I guess it's only natural for her to want a father." Theo's calm words didn't match the nervous way he drummed his fingers on the table that held the breakfast tray.

Lexie looked at her daughter. "As I explained to you before, Mr. Powers—I mean, Theo—is just a good friend of Mommy's."

"Oh." The corners of Piper's mouth tilted downward. She stared at the doll so that Lexie could only see her long eyelashes.

Lexie wondered why Piper seemed so disappointed. Sure, Theo had brought her a gift, but she already owned plenty of dolls. And of course he was handsome and kind to her and apparently liked her. But Lexie couldn't believe Piper wanted Theo to take Curt's place. Not that she remembered Curt. Still, most of the other children at Piper's preschool had daddies. Wouldn't it be normal for Piper to wish she had a daddy, too?

No, she couldn't be so captivated with Theo himself. Like any little girl, Piper's romantic fantasies carried her into a world of ease and fun. The idea of having a daddy—any daddy—played a role in the little girl's dreams. Theo embodied the idea. That's all.

Just make sure you don't fall in love with the idea yourself—or with the thought of having a husband again. If you do, you'll be on dangerous ground.

❧

That afternoon at the Downeys' house, Theo tried not to look too enthusiastic about the thick steak Lexie's dad had grilled. With the outer layer cooked to a deep brown and the inside warm and pink, Theo could hardly wait to savor a big chunk.

"So do you think you'll be going back to work this week?" Mrs. Downey asked.

"I haven't decided yet." He wondered if her question was a hint that she hoped he'd be leaving soon.

"I think he's going to wait for me to go back," Lexie said.

"That's awfully nice of you, Theo, but we can take Lexie back to Richmond ourselves," said Mrs. Downey. "Assuming she hasn't changed her mind about living so far away from home."

Theo's throat tightened. Had Lexie changed her mind? Did she plan to stay in North Carolina? His deep disappointment at the possibility surprised him, even though he knew he had strong feelings for her.

Lord, I haven't felt this way since Lexie and I were in college together. Should I follow my heart? I want to follow Your will, though, not my own.

Lexie's sweet voice broke into his silent petition. "I'm glad you want me to be home, Mom, but I think I'll stay in Richmond. I really like my work, as I told you before."

"That's what you say now," she muttered.

Theo wondered what Mrs. Downey meant. He glanced at Lexie, but she had become absorbed in finishing her tossed salad.

"Theo, you've gone to enough trouble," Mr. Downey interjected.

"I do appreciate everything you've done," Lexie added, finally looking at him.

"But we understand," Lexie's mother said, "if you have to leave."

"You're not leavin', are you, Theo?" Piper asked. "You promised you'd look at my rock collection."

"Of course I'll look at your rock collection. I wouldn't dream of leaving before I see that!" Theo assured her.

Piper pushed back her chair. "Let's go now. It's in my room."

"Not yet, young lady," Lexie said gently. She pointed to Piper's plate, which still had salad and carrots on it.

The little girl shifted in her seat. "But I don't wanna eat that stuff. I don't like vegetables."

"I know you don't, but you have to get some nutrition. You can't live on cookies and ice cream."

"But I ate my hot dog."

"I know. But at least finish your salad, okay?"

Piper nodded but with a frown.

"I hope you didn't want me to see your rock collection so you could get out of eating your vegetables," Theo teased.

The other adults laughed. Even Mrs. Downey chuckled.

"What's so funny?" Piper asked.

"You'll understand someday," Lexie said.

After dinner, Theo helped clear the dishes.

"If you think this will get you on my good side, you're right." Mrs. Downey smiled.

Theo felt someone tugging on his free hand.

"Will you come and look at my rocks now?" Piper asked, smiling up at him. "See this!" She held up a stone angled into the letter *L*. "I found it in the backyard yesterday. Pops said we should try to find the whole alphabet. I already found *D* and *T*. Wanna see?"

"Sure, as long as I'm finished here in the kitchen."

Lexie hung the dishtowel on a rack. "You're done." She smiled and nodded toward a hallway just off the kitchen. "Let's go."

"Race ya!" Piper squealed.

"Okay, honey! Are you in, Theo?" Lexie grinned.

He had no idea how two adults and one child could race through the narrow hall. "Um, sure."

They lined up; then Piper stretched out her arms, holding the adults back. "On your mark. Get set." Piper started running. "Go!"

Piper laughed as she set off. Lexie followed closely behind, with Theo coming in a distant third. Piper ran into her room and over to the bed, hopping on top of the covers.

She knelt on the bed and extended her arms toward the ceiling. "I win!"

"I don't know about that, young lady. You held us back and started before you said 'go.'" Lexie shook her finger in mock chastisement.

Piper giggled. "I still won."

"I don't know, either." Theo shook his head, his eyes twinkling. "I think your mom's right."

"I don't care. I win anyway." Piper's laughter filled the room. She leapt off the bed and bounded toward a small white dresser with pink handles. Among a menagerie of miniature toys and trinkets, Piper found a cardboard box. She opened it, peered inside, and extracted two rocks.

"Look!" She held them up for Theo to see.

"I see!"

She showed him a jagged gray rock. "See, this one looks like a *D*."

Theo studied the rock, trying to figure out how she could conclude it resembled the letter. Using his vivid imagination, he thought he could see the possibilities. "Uh-huh! How about that?"

"And look at this one. I found it in the parkin' lot of the grocery store yesterday. It looks just like a *T*."

Theo nodded. This rock looked more like the letter Piper suggested. "I see. Good job!"

"How long do you think it will take to find the whole alphabet?"

"All twenty-six letters?" Theo rubbed his chin as if in deep contemplation.

"How many is twenty-six?"

"A lot!" Lexie exclaimed. "I think it will take you at least a month to find that many, and at that pace you'd be finding a new letter almost every day."

"A month?" Piper asked. "How long is that? Till Christmas?"

"Oh, it's several months before Christmas," Lexie told her.

"Oh." Piper frowned. "That's a long time."

"It's not even cold yet," Theo said. "We have the rest of the summer, and then the leaves have to turn red and orange in the fall. Then there's Thanksgiving. And only after that can you have Christmas."

"That's forever!" Piper said.

"It will be here sooner than you think," Lexie said. "You'll be having a birthday before Christmas comes."

"Not until after Turkey Day," Piper said.

Theo and Lexie looked at each other and laughed.

"It's not funny! That's a long time."

"But you can pass the time by finding all your rocks," Theo pointed out. "A lot of the letters will be hard."

"Which ones?"

"Oh, like *Q* and *S* and *W*. But you'll find every letter before you know it. Maybe I can help you."

Maybe I can help you? Why did I say that?

Theo kicked himself mentally for suggesting something he might not be able to follow through on. He never wanted to hurt the child by making a promise he couldn't keep.

He watched Lexie stroke Piper's hair. In college he'd thought she was nearly perfect. He never expected to find her even more appealing in her role as a mother. But he did.

He wanted to stay. He never wanted to leave. But he had to.

"We can look all day tomorrow," Lexie said.

Her words consoled him. Looking for rocks tomorrow would be in keeping with his promise. Theo held back an audible sigh of relief.

"That'll be fun," he said aloud.

Assured they would hunt for rocks the next day, Piper asked Lexie to read her a bedtime story.

"I'll leave you two alone," Theo said. "See you tomorrow."

"I guess you'll have to go back on Monday," Lexie said quietly.

"I'm going to call in on Monday morning. I'd like to take a few days off. We happen to have a lag in work at the office now, and I have the time coming to me."

"Really? You're gonna stay?" Piper clapped her hands.

Lexie's face lit up. "Are you sure it's okay? I don't want to cause you to run into trouble with your boss."

An image of Ms. Thorndike, his supervisor, popped into his head. Theo couldn't envision her as a mother, though pictures of four children adorned her desk. She carried out her role at the office in a tough manner, but she appreciated Theo's work. The government had been facing lean times recently. As one of the younger employees, Theo made sure he didn't gripe or complain about taking on more work to make up for those who had retired or moved on, whose positions were left unfilled indefinitely.

Since he hadn't taken a vacation in over a year, he didn't think it would be a problem to have a few days off. Besides, the situation had developed into a life-altering event—for all of them. If he ever planned to renew his relationship with Lexie and get to know her little girl, he couldn't dawdle. He was certain his reluctance to speak up, to express his feelings to Lexie, had contributed to his losing her in college.

Theo shrugged. "She's cool. She knows I work hard. She'll approve a few days of leave for me so I can stay awhile."

Lexie spoke just above a whisper. "That would be wonderful."

⤜⧓⤛

By the following Friday, Theo felt as though the Downeys' place was his second home. Even Lexie's mom didn't seem to mind his presence.

Each day had passed quickly, filled with fun activities. Piper's preschool had already let out for the summer, so they had no particular schedule to keep. Instead, they found something new to do each day.

"I don't know when the last time was I went to the zoo," Lexie told Theo as they left nearby Asheboro. "We always lived so close, but I never seemed to find the time."

"That's what they say. The people who live near the tourist attractions never seem to visit them. Most of the people I know who live in Richmond haven't seen the Edgar Allan Poe, Valentine, or Confederate museums."

"Museums. Yuck. They're boring," Piper said, hanging on to her mother's hand.

Lexie chuckled.

"Museums have pretty pictures," Theo said.

"I don't care. I'd rather go to the park."

Theo tousled Piper's hair. "You did that, too."

"Yeah!" She looked up at him. "Can we go back today?"

"Hmm." Lexie smiled. "I see she's asking you and not me. She's already found out you're a soft touch."

"What's a soft touch?" Piper asked.

"It means he lets you have your way," Lexie explained.

"He doesn't always let me have my way. He didn't take us to the toy store yesterday."

"I guess you're right," Lexie observed. "You had just been to the store the day before."

"But I like to go every day!"

"It's a good thing we have to go back tomorrow," Lexie told Theo. "Otherwise we'd all be broke."

"So can we go to the park now?"

Lexie looked at her watch. "I wish we could, but it's getting too late. You need to be in bed before long."

"Aww! But I don't want to! Can't I stay up?"

"Not tonight, unless Grammy says it's okay. You'll be staying with her for a little while."

Piper stopped. "You mean you're leavin' again?"

❧

She hadn't anticipated telling Piper about her plans while they were still in the parking lot, but she knew her daughter wouldn't be put off. Lexie bent down in front of her child. She kept her voice low. "Yes, but this time I want you to go with me. Would that be okay?"

"Can Grammy and Pops go, too?"

"I wish they could, but they have to stay here. Pops has to go to work."

"Oh. I wish there wasn't any work."

"I know." Lexie rubbed her palms against Piper's forearms, a gesture that always seemed to calm them both. "So you want to come with me, don't you?"

Piper nodded.

"Good!" Lexie spread out her arms, and Piper rushed into them. They held each other tightly.

Lexie stood and motioned to Theo. He had been walking around in slow circles, studying the trees and the other cars in the lot. She wondered how much of their conversation he'd heard.

Theo had been the picture of amiability during their time together. He seemed to slide naturally into a role of caring for Piper. Yet the setting was idyllic. No work or school responsibilities hindered their time together. Each day was free, a gift to do with as they would. In reality, every day couldn't be filled with trips to the zoo, informal dates with Theo, or visits to the toy store. How was Theo feeling? Was he as fond of Piper as he appeared to be? Or was he just being the nice gentleman he always was, showing them a good time since Piper's life had been endangered? Did she dare let herself fall in love with Theo?

Lexie wished she could hold on to these days forever and never have to return to her new home or her job or to finding day care for Piper or confronting the mound of debt that awaited.

But she couldn't. It was time to grow up. Time to take full responsibility for her little girl.

She only hoped Theo would be there, too.

Chapter 12

Theo tried to concentrate on lifting weights but kept losing count during each set of repetitions. Ever since he had driven Lexie and Piper to Richmond, his thoughts were never far from them. He tried calling several times, only to reach Kassia's answering machine. Perhaps that was best. They needed time to settle into their new lives.

He sat up on the weight bench and wiped his face with his hand towel. Never did he think he would love a child, especially one that didn't bear his last name, as he loved Piper. Surely Lexie could see he adored her and would be a good father to her. But something was holding Lexie back. His own selfishness perhaps? Why wouldn't Lexie think him selfish? He had done nothing but talk about a life without children since they reunited—an extension of the feelings he had expressed all through school. Why would she think bringing Piper presents and taking the two of them on day trips for a week would change anything?

Lord, do You want me to be a father to Piper? And if that is Your will, how can I convince Lexie I'm worthy of her? Or of Piper?

A week had passed since Lexie and Piper had settled into Kassia's apartment. Although the days weren't as idyllic as they had been with Theo, Lexie felt cheered to have Piper with her. She'd been able to place her in a reliable day-care situation, and the evenings, for the most part, belonged to the two of them.

At the same time she missed Theo. With the adjustments of three people living in an apartment meant for one, Lexie had managed only to leave a message on his phone. She resolved to cook a nice dinner for him soon. That was the least she could do.

But now a stack of mail awaited on the desk in the bedroom. She had put off looking through it, knowing she would only feel discouraged. She sorted through the junk, throwing out catalogs that might tempt her to buy items she couldn't afford. Even the ones that offered inexpensive dresses, sometimes with the mom's dress to match, or the ones that screamed "Summer Sale" in red letters.

She sighed. She had never been one to spend money with abandon, but she wished she could at least buy a few little luxuries. If only she could pick up a pretty dress for Piper without worrying about her tight budget. Even when Curt was living, finances had been lean. Now that he was gone. . .

Lexie held back her tears. The catalogs had been trying enough. She was in no mood to tackle the stack of bills.

Piper chose that moment to burst into the room they shared. "What's wrong, Mommy?"

Lexie wiped away a stray tear and swiveled in her chair. "It's okay, honey. Mommy had something in her eye."

I did have something in my eye. A tear.

"Oh." Piper yanked a tissue out of the box on Lexie's desk and handed it to her mother. "Here you go."

"Thanks." Lexie accepted the tissue and swiped at her eyes and nose. "What are you up to now?"

Piper shrugged. "I dunno. Miss Kassia said to come in here with you 'cause there's something on the TV that wouldn't be good for me to see."

Lexie glanced at the clock. "It's eight o'clock and time for you to go to bed anyway."

"Aww! I knew you'd say that. Can't I help you instead?"

"Maybe someday, when you're old enough to write."

"I never get any mail."

"Grammy writes every week."

"But that's all I ever get. I wish I got as much mail as you do."

"No, you don't." Lexie smiled. "Now come on—let's get you into bed."

Since the room was small, Lexie and Piper shared a bed. Lexie worried that Piper might grow too accustomed to such an arrangement, but the situation couldn't be helped. Kassia's couch wasn't available since she spent most evenings in front of the television. Lexie didn't care to toss and turn on the uncomfortable cushions after Kassia turned in, which was usually past midnight.

Brad had been scarce since that one night he had come to the apartment. Lexie supposed Kassia's mindless television viewing was better than her spending her evenings with Brad. Kassia surely didn't need him in her life. Although she hadn't complained about Lexie's new roommate, the atmosphere around the apartment had changed after Piper's arrival. Before, Kassia and Lexie could more or less come and go as they pleased. If they chose to eat out together or even double date, they could.

Holding back a sigh, Lexie determined to find a better place soon—when she could round up enough money for a deposit and budget for a full month's rent.

Piper had barely said "amen" after her evening prayer when she pulled on the cuff of Lexie's blouse. "Can you stay here and go to sleep with me?"

"Not quite yet. I'll be back soon." Lexie grabbed Peanut Butter from the top of the bedside table. The bear had never been far out of reach since Piper's hospital stay. Lexie handed the toy to her daughter. "Peanut Butter will keep you company until I get back."

"I guess." The little girl frowned. "Can you stay home tomorrow? I don't want to go back to the center. I don't have any friends there."

"I know it's hard at first since you're new. But you'll make friends soon. And just think—you'll go to kindergarten next year. You'll make lots of new friends there."

Before Piper could argue, Kassia called to Lexie. "Telephone!"

Lexie had been so engrossed in putting Piper to bed that she hadn't heard the phone ring. "Okay."

"Who is it?" Piper asked.

"Well, Grammy called yesterday, so it's probably just someone wanting Mommy to buy something. I'll have to find out. Now you go to sleep—okay?"

Piper nodded.

Lexie wasn't eager to take the call. Lately she had lagged behind on a department store credit card bill, which resulted in interest plus late fees, increasing the debt even more. So much for trying to save a few dollars at a sale. She wished she hadn't accepted the store's offer of ten percent off for their credit card. She remembered the promotional gift—a water bottle—that sweetened the deal. She'd taken the bottle with her on two jogs before the straw broke, leaving it useless. Though the gift was long gone, credit card bills arrived at brutally regular intervals. The store had already called once. She hoped it wasn't them again. Kassia was sure to be upset if bill collectors made a habit of calling the apartment.

"Hello?" she asked hesitantly.

"Hi, Lexie. It's Theo."

She let out her breath. "Oh, good."

"I'm glad it's good to hear from me, but that's a funny greeting. Were you expecting bad news?"

"Uh, not really. I don't know." *So much for wit.*

"I saw an apartment for rent near my house. I was wondering if you'd like to look at it."

"Near your house, eh?" She smiled into the phone. "Do I sense an ulterior motive?" *I hope.*

"Who, me? Ulterior motive? I've never heard of such a thing." He chuckled. "Okay, I guess I'd like to know you're not having to bunk up with a roommate anymore. And I know this is a good neighborhood. But even though it's nearer to me, I promise not to pester you."

Lexie laughed. "You never pester us. Piper has been asking about you. She misses you." *And so do I.*

"Tell her I miss her, too," Theo said. "It's been crazy at work since I missed so much time. I've had to catch up."

"Sorry."

"Don't be. So would you like to take a look at the apartment? Maybe tomorrow? I can go with you if you like."

"So we'll look like a family—a reliable bunch?"

"I was thinking more that you might want another opinion. I bought this house by myself, and I would have liked having a little moral support."

"How can I pass up such a good offer? Okay. I'll meet you after work."

※

Lexie turned the key and opened the door to the vacant unit. The landlord had given it to Theo and Lexie so they could view the apartment by themselves.

As Lexie stepped across the threshold, Theo imagined her coming in from a hard day at the office to her own place. He entered behind her.

The small room had bare, off-white walls and a beige carpet. Off to one side, on a patch of beige vinyl flooring, was a kitchen. Directly opposite, beige floor length curtains hung in front of sliding glass doors. Beside the kitchen, a hallway led to the rest of the apartment, which the landlord said contained two bedrooms, a powder room, and a full bathroom.

"I love it already!" Lexie lifted her hands to the sky and twirled around the vacant room.

"Really?"

Lexie rushed to the kitchen area and opened the microwave. "Wow! It has a rotating dish. Even Kassia's doesn't have that." She peered into the dishwasher. "Looks almost new. No rusted spindles or anything."

"Great." He tried to remember all the details the landlord had mentioned. One negative item came to mind. "I just wish each unit had a washer and dryer for you. That would be so much better than having to do your laundry in the next building."

"Yes, but I can manage."

Theo surveyed the area with a more critical look. "Of course, most places you find will have a dull beige carpet and lackluster color on the walls." The area seemed so small. By the time she'd moved in furniture, it was bound to seem even smaller. "This is where you'll be doing most of your living, and it isn't nearly as big as Kassia's apartment. The kitchen opens into the living area, and you won't have a dining room."

"I don't care. I'm just happy to find a place this reasonable where I can feel that Piper is safe." She turned her face toward the sliding glass door. "And look. A balcony." She motioned for him to join her. "Come on."

She drew the curtain to one side, then walked out onto a small slab of concrete surrounded by black metal bars that reminded Theo of a prison.

To his surprise, Lexie was still smiling when he joined her. He tapped the top of the bars. "Gorgeous, huh? Early Alcatraz?"

"Maybe so." She patted the bars, which were no farther apart than the width of her hand. "I can tell this is good enough to keep Piper safe out here, especially since we're just on the second level. Her safety is the most important thing."

"That's true," Theo said, nodding.

Lexie pointed to the corner. "I think this is wide enough for me to put a couple of patio chairs here."

"You may be right." He leaned on the railing. "Beautiful view of the parking lot."

"I always did like cars."

He couldn't help but laugh. "You're determined not to find a thing wrong with this place, aren't you?"

She laughed. "Well, let me look in the bedrooms."

"Okay. I'll stay out here."

"Are you sure?"

Theo nodded. Perhaps if Lexie could have a few moments alone, she could look at the place objectively. At least she hadn't brought Piper. A child's emotional response to a new place would be far more compelling than any other factor. Lexie needed a clear head if she was going to commit to an apartment for a year.

"I'll be right back."

Theo watched the people who might soon be Lexie's neighbors as they came and went. When he'd first learned about the vacant apartment, he had made sure the complex welcomed children. A well-maintained playground awaited Piper upon her arrival. Not many children were playing there when he'd come, but the day was hot. Theo just hoped Piper would soon make friends.

And Lexie?

A lump formed in his throat. A feeling he didn't like. Lexie was still young. She was sure to meet plenty of men, maybe even single fathers with children similar in age and temperament to Piper.

What is wrong with you? Don't you want her to be happy?

Yes, but not with someone else.

The declaration from his conscience no longer surprised him. Old and new feelings had stirred during their time together. He had given her some space when they returned home. Too much space, maybe. When she hadn't called, he'd found an excuse—this apartment—to contact her.

He drummed his fingers absently on the railing. His first thought was how ugly it looked. Lexie's first thought was how it would be safe for her daughter.

Sure, I love Piper. Who wouldn't? But am I ready to take on a woman with a child? I feel like a child half the time myself.

The doubt that clouded his mind felt worse than the lump in his stomach. He didn't want to think about anything now, at least not anything except making Lexie happy.

He heard the sliding door moving on its track. "So what did you think?" he asked, turning to Lexie.

"I can't believe how large my room is. It has a walk-in closet!" Lexie's face was flushed and her voice excited. "Piper's room is a little smaller, but it's plenty big for her needs. Much larger than the room she has at Mom and Dad's."

"Great! Then you're all set."

"I think so. I'm a little nervous about signing my life away on the lease." She rushed back through the sliding glass doors and into the living room.

Theo followed her inside. "You can afford this place, can't you? I mean, if it's okay for me to ask. If you don't want to tell me, that's fine. I understand. I know you haven't been on your new job long, and you've had a lot of expense. But even if the rent is absolutely no problem, don't think you have to take this place because I mentioned it. This surely isn't the only complex in town." He knew he sounded like a babbling idiot. He was talking and couldn't stop. "Trust me—I won't be offended if you decide to walk out the door this instant and never look back."

"Whoa! It seems you're having buyer's remorse instead of me." She placed her hands on her hips and cocked her head. "What is it? I know. You don't want me to blame you if this turns out to be a big mistake. That must be why you've had nothing but bad things to say about this apartment from the moment we walked in."

Theo thought for a moment. "You know, maybe that's it. I just didn't realize it."

"Well, you don't have to worry. I appreciate your going to all the trouble to find this place for me and now coming out here with me to check it out." She held up three fingers. "Girl Scout's honor, I promise I won't blame you if the toilet leaks or the stove doesn't work or if the neighbors argue all night."

He shuddered. "Don't even suggest such a thing. It might turn out to be a self-fulfilling prophecy." He looked toward the bathroom. "And come to think of it, you'd probably better flush the toilets and turn on the appliances, just in case."

"Oh, I'm sure everything works fine." She opened each cabinet door and looked inside as though she were a small child with her first dollhouse.

"You have fun here then. I'll go check out everything for you."

"Don't worry about it." She turned toward him and took his hands in hers. Their warmth sent a pleasant wave through him.

"I really appreciate everything you've done for Piper and me. You've gone way beyond the call of friendship. I don't know what I would have done without you."

He moved closer and put his arms around her. Though small, Lexie's body had just enough flesh on her bones so she felt soft. He wanted to kiss her, more than he ever had, a feeling he hadn't thought possible after that first night at the restaurant. Theo hoped she felt the same. He lowered his face toward hers.

Suddenly she pulled away. "Theo."

"What?" He stepped back.

"I'm sorry." She folded her arms and stared at the carpet. "It's my fault."

"What do you mean, it's your fault? I don't see anything wrong here. Aren't you happy?"

She nodded but clasped her arms more tightly around herself. "I like you. I like you a lot. But we can never be more than friends."

Why didn't she simply take a knife and lance his heart? "Okay, maybe I've been too pushy. Maybe I should have given you more space. But you don't have to give me that 'let's just be friends' line."

"It's not a line. I wish things could be different."

"But they can be."

"No, they can't." She sighed. "Look—you've been wonderful to Piper. I couldn't have asked for anyone nicer. But I also know what's important to you. You've already made it clear to me time and time again that you don't want a family. You even said you weren't sure if you wanted children at all."

"But what about the time we spent together?"

"That wasn't reality. Life is not an endless stream of free time to visit zoos and museums and have picnics," she said. "Life is getting someone else ready for day care and going to work. Then rushing out of the office to be sure Piper is picked up in time so there's no extra charge. Along with those things is the guilt I feel because I'm not doing enough at work—or at home, either. Then there're the bills. I shop at consignment and thrift stores trying to keep us looking decent, and I buy everything I can on sale. Piper gets a little Social Security check every month since Curt died, and that helps. But most of the time there is more month than money at our house."

Theo glanced around the apartment. "Maybe I shouldn't have mentioned this place."

"No. Don't think that. I'm glad you did. I have to leave Kassia's place. She's a lot like you. She wants to live the single life, to have adventure, to come and go as she pleases. Look at the situation with Brad. It was bad enough when I was the only one there; but now that Piper has joined us, I'm sure I'm cramping her style."

"I don't know about Kassia, but who said you were cramping my style? I want you in my life, but not just as a friend." As soon as the words left his mouth, he felt a mixture of relief, anticipation, regret, and angst.

Lexie looked down at the carpet for a moment.

"You say that now," she finally answered, "but no one understands the reality of raising a child unless they've done it."

"Piper is a sweet little girl. She'll be a breeze to raise, I'm sure. And what we don't know, we can learn together."

"I doubt if any child is a breeze to raise, although I have to admit Piper is pretty special," Lexie said. "But being a parent isn't the same. We can't expect to take her climbing up the Swiss Alps during the school year or parasailing in the Caribbean." She returned her gaze to the floor. "You have a right to find someone else, someone who is free to go with you, without a child, at least at the start. Then when you've had your adventures, you can have your own family together."

"So I have no say in this at all? You've made this decision based on a perception of me you formed during college?"

"No, I've made it for all of us." She blinked, her eyes moist. "We'll only hold you back. You need to pursue your dreams. Dreams you've held for a long time. If you don't, you'll only resent both of us."

"No, I won't."

"I think you will. Come on—let's go. I have to sign the papers, and I promised Kassia I wouldn't leave her with Piper too long." She retrieved her bag from the top of the stove and headed out the door before he could say another word.

Theo could see he had no choice but to follow her. If only he could make a good argument. But he knew in his heart that she spoke some truth. His life was still stuck in the post-college style. He had a house, but he occupied it like an apartment. It was temporary. "Committed" was not a word he would use to describe his life now.

I must change my life, Lord. Please guide me, he prayed.

Chapter 13

Several weeks later, Lexie was filling out a new form at work when she glimpsed Darren sauntering over to her. She hunched her shoulders over the document and stared at it in hopes he would take the hint. Since Lexie's first day on the job, Darren often stopped by her desk on some pretext. Her chilly civility, rather than turning him off, attracted him even more. Just like the authors of *The Rules* promised. If only they hadn't been right!

Ignoring her concentration, Darren leaned over her desk. "So how about a day at King's Dominion? This Saturday. It'll be fun."

Even though Lexie had been expecting Darren to ask her out for some time, she was still taken aback by his abruptness. "You get right to the point, don't you?"

"No reason not to. You never get what you don't ask for. Isn't that right?" He took a sip of coffee from his mug.

"I suppose so."

Darren seemed pleasant enough, and riding roller coasters and seeing shows would be a nice diversion. Maybe enough to keep her mind off Theo for a day.

But the diversion would come at a price. She would either have to ask Kassia to sacrifice a Saturday or come up with money she didn't have for a babysitter she hardly knew. She didn't dare ask Darren if she could bring her four-year-old, which would mean they'd have to spend the day in the children's section.

She looked at her desk calendar. Piper was supposed to be at a birthday party at three o'clock. Asking someone else to take her, or asking Piper to miss it, would be out of the question.

She shook her head. "I don't think so, but thanks."

"I won't make you ride the roller coasters if you don't want to."

"I know." She smiled. Darren and she were equals, so she knew her job wasn't on the line if she didn't accept. Still, she sensed he wasn't a man who took rejection well. "I'd really like to go, but my little girl has something going on just about every weekend."

He studied the photos on her desk. "Oh. That's your little girl? I never pictured you as a mom. I thought she was your niece or something."

"Well, I'm a mom—and proud of it." She picked up the most recent photo, a snapshot of Piper hugging Peanut Butter. Every time she saw the picture, she was reminded of Theo. She handed it to Darren so he could take a closer look.

"Yeah. She's cute," he said in a flat voice and returned the photo.

Lexie replaced it on her desk. She couldn't help but compare Darren's off-handed remark to the way Theo's eyes lit up when he saw Piper.

"I don't mind that. I'm divorced myself. My ex has custody of our boys. I didn't know you were divorced, too. I'll bet you're a lot nicer about child support than my ex." He gritted his teeth and rolled his eyes. "Maureen—that's my ex—she's constantly harassing me. I do the best I can, but she doesn't seem to understand."

"I'm sure you do. I don't have any of those issues, though."

"Oh." An embarrassed look crossed his face. "You're just a single parent? That takes some courage."

"I had a husband at one time. He went home to be with the Lord a couple of years ago."

"He went where?"

Lexie tightened her lips. "He died." She wished she could keep the unpleasant tone out of her voice.

"Oh. I thought you said he went home. Sorry." He drummed his fingers against the side of the partition. "So I guess it's okay for you to see other people now?"

"Yes."

"So how about Sunday? We can be there when the park opens."

"We try to go to church on Sundays."

A blank expression crossed his face. "Can't you skip one Sunday?"

"I don't like to. Besides, Piper—that's my little girl—enjoys Sunday school."

He stepped back. "Too bad. You can go to church any time, but I don't have every weekend open."

How am I to respond? Thank you for making time in your busy schedule to ask me out? How arrogant can you get?

Feeling that almost anything she could say would be wrong, Lexie simply smiled and turned away to concentrate on one of the many forms she needed to complete before the end of the month.

Darren left her desk quickly enough. Lexie tried to think about her work, but focusing on paperwork was difficult when all she could think about was what Darren could be telling the rest of the office about her. Maybe she should tell everyone she made it a policy not to date anyone at work. But that might fuel the gossip mill even more.

She stared at the form but saw only lines. Was her mother right? Was she betraying Curt even to be thinking about other men? Then again, Mom had warmed up to Theo during their time together.

I don't know what to think. I'm so confused.

She glanced at Darren's workstation situated on the other side of the maze of desks. He was away, probably telling his friends how snobby she was. For the hundredth time she noticed on the wall near his desk a poster of an attractive model running along the beach, a revealing bikini advertising—what? The suit? The beach? The model? She didn't want to know.

Shuddering, Lexie realized that, as attractive as Darren appeared, he had offered little to cause her to want to be with him.

But Theo did.

Ever since she'd rebuffed Theo at the apartment a few weeks ago, her heart felt as though it were leaking out a little bit of love each day, love that only he could capture and refill. But she couldn't let him.

He had wanted to kiss her. She knew it. She had wanted that kiss as well, maybe even more than he had. But she had turned him away. The hurt look in his eyes made her wish things could be different. Sure, she gave him the standard excuses—the ones that made it seem as if she were thinking only of Theo and his need for adventure. And she was. Up to a point. But she didn't want Theo to resent Piper and her. He didn't need to be tied down to her financial debt nor watch years pass before he could go on the exotic adventures he so wanted. But her own guilt—the constant guilt her mother had placed in her mind over being unfaithful to Curt—was a factor as well.

Father in heaven, am I making a mistake? Maybe the biggest mistake of my life—?

Jennifer tapped on her shoulder, startling her from her thoughts. "I hear you shot down Darren." She grinned.

Lexie moaned. "So he's already told everybody in the office?"

"He didn't tell me. Cindy did."

The biggest gossip in the office. That was just great. "What's he saying about me?"

"Who knows? Who cares? Nobody will believe him anyway. All I can say is, good for you. Ever since he got divorced, he thinks every woman in the office wants him. He'll know better now." She rapped her pen against the top of Lexie's desk. "And so will the other guys. Let's see—first you threw Theo out of your apartment. That reminds me—when are you going to set us up?"

Lexie held back a groan. Even though Theo wasn't hers, she hardly wanted to arrange a match between him and someone else.

She was thankful Jennifer was enjoying the conversation too much to dwell on the question. "So first it was Theo, now Darren. How many men does this make now that you've turned down since you got here?"

Lexie counted four in her mind, including Darren. That made almost every single man under the age of forty in the office. Modesty precluded her from giving Jennifer an exact count, so she simply shrugged.

"You must be going for the big boss."

"Mr. Brooks?" Her eyes widened. "You have to be kidding. He must be at least fifty."

"But he's rich," Jennifer pointed out.

"Thanks, but I'm not interested."

"If you're not interested, maybe I should be." She smiled, then turned to go back to her work. "Have a good weekend. If you can."

Lexie let out her breath like a sharp breeze across the stack of papers. No way would she get any more work accomplished this late in the day or in the mood she was in. She started to put away her things. Maybe she could tidy up a bit until the clock struck five.

Emily interrupted her musings. "I see you had a visit from Jen."

Lexie closed her mouth and wished she hadn't confided in Jennifer about Theo.

"What did she want, to catch some of your leftover men? You're breaking a lot of hearts, you know," Emily persisted.

Lexie glanced at her coworker. "It's nothing to joke about. I just told Darren I have plans for the weekend, and word's spread around the office already. I honestly don't need this drama. I'd simply like to come to the office every day, do my job, and go home."

"Then you'd better find something to make yourself ugly, because right now you're like a magnet."

"I wish I could laugh with you. At the rate I'm going, I won't have a male friend in the office."

"At least the women will like you." Emily watched Darren walk to his desk. "Hmm. Maybe I should find an excuse to go over to his desk and let him cry on my shoulder."

An hour later, Lexie arrived at the day-care center in the nick of time. Another minute and she would have been charged an aftercare fee. The daily stress of the thin time margin between her job and the day-care location was putting a strain on her. But Piper had already made friends, and the center was on the bus route for Piper's preschool, which helped. Changing seemed to be out of the question.

Tired from a full week, Lexie looked forward to getting home. She took Piper by the hand and was heading out the door when the center's owner stopped her. "Mrs. Zoltan, I need your payment for this month."

This month! Already? Had the time passed by so quickly?

Lexie knew writing a check for the full amount would be foolish, considering the balance in her checkbook. "I'm sorry, but I don't have the money with me today. May I bring it to you next week?"

"Mrs. Zoltan, I've let you slide this long. You must catch up, or I'm afraid—"

"I know. And you're right. I'm sorry. If you can wait until I get paid next week, I'll pay you for this month and the next."

Lexie wished she didn't have to make such a rash promise. Keeping it meant she would have to be late with her electric bill. Yet she had to make sure Piper stayed in a good day-care situation.

"All right. I can live with that."

She took Piper's hand again, drawing her away from another little girl whose mother was sure to be charged a late fee. At least Lexie had been spared that much.

"Mommy," Piper said on their way to the car, "don't we like Theo anymore?"

Lexie was used to Piper's talking about what happened in preschool that day. The question about Theo took her by surprise. A tear formed in her eye. She managed to wipe it away before Piper could notice. Lexie turned her head and pretended to study the summer sky, then hurried Piper into the car, hoping she might forget her question.

"Well? Do we?" Piper persisted.

Lexie started the car. "Of course we do. What makes you ask such a silly thing?"

"We never see him anymore—that's what. He's supposed to help me find more rocks."

"I know, honey. But Theo is just a friend of ours. He was there for us when we needed him. But now we can't expect him to come over every single day."

"But can't he come over sometimes?"

"Maybe. We'll see."

"That means no."

Lexie was thankful she spotted a fast-food restaurant at that moment. She pointed to the colorful sign. "Look. Want a hamburger?"

Piper clapped her hands. "Yay!"

Lexie pulled in to the parking lot, choosing the drive-through so she could take the food home. A glass of water at home was cheaper than a beverage at the restaurant.

As they waited in the long line, Piper hummed a little song to herself. Lexie wiped away another tear and wished she were happy enough to sing.

Why am I so weepy?

She fumbled through the ashtray, which she used to hold her spare change. Enough had accumulated for her to pay for dinner.

Money. Why does everything have to be about money? *Because I don't have enough—that's why.*

She mentally reviewed her financial situation. Social Security checks had been arriving for Piper since Curt's death, but of course they weren't enough to cover their living expenses. The most worrisome at present were mounting credit card bills. She had been putting the minimum toward them each month, which was enough to keep those creditors from calling her at work or at home. But she had failed to pay anything on two other bills the past month. And interest on the debt kept her from making much progress toward paying off the bills.

But how could she ever hope to catch up? Food, rent, and utilities had to come first. Living with Kassia had helped initially, but that could never have been permanent. Not as long as she wanted Piper to be with her.

She took a moment to listen to her daughter's excited voice. So much time had passed since Lexie had been that happy. Not since—

No. She wouldn't think about Theo. He hadn't called since that day at the apartment. By now he had probably forgotten about her. Maybe he was sitting on the beach at that moment. Maybe he'd already met someone else. Maybe they were sharing an umbrella, drinking ice cold drinks, laughing together—

No. I can't think about it. I set him free—practically threw him out on his ear. He has every right to go wherever he wants, to see anybody he wants to see. He deserves better than to be stuck dealing with my problems.

Lexie added the numbers in her head. Even with the new apartment, her salary at work and Piper's checks should have provided enough. They'd never live in luxury on their income, but they should be able to live well enough. With a little bit of money management.

Money management. That was something she had never mastered. Finances had always been tight for Mom and Dad, which meant Lexie knew how to shop for her needs on a slim budget. She had picked up a few tricks by watching them, but she still couldn't understand how Mom managed to turn an old chicken carcass into a delicious soup that could last a week or make a pair of socks last forever. She did remember one big piece of advice. Dad said that a new car smell was the most expensive perfume in the world.

The car payment! How could she have forgotten? The long white envelope was sitting on her desk at home, waiting to be stuffed with the month's check that was due in three days, a week before her next paycheck would arrive.

Maybe she should write the check and "forget" to sign it. Or she could tell the company that the statement got lost in the mail.

Dear Father in heaven, have I become so desperate? I know You'll find a way. I don't have to dishonor You to meet my bills.

"Help!" she whispered.

"What, Mommy?" Piper asked from the backseat.

The child who couldn't hear her mother ask her to pick up her toys could hear a softly spoken prayer.

"Nothing, honey." She pulled up behind the car in front of her, which had just moved up so Lexie could take her turn at ordering from the menu. She rolled down the window. "One child's meal. Hamburger. That's it."

Lexie hardly felt like eating, so what was the point of ordering anything for herself? Instead she thought about how to solve her car payment problem. She had to keep the car so she could drive to her job. She had to get help from somewhere.

Theo's face flashed through her mind.

No. I won't call him, especially not after the way I've treated him. I'll call Kassia. She's smart. She'll know what to do.

❧

Theo heard his phone ring as he was about to sit in front of the television with a cup of tomato soup. He'd been engaged in mind-numbing paperwork all day at the office and was in no mood to explain to a telemarketer that he didn't need replacement windows, a heating system checkup, or a free trip to some exotic locale just for listening to a brief sales presentation.

He glanced at his watch. Six in the evening. Yep, it had to be a telemarketer. Who else would call at dinner? Theo remained in his chair, turned up the volume on the TV, and swallowed a spoonful of soup.

He listened to the announcement on his answering machine, then heard the beep.

"Theo, if you're there, pick up."

"Kassia?" he exclaimed as if she could hear him. "What are you doing calling me?"

"Okay," Kassia said. "I guess you're not there. Umm...listen, when—"

He scrambled to reach the phone. "Hey, Kassia. I'm here."

"Screening your calls, eh?"

"I thought you were a telemarketer."

"When are you going to join us in the twenty-first century and get caller ID?"

"As if that would help. It would just read 'out of area' for most of those unknown callers, and I'd still be screening my messages."

"Well, you have a point, but it works great the rest of the time."

"Now if you were planning to sell me caller ID or anything else, for that matter, I'd be forced to hang up."

"After I finish, you'll probably wish I were selling vacuum cleaners."

Theo set down his soup, bracing himself for what was certain to be bad news. "What's wrong?"

"It's Lexie."

"Lexie?" His heart seemed to skip a beat. "Is she all right?"

"Yes."

"Oh, no. Something's happened to Piper."

"No, it's nothing like that," Kassia assured him. "Calm down."

His voice turned serious. "How do you expect me to react when you call and act like the world's ended? And if it's not an emergency, why isn't Lexie calling me herself?"

"She's too embarrassed," Kassia said. "She doesn't even know I'm calling you. She'd probably kill me if she knew."

He had a thousand questions, and he wanted answers to them all. "So what's up?"

"It's her car. She's behind on her payments, and now the finance company is threatening to repossess it."

Theo couldn't suppress a laugh. "That pile of junk? I can't believe they'd bother."

"I know. But apparently they are bothering. And they've started calling her at work and at home."

"No wonder she's embarrassed," Theo agreed. "I guessed she wasn't in the best financial shape, but I had no idea things were that bad."

"Neither did I. Apparently she got into the apartment you suggested before things got out of hand. She called me earlier. I could tell she was crying, but she wouldn't admit it. This is really serious, Theo. If she doesn't have a car, how can she get to work?"

"How long have they given her to pay?"

"I'm not sure."

"Why did she call you? Did she ask for money?" He hoped Kassia would answer in the affirmative. Theo could lend, or even give, Lexie a few hundred dollars to get her out of such a predicament if necessary.

"She didn't ask, but I offered a couple of hundred dollars. That's all I can spare at the moment. She wouldn't take it," Kassia said. "She only wanted advice."

"What did you tell her?"

"I didn't know what to say. I told her things were bound to get better. As soon as I hung up the phone, I called you."

"I'm glad you did."

"Don't tell her you heard from me, okay?"

Theo wasn't sure how he would manage that, but he'd figure out a way. "Sure. But I'm not sure what you want me to do."

Kassia didn't answer right away. "I don't know. Just check on her, I guess. See how she's doing. Maybe if you do, she'll open up."

"Maybe so." Theo remembered how he had been in prayer for Kassia. "Speaking of opening up, how are things with Brad?"

"What's that supposed to mean?" Kassia's voice was sharp.

"Nothing. I just wondered if you'd like to talk about it."

"There's nothing to talk about," Kassia snapped. "And I'm in no mood for a lecture. I've had plenty of advice from her, thank you very much."

Whatever Lexie said must have hit a nerve with Kassia. Theo decided levity was the only way to go. "Did you ever see the T-shirt slogan that says, 'I yell because I care'? Well, Lexie and I lecture because we care."

"Very funny."

"Throw that stone down, Kassia. Remember—you're the one who called me about Lexie, and you didn't even tell her first."

Kassia groaned. "Why can't I talk to either one of you without feeling thumped by a Bible?"

"Maybe God's trying to tell you something."

"If He is, I'm not sure I like it very much."

"I don't like everything He tells me, either."

"Really?" Kassia sounded surprised. "I can't believe that. Not as devout as you are."

"I can't vouch for what other people have found out, but in my experience the more I sense the Lord's presence with me, the more He seems to communicate with me. Maybe it's just that I can hear Him better."

"That sounds like something you'd say," she answered. "Anyway, if it makes you happy, I'll have you know I'm not seeing Brad."

"That's probably a good thing."

"Whatever. See you later."

Before Theo could respond, Kassia hung up.

Normally he might have called Kassia back and apologized, but Lexie's situation was more urgent at the moment. Theo didn't waste time. He gulped down his soup and decided against the pint of ice cream he'd planned for dessert. Instead he logged on to his computer and stretched his fingers. If knowledge was power, Lexie would be fully armed if he had anything to say about it.

Chapter 14

Lexie was about to tuck Piper into bed when the doorbell rang. The little girl jumped out of bed and ran to the door, all the while shouting, "We have company! We have company!"

"Shh, Piper," Lexie told her. She wanted to look through the peephole and see who it was before opening the door. Now that Piper had yelled loudly enough for the neighbors in the surrounding apartments to hear, ignoring their caller was no longer an option.

Theo! What's he doing here?

"Who is it, Mommy?" Piper asked.

"You'll see." Lexie turned the deadbolt and opened the door.

Piper gasped. "Theo!"

Without hesitation she ran into his arms. Lexie couldn't believe how natural they seemed together.

Theo nodded at Lexie, then spoke to the child. "Hey, how's my little archaeologist?"

"Arkee—arkee." She wrinkled her nose. "Huh?"

"Archaeologist. They dig in the ground to find neat things like rocks."

"But I find things, and I don't dig in the ground." Her head turned in Lexie's direction. "Can I dig in the ground, Mommy? I'll find lots more rocks then."

Lexie groaned. "I'm sure you will, but you can find plenty of rocks without digging." She smiled and shook her head at Theo. "Did you have to give her more ideas?"

"Sorry." Theo chuckled. "Here's an idea, Piper. Shouldn't you be in bed by now?"

"No! Mommy was gonna read me a story," Piper said. "But now you can read it with us. Like you did at Grammy's."

Piper had missed Theo as much as she had! If a heart could flip-flop and melt all at once, Lexie's heart did at that moment. "Piper! Just because Theo's here doesn't mean he has to do whatever you want him to."

Theo bowed to Piper as though she were a princess. "If your wish is for me to read a story to you with your mom, then your wish is my command, young lady."

"If you want to do that, you'll have to come in," Lexie said over Piper's laughter. She opened the door wider and watched Theo enter. Her heart betrayed her with its rapid beating. "It's been awhile. Where have you been?"

"Where have I been?" Theo gave her a questioning look, then shrugged before offering an answer. "Work. Home. Same old treadmill."

"Me, too. I'm glad you stopped by," she ventured.

"Really?" His voice was little more than a whisper.

She nodded. "It's nice to have a break."

"Oh."

Seeing his crestfallen expression, Lexie touched the top of his hand for a moment. Her fingertips tingled at the slight contact. "I'm really glad you came by."

"Then so am I."

Lexie made coffee for the two of them, then gave Piper a bedtime snack of milk and an apple. Theo talked about nothing in particular; yet she found his conversation pleasant. As usual they agreed on everything that mattered. Since she'd been working in the office, Lexie realized the rarity of an agreeable friend.

Was his visit a peace offering? Or did he have some other reason for stopping by?

Lexie glanced at her watch. "Well, I can't believe it, but it's after eight." She shook her finger playfully at Piper. "It really is bedtime for you now. Way past your bedtime, in fact."

"Story! Story!" she called out, then dashed into her room.

Lexie stood. If Theo sought a relationship other than friends, she couldn't offer him that. And allowing him to linger after Piper was asleep was too risky—for them both. "Guess I have the rest of the night planned out for me."

"Don't you mean for us?"

"Us?"

He stared at her. "I promised to help read the story, remember? If I don't, she'll never forgive me."

Lexie wished she could think of a good reason to insist he leave, but she couldn't. "True. Piper has a long memory."

"Come on!" Piper shouted from her room. "I picked out a story."

"I hope it's not *Green Eggs and Ham* again," Lexie whispered as they both headed for the little girl's room. "As much as I like Dr. Seuss, I don't think I can take another night of the same thing."

Lexie was relieved to discover Piper had chosen *The Three Little Pigs*.

"But this story doesn't have a princess," Theo teased.

"I know. But I want to see you be the Big Bad Wolf."

"But I want to be the Big Bad Wolf," Lexie complained.

Piper shook her head. "I'll bet you aren't as good as Theo. Isn't the Big Bad Wolf a boy?"

"I suppose," Lexie agreed.

"We don't always have a boy here to be the Big Bad Wolf."

Lexie felt both grief and regret at her daughter's statement, but Piper's little face didn't change expression. Funny how children could say things and not seem to feel the same effects as the adults around them. Lexie supposed such obliviousness was a gift.

Theo and Lexie sat on each side of Piper and put on a show for the delighted little girl. Lexie read the parts of the three little pigs, and Theo gave an enthusiastic portrayal of the Big Bad Wolf. His voice was gruff when he spoke. He inhaled with gusto as he promised to blow down each house.

Despite protests from Piper that they should read another story, Lexie convinced her there was always tomorrow night.

"Time for prayers." Lexie and Piper knelt beside her bed as usual. Lexie realized she might have been shy kneeling in front of anyone else, but she didn't mind Theo's presence. When he joined them, she felt closer to him than ever.

Lord, I wish things were different. I wish I could be the wife Theo needs. But I still wouldn't give up my little girl for anything. Not even Theo.

Lexie only half listened to Piper's familiar recitation thanking God for a long list of friends and family—until she heard Theo's name. Opening her eyes, she glanced at Theo and saw a sad smile on his face.

As they stepped out of the room, Lexie deliberately set a light mood. "Ever thought of going into theater?"

"Only if I can be the Big Bad Wolf," he replied. "Or maybe Prince Charming."

"You'd have no problem with either of those roles." As soon as the words left her lips, Lexie wished she could take them back. She had promised herself she would do nothing to encourage Theo. So why did everything she say seem to contain the underlying message that she wanted to be with him?

She didn't sit down when they reached the living room. Her heart didn't want Theo to leave, but her head overruled. "Well, I have a big day tomorrow, and so do you, I'm sure."

"I guess so. At least it's past Hump Day."

"Hump Day?"

Theo's eyes widened. "You've never heard of Hump Day? It's Wednesday, of course. We've gotten over the hump of the work week."

"Oh. I guess I probably heard that somewhere before. I'd just forgotten." She folded her arms and tried to think of another excuse to urge him to move on, but nothing came to mind. Apparently she was stuck with company for a while longer. Not that she minded.

"Piper and I made some brownies yesterday. Want one?" she offered.

"Sure—why not?" He plopped down on the sofa as though he belonged. Studying him, she realized he fit well into the picture.

"How about a soda, too?" he asked.

"I don't know. I'm afraid that might not be enough sugar for you." Nevertheless, she headed toward the refrigerator to fulfill his wish.

"I doubt it."

Lexie searched for the last soda she thought she had saved. "Looks like it's milk for you. I ran out of soda. Sorry."

"Is this a conspiracy?"

"Maybe it is." She smiled at him and poured a glass of skim milk instead. "This will go better with a brownie anyway."

He bit into the square. "Mmm. You and Piper make a good team."

"I know. Sometimes I feel as if it's just the two of us against everybody else."

"Against everybody? How can you say that? You have lots of friends and family to support you."

"Emotionally, yes." She crossed her arms over her chest, a gesture she knew looked defensive, but she didn't stop herself. "And financially, too."

"Are you sure about that?"

"So that's what this visit is all about? You're afraid I can't handle the rent on this apartment, and you've come to make sure I'm still living here?" She kept her voice light and teasing, though she knew Theo would see the truth in her words.

"I'm sure you can handle anything. You've done better than I would have in your position, with the move, getting settled in a place you haven't lived in a long time, and now getting Piper settled in."

"It's been a struggle, but we manage."

"Are you sure?"

She set her own brownie on the side table. "Okay. Spill it. What do you know?"

"Is there anything to know?"

Lexie had confided in only one person who knew Theo. "Kassia. You've talked to her, haven't you?"

"What makes you say that?"

"The fact that you answer every question with a question, that's what." She narrowed her lips. "So what did she tell you?"

"Now don't get mad at her. She's just concerned, that's all."

Lexie's stomach suddenly felt like a ball of lead. So Kassia had run to Theo and told him her troubles. "Tell me what she said."

"She just hinted that you're having a little bit of difficulty meeting your bills."

"Well, I have to admit—that's an understatement. I'm not doing too bad, really, except right now I'm worried about the car. I got behind on my payments, and now they want to take it. I'm not too proud to take a bus to work, but having to drop off Piper and pick her up from day care is the problem. I really need a car if I want to function with any efficiency." Lexie realized she was babbling. "But why did Kassia tell you? It's not your problem."

"She thought I could help. And I can. Well, sort of." He lifted his forefinger in a way that reminded her of a teacher. "Did you know that some day-care centers are funded by a charitable organization? Others are subsidized by the government."

Lexie remembered how much money she owed Piper's center. She shuddered at the mess she had made for herself. "I don't guess our center is subsidized. No one said anything."

"Do they know you're a single mother?"

She nodded. "I had to put all the information on the emergency contact form."

"Then they should. Maybe they just didn't pay enough attention to your form. But as far as I know, you're eligible to apply for low-cost daycare since you're a single mother," he said. "Who knows? You might even be able to get good care for free."

"Free?" Lexie didn't like the idea of charity, but she was in no position to be picky. "Really? I had no idea. But how did you know?"

"One of our secretaries is a single mother. We took her out to lunch for Secretaries' Day, and she was talking about how she had to get subsidized day care. She said she didn't know how she'd make ends meet without help."

"I'll definitely look into that. Thanks, Theo."

"Problem solved then." A big grin spread across his handsome face.

"I wish! Sure—if I'm able to get help with day-care expenses, that would be great. But that's only part of the picture. I have other bills, and I'm way behind."

"On more than just the car?"

She nodded. "I'm afraid so."

"You're not making the minimum payment each month, are you?"

"I try to pay a little more, but it's hard."

Theo gulped, a gesture that left Lexie embarrassed.

"I don't want to talk about it. Let's change the subject."

"Changing the subject won't make it go away. Let me help you if I can."

"I don't see how you can help any more than you already have." Lexie rose from her seat and took her plate into the kitchen. Their discussion seemed to be degenerating into an argument, something she didn't want to happen. She had argued too often about money with Curt. Why was she repeating the pattern with Theo—even if he was just a friend?

"My dad's a banker, and I learned a lot from him. Maybe I can help you sort things out. For instance, do you buy things on sale?"

Now she had him. Lexie strode toward the couch and sat beside him. "I certainly do. In fact, I buy almost everything on sale. I make sure to use plenty of coupons at the grocery store."

"That's great, but I don't just mean food. I mean clothes and things like that."

"Of course. Why, just this week I bought a new pair of shoes on sale. In fact, it was a sale with an additional 20 percent off." She was certain he would agree she was a smart shopper.

"That's great. But you charged them."

How did he know? "Yes." She almost blurted out that she didn't visit the consignment shop because she didn't have the cash. Perhaps the shoe purchase could have waited; but they were perfect for work and church, and the sale had been too good to resist. "My church shoes have some wear on them, and I have to keep my wardrobe looking halfway decent for work."

"I know. You have to present yourself well if you want to hold an office job," Theo agreed. "But if you buy things on sale and pay the credit card companies interest on what you buy, you're not saving the first cent."

Lexie didn't answer right away. She hadn't thought of it that way. "I guess you have a point."

"I hope you don't mind my saying so, but the first thing you should do is pay off as many of those cards as you can."

"I would if I could."

"You could use your savings. You'd still be ahead on interest, unless you have some kind of deal I don't know about."

"Sorry. My savings are gone."

"You were married awhile. Did you and Curt buy any real estate, maybe a piece of land in North Carolina you could sell now?"

"If only we had. No, we always rented." The next part was difficult to say, but Lexie had to tell him. "Curt's funeral expenses ate up everything we had accumulated, which wasn't much. I couldn't believe how much everything cost."

"Oh, that explains it then."

Lexie looked at him. "That explains why I seem so irresponsible?"

"You don't seem irresponsible. Who would have thought you'd have to even be thinking about a funeral for your husband at your age?"

Lexie nodded and looked down. She turned away and grabbed a tissue from the box on the side table. Maybe if she wiped her eyes now, she could keep tears from falling and mascara from running.

She was so absorbed in getting the tissue that she didn't realize Theo had moved closer to her. He put his arm around her shoulder. His arm felt warm, protective. Close like that, she could smell his citrus cologne. As she inhaled the pleasant aroma, she felt as though she had arrived at a familiar place. A place she liked.

"I'm sorry. I know it's painful still for you to talk about Curt. And it probably always will be. Especially because of Piper. My heart goes out to both of you." His voice, barely above a whisper, offered comfort.

So he thought of Piper, not just me.

She patted his hand. "Thank you."

He squeezed her shoulders, then moved back until their gazes met. "I have an idea. You say you and Curt never owned a house, right?"

"You say that like it's a good thing."

"It might be," he said eagerly. "All you have to do is exercise a little bit of discipline and pay off your cards, or at least get the balances manageable. Then I can ask my dad about finding a home loan for you. First-time home buyers get a lot of breaks, especially if they don't make much money. You won't be able to buy a mansion, but something reasonable in a good neighborhood will help you in many ways."

Lexie raised her hands. "That sounds great, but hold on. I don't think you understand. I'll never qualify for any kind of loan with my credit as it stands now. Not counting what I owe on my car, I'm more than ten thousand dollars in debt."

"Ten thousand dollars?" Theo's eyes widened, and he took in so much air Lexie thought he might suck all the oxygen out of the room. "You're kidding."

"I wish I were. The only reason I could get in this place is because Mom cashed in a CD that was due and loaned me the money for the security deposit. I'll be paying her back—with interest."

She watched as he looked around her apartment. The furniture was a mishmash of castoffs, rentals, and pieces of cheap veneer that Curt had assembled himself. "I know. It's hard to believe I owe so much, isn't it? I sure don't have a thing to show for it. Except a decent burial for Curt."

"I'm sorry. I didn't mean to seem as if I were passing judgment," Theo said. "You've had some tough breaks. I can only imagine what that's been like for you."

"That's okay. I don't expect anyone to understand if they haven't been through it."

"I wish I could write a check for the whole amount and make your money problems disappear like that." He snapped his fingers. "But I can't."

She took his hand in hers and squeezed it gently. "I appreciate that. I really do. But even if you could, I wouldn't accept your money. I don't need a knight in shining armor." Fresh tears betrayed her, flowing down her cheeks. "Theo, I don't know how I'll ever be a good mother to Piper. At least, not the mother she deserves. She deserves a responsible woman, someone who has everything all together. She doesn't need someone who's made such a mess of her life, like me."

"I wouldn't say that."

"Don't try to defend me," she said. "When I first came here, I thought that with the salary I was making I'd be in good shape in less than six months. But I hadn't counted on everything being so expensive or Piper's going to the hospital or our having to move out of Kassia's place so soon. I don't own a thing of value, really. Even the couch you're sitting on is rented."

"That's nothing to be ashamed of."

"I'm not ashamed. It's just that, well, I came here in part because I didn't want to depend on my parents so much. After Curt died, Mom kept Piper for me so I could work. I was living rent free, too. I see now that I didn't know what a good deal I had. I guess I never grew up. I'm beginning to think I never will."

"Yes, you will. You're just finding out—a little late in the game—that the price of independence is high. But maybe it's not as high as you think." He thought for a moment. "What about insurance? Maybe Curt left you some money you don't even know about."

Lexie cried even more at Theo's suggestion. "He didn't have any insurance. There was no money when he died."

"What?" His face was flushed. "How could he have been so irresponsible? He knew he worked in a hazardous field and that you had Piper to take care of!" He let out a sharp breath. "You know something? Since that accident was work-related, the construction company should have offered you a settlement at least. If they didn't, I think you should hire a lawyer first thing tomorrow."

"No, it's not like that at all." She placed her hand on his arm. "Curt's death had nothing to do with the construction company. It was my fault."

"What did you say?"

Lexie swiped at her eyes. She had given up on not smudging her makeup. She could only imagine what she must look like, with brown mascara and gray eye shadow running down her face. "It's true. It's my fault he died. Neither one of us was good at managing money. No matter how much Curt earned, we barely got by. We never could get ahead. We both wanted what was best for Piper, so she could grow up and have a nice childhood. We didn't want her to remember us scrimping on everything and fighting about money—which we did all the time. I even thought if things got better, we might have another baby." She paused. Making such a confession to Theo seemed strange. She almost wished she hadn't.

"That's only natural," he said without rancor in his voice or face. "Everyone wants what's best for their families."

"Well, I went too far. I suggested that Curt start his own business. At first he resisted, but the more we talked about it, the better of an idea it seemed to be. Then, when he started not getting along with his boss, I insisted. At first he was happy being his own boss. But soon we found out owning a business wasn't Easy Street as we'd thought. He freelanced and took whatever jobs he could. He didn't always win the bid for the work, and the paperwork required to put in all those bids consumed a lot of time for nothing. Everything was so insecure. The work wasn't as regular as we'd expected it to be. Then when we got walloped with more taxes than we anticipated, plus insurance bills for our employees, we were in a mess. We were beaten emotionally, physically, and financially."

"The construction industry was booming, though. He couldn't get his old job back?"

"No. He was in competition with them on several small jobs."

"Since he didn't like his boss, they probably wouldn't have taken him back anyway."

"That's what Curt thought," she agreed.

"So you weren't working?"

"I tried to find something, but the salaries I was offered were too low to justify the expense of working. I was too proud to ask Mom to take care of Piper for me. So Curt took a second job with no benefits. The day of the accident Curt was functioning on four hours' sleep. I think if he hadn't worked so hard, he'd be alive today. I wish I hadn't pushed him so much. I wish I hadn't been so greedy." By now her tears had turned to sobs.

"Don't be so hard on yourself. Curt was a grown man, and he made his own decisions to work so much. You didn't force him."

Regret washed over Lexie. Curt would have died a thousand more times if he could have witnessed her spilling every bad thing about their lives to Theo. "I didn't mean to tell you so much. Curt would have a fit if he knew. He always was afraid of you, you know."

"Afraid of me?"

"He thought you were too much competition. I tried to tell him we were just friends."

"Are we? Are we really just friends?" Theo's voice held no expression.

Lexie's heart skipped a beat.

"I think we are more than friends, and I think you believe that, too." He leaned closer to her. "What are you afraid of, Lexie?"

What was she afraid of? So many things.

She drew in a breath. "I won't ruin your life the way I did Curt's. I want you to leave. And don't bother calling. For your sake, please don't call again."

He rose from the couch. Standing tall, he turned toward her and looked her in the eyes. Lexie held her gaze steady. She couldn't falter. Not now.

Please go. Just go!

The words she screamed in her head refused to leave her mouth.

"I know I came here uninvited tonight. I know I'm the one who's been pursuing you. But I don't believe you don't want to see me again."

She stood. "You're wrong. Just plain wrong."

Theo looked into her eyes. "Am I?"

Theo drew her toward him and wrapped her in his arms in one quick motion. Even though his gesture took her by surprise, he was neither forceful nor demanding. Instead his arms around her felt—natural. As natural as Curt's.

No. I can't.

She wanted to voice her protests but couldn't, not with Theo's lips pressing against hers with a fervor she had forgotten could happen between a man and a woman. As her initial resistance gave way, she softened, dissolving into his embrace as though she were destined to be his forever.

She returned the kiss, her lips touching his clean-shaven face and his mouth that was both soft and strong. How long had she been waiting for this moment?

She was about to savor another kiss when, without warning, he pulled back. "I'm sorry."

Sorry? She wasn't sorry.

"I shouldn't have. I–I have to go."

"But—"

Theo shook his head. "I'll talk to you later."

She reached out to grasp his shirtsleeve but missed.

He had moved fast. And now he was gone.

Chapter 15

The following weekend, Theo looked at the telephone for the hundredth time. He was due to arrive at the church clothes closet at noon; he had volunteered to help with it the second Saturday of every month. The time was almost eleven. If he called Lexie now, he might slip in an invitation to dinner.

"No," he muttered. "I can't call her. I already took advantage of her."

The image of their kiss entered his thoughts. He wished Lexie were there, so he could touch her, hold her, as he'd wanted to for so long. He was sorry he had given in to his longing, a longing he had felt ever since seeing her again. Then again he wasn't sorry. For no matter how many times she told him to get out of her life, he would have the memory of her sweet kiss.

"No. I can't think about her."

He looked at the phone one last time. Resisting the urge to call, he shook his head and hurried out the front door, shutting it behind him.

Lexie sat at her kitchen table and stared at the bills that begged for her attention. How would she manage to get by this time? The juggling act was growing harder and harder.

"Here it is, Saturday night, and instead of getting out of the house and having a good time, I'm alone with a mountain of paperwork, wondering how I'll get by," she mumbled.

At times like this she missed Kassia. Her old roommate would have taken her by the arm and insisted they go out for a few minutes—if only to eat a fast-food meal. Or they would escape with a rented movie. At a bare minimum, Kassia would offer a few moments of adult conversation.

Her gaze rested on the nearby phone. Ever since Theo had kissed her, a picture of him was not far from her thoughts. If she harbored any doubts that Theo wanted to be more than friends before, his kiss left no doubt in her mind now. No man had affected her this way since Curt.

Curt. What would he think about Theo? She knew the answer. He would want her to be happy. But did she deserve happiness, after her greed caused his death?

Father in heaven, thank You for forgiving me! But, Lord, can You help me forgive myself?

If only she could take her mind from her unwelcome thoughts. Maybe if she stared at the phone long enough, it would ring. And maybe if she added a wish, the caller would be Theo.

"Yeah. And maybe if I kiss the blarney stone, I'll attract a leprechaun—and if he doesn't trick me instead, he'll show me the pot of gold at the end of the rainbow."

Piper interrupted her musings. "What's a leprechaun?"

"A leprechaun is a—oh, never mind what he is."

"Is there a pot of gold at the end of the rainbow?"

"Only in the minds of those who wish it were so," Lexie told her. "That's just an old legend."

"Can we look for it the next time we see a rainbow?"

Lexie laughed. "The trick is, no one can find the end of a rainbow."

"We can try!" Piper insisted.

"Honey, if you show that much determination in all your efforts, you'll be a great success in life. And you'll also succeed if you get enough sleep. So I want to know why you're up at this time of night. You're supposed to be in bed."

"But I'm thirsty."

"You can drink some water from the cup in the bathroom."

"But I don't want water. I want lemonade."

"It's too late for all that sugar. Go to bed, please."

Piper's mouth formed a pout. "You're always grumpy when you read the mail. I hate the mail."

"Some days I don't like it much, either." She stretched out her arms for a hug. Piper ran into her arms and shared a brief embrace. "Now can I have a glass of lemonade?"

"I'm sorry—but I said no, and I mean it. Now run along to bed as I told you. Mommy's busy."

"Okay."

"Remember—it's 'yes, ma'am.' "

"Yes, ma'am." Her shoulders drooped, along with her voice. "Mommy?"

"Yes?"

"I miss Theo. You were happy when he was around."

Piper's observation tugged at Lexie's heart and mind. "I know, honey."

"Can you invite him over?"

"Maybe sometime. Now go to bed."

Piper nodded and headed back to her room. Lexie wished Piper didn't have to go to bed, even if their conversation centered on lemonade. She returned to the stack of papers.

At least she could claim one small victory. Because she had always been prompt in the past with her car payments, the bank had agreed to wait another month, but that was it. If she didn't come up with the payments this time, she could kiss her old car good-bye.

And then there was the day-care center. She had to bring her payments with that up-to-date, too. Theo was right. The price of independence was high.

Theo. She wished he hadn't left. In her heart she had wanted him to protest, to insist he'd never leave her side, no matter what. But why should he have stayed? She had been nothing but rude to him, even though he had spent the evening entertaining Piper, then giving her the best advice and help he could to get her out of this mess. Now she didn't even have his friendship. And it was all her fault.

Under normal circumstances she could call Kassia, but she hadn't spoken to her since Theo's visit. Kassia had betrayed her by running to Theo with the whole story. Sure, she thought she was doing Lexie a favor, but she had only made things worse.

Lord, why do I keep creating chaos in my life? I can't keep money in my pocket or friends by my side. Is it my guilt?

The answer came to her.

The guilt is just an excuse. Your false pride is holding you back.

She recalled a verse from Proverbs. *"Pride only breeds quarrels, but wisdom is found in those who take advice."*

The truth of those words struck her.

When she refused to listen to Theo, they argued. And why didn't she want to listen to him? Pride. Her pride didn't want her to admit she was struggling. Theo only wanted to help, and what did she do? Ask him to leave her apartment—the same apartment he had found for her. And what about Kassia? She had shown Lexie nothing but kindness, and what was her reward? To listen to Lexie's judgment of her and then be cut off after she asked Theo to help.

Lexie knew she'd had to tell Kassia how she felt about her behavior with Brad. Even though Kassia promised she hadn't let Brad go too far that night at the apartment, their public display of affection at the restaurant made them seem too close for a couple on their first date. In hindsight, Lexie saw she should have been more loving in the way she'd spoken to Kassia. She wished she hadn't let her anger control her. Spiritual pride must have made her arrogant.

Lord, will You help me overcome this pride?

❧

Theo couldn't keep his mind on the article he was trying to read in *The Richmond Times-Dispatch*. The machinations of the latest events in the Middle East were complicated enough to require his full attention, so he couldn't hope to glean much from the article unless he concentrated.

His gaze drifted from the article to an ad for a diamond ring. He thought of Lexie's left ring finger, now bare. He couldn't help but wonder if she would enjoy wearing a ring with three diamonds, representing the past, present, and future.

He had abandoned Lexie. She was alone now, with no one to help her sort out the mess she had made of her finances.

"Maybe I was a little bossy," he mumbled. "Maybe that's what turned her off."

The phone rang. It was a little after eight. Didn't the sales calls ever end? Or maybe it was his boss, hoping to pile on extra work. Since Theo was single, everyone seemed to assume he had no life outside work and would be glad to devote plenty of unpaid overtime to the job. Well, they were wrong. Dead wrong. In fact, the previous night he'd gone to a movie with a bunch of the guys. And as soon as he arrived home every day, he took a nice, long jog and often lifted weights.

Then again there he was, staring at a newspaper he didn't want to read, refusing to answer the phone to avoid a sales call and watching the neighborhood kids run through his yard. Maybe his coworkers were right. Maybe he didn't have much of a life. At the same time, mothers and grandmothers of grown women looked upon him as a catch. They were always hinting around, wondering if he had a girlfriend. If only they knew. Would they think he was such a great catch if they could have witnessed Lexie asking him to leave her apartment?

His mood now foul, Theo listened to his message play on the machine. The caller hung up without a word.

Must have been a salesperson after all. His mother would never hang up, and neither would his friends. Not even Lexie.

Lexie. Was there ever a second when he didn't think about her?

For one moment he had thought he might have a second chance at a life he could be proud of. A chance to show love to Lexie and to be the father her little girl so desperately needed.

"Looks as if that's not going to happen," he muttered.

The phone rang again. This time he answered, snarling a greeting into the receiver.

"Hi. Did I call at a bad time?"

"Lexie!"

"I can call back later." Her voice was enough to cheer him.

"No," he protested. "That's fine. I'm fine. What's up?"

"Oh, I don't know. What's up with you?"

"Nothing much. Just reading the paper." If Lexie had called for a reason, she was having trouble expressing it. Not that he was showing himself to be a great conversationalist, either.

"Hey, I was thinking—I want you to know I'm sorry about the other night."

Theo let out his breath. "I'm sorry, too."

"You were just trying to help. I see that now. Actually I saw it then, but I guess I was too caught up in pride to listen."

"Don't lay all the blame on yourself. I was being my usual bossy self."

She chuckled. "Well, boss, would you care to make up over a cup of coffee sometime? I'd invite you out to a café, but I'm afraid I can't afford a sitter for Piper. Wait. Let me rephrase that." She cleared her throat. "In light of my current financial situation and my efforts to strive toward total financial freedom, I am choosing not to afford a sitter at this time."

"You sound as if you're reading a self-help book. I'm impressed."

"I'm not really. It's a compilation of advice from a lot of books I've been reading lately. I developed a list of guidelines for myself. For instance, instead of saying I can't afford something I want, I say I'm choosing not to afford it. That makes me feel less deprived. So far it's helped. But making up the list was a lot more fun than trying to live by my new rules," she added.

"It's only been a week and a half," he pointed out.

A very, very long week and a half. A week and a half without you.

Aloud he added, "You're not giving up already, are you?"

"I'm trying not to get discouraged. I did have one side benefit, though. Instead of buying them over the Internet or in a store, I went to the library to check out the financial books—"

"Good for you!"

"Thanks. Going into a bookstore is trouble for me. I always end up buying far more than I intend."

"Me, too," he admitted. "So what was your side benefit?"

"Piper wasn't interested in visiting the library before, but when we started going, I let her check out some books. She can't believe she can borrow all those books. Now she begs to go back."

"That's great! Isn't it funny how situations that upset us so much can end up having a silver lining?"

"Sometimes."

The pensive tone in Lexie's voice took Theo by surprise. What was she thinking?

"So can you come by after work?"

"I wish I could, but I have a church committee meeting. How about after that? It shouldn't run too late."

"Sounds great. Maybe I can fix you a bite to eat?"

"Sure! I never turn down a home cooked meal. Even a sandwich."

❧

The following evening, Theo was glad to sit on the couch with such a beautiful companion. The rusty color of her blouse was a tone he hadn't thought contemporary women would consider fashionable, since it was a throwback to past decades. He'd noticed women favoring rust-colored clothing and wondered why they let designers tell them to wear that shade. Yet no one looked as good in the color as Lexie. The blouse, with a pointed collar—another reminder of past fashions—flattered her light skin and captured the reddish highlights in her golden blond hair, swept away from her face to accentuate her fine cheekbones. When she smiled, her perfect teeth and sparkling blue eyes couldn't compete with the obvious inner beauty she held. How did Lexie manage to look so fresh long after the end of a workday?

"I'm glad you called me and not just because that chicken and rice was so good," he said. "I'd been praying you'd call."

"Really?"

"Well, sort of. I asked the Lord to guide us both. I told Him that if you called, I would take it as an indication He wanted me to give you this." He felt suddenly nervous as he withdrew a check from the pocket of his blazer.

Lord, please don't let her think I'm demeaning her in any way or insulting her. Or worse, don't let her think I'm using You for my will.

"What is that?" Her voice held an edge.

He hesitated. "This will help you bring your car payments up to date, if it's not too late."

"No." She looked down at her hands. "I thought we had this discussion."

"We did. And this is not a handout. This is to help you get to work. It's a lot easier than driving you to work myself every day, although not nearly as much fun as being with you." He smiled, and she glanced up in time to see his expression.

"That's true," she agreed.

"I wish I could bring you up to date on all your bills, but I can't."

"And why not?" Her eyes were twinkling.

He handed her the check, but she still hesitated. He set the check on the table. "Please accept this from me."

"I know you're trying to help, but how can I ever be independent if I take your money?"

"I see your point. Look—if it will make you feel better, you can pay me back with interest."

"Great." She rolled her eyes. "Another debt."

"But not one with a due date."

"I don't know. . . ."

"Don't take it for yourself. Take it for Piper. Ask yourself, are you being the best mother you can be if you pass up this chance to stabilize your lives? Everyone needs help getting started in life."

"You don't mind using guilt, do you?"

"If I have to." He smiled.

Lexie placed her fingers on top of the check and slid it toward her. She picked it up, noted the amount, and nodded. "Yes, this is about what it will take to get me caught up."

"So you'll take it then."

She looked into his eyes without flinching. "Only if you promise to work out a repayment schedule and hold me to it."

He had seen that look in her eyes before. No way would she consider any other option. "All right then. I'll give you a schedule in the next few days, and if you can't live with it, we'll try again. But don't put off cashing that check and paying the bank. If you let them repossess the car, you'll be in trouble."

"I know."

"I don't want you to worry. No matter what you say, I consider the loan a gift."

"But why?"

"Remember Luke 6:34? 'And if you lend to those from whom you expect repayment, what credit is that to you? Even "sinners" lend to "sinners," expecting to be repaid in full.'"

Lexie grinned. "You memorized that verse just for today, didn't you?"

He cleared his throat and smiled. "I prefer to think the Lord led me to memorize that verse for today."

"What about the verse that follows? 'But love your enemies, do good to them, and lend to them without expecting to get anything back.'"

"All right. You win a gold star."

"Maybe so. But I have a more important question. Am I your enemy?"

He stood up and extended his hand toward her. Despite the puzzled look on her face, she accepted it and stood.

"I think you know the answer to that."

Lexie pushed him away. "If you're talking about what happened the other night—"

"I am. And if you're waiting for me to say I'm sorry I kissed you, don't hold your breath," Theo said. "I'm not sorry."

"You know something? Neither am I." Her eyes were moist.

"I love you," he said. "I always have, and I always will."

She didn't answer with words. Instead she stepped closer to him. He leaned down to kiss her when the noise of little feet scuffling through the hallway interrupted them. Lexie broke away.

Piper peeked in. "Mommy!"

"Piper, I'm wondering why you're up at this hour."

"I want a glass of water."

Lexie glanced at Theo. "This is our routine, I'm afraid. She goes to bed, and then like clockwork she comes back out asking for water."

"I'd say she's normal," Theo observed.

Lexie shook her head and took Piper by the hand. "I'll be right back."

"Aww!" Piper protested. "You're visiting with Theo. Why can't I?"

"Because it's late. Now come along." She threw him a look of apology.

"I'll be back another time," he promised.

Lexie returned a few moments later, looking a bit irritated and frazzled.

"Now where were we?" Theo asked, hoping to lighten her mood.

Instead of returning to his arms, Lexie stood by the couch. "Don't you wonder sometimes how any couple manages to stay alone long enough to have more than one child? As you can see, living with a child means a life full of interruptions."

"And you wouldn't trade it for the world."

"I wouldn't. But then again, I'm not writing a book or traveling the world."

"Neither am I."

"But you hope to someday. Admit it."

Theo shrugged.

"Oh, no. Don't tell me you've given up the idea, especially if you say it's for us. That would be worse."

"I'm not so sure."

"Theo, you've always said you never wanted children."

"I did?"

"Yes. Don't you remember? All through college you reminded me time and time again."

"I did?"

"You're starting to sound like a recording."

"Sorry. I don't remember saying those things. But that was a long time ago. We've both changed a lot since then. Surely you won't hold me to things I said when I was twenty."

"But you also said them when I first came back to town. Especially the part about not wanting children. That's why I didn't tell you about Piper right away."

Theo cringed. "If I said that, I'm sorry. I must have sounded incredibly selfish."

"You're not tied down. You have a right to be selfish. In fact, if you don't want children, you certainly shouldn't have them." She looked him in the eyes. "And that's a shame, too. Judging from the way you are with Piper, you'd make a wonderful father."

"Maybe she brings out the best in me. Sort of the way you do. I must have known that back in school. My heart was broken when you married Curt. But you already know that."

"Theo," she answered, her voice soft. "Don't you realize we parted because our dreams were so different? I knew I wanted a family. Curt had four brothers and three sisters. He wanted to carry on that tradition with me."

"You were planning on eight kids?"

Lexie smiled shyly. "I'm not so sure we would have kept going after three or four, but our house would have been full of love and laughter."

"And you thought mine wouldn't." Despite the harshness of his words, Theo's voice was not condemning.

"Oh, I could tell you had—and still have—lots of love in your heart. But the life you wanted was so different. With Curt, I knew I'd be a mother. With you I'd be footloose and carefree, available to pick up and go anywhere on a moment's notice. Sort of like the girl I was in school. I guess I thought you wanted to keep me that way."

"Maybe I did."

He remembered the Lexie of so many years ago, when she was a young woman who seemed to have no end to options in life. Even now, after the tragedy of losing her husband and with her financial troubles, Lexie never seemed unhappy, bitter, or cynical. Over the years she had matured from a spindly teenager to a shapely woman. Her youthful face wore no wrinkles but the look of kind wisdom.

"I'm sorry to disappoint you, but that girl is gone now," Lexie told him. "She'll never return, I'm afraid."

"That's okay. I'm not the least bit sorry to see her go," Theo assured her. "Because the woman who replaced her is far more lovely."

Lexie looked at her feet. "I—I don't know what to say, Theo. As much as I love you, I can't tell you I wish things were different with Piper."

"And I wouldn't want you to." Suddenly Theo understood why Lexie was acting so strangely. "Did I hear you say you—you love me?" His voice was so low and soft he barely recognized it himself.

Lexie nodded. "Don't make me say it again. It hurts too much."

Theo rushed over to her and tried to take her in his arms. She twisted herself out of his reach.

"Do you have to make this any harder than it already is? You know it will never work. We've already had this discussion."

"I remember what you call a 'discussion.' You asked me to leave the apartment."

"Only because I had to. I can't marry someone who doesn't want children."

"Lexie, what will it take for you to understand I've moved past that? And that's all because of Piper. You know I was the youngest in my family. I never was around kids very much. I always was the baby myself, so to speak. I always will be, as long as my sisters have anything to say about it."

"So Piper hasn't scared you?"

"Not at all. My mom said children don't make your life easier. They make it better. Now I finally see what she means." Theo narrowed his mouth. "Until you came back into my life, I was a pretty selfish person. You and Piper have helped me be a little less self-centered and more outwardly focused. At least I hope so."

She hesitated.

"What's wrong?"

"Nothing."

He knew better. "It's Curt, isn't it? You're afraid you're going to hurt him somehow."

She looked up. Her mouth had formed a surprised *O*. "How did you know?"

"It's only natural to have some doubts. But, Lexie, please don't make me compete with a man who's already gone home to the Lord," he said. "Look—I know this sounds like a cliché, and it probably is, but I don't want to replace Curt in either your life or Piper's. I never want to intrude on the place in your hearts you'll always have for Curt."

"Thanks. I needed to hear you say that. And Piper has helped me realize that. She loves you, you know. She always asks about you if we're apart too long."

"Really?"

"Really."

"And you want me to trade all that just so I can travel and write?" he scoffed. "There will always be time for those things."

"How do you know?"

She didn't have to explain to him what she meant. He knew she was remembering Curt.

"I know the Bible says God doesn't promise us tomorrow. And maybe I won't have time to travel and write. But if not, I can accept that outcome as the Lord's will."

"Are you sure you want to get any more involved with my complicated life?"

"I'm positive. I won't abandon you and Piper. Ever."

Lexie looked around the apartment. "So where is your white horse?"

"He's parked outside." This time, when Theo reached for Lexie, she didn't resist.

Epilogue

Lexie took in a breath when she and Theo reached the mountain summit on horseback. The view proved to be everything the trail guidebook promised. A cluster of homes below looked smaller than dollhouses from such a high vantage point. She wondered about the people who lived in them and what their lives were like. Autumn leaves were at their peak in color. A brisk breeze wafted through Lexie's hair, reminding her that winter would touch its icy hands upon them in a matter of weeks.

Lexie couldn't remember a time when she felt freer. Lexie's parents were up for a visit and had taken Piper for the day. Over the past year, Mom had been somewhat chilly toward Theo, and even now she was still reticent about Lexie's relationship with him. Yet her objections lessened as she saw how well Theo interacted with Piper. Mom never said it, but Lexie suspected she could see the happiness in Lexie's eyes as well. How could she not want what was best for her daughter?

Over time Lexie had begun to chip away at her bills. She wasn't completely out of debt, but because of discipline and getting the subsidy for Piper's day care, she had finally retired the smaller debts on department store credit cards and was making well over the minimum payments on the major credit cards. She had even cleared her debt with Theo and her mom.

She had proven to herself she wasn't helpless, that she could survive on her own. As she became more comfortable with this fact, she found she felt more at ease with Theo. She could love him unreservedly, without thinking he felt only compassion and sympathy for her. While she didn't want a man with no compassion, she didn't want Theo's love out of pity, misplaced or not. Now she could look him in the eye, knowing she was responsible, not dependent.

"This view is something, isn't it?" Theo asked.

She was grateful his observation brought her back to the moment, so she could savor the feeling. "Yes. We'll have to bring Piper here sometime."

"Maybe one Saturday this spring," Theo suggested as he dismounted.

"Or maybe sooner." Lexie dismounted also. After riding, her feet felt strange for a moment as they touched the ground. She shook her legs out before taking the few steps that brought her to Theo's side.

"Yep, God did a pretty good job of creating the world," Theo said.

"I'm sure He's happy to hear that from you," Lexie joked.

"Don't kid yourself. He knows I'm more awestruck than I let on. He knows I think He did some of His best work when He made you."

"Thank you, although I'm sure He's made lots of people who look better than I do."

"Name one."

"I'm looking at him."

Theo laughed out loud. "Okay, so He didn't make you perfect. Your eyesight leaves a lot to be desired."

"You know something? I'll bet if you realized how wonderful you look, you would have seen all the women who wanted to be with you, and you'd never have wasted your time on me. So maybe your eyesight isn't so good, either. And I'm glad." She grinned.

"Well, if neither of us can see well, maybe I should have saved my money and bought a cubic zirconia." He reached into his jeans pocket and drew out a black velvet box.

Lexie gasped but found herself unable to make another sound.

He opened the box and showed her a modest solitaire that sparkled as the rays of the sun hit it. "So did I spend my money wisely?"

"I don't know. Who is it for?"

"Who is it for?"

One of the horses whinnied.

"No, it's not for you, Lancelot," Theo answered as they both laughed. He looked at the craggy ledge. "I'd get down on bended knee, but—"

"That's okay. So what was your question?"

"As if you didn't know. You're really going to make me take this to the *nth* degree, aren't you?"

"Yes. Yes, I am."

"All right then. Alexandria Marie Downey Zoltan, will you marry me?"

Lexie pulled on her chin as though she were trying to reach a decision. "Theodore Evan Powers, umm, I'll have to think about it."

Theo's face fell.

"Okay, I've thought about it. Yes, I'll marry you!"

"Yes!" Theo pulled her into his arms in a bear hug, though not too strong or hard. He took the ring out of the box and slid it on her finger.

Lexie laughed with happiness at the sight of the diamond sparkling in the sunlight.

He took her face in his hands. When his lips brushed against hers, even such a slight touch sent sparks through her being. Sparks she wanted to feel forever. To show him, she returned his kiss with fervor.

"Let's get married tonight," she muttered.

He drew his face away until their gazes met. "Tonight? But I, Sir Theodore, your knight in shining armor, won't have time to prepare the castle!"

"Knight in shining armor, indeed!"

"You don't believe me?" He tilted his head toward his horse. "Look."

For the first time, she realized Lancelot's coat was solid white.

The Thrill of the Hunt

Chapter 1

Enid Garson was about to do something wrong. Terribly wrong. When Reece Parker walked through the door of her office at Prince of Peace Church, she planned to give him his aunt Agnes's key.

She had read and reread Agnes's note. She didn't need to retrieve the lavender-scented paper from the side drawer of the substantial computer desk that dominated her cramped office. The message was branded into her memory.

Dear Enid,
*   The key in this envelope is critical to my nephew's inheritance. However, you are not to relinquish it to Reece until he proves to your satisfaction that he has read the Bible. I trust you will respect my wishes.*

Lovingly,
Agnes

Why did Agnes have to drag me into the middle of all this? Enid sighed as she placed her elbow near the mouse pad that pictured a dove flying through a blue sky. She stared at the computer screen, which displayed page two of *The Prince's Epistle*, but her mind didn't absorb the meaning of the words. She twisted a short blond curl around her forefinger, praying silently that the Lord would forgive her for violating the trust of her dear friend.

"I wish I could talk to her now." Enid looked up at the ceiling, as if Agnes could hear from heaven. "If only I could explain."

"Explain what?"

Enid recognized the voice as the same baritone that had read a poignant poem at Agnes's funeral. Her heart pounded when she turned and saw the tall blond whom she had met before only briefly. He was leaning in the doorway, arms folded across his casual blue shirt.

"Sorry. I didn't mean to scare you, Enid."

"That's what I get for daydreaming instead of doing my work." She tilted her head toward the newsletter waiting to be edited.

His chuckle made her want to amuse him again so she could hear his pleasure. "It's not my habit to interrupt people in the middle of their workday, but my aunt's lawyer told me I could find you here."

She arched an eyebrow but made sure to keep her expression friendly. "Every

247

Monday through Friday, from nine to four."

"I won't keep you long." He shot her a winning smile.

"The work can wait." Swiveling in her chair, she waved an inviting hand toward an empty chair near her desk. "Won't you have a seat?"

"I really can't stay." Despite his protest, he positioned his lanky frame in the chair. "I'm on my lunch hour, and I've got to be back at the pharmacy by one." Regret was evident in his tone.

Enid glanced at the electric wall clock. "It's only a few minutes past noon. Don't you have time for a cup of coffee?"

"Sure. Why not? Sugar and cream, please."

"So you're a pharmacist?" she asked as she poured the hot brew into a clean Styrofoam cup.

"Nope. Just a clerk. Hope you're not too disappointed."

Enid poured herself a cup of coffee. "How can I be disappointed when you obviously appreciate the medicinal benefits of coffee?"

"An energy booster, sure enough." He accepted the coffee, then lifted the cup in a toast. "To cure what ails you."

Chuckling, she touched her maroon ceramic cup to his Styrofoam rim. The abrasive scraping sound was hardly as rewarding as the tinkle of fine crystal.

After taking a sip, Reece became pensive. "If only some miracle medicine could have helped Aunt Agnes."

"I know," she agreed, her mood matching his. "But she had lived a full life, and it was her time to go home to the Lord."

"I suppose you could look at it that way." He took another sip of coffee. "She thought highly of you, you know. She always had something good to say about you."

Unable to return the compliment, Enid could only nod. Agnes had worried about Reece and how his haphazard upbringing hadn't left him grounded enough to find spiritual direction in his life.

"I suppose you've figured out I'm here for my inheritance. Although I don't know why she left the check with you instead of her lawyer."

"The check?"

"My inheritance is in the form of a check, isn't it?" His shoulders slumped and he began to stare at the ceiling. "Unless she left me some odds and ends I'll just have to sell."

"I doubt she'd bother to bequeath worthless bric-a-brac to anyone in her will—"

"Sorry, I didn't really mean that. It's just that I don't have room for a lot of knickknacks. Nor the patience to dust them." He scrunched his nose in displeasure.

She chuckled. "Don't worry. You don't have to dust a key."

"A key?" Reece tapped his fingertips on her desk. His brown eyes took on a light that told Enid he was contemplating the possibilities.

"Yes. She left me an envelope with a key in it."

"The key to her '57 Chevy?" Hope colored his voice. "That car's a classic."

She clenched her teeth. "No doubt. As much as I hate to disappoint you, this envelope doesn't seem to contain a car key."

"So you held the envelope up to the light, huh?" A frolicsome twinkle in his eyes told her he was jesting.

Enid lifted both hands in surrender. "Okay, I'm busted."

"That's all right," he laughed. "I would have done the same thing. You know, isn't it just like Aunt Agnes to send me out here on a wild goose chase? She couldn't just leave a will like a normal person."

"She definitely had a sense of humor." Enid swallowed, unhappy with the prospect of having to break the cheerful mood. "You do realize I'm not supposed to give you the key yet."

Reece placed his empty cup on her desk. His eyes widened and he clutched the arms of his chair as if he were steeling himself for battle. "Why not?"

"Reece, you've read the Bible, right?"

A blond eyebrow arched. "Some of it, I guess."

Enid pursed her lips. She was hoping Agnes had been wrong about Reece—that he had already read the Bible from cover to cover. Then her job would be easy. However, it wasn't turning out that way.

"Why do you ask?"

"Because she wants you to read it before I give you the key."

"What? You've got to be kidding." His lips narrowed. "You mean she expects me to trudge through the whole thing?"

"I'll answer both questions. No, I'm not kidding. And, yes, she expects you to read it all."

Reece drew his eyebrows close together, causing the space in between to scrunch. "This is going too far. Who does she think she is?"

Enid coaxed her voice into a gentle tone. "A person who cared about you a lot. A whole lot. That's who your Aunt Agnes was."

Her ploy must have worked, because Reece's brows returned to their original position and his mood softened. "I know she did. But why does she have to put a condition on my inheritance? It just isn't fair."

Seeing his point, Enid sought to console him. "But you know something about the Bible, don't you? I mean, did you go to Sunday school while you were growing up?"

"Look, just because I didn't grow up in the church like you did—"

"What makes you think I grew up in the church?"

"Well, I, uh—" he faltered, then swept his gaze around her office. "You work here and everything. I just assumed the church would want someone who's been a Christian from day one."

"Unfortunately, you assumed wrong. I didn't have a strong Christian upbringing. My parents divorced when I was still a baby. I was with Dad, and he was too involved with making a living to worry about church."

"So we have something in common." Reece's voice filled with sadness as his gaze fell to the gray carpet. "I was raised by my dad too. Only, my mom died when I was ten."

"Oh, I'm so sorry."

"Thanks." Reece's face took on a faraway look. Then, as though he remembered he should be back in the present, he sent Enid a half smile. He appraised her from head to toe and nodded approvingly. "Things were tough for you as a child, but just look at you now." He waved a hand as if presenting Enid to a jury. "First of all, you're well dressed."

Enid looked down at her olive green and black tweed suit. The thick, nubby material offered warm comfort against the chilly office, inadequately heated against a brisk Virginia spring. The stylish outfit was a castoff from a successful friend, but Enid wasn't about to share that fact with Reece.

"And you're obviously a model citizen," he continued. "A church secretary. Somebody must have seen to it that you got religion."

She tried not to cringe at the negative expression. "Like I said, it sure wasn't Dad. He never put much faith in religion. Maybe it was because of the way he was treated by my mother. I don't know." She shook her head. "But I never went to church until a few years ago."

"Did some tragedy bring you to church?"

"Fortunately, no. One of my friends from high school invited me to the youth group here." She shrugged. "I guess you can say I never left."

"So good old Aunt Agnes took you under her wing."

"Precisely. She even recommended me for this job."

The sound of his endearing chuckle caused Enid to forget why she was miffed with him. "She always did want to save the world."

"Only Christ could do that."

The way Reece folded his arms made Enid wonder if he considered her words bullets to dodge.

"I don't mean to preach, but it's the truth."

Reece looked heavenward. "What should I expect? After all, this is a church."

"A place you suddenly seem eager to leave," she noted.

"Ouch! That hurt!"

Culpability tugged at Enid. Who was she to make someone else feel wretched? "Look," she said, "I've got an idea that will help you get your inheritance today so you won't have to wait. Why don't I ask you a few questions about the Bible? If you know them, I'll give you the key. How does that sound?"

"Sounds like the best offer I've had all day." Relaxing in his chair, Reece placed an elbow on each knee and clasped his hands as he leaned toward Enid.

The motion caused a trace of musk cologne to waft her way. Before she could stop herself, she tilted the upper portion of her body toward him, in part to breathe more of his masculine scent. At that moment, his eyes met hers, flaring with such intensity that her concentration tottered.

"What is the first question?" His voice wavered ever so slightly. Enid couldn't be sure the hesitation didn't result from his study of her rather than nervousness at the pop quiz.

She set the small of her back against her chair in a deliberate attempt to regain her focus. "I'll start out with something easy. What was the name of the giant David killed?"

"Um, Goliath?"

"Right. See? Now that wasn't so hard." Enid smiled at her student.

"Maybe I do know more than I thought." He leaned away from her, resting the back of his head in the palms of his hands.

"We'll see. Now, how many books are there in the Bible?"

"That's easy. Eighty-eight."

Enid shook her head. "You must be thinking of the keys on a piano."

"Right." He gave his forehead a gentle slap and folded his arms.

"Can you try again?"

After he thought for a moment, he shrugged. "Not sure."

"Sixty-six. But not everybody knows that off the top of their head." Drumming her fingernails, coated with clear polish, on her desk, Enid tried to think of a no-brainer. "All right, here's one. How about naming the four Gospels?"

Reece lifted his right forefinger. "John, Paul, Ringo, and George." He grinned, obviously pleased by his thought to name the Beatles instead of the Gospel authors.

"Very funny." Indulging him with a half-hearted smile, Enid hoped his attempt at humor was a retort to the ease of her question.

Instead, he squirmed. "Matthew, Luke, and, uh," he paused. "James and Paul?"

Enid shook her head. How could she justify giving Reece the key when he didn't possess even a passing knowledge of Bible basics?

"Wrong, huh?"

"I'm afraid so. The four Gospels are Matthew, Mark, Luke, and John."

"I knew it was something parochial like that." Reece placed his palms together in a pleading motion and gazed at her with widened puppy-dog eyes. "Could we try one more question? Please?"

"How can I resist?" She took a moment to think. What question would be so easy he couldn't miss? "All right. Who wrote the first five books of the Old Testament?"

"Paul."

"Not the New Testament," she responded, determined to give the benefit of the doubt even though the saint was not the author of the Gospels or The Acts of the Apostles. "The Old Testament."

"Oh." He let out a heavy breath and shook his head. "I give. I guess I should be ashamed of myself. You'd think somebody thirty years old would have had enough time to learn something."

"I'm sure you know a lot." She kept her voice bright.

"You're too kind." He sighed. "Now that I've proven myself a doofus, I guess you've been told to move on to Plan B. To let the church have my inheritance. That is Plan B, right? Since my father died, she has no other family to leave her money to."

Enid let out an expression of surprise. "I had no idea your father had passed away too. I'm sorry."

Reece's blond eyebrows rose. "I can't believe you didn't know. Aunt Agnes never said anything, huh?"

"Agnes didn't talk much about her family."

"I'll have to fill you in some time. My life story is a good substitute for a sleeping pill." His grin was semisweet. "In the meantime, let the church enjoy her money. Hope they do lots and lots of good things." With his shoulders slumping, Reece turned to exit.

"Wait a minute."

Her voice stopped him cold, and he spun around to face her. The heartened look in his eyes told Enid she had made the right decision. "I never said I wouldn't relinquish the key."

"But I failed the test."

"I know. But I'm going to give you the key anyway."

His mouth dropped open, forming a large *O*. "You'd actually do that? Why?"

"Because Revelation 22:17 says, 'And whosoever will, let him take the water of life freely,'" she answered.

"Huh?"

Enid chuckled. "Agnes influenced me to love the King James Version."

"Oh. So what are you saying?"

"The stipulation of your aunt's will coerces you to read the Bible. As much as I'd like to see that happen, I disagree with her idea of forcing the Word on you. So I'm going to let you have the key anyway." Extending her hand, she gave him the envelope. "Don't think this decision was made lightly. I didn't want to betray your aunt. You have no idea how long it took me to pray my way to this point. But I'm convinced this is what the Lord wants me to do."

Reece hesitated before taking it, as though he felt an attack of conscience. After a brief pause, he accepted the gift. His brown eyes met hers. "Thank you."

"You're welcome."

Watching Reece depart, Enid was almost sorry she had relinquished the key so easily. Her sacrifice meant she would never see him again.

Connie ran into Reece's waiting arms and gave him a sloppy kiss on his cheek. Sending her a broad grin, Reece rose to his feet. Connie squeezed him tightly around his upper calves. Her head, covered with chestnut brown curls, rested on his thighs. Reece patted the four-year-old's back, tapping her thick red fleece shirt and the strap of her denim jumper. Then he crouched to the ground and returned the hug.

"Look what I did, Weece!" She handed him a drawing of a lamb. Taking the paper from Connie, Reece marveled at the cotton balls glued onto a sheep's body, forming a facsimile of wool. "Very good, sweetheart."

"Don't forget your book bag, Connie." A stout woman handed Reece a blue parcel decorated with a picture of Cinderella.

"Thanks, Mrs. Jones." Just then, he remembered an errand he had neglected in his rush to arrive on time for work that morning. "Oh, before I forget." He reached into his black vinyl wallet for the check he had written that morning. The expense for Connie's day care consumed a hefty chunk of his budget, but he wanted her to have the best of everything he could afford on his modest salary. The program at Jones Day Care, with emphasis on constructive play, was a start.

He lowered his voice so Connie couldn't hear. "I'm sorry this is late. I appreciate your waiting for payday."

Mrs. Jones gave him a sympathetic nod. "I know you're good for the money, Reece." She looked down at Connie, who was chattering with a playmate. "And Connie is such a sweet girl," she cooed.

"She sure is."

Moments later, Connie skipped out of the day-care center, resisting Reece's attempts to take her hand. "What's for supper?"

He mentally rummaged through the food in the refrigerator. "I think there's some macaroni and cheese left over from yesterday."

"Yum!"

Though Reece didn't share her partiality for cheese-coated noodles, he was glad Connie was so easy to please. At that moment, he caught a glimpse of one of the mothers waving to him as she hurried to her van with a toddler by her side. Smiling and waving in return, he wondered what she planned for dinner. His mind wandered to what it would be like to have a wife waiting at home for him, with supper already prepared. Reece had indulged in such thoughts in the past, but an image of the wife never materialized. This time, his mind formed a picture of the stunning blond, Enid Garson, her green eyes shining with pleasure upon seeing him return home from another day of work.

Enid! What made me think of her?

Feeling a catch in his throat, Reece realized Enid's unwanted effect on him. He had no time to harbor such emotions. He had a living to make, for himself and for Connie. He wanted to give his little sister the opportunities she deserved, opportunities he never had. Maybe the inheritance would be the answer.

Chapter 2

During a dinner of boxed macaroni and cheese and hot dogs, Reece thought of little else but the key.

"Weece!" Connie interrupted. "Are you lis-en-in'?"

A surge of guilt shot through him. He looked into her vulnerable face. "Sure, I'm listening."

His generic response didn't fool her. Connie easily freed her hands so they could sail to her little hips. "You're not really lis-en-in'.'."

"All right. I'm listening now." He set his fork down and folded his arms across his chest to show her that he was serious about paying attention to her.

"That's better." After giving Reece a satisfied nod, Connie reiterated a long-winded story about lunch. She could recall the flavor of fruit bar each person was given at day care and how Josh and Tim fought over a container of cherry yogurt. Studying the girl, Reece wished sometimes he could forget his cares long enough to relive the minute details of life as meticulously as his little sister. If only his main concern was what flavor of yogurt to have for lunch!

Reece decided to devote his full attention to Connie until her early evening bedtime. The envelope could wait, no matter how anxious he was to open it. He couldn't reveal its contents in front of the child. Her natural curiosity would lead to too many questions. Not that she would understand money. Connie presumed a penny could buy as much as a hundred dollars. Still, Reece thought it better to keep the key to himself for the time being, lest something go wrong and the little girl be disappointed.

Sitting at the kitchen table a few minutes after seven, he ripped open the plain white envelope. Out fell the key, along with a sheet of notebook paper. Eyeing a phrase written in blue ink, Reece recognized the shaky handwriting of his elderly aunt. He read the simple message: 2 Kings 9:3.

"What does that mean?" Hoping to find more information, he flipped the note over, only to discover the back was blank. Reece turned the open envelope upside down. He shook it, hoping another clue would fall onto the table. Still nothing. Running his fingers along the inside offered no reward either.

"Now what game is my aunt playing?" He let out a breath of frustration. Tapping his fingers on the table, a moment of contemplation revealed what his aunt was trying to do. "I have no idea how anything in Second Kings relates to me." He let out a sigh. "I can see she's determined I'll read the Bible one way or another."

Shaking his head, Reece walked to the bookshelf in his living room. Scanning the titles, he spotted his unread copy of the King James Bible in the middle of the bottom shelf among a few horror novels he had acquired as a teenager.

Plopping himself into the only cushioned chair in the apartment, he flipped to the table of contents and then to the second book of Kings, where he read the third verse of the ninth chapter:

> Then take the box of oil, and pour it on his head, and say, Thus saith the LORD, I have anointed thee king over Israel. Then open the door, and flee, and tarry not.

Rereading it several times only brought more puzzlement. "What could she possibly mean by such gibberish?"

In one of the rare times in his life, Reece uttered a silent prayer. The next few moments he sat alone, listening to sounds of life he could hear through the walls and ceiling. The smooth sound of drawers opening seeped through the ceiling. He supposed his upstairs neighbors were in their kitchen, washing the day's dishes. Tom Warner, the neighbor in 3B, was treating the building to rock music, courtesy of a stereo much too powerful for tight quarters. Still others, unknown, walked by his front door, chattering as they passed. Despite the noise level, after his prayer Reece didn't feel the usual compulsion to turn on his own television to drown out the neighbors' unwanted clamor. Instead, the fullness of silence entered him, as if making room for God's answer.

A name came to mind. "Enid," he blurted. "That's it! She knew Aunt Agnes better than anyone else. Enid's the one who can help me."

Reece muttered a "thank you" to the God he had long neglected.

❧

Reece decided not to wait. The next day, he took a few minutes of his lunch hour and drove to the church. He entered through the side door, and his heart fluttered when he spotted Enid. She was dressed in soft pink. Her hair was pulled back, revealing the nape of her neck. To Reece, she seemed more like a princess than a church secretary as she typed rapidly on the computer keyboard.

She looked up from her work. "Back already?" Her voice betrayed a mixture of surprise and, he hoped, pleasure.

"Like a bad penny."

As Enid let out an appealing chuckle, he noticed she had ever-so-slightly tinted her lips with silky lipstick in a shade of pink that reminded him of the strawberry ice cream that Connie liked so well. "If you're here to say you've already read the Bible, you must have set some kind of record."

"If only I could read so fast. But your guess isn't totally off. I do want to see you in relation to my aunt's letter." He hoped he didn't sound too eager.

The place between her thin blond eyebrows wrinkled into two vertical lines. "Letter?"

"The letter in the envelope. It was there along with the key." Already holding the paper in his hand, he surrendered it to her.

After she accepted the letter, Enid scanned it. She didn't look up. "Oh."

"Is that all you have to say?"

"Well, this does add a bit of interest to things, doesn't it?"

"I'll say. So much interest, I might not ever earn my inheritance." He paused. "Unless you can help?"

Enid's mouth twisted, indicating her doubt. "I take it you looked up the verse."

He nodded. " 'Then take the box of oil, and pour it on his head, and say, Thus saith the Lord, I have anointed thee king over Israel. Then open the door, and flee, and tarry not.' "

"Committing scripture to memory already, I see. I'm impressed."

Reece swallowed. No doubt Enid wouldn't be as dazzled if she knew how badly he wanted the inheritance. "So what do you think it means? I've been turning it over and over in my mind, and I can't come to any reasonable conclusion."

Enid hesitated. "I'm not very good at puzzles. But I suppose I could try."

"Are you really saying you don't have the answers?"

Her clear green eyes widening, Enid shook her head. "What would make you think I have them?"

"I thought she'd write them down somewhere and leave them with someone she trusted. You know, in case I failed her test."

"Apparently she had more confidence in you than you do in yourself." She flashed him a captivating smile. "I wish I had more time to help you, but I've got to finish this bulletin."

"Oh." He knew his voice didn't conceal his disappointment.

"But maybe I can help later?"

"Could you? That would be great." He tried to think of the best time. "How about if we meet tomorrow morning at nine o'clock?"

"Nine in the morning?" Her blond eyebrows rose.

"That's when Connie has her tumbling class. We'll have a child-free hour to concentrate."

"Child-free?" She averted her eyes to the keyboard. "Agnes never mentioned you were married."

"I'm not married," he hastened to inform her. "Look, why don't we meet at the diner, and I'll treat you to breakfast. One with loads of calories. Is it a deal?"

"Sure." She looked up at him, her eyes sympathetic. "It was nice seeing you again, Reece, but I've really got to get back to work." Enid swiveled her chair so her back was turned to him.

"Okay. See you then." Wishing he could find an excuse to linger, Reece left. *Wonder what's eating her?*

The next morning, Enid swung open the door of the diner called Katie's Kookin' and walked inside. She felt her stomach somersault when she spotted Reece waiting in a red vinyl booth. Elbow resting on the laminated particleboard table, he leaned his handsome face on a firm hand. Reece stared out the window and watched a spring breeze whip newly grown grass and budding trees, pollinating the earth for future growth. Winds always made Enid think of God's simple yet brilliant ways of accomplishing the mechanisms of His world. She wondered if Reece contemplated such ideas.

"A good day to fly a kite," Enid remarked as she took her place in the booth opposite Reece.

As he turned to her, Enid was almost certain she saw a flicker of interest in Reece's brown eyes before he returned his stare back in the direction of the outdoors. "Yeah." He let out a resigned sigh. "I promised Connie we'd fly kites after her class."

The mention of Connie caused Enid to remember why she wasn't sure she wanted any romantic attention from Reece. "Why do you seem so blue?" she asked. "I think it sounds like fun."

"It might be, except my kites seem to get stuck in a tree every time."

Enid laughed. "Don't be silly."

"Believe me, I'm not exaggerating," he answered as the waitress poured each of them a cup of coffee without bothering to ask. "I went to the store and paid almost twenty bucks for a kite yesterday. I'd hate to see all that money wasted."

"Twenty bucks?" The waitress hooted. "Me and my brothers used to make kites out of old newspapers. What's the matter with you, Reece, throwin' money down the drain like that?"

"Up a tree is more like it," Enid muttered, unable to resist a grin.

"Very funny." Reece's lips formed an irritated line.

The waitress looked at Enid. "This one wants nothin' but the best for his little Connie. Even if that means spendin' way too much money."

"What's the matter, Sarah?" Reece wanted to know. "Afraid that I spent your tip?"

"Now you hush your mouth, or I'll make sure Katie fries up your eggs hard as rocks instead of over easy, the way you like 'em." Sarah's teasing expression belied her threat.

Enid wrinkled her nose at the thought of eggs with runny yolks. "I'll pass on the eggs, thank you. Although I wouldn't mind grapefruit."

"Grapefruit?" Sarah tapped her ballpoint pen on the small pad in her hand. "Are you on some kind of diet, hon?"

"No, I always—"

"Sorry. We don't carry grapefruit. Not enough people who come here seem to like it. How about a nice waffle? We can put some pecans in it. Maybe even some chocolate chips." Her eyes pierced Enid's thin frame. "A few extra calories wouldn't hurt you none."

"Sounds tempting, but I think I'd better stick with a bowl of cereal." Enid flashed what she hoped was a soothing smile. "Something sugarless, if you have it. And skim milk."

"I'll see what I can do." Sarah rolled her eyes and then threw Reece a look as if to ask him why he was with Enid.

Reece chose to ignore her unspoken question. "I'll take a large glass of orange juice too."

"Me too. Only make mine small."

Reece shook his head as Sarah ambled to the kitchen. "You'll have to excuse Sarah. Ever since I started coming here every Saturday for breakfast, she's sort of adopted me."

"I guess she thinks I'm an intruder, then."

Reece chuckled. "To Sarah's way of thinking, everyone is, until they become one of the regulars." He glanced at his black digital watch. "We'd better get started on this puzzle before the food comes."

Enid nodded. "Have you thought up any more ideas?"

"Not really. I was pretty desperate by the time I saw you yesterday."

"I've been thinking. The verse is about the anointing of a king. And then there's a box."

"I noticed that. Is there a box that was special to Aunt Agnes? Maybe since the verse talks about a box of oil, she kept anointing oil or holy water somewhere in a box?"

"Good guess." Enid mulled the idea over in her mind. Coming up blank, she shook her head. "I don't know of any time Agnes used holy water or oil. And of course, kitchen oil doesn't come in a box."

Reece laughed. "I can imagine what a wad of bills would look like soaked in a bottle of vegetable oil."

"Unless the inheritance isn't money, but something else." She let out a giggle. "I can't imagine Agnes drenching anything in oil, except a frying chicken. No, it must be something else."

"What about the king? A chess game has king pieces."

"That's a logical idea for just about anyone else except your aunt Agnes. She never played chess. I can't imagine that she owned a chess set."

"Checkers, then?"

"That's a stretch, but not an impossibility," Enid observed. "I was thinking, maybe she could have hidden something underneath a statue or portrait. Since the scriptural reference is from Kings, I was trying to remember if there are any images of the King in her house."

"The king?" Reece's mouth dropped. "You mean she liked Elvis?"

Enid threw back her head and let out a hearty laugh. "Not that king! The real King."

"The real king?" Reece lifted his eyes skyward. Enid could visualize the cogs in his brain spinning as Reece tried to recall all the kings of the world.

"By the 'real King,' I meant Jesus."

"Oh." Chagrin flickered over his good-looking features before he composed them into a poker face. "I knew that."

Sure you did. Aloud, Enid sighed. "Too bad we can't go in and take a look."

"Who says we can't?" Reece asked. "I have the key to her house."

Enid leaned closer. "You do?"

"Sure. Aunt Agnes gave me one in case I ever needed it."

"After we eat, let's go take a look. We're bound to find the answer!"

Chapter 3

Since Reece needed to pick up Connie from class, Enid agreed to meet him at Agnes's house on the edge of town. Reece had given her the key so she could explore as she waited.

A catch formed in her throat as Enid pulled her white economy car in front of the bungalow. Not so long ago, the sound of her car would have brought Agnes to the window. But this time there would be no Agnes peeking through the white lace curtains. No Agnes stepping onto the porch, eager to greet her.

Enid trod over the short walk, with its concrete cracked and broken in several spots from age and weathering. Wind whipped the leaves of four mature oaks, causing them to swish against each other, creating a fluttering sound. Gusts caught Enid's hair. Her blond curls blew into her face. She reacted by tucking the front locks behind each ear so strands wouldn't land on her lipstick and leave pink spots. The wind played with the unrestricted hair in the back, blowing it fully to one side.

Moments later, Enid felt a sense of emptiness as she turned the key in the tarnished brass lock. In the past, the door would have been open. Agnes had been one of the few elderly ladies Enid knew who refused to secure her doors. Enid could hear Agnes's voice as clearly as though she spoke yesterday. "Child, I've lived here in this house all my life and kept my doors unlocked all these years. I'm too old to change my habits now. Besides, if anybody really wants to take what little I've got, it will be the good Lord's will, and it's not for me to put up a fuss about it."

Enid wasn't sure she entirely agreed with the older woman's sentiments, but she kept her opinion to herself. She knew from experience that no amount of coaxing, begging, or debate would change Agnes's mind once it was set.

If only she could hear Agnes lecture. Just one more time.

Pensive, Enid shut the door behind her, ignoring its protesting creak. Enid expected the house to provide welcome shelter from the frigid wind. Yet the chill inside left her shivering. Enid rubbed her forearms and then shook her short curls back into place, touching them with her fingertips.

Enid studied the living room. Decades-old furniture remained in place. A crewel bellpull, yellowed with age, hung on a narrow wall. She stared at her favorite photo, still in its usual spot on an end table. Black-and-white and framed in silver, it showed a group pose of a family reunion that took place soon after World War II, capturing forever a moment now lost to history. In the center stood Agnes. Then thirty years old, she wore her coal black hair twisted into the off-the-face style which was popular at the time. Her fashionably full skirt had come into vogue with the advent of Dior's "New Look," made possible by postwar prosperity that included plenty of available fabric after years of rations and shortages of every kind of good.

The only clue that Agnes hadn't been home for a while was the layer of dust that had accumulated on the coffee table, visible only because the sun's unforgiving rays shone through the picture window, exposing this imperfection. Otherwise, everything looked just the same.

Enid inhaled in sorrow, causing her to notice that Agnes's gardenia perfume still lingered in the stale air. Suddenly she knew she would never be able to smell gardenias again without remembering her friend. A tear formed at the corner of her eye. Enid wiped it away.

"It's not easy to come back here, is it?"

"Wow!" Enid jumped, startled by Reece's voice behind her. She placed a hand over her heart and turned to face him. "You really have a way of sneaking up on me."

"Sorry. Bad habits die hard, I guess."

A little girl with curly brown hair and eyes like Reece's pointed at Enid. "Who is that?"

"It is very rude to point, Connie." Reece kept his voice gentle but resolute.

"Oh." She set her gaze upon the dusty hardwood floor.

Enid could tell by her regret that this wasn't the first occasion Connie had been corrected about a motion that comes naturally to children. "That's perfectly all right, Reece." When his mouth tightened, Enid could see she had said the wrong thing.

"This is Miss Enid," he told Connie. "As you can tell, she is a very nice lady. Can you say hello?"

Connie lifted her cherubic face just long enough to speak. "Hello." Her attention returned to the floor.

"Hello, Connie."

Connie tugged the side of Reece's pants leg. "Where's Aunt Agnes? It's spooky here without her."

Looking down at Connie, Reece stroked the back of her head. "I told you, honey. She's with Jesus now."

"But when is she comin' back?"

The way Connie's voice rose at the end of the sentence made Enid realize that if she wasn't calmed right away, the child could become hysterical. "Don't worry about your aunt. She's just fine."

Connie gazed into Enid's eyes without flinching. "Weally?"

"Really." Enid knelt so that her face would be closer to Connie's. She touched Connie's shoulder to draw her attention to the pink leotard she wore.

"This is so pretty. I like the gold stars on the front."

"Me, too." Connie's brown eyes brightened.

"I understand you take tumbling lessons."

She nodded. "I did a flip today." Her face showed her pride.

"That's wonderful!"

Obviously encouraged by Enid's compliment, Connie ran farther into the living room, onto the only portion of the floor that wasn't consumed by furniture. "Wanna see?" Before Enid could answer, Connie rolled on her back and executed a perfect somersault. Jumping to her feet, she rubbed the back of her neck. "Ouch!"

"You're not supposed to tumble on such a hard floor," Reece advised. "That's what you get for being a show-off." Despite his admonition, Enid could see Reece was pleased by Connie's ability.

"What's the point of taking tumbling classes if you can't show anyone what you can do?" Enid added.

A beaming smile from Connie was her reward.

"All right, we've seen what you learned today. Now, why don't you run into the den and watch a little TV?" Reece instructed.

"TV? Yay!" Connie ran into the next room without a pause.

"As you can see, television is quite a treat for her. I allow her to watch very few programs."

"I'd say that's a good thing," Enid noted. "Although, I'm surprised the electricity hasn't been turned off."

Reece shrugged. "The house will have a much better chance of selling with the electricity on, don't you think? Especially if it's dark when prospective buyers come to look."

"You've got a point. Well, since you and Connie have a date to fly kites, let's say we get started?"

"Get started? I take it you mean nothing in the house has inspired you?"

"Not much, I'm afraid." She swept her gaze over the room. "I guess I've wasted too much time reminiscing. I haven't been here since the funeral."

"It seems like she's just gone on vacation for a while and she'll be right back, doesn't it?"

"Yes. Except for the door being locked." Enid felt a bittersweet curve touch her lips. "I wonder who'll end up buying this place?"

Reece shrugged. "Beats me. But her lawyer isn't in any hurry to sell it as far as I can tell. No FOR SALE sign is up yet. And they're still delivering newspapers every day, even though I've called twice asking them to discontinue the service. Maybe if I don't pay the bill next time, they'll get the message."

"Don't even consider such a thing!" Enid warned. "Agnes would have a fit if she knew."

"I'm sure she has more important things to worry about in heaven." Enid was about to argue that there are no worries in heaven when Reece continued, "Speaking of worries, I'd better look on the kitchen table and see how big the pile of mail and papers has grown since I last checked."

Enid followed. Lacking the odors of freshly brewed coffee and delectable food simmering on the harvest-gold stove, the kitchen didn't seem to belong to Agnes anymore. If that weren't enough, a mountain of materials amassed on the table left no doubt. Agnes had always tended to her mail and papers so promptly that Enid never saw a stray scrap anywhere in her house.

Marveling at the pile, Enid whistled. "It'll take forever to go through all this."

"I can throw away most of it right off the bat," Reece said. "I'm just glad Mr. Morgan next door has agreed to pick up the papers and the mail at her post office box uptown. Otherwise, I'd be running the whole day, trying to keep up with it all."

Enid thought about how Mr. Harris was always willing to help Agnes. One day, Enid had ventured that the widower and Agnes should have made a match, but Agnes would have none of it. "I've been single this long. No need in me ruinin' somebody else's life at this late date."

The thought caused Enid to chuckle.

Reece looked up from sorting the mail. "What's so funny?"

"Oh, just thinking about your aunt."

"She could be a character. Did you know she went to the post office every morning at nine sharp and every afternoon at three to get her mail, knowing those were the times they filled the boxes each day?"

"No, I—" Enid paused. "Wait a minute. Did you say 'boxes'?"

Reece twisted his mouth as though he thought she had lost her mind. "Yes, why?"

"I just remembered. The post office is on King Street. You don't think the clue might be in that stack of mail, do you?"

His mouth dropped open. "Maybe it is! Come on, help me look."

Enid and Reece spent the next few minutes rummaging through the stack of bills and solicitations. Not a single personal letter was to be found. Just as they were about to give up, Enid spotted a yellow slip of card-stock paper. It was a notice for Reece to appear at the post office to pick up a package in person. "This is it! There's something waiting for you!"

Taking the paper from Enid, Reece read it and shook his head. "All this intrigue for nothing. Didn't she know I'd find this sooner or later anyway?"

"If you hadn't asked me to help you, I have a feeling you would have found it later."

Reece smiled. "Somehow, I think you're right."

At that moment, Connie bounded in. "There's nuttin' good on TV anymore. Can we go now?"

"Sure."

Connie jiggled up and down and clapped her hands. "Yay! Let's go fly kites!"

"We will," Reece assured her. "But first, we have to go by the post office."

"Nooooooo!" Connie tugged on Reece's pants leg. "You pwomised! I wanna go now!"

"The post office can wait," Enid said.

Connie looked at Enid. "You goin' to fly kites with us!"

"Oh, no, honey."

"Please!" The light in Connie's brown eyes was hard to resist.

"That's a great idea, Connie," Reece agreed. "Miss Enid was telling me just this morning how much fun it is to fly kites." He shot her a teasing look.

Enid decided it best not to respond to his playfulness. "Really, Reece, I don't want to interfere."

Connie would have no part of Enid's protests. "Please, Miss Enid?"

"Maybe Miss Enid has other plans for this afternoon," Reece explained to Connie in a gentle tone.

"No," Enid blurted.

"Then come along with us."

Enid looked for signs that Reece was merely trying to be polite, but she found none. Instead, he seemed relaxed and actually eager for her to join them.

Still, she hesitated. Where was Connie's mother? Obviously, Reece wasn't married with a wife waiting at home or the little girl wouldn't be so enthusiastic about Enid spending time with them. And she somehow didn't sense he was a widower. Perhaps Reece was divorced, with custody of Connie on the weekends. But if that were so, why didn't Connie want Reece all to herself? And certainly if Reece had Connie in his custody for such a short time, he wouldn't be wasting the day sorting his deceased aunt's mail. Or maybe the mother was a girlfriend, someone Reece never bothered to marry at all.

I really shouldn't go.

Connie's voice broke into her internal debate. "Please! Please go with us, Miss Enid?"

"Well. . .I suppose I could follow you to the park in my own car. . . ."

"That means you'll go. Right?"

Her better judgment abandoning her, Enid gave in to the little girl's prodding. She would have to wait to find out the details of Reece's tangled web of a life.

Chapter 4

I don't remember the last time I had so much fun!" Laughing, Enid sat under a tree and leaned back against its massive trunk. The exertion of kite flying had left her tired and winded, but seeing Connie's delight made it worth every breath.

"Speak for yourself." Taking a place on the chilly ground beside her, Reece watched the branches sway. "You weren't the one who had to get the kite out of this tree more than once!"

"Are you saying you didn't have any fun?"

Looking into her face, Reece grinned. As his sparkling eyes met hers, Enid felt a quiver—a thrilling tingle not attributable to brisk weather. "No, I really can't say that," he answered. "In fact, I've had more fun today than I have in eons."

Taking his gaze away from Enid, Reece looked contemplatively at the little girl. She was trying to wrap the kite string in a ball, but was doing a better job of tangling it than anything else.

"At least she's trying," Enid remarked.

"You can say that again."

"I'll bet every day is an adventure with her."

"I have a lot of fun with Connie." Reece looked back at Enid. His eyes held a wistful light. "But I haven't had this much fun with someone my own age. Not lately." As soon as the words were out of his mouth, Reece averted his eyes to Connie's direction. Was he avoiding her because he was afraid of what Enid's answer would be? Quickly, Reece called Connie. "Come here and let me wind up that string for you."

She didn't answer, but kept rolling the thread.

"I don't think she heard you," Enid said.

Reece's lips curled into a wry line. "More likely she's pretending not to hear." He shouted, though his voice betrayed not a touch of impatience, "Come here, Connie!"

Connie shook her head. Still holding the ball of string, she put chubby hands on little denim-clad hips and shouted back, "No! I can do it!"

"You'd better let me," Reece protested from his position under the tree.

"No! I'm not a baby! I can do it!" Attempting to prove her point, Connie resumed tangling the string.

Finally realizing he couldn't win the battle in such a far away proximity from his charge, Reece rose to his feet. "I'd better take care of this before she gets the string so tangled we'll never be able to use it again."

An instant later, Enid watched Reece try to wrestle the ball of twine from Connie. She couldn't hear what they were saying, although Enid could see from Reece's body language that he was treating her gently. The more patience he tried to exhibit, however, the more Connie pouted and stamped her feet. Enid decided it was time to rescue the tired little girl—and Reece. She made her way over to them.

"How are things going?" she asked Connie sweetly.

Connie stuck out her little pink lips as far as she could force them. She shook her head until her brown hair swished back and forth and pointed an accusatory finger at Reece. "He won't let me fix the stwing."

"You know what that string reminds me of?" Enid asked, kneeling so her eyes could be closer to Connie's.

"What?"

"How a spider catches lunch."

"Huh?" Connie asked, her big eyes growing even larger.

Enid cut her glance to Reece. He seemed just as intrigued as the little girl. She cupped her hands and extended them to Connie. "Will you let me show you?"

Nodding, Connie relinquished the twine. Enid pointed to the end of the black spool that was visible at each end of the ball of string. "See this? This is like a big old fly that the spider catches in her web. Do you know what happens to a fly after it gets stuck in the web?"

She shook her head. "Uh-uh."

Enid began winding the string around the spool. "The spider winds a sticky string around and around and around, sort of like this, until the bug is all covered up."

"It does?" Connie placed a little forefinger on her chin. "How come?"

"To save him for lunch." Enid looked at Reece. She hoped her pleading expression told him how much she hoped he didn't mind her analogy. To her relief, he didn't seem to be angry, but amused. Enid wound the string until the ball was about a foot from the kite. She showed Connie her handiwork. "See? Just like that."

"Wow!" Connie had become so engrossed in the story, she had forgotten how hard she had fought for the privilege of wrapping the string around the spool herself. "How come?"

"How come what?"

"How come the spider saves the bug for lunch?" Connie wanted to know. "You mean the spider and the bug eat lunch together?"

Enid searched for an explanation that wouldn't upset the child, but came up blank. "Not exactly."

"The spider keeps the bug warm until lunchtime?"

Enid looked again at Reece. "Sort of."

"How come?" Connie inquired.

Another pleading look to Reece proved futile. He grinned and folded his hands across his chest, all the while lazily crossing one foot in front of the other so his legs formed a triangle. "You got yourself into this one. You'll have to get yourself out of it."

"I guess that's only fair." Taking Connie's soft little chin into her manicured hand, Enid gave Connie the best answer she knew. "Because that's God's plan."

"It is? Ooooh!" Connie answered.

Enid smiled. Finally she had given an answer that satisfied Connie's curiosty well enough.

"How come that's God's plan?" Connie asked.

Stemming the stream of questions wasn't going to be as easy as she thought. "Um, because," Enid tried to answer. "Because God has a plan for each and every living thing. He loves people especially. He loves you and Reece and me. The Lord especially loves little children like you, and He wants to know you. Did you know that?"

She shook her head.

"Well, He does."

"That's cool!"

Enid chuckled. "You sound just like a teenager."

"That's cool, too! And so are you, Miss Enid." Connie wrapped her little arms around Enid.

Enid squeezed her in return. She didn't realize until that moment that a hug from Connie would affect her so deeply. Fighting the mist in her eyes, Enid answered, "I think you're pretty cool, too."

Reece interrupted. "I hate to break up this little moment, but it's getting late." His expression revealed he was pleased with what had just transpired.

Connie let go of Enid and tugged at Reece's sleeve as they walked toward their cars. "Can we have hot chocolate? Please?"

"Not before lunch."

"Can we have it with lunch?"

"Maybe after I run my errand," Reece offered.

"What's an ewan?"

"A little job that has to get done."

As they were flying the kite, Enid had forgotten the real reason she was with Reece—to help him discover the whereabouts of his inheritance. She'd hoped he would let her see what the post office box contained, but apparently he had no plans to include her.

Her stomach tied itself in a dejected knot when she remembered that she wouldn't have been included in this excursion at all had Connie not extended the invitation. Enid had to face facts. She was no longer welcome. She had intruded long enough.

As they began walking to their cars, Enid felt a little hand tugging the hem of her jacket. "Can you come to our house an' eat lunch? We got hot dogs and macawoni and cheese again."

Again? How many times a week did Reece serve her such fatty, processed foods?

"And maybe even ice cweam for dessewt!" Connie promised.

More sugar-laden, empty calories. She tried not to grimace at the thought. "Do you take a vitamin every day, Connie?" She knew she was prodding, but Enid couldn't resist asking. She made sure not to look at Reece as Connie answered.

"Yep. I like the owange ones." Connie bounded into Reece's small automobile and hopped into the car seat in the back.

"Good." Enid knew most children's vitamins were loaded with sugar, but she supposed she should be glad that Reece was at least making an effort to see to it that the little girl was getting a few nutrients. "You keep on taking your vitamins every day. Promise?"

"I pwomise."

Enid watched Connie strap herself into her seat. "Wow! I'm impressed! You're such a big girl!"

Connie beamed at the compliment. "So. You comin' home with us?" she asked again.

"I really appreciate you asking me, but I need to get home."

"Oh." Connie didn't try to conceal the hurt expression that clouded her brown eyes. Soon, she brightened. "If you come and eat wif us, you don't have to take a vitamin."

"She knows that, Connie," Reece answered as he started the engine. "But we've kept Miss Enid out all morning. She probably has things to do."

"Can't you do ewans tomowow?" Connie asked.

"Tomorrow is Sunday. Ever since Pastor Ben preached a series of sermons on keeping the Sabbath holy, I try not to do any shopping on the Lord's Day."

"You don't?" Connie looked up at Enid as though she had just sprouted a mass of purple hair. "Then what do you do for fun on Sunday?"

Enid chuckled, being careful not to look in Reece's direction. "Oh, I have lots of fun."

Reece corrected Connie. "You don't need to ask so many questions. I'm sure Miss Enid has lots of things to do tomorrow."

Enid wished Reece had made at least a feeble protest to encourage her to join them for lunch. She kept her voice perky in spite of her disappointment. "I do need to be up early tomorrow morning. It's my turn to help out with the babies in the church nursery."

"Can I come?" Connie asked. "I like babies."

"No," Reece said.

"I'm sure you have your own church to go to," Enid added.

Connie shook her head.

"We'd better get going." Reece's voice seemed too eager. "Thanks for flying the kite with us today. Connie really enjoyed having you along."

"Yep!" the little girl agreed.

"Thanks. I had a great time." Reluctantly, Enid opened her car door.

She noticed Reece commented that only Connie was glad she had been along. All day she had thought Reece was enjoying himself. She felt comfortable in his presence, and she thought he had felt at ease with her. Had she misread Reece's body language?

She slid behind the wheel of her car, but didn't start the engine right away.

Watching them pull away, she thought about Reece and Connie. What would they find in the post office box? Perhaps cash? Stock certificates? Jewelry? A deed to property? Or maybe just an admonition to keep reading the Word. Reece would be pleased with that! She chuckled aloud in spite of herself.

Would Reece even bother to tell her what the package at the post office contained? Perhaps not. Though letting her know would be thoughtful, she didn't count on it. Most likely, handsome and personable Reece—and darling little Connie—had just slipped out of her life.

◈

Connie chattered all the way to the post office, but Reece was only half listening. He was too busy thinking about Enid. Images of the beautiful blond had lately taken precedence, even over his wildest fantasies about a large inheritance.

Though she certainly was beautiful, Enid possessed qualities far more important. She seemed to be so comfortable with God as a part of her life. The radiance and peace she possessed weren't the result of cosmetics. That much even he could see. How he wished for, longed for, Enid's confidence, her assurance!

Reece willed his mind to return to more practical matters. Enid had obviously connected with Connie, which was a good thing. Before Connie came into his charge, Reece had gone out on a few casual dates, but hadn't been too serious with anyone. Lindsay was the closest he had been to a meaningful relationship, but as soon as he gained custody of his little sister, Lindsay bolted. Since then, Reece had no opportunity to date, even casually, much less to form a lasting relationship. Keeping up with the toddler as she grew into a preschooler was enough to try the stamina of a pair of seasoned parents. Connie was truly a challenge for a bachelor with no previous experience.

Reece's thoughts returned to his love life—or lack thereof. Even when, on rare occasions, he did strike up a conversation with an attractive woman, she proved either to be married or turned off by the prospect of becoming an instant mother. Not that he blamed them. He hadn't been enamored with the prospect of imposed fatherhood at first, either. He was only in this situation out of necessity. Any woman he became interested in would be entering instant motherhood voluntarily.

Enid was the first woman who seemed the least bit interested in the package deal he offered. Not that he was anywhere close to making an offer. He had to get to know a woman first. Even worse than a woman loving him and not wanting Connie would be a woman falling in love with the little girl and being less than enchanted with him as a husband and father.

In his view, a successful family life meant marriage to a woman whose goal was to nurture Connie and any future children they might have together. After that, Reece hoped he and his wife could enjoy their golden years, relishing each other's company alone and eagerly anticipating family events. He pictured traveling, lolling about leisurely, pursuing hobbies—maybe even continuing education. For those dreams to come true, his future wife must be as committed to him as she would be to the children. Maybe even more so.

Reece remembered how Enid had included God in her explanation of a spider web when she was talking to Connie. He had never formed a significant relationship with a woman who talked about God as though He were a real part of her life.

How did religious people like Enid juggle their self-interests with their faith? And if he formed a romantic relationship with Enid, could he live with the knowledge that he wasn't first in her life?

Reece could see that if he wanted to be more than acquaintances with Enid, he would have to join a church. Maybe that was because she worked in a church, and so she must be around religious fanatics all the time. Maybe that's why she asked Connie about church. That question puzzled him. Enid seemed normal, having grown up in a broken home. So why didn't she understand that not everybody was turned on to church?

He didn't have anything against church. He even went so far as to say he was a Christian. Reece felt no qualms about his proclaimed faith. He knew other people who said they were Christians. Most were straight arrows, but others partied with the best of them.

Still, as far as going to church every week, the whole thing seemed to be a waste of time. The preacher always said Jesus died on the cross for everyone. No doubt such an act was a brave thing to do. But that was over two thousand years ago. How was that sacrifice supposed to help him today?

Reece felt his lips tighten. He didn't like how Enid implied that Connie needed to know about religion. Maybe she should. But how could he begin to teach Connie about something he really didn't understand?

His thoughts were in turmoil as he parked in the post office lot. With Connie in tow, still babbling, he rushed to the window.

"You just made it." The clerk pointed to a wall clock behind him. "It's one half minute to noontime. I'm ready to close for the day."

"I'm sorry. But if you could be so kind as to get this package for me—"

The clerk shook his head and muttered, "If we stayed open until three in the morning, someone would come running in here at 2:58 wanting me to find a package."

"We went flyin' kites!" Connie piped up. "Weece's fwiend, Miss Enid, went with us. She's pwetty."

"That's enough, Connie."

The man's face softened upon seeing the little girl. "No wonder you're running late, then." He took a chocolate candy out of his shirt pocket. "You don't mind if she has a piece of candy, do you?"

"Well, I—"

"Please?" Connie asked.

"Now how can you turn down that cute little face?" the clerk asked.

Reece shook his head helplessly. "I guess it's all right."

Obviously pleased, the clerk handed the candy to Connie.

"Thanks," she said, without prompting. Eagerly she began unwrapping the foil.

"You're welcome."

Grinning, the clerk took the yellow slip from Reece and disappeared into the back. Reece watched the clock tick five minutes away while Connie ran all over the lobby, investigating the mail slots and putting her hand in the stamp machine coin return to see if anyone had left spare change.

"Here you go. It took me awhile to find it." He slid a large box across the counter.

"Thanks." Reece's hands shook as he took the box. He hoped the clerk didn't notice.

"Thank you for the candy!" Connie chirped.

"You're welcome." The man waved and smiled before he let down the aluminum shield that indicated the post office was closed until the following Monday.

"Whazzat?" Connie asked as soon as she realized Reece held a box. "Is it fo' me?"

"I don't know yet. Maybe."

"Let me open it! Let me open it!" She jumped up and down, rays of hope beaming in her brown eyes.

"How about we open it together?" He motioned for her to follow him to the car.

"I don't wanna wait!"

Since no one else was watching, Reece figured it wouldn't hurt to open the package right away. He didn't want to admit it, but he was as eager to see its contents as Connie.

"I wanna open it. Please?"

Reece doubted the contents were fragile. "Oh, all right. But be careful."

Ignoring his admonition, she tore the brown paper off the box. Printed inside was the logo of the local grocer. Reece chuckled. Leave it to Aunt Agnes to economize by using an old grocery bag instead of buying packing paper from a store. However, the shirt box inside indicated that, at some point, his aunt had patronized an upscale department store. Or someone had given her an expensive gift. Upon contemplation, he decided the second scenario was more likely.

"Bet it's jus' clothes." Connie grimaced. "I wanted a teddy beah. A big bwown one. Or pink. Or white. Or maybe blue. Blue is for boys. Yuck. I wish I had a big pink teddy beah."

"Maybe you'll get one soon."

She gave him a beseeching look. "Can I have a pink teddy beah for Chwistmas?"

"Christmas is a long time off. Nine months away, to be exact."

"So it's tomowow?" Connie's voice lilted.

"No. Longer than that."

"How much longah?"

"A long time." He was becoming anxious, but attempted to keep the impatience out of his tone. "Come on. Let's enjoy today. Open the box."

The box wasn't taped shut, so Connie's frustration was kept to a minimum. She managed to turn the box upside down and let loose the bottom from the top. The top fell to the floor, along with tissue paper and whatever was inside. Connie was left holding the bottom of the box, but not for long. With a flourish, she threw the box bottom to the floor and made a dive for the crumpled white tissue paper. Upon exploring each piece, she threw it gleefully on the floor. Finally, after investigating each sheet of paper, she discovered an envelope.

The treasure turned out to be white, business-sized, with no label. Connie held it up for Reece to see. Puppy-dog eyes and a slight frown indicated her disappointment. "It's jus' an ol' lettah." As disgusted as is possible for someone so small, she tossed it on the floor.

"That's not polite." He held out his hand. "Let me see that, please."

She obeyed by handing him the envelope, pouting all the while.

Reece was hardly as distraught as Connie over the prize. He could only guess the many possibilities the envelope contained. With one eye, he watched her look for coins on the floor while he slipped his fingers under the sealed flap to open it. Maybe there was a letter inside. Maybe it told what the key opened!

Reece was conscious of his rapidly beating heart. To his delight, he discovered a piece of white notebook paper with a message written in Aunt Agnes's familiar scrawl:

Deliver my soul from the sword; my darling from the power of the dog (Psalm 22:20).

He groaned and kept reading:

Be not afraid, I say to thee
It is a friend who holds the key.

A friend? Which one of my friends does she mean? Surely it can't be Enid. Distraught, Reece exhaled angrily.

"What's the mattah?" Connie's eyes were wide.

"Nothing, Connie." After he picked up the torn box and discarded paper from the post office floor, Reece took her little hand in his. "Come on. Let's go home."

Chapter 5

"Are you busy?" a familiar voice asked Enid from behind her desk the following Monday. She swiveled her chair to face Reece. He was leaning in the doorway, just as he had on his last impromptu visit. As soon as she saw his bright, even features, she felt her stomach jump the way it did when she was little and had gotten an unexpected, but especially coveted, present on Christmas Day.

She more closely observed today's pleasant surprise. Reece's blond hair had been cut sometime since the past Saturday morning. The newly cropped style flattered the square jaw that looked as though God had taken extra care to chisel Reece's face into perfection. Reece wore an expression of anticipation. Had he stopped by on more than just a mystery-related errand?

"I'm not terribly busy today," she finally answered. "The monthly newsletter went out to the printer last week, and this week's bulletin for the worship service won't be ready until Thursday." She shrugged. "I'm basically answering the phone and holding down the fort today."

"Good. I come bearing gifts." He held up a paper bag from a fast-food chain and approached her desk. The smell wafting from the package promised delicious, grease-laden fries and juicy, fatty burgers. Enid knew she had no business eating either, but the scent promised a treat much more appealing than the cold turkey sandwich and yogurt she had packed in her lunch.

Reece unpacked the bag, laying its contents on her desk. "Hope you like their flagship burger."

Enid unwrapped the paper. Inside was a monstrous hamburger loaded with ketchup, mayonnaise, mustard, pickles, lettuce, tomato, onions, and bacon. She tried not to make a face. "I usually don't eat burgers this large, but I'll make an attempt."

"You can toss anything you can't eat. But don't let Connie know I told you that. Otherwise, she'll want permission to throw away all her vegetables except mashed potatoes. And speaking of potatoes," he said, reaching into the bag, "I got a super-sized order of fries for each of us."

Enid was astounded by the size of the pouches. Each contained more fries than she could hope to consume in a week.

Reece didn't seem to notice her wide eyes. Instead, he gave her a sheepish look. "I was hoping you wouldn't mind springing for coffee."

Eyeing the coffee pot, she gratefully realized it was nearly half full. "Looks like I can manage that." She smiled.

Enid was conscious of Reece watching her as she rose. She was glad she'd decided to take the time to set her shoulder-length blond hair with hot rollers that morning.

On impulse, she had worn a flattering and stylish fuchsia shift she had snapped up at an end-of-season sale the previous year. An unusual splurge on shoes in a matching deep pink color had paid off, taking the ensemble over the top in elegance. Never mind that blue jeans and a sweatshirt would be sufficient attire for her job. Enid believed since she faced a portion of the public—no matter how small—each day, she should try to look her best. And when she looked her best, she felt her best. An added reward was a sense that Reece was judging her appearance favorably. She allowed herself a triumphant little smile.

"So did you come by to tell me that Agnes left you a big check?" Enid asked as she poured the hot brew.

"I wish! All she left was another clue."

Enid's heart fluttered. As long as he needed her help, she would keep seeing Reece.

"I'm not surprised," she noted, managing to keep her voice casual. "I didn't think she'd let you off that easy. After all, she wanted you to read the Bible." She handed him his coffee, motioning for him to take a seat. "How's that coming along, anyway?"

"I'm still plodding along in Genesis. I haven't had much time to read." His tone was contrite.

"No need to apologize. There's a lot of wisdom to absorb in every book. I'm reading the Bible for the second time myself, and I'm taking away more wisdom from it now than I did the first time." She returned to her desk chair.

Reece's mouth dropped open. "You've already read it? The whole thing?"

She nodded. Realizing she may have appeared to be boasting, she looked at her lap. "And I plan to read it many more times, Lord willing."

He let out a low whistle. "I think I'll be lucky to get through it once."

A chuckle escaped her lips. "I know how you feel. You know what? I'm really humbled when I hear about people who've read the Bible all the way through twenty or thirty times. I think your aunt had read it through over thirty times."

He raised his eyebrows. "Maybe she was a fast reader."

"Maybe so." Enid poured a packet of ketchup over a few of her fries. "But I don't think she'd want you to hurry through it. My best advice is to take your time so you'll get the most out of your reading."

"I guess." He took a swig of coffee. "I'm amazed how many stories Genesis has in it. Seems like it has most of the stories I remember hearing as a young child."

"Quite a few, I'm sure. Although I'll bet your favorite isn't in Genesis," she remarked as she took her seat.

"Which one is that?"

"The story of David and Goliath."

He grinned. "Come to think of it, that always was one of my favorites. So it's not in Genesis, huh?"

"Nope. First Samuel." She took the last bite of her burger. Since she rarely indulged in burgers, she discovered they didn't taste quite as good as she recalled. However, Enid didn't have the heart not to finish the meal that Reece had been nice enough to provide. She washed down the last bite with what was left of her coffee. After leaving her seat, she offered Reece another cup.

He shook his head. "I have so much to learn. It's all so overwhelming." Reece took a bite of his burger, but Enid could see from his discouraged look that lunch was the last thing on his mind.

A twinge of guilt shot through her mind as she became conscious of the fact that she hadn't suggested they say grace before the meal. The feeling quickly melted when she realized the idea might have made him uncomfortable.

"All of us start out having to learn a lot. No one asks you to learn everything in one day." Enid stirred her fresh coffee. "So, what version of the Bible are you reading?"

He didn't answer right away. "The International something."

"The New International Version?" she asked.

"That sounds right. I hope Aunt Agnes doesn't mind that I'm not reading the King James Version. I started out with it, but I gave up after the first three chapters because I realized I wasn't taking in anything I was reading. I can't seem to get past the archaic language."

She chuckled. "I have a feeling your Aunt Agnes wouldn't mind a bit. She'd just be pleased to know you are reading any version of the Bible."

"That's a relief."

"I have some good commentaries if you'd like any passage clarified. I'd be happy to loan you one."

He nodded. "I might take you up on that. But first, I have another favor to ask." He withdrew a piece of paper from the pocket of his blue shirt. "Do you think you could help me with this?"

Enid took the paper from him and read:

> *Deliver my soul from the sword; my darling from the power of the dog (Psalm 22:20).*

> *Be not afraid, I say to thee*
> *It is a friend who holds the key.*

Enid creased her eyebrows together and shook her head. "I have no idea what she means. This truly is a puzzle."

Reece's crestfallen expression said it all. "Is it really? I was hoping maybe you were the friend?"

"Me?"

"Yes. She didn't know any of my friends well enough to leave them anything." His eyes rolled skyward. "And if she did, she'd know there's no way she could trust them to keep something like this from me. So naturally, I thought about you. You're the only mutual friend Aunt Agnes and I have. Or had." He shook his head as if to clear his brain. "Whatever."

"I'm flattered you thought of me, but I'm afraid I can't help you. She didn't leave anything with me. She probably knew better. I never could keep a secret either." Enid tittered and then realized Reece's expression revealed a broken heart. She was left with an unbearable feeling of disappointment. "I'm sorry. I wish I could do something to help. This inheritance is really important to you, isn't it?"

Reece balled up his burger wrapper and tossed it into the wastebasket. "It's not so much that I want it for myself. Even though I'd be lying if I tried to say I wouldn't mind having a few extra dollars to my name. The real reason I could use the money is for Connie. If my financial situation doesn't change much between now and the time she goes to college, I'm not sure how I'll pay for it. I know she can take out a loan and we could get some financial aid, but it sure would be easier on everybody if we didn't have to worry about it. I'd like for her to go wherever she wants to—to pursue whatever dream she has."

"But she's not even in kindergarten yet."

"Have you checked the price of tuition lately? It's not too early for me to be thinking about it."

"I can understand why you want her to go to college, but she might not have the same idea. When she's eighteen, she might want to travel instead or pursue a career that doesn't require so much schooling."

"On the other hand, she might want to be a pediatrician." A wry grin lit his face. "At least, this week she says that's what she wants to be when she grows up. That usually happens about this time of year, when I take her in for an ear infection, strep throat, or whatever's going around at day care. Next week she'll want to be an actress or a ballerina or a police officer."

Enid responded with a hearty laugh. "She's the typical girl, isn't she? Reece, I admire you for wanting to keep her options open. Whatever happens with the inheritance, I'm sure the Lord will provide."

"What if I decide I'd like other children one day? Will He provide for them?"

Enid wasn't sure how to answer. She hadn't considered he might want more children, and he hadn't even mentioned whether or not they'd arrive within a stable marriage. As for the Lord's provision, Reece's aggressive posture as he leaned toward her indicated he was asking as a skeptic.

"I–I'm sure He will. He's always been there for me. That's all I can say." She searched for safer verbal terrain. "And you'll learn about His faithfulness as you journey through your Bible reading."

"I know. I already have." Reece set his back against the seat, his posture relaxing as though he was no longer eager for verbal sparring. "I have to admit, I don't understand why He let Noah look like a fool building an ark in the middle of the desert."

"How else could He have worked His plan?" Enid asked. "He couldn't very well send the flood first, then tell Noah to build the ark."

"I guess you're right." His expression softened. "I'm sorry if it seemed like I was jumping on you. I didn't mean to. As long as I lived alone and my finances didn't affect anyone but myself, I didn't mind. I've never been a person who wanted to spend my whole life chasing a dollar. Now, being responsible for Connie, my outlook has changed. The older she gets, the more I realize I've got to provide the best I can for her. Any financial windfall would help."

"I thought you wanted the car."

"You've seen my car. Don't you think Aunt Agnes's is better?"

"I'd better not answer that." Enid let out a good-natured chuckle.

As he laughed in agreement, Reece's eyes focused on the wall clock. "Uh-oh. I'd better get moving if I want to get back to work on time."

"Thanks for lunch."

He rose from his seat. "No, thank you."

"I didn't do anything."

"You let me talk to you. That was enough. And I hope you'll call me if you think of anything."

"Of course."

He dictated his number to her so she could add it to her Rolodex file. As she watched him exit, she wished he had a better reason to give her a call.

❧

That evening during her quiet time with God, Enid felt burdened to pray for Reece and Connie. Bowing her head, she closed her eyes and sent up silent thanks and petitions. The prayers she uttered seemed inept and insufficient, yet in her solitude, she could feel the Lord leading her to remain available to both of them. She sensed the Lord had a plan to reveal. A feeling of peace poured over her.

As she dressed for bed, Enid wondered what the latest clue could mean. If she wasn't the friend Agnes referred to, then who could it be? Then she remembered what Reece told her about his thought process. He'd eliminated the possibility that the clue referred to a friend of his. But what about a friend of Agnes's? Maybe the friend was someone in the church who knew Agnes, but didn't know Enid well.

"That's it! I'll look through my Rolodex file tomorrow. I'm bound to come up with someone." Plans in place, Enid finally drifted off to sleep.

Chapter 6

T he next evening, Enid was exhausted after several hours on the telephone with Agnes's friends from church. Out of ten people, most of whom were dear elderly ladies who loved nothing better than a long chat, not one could help. In fact, none had even an inkling that Agnes had come up with such a scheme to bestow her belongings on her nephew.

Enid let out a tired sigh. Her clock told her the time was ten in the evening. Though the hour was later than when she usually initiated telephone calls, she decided to take a chance on Agnes's best friend, Inez. Everyone in church knew that each Tuesday night without fail, Inez went to her bridge club. Enid knew that trying to reach her early in the evening would be futile, but surely Inez would be home by now.

Agnes had told Enid many times that she and Inez had been among ten charter members of their church and had been close friends for forty years. Enid wondered why Agnes hadn't left Reece's letter with Inez.

If Inez couldn't help, then Enid would be forced to give up. She had exhausted her list and had no other leads.

"Yes?" Inez's pert voice answered on the fourth ring.

"Hello? Miss Inez?"

"Yes?"

"This is Enid. How are you this evening?"

"Enid! How wonderful to hear from you!"

Enid wondered why Inez seemed so excited to speak with her. They had just seen each other the previous Sunday, and though Enid harbored great respect for Inez, they had never been close. "Thank you. It's wonderful to hear your voice, too."

"How is your mother?"

"She's doing fine." Enid appreciated the kindness of the query but wondered why Inez asked about her since they'd never met.

"Is her arthritis any better?"

"Arthritis?" Enid's curiosity had progressed to puzzlement. "My mother doesn't have arthritis."

"Oh?" Inez paused, leaving the phone line filled with silent wonder. "You don't mean them doctors down there at Duke University found a cure for arthritis, do you?"

"Duke?" The puzzle was solved. "I'm afraid you must have me mixed up with someone else, Miss Inez. I'm Enid Garson. The secretary at church."

"You mean, you're not my cousin Maggie's daughter?"

"No, ma'am."

"Then who are you? You're not one of them salespeople that calls up pretending to know a person just so you can sell them something, are you?" Her voice had grown suspicious.

"No, ma'am," Enid was quick to reply. "I'm Enid Garson. The church secretary."

"Well, why didn't you say so? You've never met my people down in North Carolina, have you?"

"No, ma'am."

Seizing the opening, Inez immediately launched into a listing of her family tree and some tidbits of related history, including every woman's maiden name and married name. After Inez touched upon a few more topics, Enid noticed that the time had reached almost forty-five minutes past the hour. Apparently not realizing that Enid had never gotten the chance to state the purpose of her call, Inez began to make her excuses to hang up. Only after Enid caught her attention by sharing Agnes's intriguing clues did Inez put her concentration on what mattered most to her caller.

"No, she didn't leave anything with me," Inez said. "You say you already tried all of Agnes's other friends at church?"

"Yes, ma'am. Was she friendly with anybody in your bridge club? Maybe she left the inheritance with one of them."

The older lady cackled. "Never! If there was one thing Agnes hated, it was any type of card game. She always told me that playing cards was a big waste of time. We used to go back and forth, arguing about this, us two old ladies with nothing better to talk about. Well—unless we talked about our doctor visits and our health. You'll find the older you get, the more fascinating doctors become. And they get younger, too. Younger and younger every day. Kids, in fact. I just don't see how these little kids graduate from medical school."

"Yes, ma'am," Enid interrupted, hoping Inez wouldn't think her terribly disrespectful. Yet if she didn't get Inez back on topic soon, she'd be up all night. "You don't think she could have left the inheritance with a doctor, do you?"

"Oh, I doubt it. She didn't trust too many of them. Not since Dr. Mahoney died back in the winter of '64. Or was it the fall of '65? I don't suspect you'd remember."

"No, ma'am. Wonder who she left the inheritance with, then?"

"Hard to tell. Fact of the matter is, I'm surprised she went to all the trouble to leave a mess of clues around just to make you young people run all over here, there, and yonder, trying to find the money. That wasn't like Agnes at all. I would have thought she'd have been more straightforward than that. And she's not even here to see you work out the puzzle, God rest her dear soul." Inez began sniffling.

"I miss her, too."

"Excuse me." Enid heard the sound of Inez blowing her nose most heartily.

"I'm back," she said after a moment.

"I'm sorry. I didn't mean to upset you."

"You didn't, girlie. It's just old age. You get kind of sentimental. Well, sorry I couldn't help you none. And as much as I'd like to talk to you all night, I've got to go feed the dog."

"A dog? I didn't know you had a dog."

"You didn't know Agnes left Hot Dog to me?"

"So that's what happened to the dog. I wondered who had her."

"I thought everybody in church knew I was the one that ended up with the dog. Agnes and I had an agreement from the get-go that if anything ever happened to her, I'd take care of her little dog. I don't know what I was thinking when I agreed to it. I reckon I thought Agnes would live forever. Seemed that way."

"She was a hearty soul," Enid agreed.

"Anyway, Agnes said Hot Dog would keep me company. She keeps me company, all right. I've got to feed her all the time and let her in, let her out, let her in, let her out, all day long." She paused. "Now, don't tell anybody I said that."

"I won't."

"Agnes was trying to do me a favor. She loved that dog more than she loved most people. Guess that dog was the only friend she had, sometimes."

"Too bad Hot Dog can't talk. Maybe she could tell us where the inheritance is."

Inez laughed, a sound Enid welcomed. "Too bad, it is."

Enid was thoughtful as she hung up the phone. Inez hadn't been exaggerating when she said how much Agnes loved her little dog. Maybe Hot Dog was the friend in question. But how could a dog have a clue or know how to tell them about the inheritance? Obviously, no note, key, or other object had been passed to Inez when she inherited Hot Dog. She certainly would have mentioned it.

Suddenly a fresh thought popped into her mind. Enid snapped her fingers. "That's it! I know exactly what to do!"

Enid hurried to bed as eagerly as a little child on Christmas Eve. As soon as she could the next day, she would see if her idea brought her closer to Reece's inheritance.

❧

The next day after work, Enid rushed to see Inez. After a telephone call earlier in the day, the older lady was expecting her visit.

"I sure hope you find what you're looking for," Inez commented as she opened the door to her unassuming cottage. Hot Dog was right by her side, tail wagging.

"I hope so, too. If I don't, I'm lost." Enid bent down and greeted the animal with a pat on the head. "Hi ya, Hot Dog. Good girl."

The little dog panted and looked as though she were smiling.

"Run along now, Hot Dog," Inez instructed her. When the dog stayed put, Inez gingerly prodded her on the side with her foot, clad in a thick pink cotton bedroom slipper. "Get going."

Inez began walking toward the back of the house. Hot Dog stayed underfoot. "I'll get her trained right one of these days."

"I think she just likes you," Enid guessed.

"Maybe that's it." The elderly widow let a little grin touch her lips as they entered the kitchen. "Have something to eat?"

"I appreciate the offer, but no thanks."

"Not even some tea? I just brewed some this morning."

Enid declined. "I try not to drink caffeine this late in the day."

Inez shook her head. "You young people and your health kicks. I been drinking tea right steady for over seventy years, and I'm doing just fine, thank you very much."

"You certainly are, ma'am. I'm afraid I don't have your fortitude."

Inez looked pleased. Pleased enough to change the subject. "So, did Agnes say she was leaving you some money, too?"

"No. Why would you ask that?"

Inez shrugged. "I don't know. Just seems like you're taking a mighty big interest in finding these clues. You and Agnes's Reece an item?"

Enid felt her neck flush hot. "No, ma'am."

"I see." She nodded as though she was absorbing what Enid said, but she wasn't quite sure whether or not to believe it. "You're helping him out of the goodness of your heart. Too bad there aren't more people like you in the world."

Enid was loath to answer. Inez's assessment had only caused guilt to wrench her gut. But why? Wasn't she being nice to Reece out of the goodness of her heart? Or did she really have ulterior motives? Motives she wasn't ready to explore—at least not yet.

Inez crooked her finger, motioning for Enid to follow her to the basement door. "The dog sleeps in the corner, right beside the hot water heater. You'll see it as soon as you get down there. Can't miss it."

The little dog ran into the basement as soon as Inez turned on the light at the head of the stairs.

"I think she's going to lead me to her bed," Enid noted.

"She thinks it's time for me to feed her. She doesn't know it's not six o'clock yet."

Enid nodded and began her descent.

"You be careful now," Inez hollered. "Them steps can be tricky at times."

"I'll be careful." She wondered how Inez managed to navigate her way up and down the rickety steps to feed Hot Dog, but she decided not to press the issue.

Inez soon proved to be right. The hot water heater was impossible to miss. The dog's bed was the same as the one Agnes had had for her—a woven basket with a custom-made green cushion. Hot Dog stood in front of it, lapping water from her familiar ceramic bowl. Glad that the dog was occupied, Enid felt underneath the cushion. When her fingers touched a piece of paper, her heart began racing. Retrieving it, she discovered an envelope with a piece of paper inside.

"Any luck?" Inez called.

"Yes, ma'am!" Enid bounded up the steps. "I found it!"

"Well, what are you waiting for? Open it up."

Temptation tried to seduce Enid, but she held tight. "I can't. As much as I'd love to, I just can't. Not without Reece being here. It's his inheritance, after all."

"I suppose you're right." Inez took the envelope from Enid and held it up to the light. "Too bad I can't read what it says without opening it up. I'm not surprised. Agnes was way too smart to leave an important message around where just anyone could read it."

Inez gave Enid a conspiratorial look. "You know, we might could steam it open."

"I have to admit, the idea is tempting. But I'd better not."

"I can fix it back so's no one would ever know. That's how I used to read my daughter's mail." Inez put both hands on her hips. "Never would have found out she was going to up and elope on us if I hadn't, either."

"Yes, ma'am." Enid could tell by the way the woman was inhaling that she was gearing up to share a long story. "I'll bet that was really something. I'd love to learn all about it sometime. But I'd really better get this to Reece." She started heading for the door, ignoring Inez's disappointed look at the prospect of losing her audience.

"You'll let me know what it says, won't you?" Inez called as Enid rushed to her car.

"Yes, ma'am. And thanks again!"

Chapter 7

Enid trembled with excitement as she pulled her car out of Inez's drive. She punched Reece's number into the cell phone, hoping she wouldn't get the answering machine. He answered on the second ring.

"Reece, it's me, Enid. Do you mind if I drop in for a visit?"

"Now?" His voice indicated surprised pleasure. "Sure. You need directions, don't you?"

As soon as Reece named the apartment complex where he lived, Enid knew he didn't need to bother with giving directions. She had passed the well-maintained development many times and could almost drive to it with her eyes shut. All she needed was the unit number.

"So to what do I owe this honor?" Reece wanted to know.

"I figured out the solution."

"To the puzzle?" The exhilaration was evident in his voice. "You found the inheritance?"

"Not exactly. But I did find out who Agnes's friend is. It's Hot Dog!"

"Hot Dog?" Only a split second passed before Reece broke out into chortles of laughter. His mirth was so loud that Enid had to hold the phone away from her ear for a moment. "I should have known. Man's best friend is supposed to be his dog. Looks like a dog can be woman's best friend, too. But I'm wondering, how did you come to that conclusion?"

Enid recounted her detective work.

"Whoa! You spent all night on the phone?"

"Not all night. Just most of it." She let out what she hoped was a good-natured chuckle.

"You didn't have to go to all that trouble, Enid, but I really appreciate it."

Suddenly feeling humbled by his obvious sincerity, Enid delivered a flippant "You'd better!" as she turned into the parking lot.

Once she hung up the phone and exited the car, Enid bounded up the outdoor concrete steps to his second-story unit. She was thankful when Reece answered the door promptly. Enid wasn't eager to prolong her stay in the chilly night air.

"Come on in!" he greeted her with a smile, an element of contagious excitement in his voice. Stepping back, he motioned for her to enter the apartment.

As she obeyed, Enid tried not to make her study of the room obvious. The living space was merely adequate for two. She wasn't surprised that the walls were painted off-white and equally neutral beige carpeting covered the floor. The living room and dining room were combined into one area, with a minuscule kitchen visible through a rectangular hole cut in the wall. Enid presumed its purpose was to allow food to be passed to the dining area without the cook leaving the stove. On the side of the kitchen was a short hallway with a linen closet. She assumed two bedrooms and a bathroom lay beyond her field of vision.

"I doubt my coffee is as good as yours," Reece said, "but I'd be glad to make a pot."

"I'm fine, thanks."

Following him to the couch, Enid noted that Reece had decorated the walls with posters of impressionistic artwork. The pictures were mounted in sleek black metal frames. Classical music was reverberating from a set of relatively high-end stereo speakers. Two loaded compact disc towers testified to Reece's love of music. Enid couldn't read the titles from her vantage point, but she assumed she could find more classical titles in his collection. Enid noticed that Reece's television set was oversized and looked to be only a few years old.

Where he had splurged on electronics, Reece had apparently economized on the other furnishings. A beige recliner looked as though it had seen years of wear. Enid wondered if the chair had been a cast-off from Reece's parents or if he had bought it secondhand. The love seat, though beige, didn't match the recliner. A pine veneer end table and contemporary lamp both appeared to be purchases from a trendy discount store catering to college students.

If Reece noticed Enid was observing her surroundings, he didn't let her know. With a sweeping motion, he offered her a seat on the couch. As she accepted, he observed, "Maybe this is it. Maybe I'll finally learn what Aunt Agnes left me."

"I have no idea what it says," Enid confessed as she relinquished the prize.

"You didn't open it?" he asked as he sat beside her.

She shook her head. "Nope. Not that I wasn't tempted, mind you. Inez offered to steam the envelope open, but I declined."

"Did she really? That's a hoot," Reece said. "Thanks for waiting for me. At least we won't have to be in suspense any longer!"

As soon as he tore open the envelope, Reece extracted a piece of white paper that looked just like the others. His shoulders slumped. "It's another clue."

"Looks like Agnes was determined to make you work for this inheritance."

"Sure looks like it. This has turned into a mystery of some complexity."

"True. But you know, this is kind of fun." She smiled.

"That's easy for you to say. It's not your inheritance we're hunting for."

"You've got a point."

At that moment, Reece looked into her eyes, sending a now familiar tingle up Enid's spine. "Come to think of it, there are some enjoyable elements."

Enid hoped her instincts were right—that he meant he enjoyed being with her. All the same, she thought it best not to answer right away. Instead, she began studying a nearby bookshelf that towered almost to the ceiling, indicating that he shared her love of printed matter. Reece's bookshelf was overflowing so that several books were piled on the floor in front of the bottom shelf. She could see from thin, brightly colored spines that two of the shelves were devoted to children's books. Obviously Reece knew the value of reading to Connie. With such encouragement, surely Connie would grow in her love of books as she grew into adulthood.

Reece interrupted her musings. "Listen to this—"

> *Behold, I will stand before thee there upon the rock in Horeb; and thou shalt smite the rock, and there shall come water out of it, that the people may drink. And Moses did so in the sight of the elders of Israel (Exodus 17:6).*

> *Water rushes over rocks*
> *Near the place I hang my socks.*

"Near the place she hangs her socks?" Reece wondered aloud. "What could that riddle mean?"

A quick thought flashed through Enid's mind, causing her to gasp with delight. "Oh, it's easy, Reece. There's a little creek near her clothesline. The note mentions a rock. The next clue must be underneath one of the rocks there."

Paper in hand, Reece folded his arms and set his brown eyes skyward. "That's just great. We'll be all night looking under every rock in the yard."

Remembering her days as a Junior Girl Scout, Enid lifted her first three fingers in the air. "I promise to leave no stone unturned to help you find the next clue."

"Very punny." Reece pressed his lips together. He seemed to be trying to suppress a laugh at Enid's lame attempt at humor, but he burst out laughing all the same.

"Like your humor isn't just as pitiful." Enid giggled along with him before turning serious. "I have a feeling there aren't too many rocks big enough to hide messages under."

"Is that you, Miss Enid?" Connie emerged from her bedroom. She was already dressed in a warm pink sleeper. As soon as she spotted Enid, the little girl's cherubic face lit with a smile. "Oh, good. It is you!" She flew toward Enid. In turn, Enid patted her lap and extended her arms. Connie bounded into her lap and gave her a squeeze, which Enid returned gently.

"Did I wake you up, honey?" Enid asked after Connie broke their embrace.

"Nope. I wasn't asleep."

Enid looked to Reece for confirmation. For a shadow of an instant, she caught him wearing a wistful expression. She wondered what he was thinking.

Apparently afraid of appearing vulnerable, Reece recovered. "She never goes to sleep when I put her to bed."

Connie wrinkled her nose. "He puts me to bed way too eawly."

"Too early? You're so slow in the mornings, I don't think I put you to bed early enough," Reece commented.

Connie shook her head. "Too eawly." She stepped over to Enid's side and tugged on her hand. "Look." The little girl held up a sheet of paper scribbled with crayon. "I dwew this fo' you."

"Ahhh!" Enid took the artwork from her hand. After studying the picture, Enid wasn't sure she could identify the subject.

"What is it, Connie?" Reece asked.

"Don't you know what it is?" Connie wondered, disappointment clouding her button-like features. "I bet Miss Enid knows."

Enid swallowed. "I want you to tell me all about it."

Connie looked at her doubtfully, but decided to comply. She pointed to a section that was predominately pink. "This is you. See the hair?"

"It's green."

Connie smiled. "I made it gween. Isn't it pwetty?"

"Um, I suppose so." She touched Connie's soft cheek with her fingertips. "What makes it special is that you drew it yourself. Thank you."

"Will you put it on the wefwigewatoh? We have lots of pictures on the wefwigewatoh." She pulled Enid's hand, leading her into the kitchen to see the refrigerator. "Come see."

Enid eyed Reece, silently seeking permission to go along.

"Don't look at the dirty dishes in there," he apologized.

"Don't worry. I won't." The kitchen provided enough space for one lone cook to barely move around. Still, the room boasted all the latest conveniences, including a dishwasher—a luxury Enid didn't have.

"Look!" Connie said. "You awen't looking!"

Enid snapped her head in the direction of the refrigerator. "I'm looking now."

True to Connie's promise, the refrigerator was covered with her artwork. Only a few bits and pieces of the appliance's almond surface were visible underneath the collage of papers held on by a variety of kitchen magnets.

"See?" She pointed to a drawing that looked like a bunny. "That's a dog."

"His ears are quite big."

"He's like Dumbo. He needs to heah."

"I see. Can he fly?"

Connie shook her head. "Only Dumbo can fly."

"I see! You're quite an artist," Enid told her.

Connie looked up into Enid's face, beaming. "I like dwawing."

"I can tell."

Reece entered the kitchen, stopping behind Enid to admire his informal art gallery. "I'm about to run out of space."

Enid laughed. "Don't worry. Your refrigerator looks like just about every other one in America."

"No, it doesn't!" Connie protested. "Nobody else dwaws pictures like mine. Mrs. Jones said so."

"That's true," Enid conceded, "and now I can start my own art gallery on my refrigerator. I'll know that I'm the only person in the world with a picture just like this one. Thank you." She knelt down and extended her arms for a hug.

"Welcome!" Connie returned the hug as though she wanted to hold on to Enid for dear life.

"All right, enough hugs for one night," Reece said after they broke the embrace. "Time to go back to bed, Connie."

"Do I have to? Can I stay up until Miss Enid leaves?"

"I'll be leaving soon," Enid assured her. Noticing a small window at the end of the kitchen, she saw that night peered through cracks in the curtain. "It's already past dark."

"Are you afwaid of the dawk?"

"Not really."

Connie expanded her chest. "Neither am I!"

Reece gently pushed Connie's shoulder. "All the more reason why you need to get back to bed, little girl."

Apparently Reece's tone, though not unduly rough, told Connie that any possibility of prolonging the argument was over. "Okay. I'll go. Will you be here tomowow, Miss Enid?"

"I'm afraid not. But I'll see you again soon."

"I wish you would be here tomowow. Mommy always used to be with me all the time."

Enid didn't know what to say. None of the thoughts that popped into her head seemed right.

Thankfully, Connie moved quickly to the next topic. "Wanna see my bed-woom shoes? They have stahs and moons."

"Another time, Connie," Reece said.

"Oh, alwight." Connie blew Enid a kiss.

Enid blew her a kiss in return. "Night-night."

"Night-night."

As he leaned against the counter and watched his young charge depart, Reece's look of sadness was unmistakable. "She always used to blow kisses to her mom every night before she went to bed," he explained.

Judging from Reece's heartrending expression, Enid deduced that rather than being Reece's former wife or exgirlfriend, Connie's mother had passed away. Enid wasn't certain how to respond, or if she should. How can one express the right sentiment to a man who had lost the woman he loved, leaving him with a child to rear alone?

As though he knew she couldn't respond, Reece sighed. "Too bad it's already dark. I'd love to search for the next clue tonight."

"How about tomorrow?" Enid hoped she didn't seem too happy about the change in topic.

"We could meet for lunch? I might even spring for another burger."

"Uh, why don't you let me bring a picnic lunch? I have a feeling you might like some real food for a change."

Connie reappeared. "Oh, can I come? Can I?"

"What are you doing back up, squirt?"

She looked sheepish. "I was thiwsty. Can I have some juice?"

"You know that's too much sugar this late at night. You may have some water, though." He retrieved a plastic cup from the dishwasher and ran some tap water into it.

"Can I go?" Connie persisted.

"I wish you could, but there's no way I can get you from day care and back and have time to eat and look for clues, too. I'm sorry." To Enid's pleasure, Reece's apology seemed genuine rather than just an attempt to appease Connie.

"I wish you could come too, Connie," Enid added. "You could be a real help to us, looking under all those rocks. I'll bet you'd find the clue even before we did." Enid placed her forefinger on the end of the child's nose. "Know what? I have a great idea."

"What?"

"How about I pack you a special supper, with lots of good things to eat and a treat, too. Then it would be just like being with us on the picnic. Would you like that?"

Connie nodded.

"Wow!" Reece agreed. "That's really something, Connie. You should thank Miss Enid for being so considerate of you."

"What's con—con—si—dwate?"

He grinned. "Considerate. It's a big word meaning that Miss Enid is being nice to you."

"Oh!" A beam of understanding lit Connie's face. She nodded vigorously. "She is!"

Her admission sent both adults into peals of laughter.

"What's so funny?" Connie wanted to know. Puckering her mouth, she looked as though she was trying to decide whether or not she should be insulted.

"You're just cute as a button, that's what's so funny." Enid playfully nudged her forefinger on Connie's pajama-clad tummy. The girl burst into a musical laugh.

289

Enid hated for her visit with Reece and Connie to end, but she knew she was keeping Connie up well past her bedtime. As she glanced at Reece to bid him farewell, once again she caught a look of yearning etched upon his features. His face had never seemed more gorgeous to Enid than at that moment. If they had been actors in a movie, Enid was certain that this would be the scene where Reece would send Connie to bed so he could give Enid a kiss goodnight. Enid imagined the kiss would be tender. . .loving. . . .

What was she thinking? She forced herself to return to the here-and-now. "See you tomorrow, Reece." Putting her feet into motion, she waved as though she were a beauty queen riding on a parade float. Dropping her gaze, she waved a second time. "Bye-bye, Connie!"

"Bye-bye, Miss Enid!" Connie waved with both hands.

Hours later, Enid was anguished as she approached her evening's devotions. She had to find the passage. Somewhere, she knew there was a scripture that would give her God's answer as to why she had to stop her troublesome thoughts. Lately, she'd been having many disconcerting fantasies that she and Reece could be more than friends.

What was she thinking? Maybe they couldn't even be friends. Not for long, anyway. She would help Reece find his inheritance. Then she would distance herself from him. Of course, she would think of him now and again, and she was prideful enough to think that maybe he would miss her, too. And so would Connie. But little girls were resilient. Connie would soon move on to new friends and new adventures. They would go on with their lives. Hopefully, Agnes's inheritance would make them richer. Reece would be at peace, knowing he could provide the best for Connie. And Enid would go on. Somehow.

She flipped through the pages. Now, where was that verse? That problematic verse? After a few moments, she discovered it in her King James Bible, 2 Corinthians 6:14: *"Be ye not unequally yoked together with unbelievers: for what fellowship hath righteousness with unrighteousness? and what communion hath light with darkness?"*

Hoping against hope that the New International Version would offer a kinder, gentler translation, she thumbed through her second Bible to the same verse and read: *"Do not be yoked together with unbelievers. For what do righteousness and wickedness have in common? Or what fellowship can light have with darkness?"*

Enid closed her Bible, her heart heavy with emotion. "Lord," she prayed, "why did You bring Reece into my life? Surely You know I don't want to disobey Your Word. I have no desire to be yoked with an unbeliever. I want to think that Reece loves You, but he's told me plainly that he doesn't know You at all. And he has the responsibility for a dear little girl. I have no idea where she came from, Lord. Is Reece divorced? A widower? Or was Connie born out of wedlock? I am not Reece's judge, Lord, but I know I can't think of him, even as a friend, when he seems so lost and unrepentant. So why do I feel drawn to him? Why must I be tempted by how handsome he is, how he looks at me when he thinks I'm not watching? What is Your answer, Lord? Please, help me!"

Enid closed her eyes, waiting for the Lord to answer. Though He didn't draw her a road map on how to handle her feelings for Reece, a rush of peace entered her. At that moment, she knew He would walk beside her every step of the way.

Chapter 8

In spite of a sense of reassurance from the Lord the previous night, Enid felt jittery the next morning as she packed the picnic lunch. She tried to make herself believe she was mainly concerned with what the next clue would reveal. But if she were to be honest, she had to admit that, in reality, she hoped Reece would enjoy the lunch—and more of her company.

She assembled two sandwiches with meat from a roasting hen she had prepared the previous day. The tender white chicken would be a lean and nutritious alternative to the burgers Reece had proposed. Enid piled Reece's sandwich high atop fortified whole-wheat bread, while keeping her own sandwich sparse. In separate containers, she included yellow mustard, deli mustard she bought just for this occasion, light mayonnaise, and her personal favorite spread for white meat sandwiches—guacamole. The fatty vegetable spread was an indulgence, but an older lady she once knew told Enid that the oil in avocados was healthy for feminine skin. Enid hadn't yet arrived at the age to be fighting wrinkles, but she hoped to hold them off as long as she could. She involuntarily touched her face. Her pale, sun-sensitive skin was still smooth and creamy. So far, the moist green insurance had worked. All the same, just in case Reece craved something green other than guacamole, she'd included a generous helping of alfalfa sprouts on each sandwich.

Sealed in a separate plastic container was a fine salad consisting of spinach leaves, red cabbage, shredded carrots, alfalfa sprouts, sun-dried tomatoes, snow peas, mushrooms, and sunflower seeds. Just to cover all her bases, she had purchased one packet of low-fat Italian dressing and one packet of fat-free ranch dressing from the grocery store salad bar. Surely Reece would like one of those flavors well enough.

Enid peered into the basket again, double-checking to be sure she'd included the berries. She didn't know which Reece would prefer—strawberries or blueberries, so she bought a pint of each for several dollars. They were the first berries she'd seen this spring, both varieties well ahead of their peak season. Even with paying a ridiculous price, she couldn't guarantee they would burst with flavor. She'd had to cut away some bruised places in the strawberries, worse for wear from traveling from a land with a hot climate, probably Chile. When she washed the blueberries, several tiny green ones had to be culled from their purple cousins. Those that passed for ripe were barely so. Still, both varieties of berries would be a treat. Enid made sure to include a small carton of gourmet half-and-half cream to pour sparingly over them, along with a few packets of sugar-free sweetener. Who could resist such a delectable indulgence?

For the grand finale, Enid had made no-bake cookies out of wholesome ingredients—nuts, rolled oats, raisins, and peanut butter. She had included a few extra in Connie's bag for Reece to take home. Enid couldn't think of a better way to sneak in a few extra vitamins in the child's diet.

One last look revealed she had everything—utensils, plastic plates and bowls, sparkling water. Enid shut the lid and fastened it. Letting out a satisfied sigh, she rubbed her hands together. What a perfect picnic lunch! So much better than the prefabricated junk he usually ate. Reece would be thrilled.

Two hours later, Reece drove Enid to Aunt Agnes's house for an early lunch and clue-hunting expedition. He wasn't sure which he looked forward to more—finding the next clue that would take him closer to his inheritance or being with Enid again. He glanced over at the blond sitting in the passenger seat next to him.

Enid. Of the two prospects, he definitely looked forward to seeing Enid more often. As usual, she was overdressed for the occasion. At first her style had put him off, but over time he found he had come to enjoy seeing a woman in something other than sweat pants or blue jeans. Not that he saw many women outside of the pharmacy, when they were usually sniffling, feverish, and hardly at their best. In the mornings he often ran into one or two executive types dropping their kids off at the day care, but even they relaxed their dress code on Fridays.

Enid never let up. Wearing pants, as she was on this day, might have even been called a stretch for her. But what impeccable pants they were, with matching blazer, a perfectly matched soft rose blouse, and one thin strand of pearls that seemed to have a pink luster. Though hardly a follower of fashion dictates, Reece could see the quality in Enid's clothing. He wondered if instead of going all over the place searching for clues, he should sign up to be a church secretary.

He considered how much a congregation of about a hundred people could pay a secretary and quickly changed his mind. Her salary certainly couldn't have been called spectacular. She was a whiz with money, that's all. Not that being a financial genius was a drawback in a wife.

Wife! He mentally kicked himself, much as he had been doing almost from the day he met Enid. If she had any idea how often his mind wandered to the subject of love and marriage, Enid would have a good laugh at his expense. Marry a heathen like him? No way!

So why did his feelings betray him? Cutting his gaze to her, Reece caught Enid staring out the window. That was another thing he liked about his lunch companion. She didn't fill the air with nervous chatter. When she spoke, there was usually a reason. A good reason. She wasn't like many beautiful women he knew who talked about nothing, or worse, focused conversation on herself.

Yes, Enid was what he looked forward to most. No need to let her know that, though. After she had a good laugh, she might decide to take him seriously. She might even get the idea he would agree to be a missionary in a jungle somewhere.

He parked the car on the street in front of his aunt's house and killed the engine. Remembering his manners, he grabbed the basket out of the back seat and hurried to Enid's side of the car to open the door for her. Her pleasured look at being pampered was his reward.

"Since we know where the next clue is," he ventured as they headed for the backyard, "why don't we go ahead and find it before we eat?"

The familiar smile he had come to love caressed her lips. "Can't wait, huh?"

"I admit it. The suspense is killing me." He sighed. "Wouldn't it be nice if this were the last clue?"

"Oh, I don't know. Somehow I doubt Agnes plans to let us off that easy."

Us. Reece couldn't resist a smile. He liked the sound of that. What a pleasant surprise, to have Enid use the word. And so casually, too—as though they'd been together for a long, long time.

Stealing a look her way, he wished they had been together forever.

"I feel badly that you're dressed so well for work, and all I'm offering you is an outdoor picnic," Reece observed. He knew the compliment about her appearance sounded half-hearted, but he was reticent to be too forward with Enid. She was only helping him because she was so kind, always evident in the way she related to Connie. After he discovered his inheritance, she'd be out of his life. The thought left him with an unwelcome twinge of loneliness.

"I don't feel bad about it. I brought an old tablecloth and plastic cushions for us both."

She seemed genuinely unworried about her attire. Reece only hoped she was telling the truth. "First things first," he said as he placed the basket on the ground beside a massive oak that had been a fixture in the yard since he was a child. "We'd better see what Aunt Agnes has in store for us now."

The trek through the backyard revealed only a few rocks of reasonable size under the clothesline. "This should be easy." Enid knelt, struggling to overturn one of the larger rocks.

"Let me." Remembering Enid's carefully polished pink fingernails, Reece hurried over to her side. "No need for you to muss your manicure."

"Really, Reece, I'm not that vain."

"That's not what I meant," he blurted. "All the same, I'd feel better if you'd let me."

She rose, stepped back, and placed her hands on her hips, posing as though she planned to watch him. "All right, my big He-Man."

With both fists, Reece beat rapidly on his chest as though it were a bongo drum. "Me Tarzan. You Enid."

Reece's lunch companion burst into laughter. "Me Enid go set up food."

As Enid spread the cloth over a level portion of newly grown, light green grass, Reece poked and prodded a few of the larger rocks. Finally, after the fifth try, he spotted a portion of a familiar looking white envelope. "Pay dirt!" Eagerly he dug through the soil until he unearthed the envelope. Thankfully, Aunt Agnes hadn't buried it too deeply. It was safely tucked inside a plastic freezer bag.

"Any luck?" Enid called from her spot on the ground.

He nodded his head in an exaggerated motion. "Yep!" He began walking swiftly toward her, holding up the envelope as though it were a first-place trophy.

Enid clapped her hands and bounced up and down. The motion reminded him of Connie. No wonder they got along so well together.

"What does it say?" she asked as soon as he got close to the blanket.

"I haven't opened it yet. I waited until you could see it, too."

"You waited the whole thirty seconds, huh? Must have just about killed you."

"Just about!" he jested in return.

Reece removed the envelope from the dirty baggie and tore it open as Enid watched over his shoulder. They read its contents together:

And unto man he said, Behold, the fear of the LORD, that is wisdom; and to depart from evil is understanding (Job 28:28).

From this box evil we see
If from its wickedness we do not flee.

"Huh?" they said in unison.

"What could she possibly mean?" Enid wondered aloud.

"Maybe she has a wicked genie trapped in a bottle somewhere. At this point, nothing would surprise me." Reece groaned.

Enid let out a melodious laugh. "If we do find a genie, maybe he'll let us know where your inheritance is. But I have a feeling we're on our own. But that's not so bad. We've gotten this far, haven't we?"

"Can't deny that." He flashed Enid his best smile. "I couldn't have done this much without your help."

"As they say, two heads are better than one. But give yourself some credit. You would have eventually figured everything out on your own."

"You have more confidence in me than I do in myself." He looked eagerly at the picnic basket. "I do know one thing. I'm hungry, and I'm confident I'll like whatever you've made. On second thought, I guess that's two things."

"Yes, it is. And I think you will!"

The light shining in her green eyes was so appealing. She was obviously proud of the lunch she had prepared. For more than one reason, Reece was glad he'd agreed to let Enid bring a picnic basket. The day was beautiful. Rain had visited their part of Virginia throughout most of the previous week, its cold droplets ranging from chilly drizzle to driving torrents. The past few days had been sunny. The ground had dried enough so that sitting on the grass, especially shielded by a cushion, didn't mean risking your good clothes to dampness. The sun was warm, but not too warm. Reece knew he was comfortable in his light windbreaker, and Enid looked plenty cozy in her blazer. For an instant, he thought that was too bad. He had no good excuse to put his arm around her.

No matter. He would enjoy a meal prepared by a woman's hands. A woman who cared for him, not just someone in a cheerful uniform who just wanted to know what number of combo meal he was ordering. Reece watched Enid open one of the containers on the blanket. She dished out a portion of salad onto a sectioned disposable plate. He wasn't sure what was in it, but some of the ingredients looked strange. What was that substance that looked like the weeds he used to pull out of his mother's garden? He tried not to grimace. When consuming a salad, Reece was a lettuce, tomato, and crouton man. In his view, three ingredients were the greatest of plenty for any reasonable human. Well, maybe he could drown the offensive vegetables in plenty of French dressing.

"I brought ranch and Italian dressing," she informed him.

Yuck. "Um," he said aloud, "I'll take ranch, I guess."

Her smile drooped into a slight frown. "Oh, no. You don't like either one."

He grinned, although he feared his expression looked like he was trying to be optimistic about major surgery—and failing. "I usually go for French, but that's fine. How were you supposed to know?" Reece reached out his hand and took the packet of ranch dressing from her. He read the label. "Fat free." He swallowed.

"Yes," she said brightly. Enid gave him a look that showed she could read his thoughts. "You know, fat-free cream dressings can take some getting used to. Would you rather have the Italian?"

"You don't mind?"

"Oh, no. I like either. Guess that's one advantage of being the chef. I can buy what I like."

"Are you hinting that I should be the chef next time?"

"I don't know. Depends on what you like." She tossed him the other packet, and he happily relinquished the ranch dressing.

Reece read the second label. "Fat-free."

Enid nodded. "You don't mind, do you? I always get fat-free dressings. Did you know that if you eat fat-free condiments all the time, you can keep off at least ten pounds a year?"

"Really?" The sacrifice didn't seem worth it to Reece.

"Well, that's what I read somewhere."

"In a woman's magazine, no doubt."

She gave him a sheepish half-grin. "Yes, I admit it. But it makes sense, doesn't it?"

He shrugged. "I suppose."

"Sorry. I'll know to get French next time."

Next time. Reece decided he could make do with substandard dressing just this once.

"And look!" She withdrew several little plastic containers filled with various concoctions. He couldn't tell what most of them were since each container was a different color.

"You're quite organized."

"I like to think so." She looked as pleased as Connie did when she brought home an especially good drawing from day care. Enid tapped her forefinger on each one. "I have mayonnaise, mustard, deli mustard." She emphasized the word "deli" as though the concept were exceedingly exotic. "And guacamole." She tapped the guacamole jar as though she were an orchestra conductor on the last triumphant note of *Beethoven's Fifth Symphony*.

"Guacamole?"

"Yes. I always put guacamole on chicken sandwiches."

"Oh." He supposed a nice, juicy piece of Southern-fried chicken was out of the question.

She handed him a sandwich, and upon unwrapping it, Reece discovered she had used wheat bread. Oh, well. She didn't know he never ate anything but white. Upon further inspection, he discovered the sandwich was loaded with white chicken meat that looked bland but tender. Too bad she had to go and ruin it with more of that grassy stuff. Did the store have a sale on that this week or something?

"I know it's unusual to use guacamole on sandwiches when most people use it as a dip. But that's me. I'm a bit unusual."

"That's part of your charm."

She giggled as though no one had ever given her a compliment. He found the gesture endearing.

"Um, is the guacamole fat-free?"

She shook her head. "Avocados are one vegetable they haven't made a substitute for. At least, I haven't found one."

"If I were you, I wouldn't look too hard," Reece quipped. He reached for the container. "All right. I'll try it." He spread the green concoction onto the bread. "What are those red things in it?"

"Sun-dried tomatoes."

"Oh." He placed the slice of bread on top of the concoction and reluctantly tasted the result. "Mmm."

"Is that a good 'mmm'?"

He nodded and swallowed. "Surprisingly good. The guacamole adds a little spicy flavor."

"That's what I think." She tapped him on the knee. "See? You learn something every day."

"That you do."

"Would you care for some coffee?" she asked, drawing a thermos from the basket.

He nodded. At least he already knew he could trust her coffee. He picked through his salad and he enjoyed the warm beverage.

"I see you ate your salad, even if you didn't have French dressing."

"Yes, but I have to admit, lettuce and tomatoes would have been sufficient. And croutons."

"Croutons? Those greasy things, drowning in all those dried-out herbs?" She wrinkled her nose in an appealing way. "Perish the thought."

"You should try them. You might learn something," he teased.

"You have a point. I do like to put a lot of ingredients in my salad, though. I read a book that said if you eat foods of all different colors, you'll get all the various nutrients you need."

"Interesting concept. You seem to read an awful lot," he couldn't resist adding.

"And so do you, I noticed."

He stopped his sandwich midair. "How do you know that?"

"From your bookshelf," she said triumphantly. "You have so many books on it, there isn't even room for them all."

"Oh, that." Reece twisted his mouth in a sign of chagrin. "I know all those books on the floor look messy, but Connie's library took over two of my shelves. I need to get a bookcase for her room. I just haven't had a chance." He didn't want to admit he didn't have the funds, either. Why was he hiding that from Enid? Surely she had a good handle on his financial situation by now. Reece supposed pride made him say such a silly thing.

"No need to apologize. I'd rather see an overflowing bookcase than one without any books at all. I think it's wonderful that you and Connie have so many books," Enid assured him. "You do read to her every night, don't you?"

Reece fought back the feeling of insult. Did she think he never paid any attention to Connie? "Of course."

"That's wonderful." Apparently oblivious to the fact her comment had seemed like a put-down, Enid dove into the basket and took out two plastic containers. She held one up in each hand for him to see. "Which do you like better, strawberries or blueberries?"

The invitation made him forget the residual negative feelings upon being insulted. "You've got berries at this time of year?" Reece let out a low whistle. He decided to explore an earlier thought. "They must be paying you pretty well at the church."

"I wish!" She laughed. "This is a definite indulgence for me."

"In that case, I'll indulge along with you. Let me have a few of both. You can mix them in one bowl."

"Sure. I think I'll do that myself." As she dished out the portions, she asked, "Sweetener and half-and-half?"

He noted that the half-and-half was labeled "fat-free."

"Um, no thanks. Say, how can half-and-half be fat-free?" He shook his head. "On second thought, don't answer that." He bit into the berries. For a moment, he regretted that he hadn't accepted the condiments. The berries were a bit sour, but he ate them anyway.

"Not bad for this early in the season," Enid remarked, stirring her berries.

"I admit, I'm not much of a fruit eater."

"Why am I not surprised?" Grinning, she took one more container out of the basket. Dessert! "Here you go." She presented him with morsels of what looked like a cross between cookies and candy.

"Treats! Yum!" he exclaimed, deliberately imitating Connie's ebullient nature, which was met with Enid's delighted grin. Eagerly, he accepted a piece of the dessert and bit into it. To his disappointment, it wasn't as sweet as he had anticipated.

"Aren't these wonderful?" Without waiting for him to answer, she continued. "Reece, they're so easy to make. No baking involved. And they're a great way to sneak a few more nutrients into Connie's diet. I packed a few extra for her along with her lunch. Or rather, dinner."

Reece consumed his last bit of the so-called treat. "She'll eat these for you, but I doubt I'll have much luck. Connie has developed a fondness for chocolate cream cakes, I'm afraid."

Enid didn't look as though she approved. "Maybe you can alternate days. Cream cakes one day, these the next."

"Maybe." Reece leaned back on his elbows. "You really have come to like Connie, haven't you?"

"How could I not? In fact, how could anyone not be enchanted by such a charming little girl?"

"I just hope she stays that way and doesn't eventually grow bitter over losing so much at such an early age." He sighed. "Thank goodness when her mom died, she wasn't really old enough to realize what happened. I don't even think she remembers her, except from a few pictures."

"Maybe that was God's way of being merciful."

For an instant, Reece thought perhaps Enid was making that point in an effort to preach at him. Yet the expression on her face, the look in her eyes, showed him that she meant what she said, yet he still felt compelled to disagree. "Maybe it would have been more merciful to let her keep her mother."

"I can see why you would feel that way." She placed her hand on his. "I don't think God sees death the same way we do. We look at it as the end of everything we know. But really, it's just the beginning. The beginning of a new existence of unparalleled happiness for those who love Him."

"I hope you're right."

"I know I'm right."

"I wish I could be so confident."

"You can be, Reece." She paused as though she were reluctant to continue. Her eyes finally met his. "Would you like to know how?"

A sarcastic "I'm sure you're going to tell me" fell silent on his lips. Suddenly, he didn't want to be flip. He found he really did want to know. "Yes," he whispered.

Enid took both of his hands in hers. Her touch was warm and inviting, but the contact went beyond something as earthly as romance. The contact caused him to sense his soul connecting with hers. He cherished the feeling.

"Do you accept Jesus Christ as your personal Savior?"

At that moment, Reece knew he wanted to, more than anything he had ever before desired. He wanted to possess a confidence as clear and true as Enid's. Reece stared deeply into Enid's green eyes. They silently beckoned him to join her in an abiding love. A love that would not be for her but reserved for the Lord. He knew that the words, once spoken, would represent a true covenant, a promise not to be broken. He hesitated. "What does that mean, exactly?"

"Do you confess that you are a sinner?"

Reece's mind flashed back to the many times he had chosen to do what was wrong instead of what was right. He hoped he was making progress in making the right choices more often. But he somehow knew he couldn't do it alone. "Yes. I'm a sinner." He looked down at Enid's hands on his.

"Do you want your sins to be forgiven?"

Reece nodded.

"To accept Jesus Christ as your personal Savior means that you believe He died for you on the cross. He died to wash away your sins. Once you accept what He did for you, you are forgiven. The slate is wiped clean." She squeezed his hands. "You are born again."

"Born again," he whispered.

"Jesus told Nicodemus, 'Verily, verily, I say unto thee, Except a man be born again, he cannot see the kingdom of God.'"

In a flash of epiphany, Reece knew the answer. "Then I want to be born again. I accept Jesus Christ as my personal Savior."

"Congratulations." Enid let go of his hands and gave him a hug.

He was too surprised to give her much of an embrace in return. "That's it? That's all I have to do?"

Breaking away, Enid nodded.

"Wow. I thought I'd have to go up in front of everybody at church or something."

"A lot of people are saved when they accept an altar call at church. But that's not the only way. As long as God hears you. . ." She smiled.

Reece didn't want to break the mood, the feeling that God was nearer than ever. Yet the hour had grown late. Besides, what could he say after such an emotional episode? With great unwillingness, he spoke. "Uh, I wish I had more time for lunch. I've got to get back to work."

Enid responded with a sad nod. "Me, too."

Reece helped Enid reassemble the remains of lunch. He enjoyed the teamwork of the simple task. He could get used to this. All too soon, he walked her to the car and loaded the basket. "Thanks for the lunch, Enid." If they had been more than friends, Reece would have taken the opportunity to kiss the gorgeous blond standing before him. But they weren't and he still wasn't going to take advantage of Enid by trying to kiss her. There was no reason to let her think all the unwashed heathens—even those who had just been saved—were uncouth on top of everything else. "Let me know if you think of the answer to the clue."

"I will."

As they drove to church so Reece could drop Enid off at her work, Reece prayed about his new commitment. He sensed that Enid, in silence, prayed too. He enjoyed the silence and was sorry to pull into the church parking lot.

"Goodbye, Reece," Enid said.

"See you soon."

She nodded and left the car.

As he watched her walk away from his car and into the church, he already missed her presence.

He hoped one of them thought up the answer. And soon.

Chapter 9

"Can I watch TV tonight?" Connie asked.

In his final preparation for dinner, Reece popped open the bottle of sparkling water Enid had sent. His gaze went to the child. Her big brown eyes, so much like his own, twinkled with a pleading light. Why was she most adorable when she was asking a favor? He stalled. "What's so special about tonight?"

"I dunno." She shrugged. "Evvybody else watches TV. Evvybody but me. Can I? Can I?" She leaned her elbows on the table in anticipation of his answer.

"That's 'may I' watch TV."

"May I watch TV?" She leaned closer.

Reece set the bottle of water on the table, then took his seat in the dinette chair. Careful to keep his voice gentle, he responded. "I'm afraid the answer is 'no.'"

Leaning back, Connie wiggled in her booster seat and folded her hands. "But I asked nice like you said to."

"I know. And I appreciate that. You were very polite. But we're eating dinner in peace." He pointed to her plate. "Don't you want to enjoy all the delicious food Miss Enid sent?"

Connie looked at the cuisine set before her. In her care package for Connie, Enid had included a small portion of salad and half of a chicken sandwich along with the bottled water. "I don't know. I don't like gween stuff." She made a face and stuck out her tongue.

"Miss Enid was nice to send all this food just for you—just so you could see what we had at the picnic today. You don't want to hurt her feelings by not eating it, do you?"

"No. But if I don't eat it, do we have to tell her?" Her face, with its questioning expression, was so adorable that Reece wanted to acquiesce, but he knew he couldn't.

"We'd have to tell her something," he answered. "And unless you want to say to her that you didn't even try it, we'd have to tell a fib, wouldn't we? Would that be the right thing to do?"

"No. But I wish it was."

Reece stifled a laugh. "Good girl." Taking his fork, Reece used it to motion to his own plate, which was filled with picnic leftovers. "See? I'm eating lots of green things, too."

"I know." With a sigh that sounded world-weary for her years, Connie picked at the food, eating bits of it, but ultimately leaving most of the food on her plate.

"Tell you what. If you eat that, I'll give you the yummy cookies Miss Enid sent."

The little face brightened. "She sent cookies?" Eagerly, Connie dug into the food. A grimace now and again was the only indication of her distaste. A few moments later, Connie tilted her clean plate toward him.

"Good job." He clapped. "See? That wasn't so bad."

"Yes, it was."

Reece chuckled, then handed her the cookies.

After she inspected her dessert, Connie's expression was crestfallen. "No chocolate chip?"

"Not every cookie can be chocolate chip." Reece placed his forefinger on his chin as though he were deep in thought. "I have to say, though, if I were a cookie, I'd want to be chocolate chip."

"Me, too." Connie smiled. "I wish Miss Enid had sent chocolate chip or peanut butter." Imitating Reece, she placed her little forefinger on her tiny chin. "I wondaw what kind of cookie Miss Enid would be?"

"I don't know. Maybe you can ask her next time you see her."

Connie still hadn't given up on her original request. "Can we—I mean, may we watch TV while we eat the cookies?"

Reece glanced at the wall clock. "Sorry. It's too late. All of the programs for kids your age have gone off for the night. Besides, it's already past your bedtime. Maybe tomorrow."

"You always say that." She let out a sigh that was obviously meant to sound as though she had cares far beyond her years. "So can—I mean, may—I stay up and watch TV with you? Please?"

"I know you're asking nicely, but not tonight. Maybe this weekend."

Connie's pout was hard to resist. Reece literally planted his foot on the floor and held his ground. He hated being strict, but his policies were for Connie's benefit. An innocent girl couldn't be expected to understand how vile some television programs could be. As her guardian, he wished the networks would continue to honor the unwritten code of keeping programs family-oriented in early prime-time slots.

"How come I hafta wait?"

Reece decided it was best to tell her the truth. "Because some TV shows aren't good for kids. Some people might even call them evil."

"But the people in the box don't seem bad." She set her eyes on the blank television screen as though it were running her favorite show. "You know, I've been wondewin'. How do they get the people in the box?"

Reece put on a serious expression worthy of a wiser big brother. "I used to wonder that, too, but they're not really inside the box."

"They awen't?"

"No, they're not." He was just about to launch into an explanation about film when he realized something. "Box. TV. Evil. That's it! The TV is the evil box!"

Connie's expression was full of questions. "What does that mean?"

"It means—" He leapt from his chair and kissed her on the forehead. "You just solved the mystery of the latest clue!"

"Huh?"

"Never mind. I'll read you a bedtime story, and then it's off to dreamland for you."

"But I don't wanna go to bed. I wanna find out all about the next clue." She began to jump up and down in her seat. "Does this mean we get to see Miss Enid again?"

"Probably."

"Oh, good!" Connie clapped.

Reece felt like applauding at the prospect himself. "That is a good thing," he said. "But first, you have to go to bed."

"We can't see her until tomowow?"

"I'm afraid not. But you know what? The faster you go to bed and get to sleep, the faster tomorrow will come."

"You always say that." She twisted her little mouth as though she didn't believe him.

"I know. That's because the next day always comes faster for me when I go to sleep early." He patted her on the head and nodded toward the rocker positioned near the bookcase. "Come on. I'll race you to the rocking chair!"

Giggling, Connie ran ahead of Reece, who didn't put up much of a contest. Connie jumped into the chair. "I always win!"

"You sure do!"

She relinquished her winning position so she could select a book from the overloaded shelf and then bounded onto Reece's lap. After they shared a story, to Connie's surprise, he asked her to pray. Together they thanked God for the day and each other. It was the best Reece, unaccustomed to praying, could do. As his young charge prayed, Reece felt more moved than usual. He was aware that his newly stirred emotions were a result of the astonishing and dramatic turn the picnic had taken. Never had he expected Enid to lead him to accept the Lord so unabashedly.

Most of the people he knew didn't talk about religion or God. Some of them went to church, but they believed faith was a private matter, best kept to oneself. So he was surprised when Enid had shown no shyness about what he needed to do. He hoped one day he could be so open and unashamed of his faith.

"Amen!" Connie said, bringing him back to the present.

"Amen!" He tucked Connie into bed and placed a peck on her smooth forehead. At that moment, Reece resolved to deepen his own prayer life.

"Good night, Weece!" the little girl called as he exited.

He turned, giving the sleepy girl one last look. "Good night."

Indulging in welcome silence, Reece read the day's paper. His mind relaxed from chuckling at the comics, he decided to take advantage of the quiet to resume his Bible reading. After trudging through two chapters of Exodus, Reece felt a sudden need to discover what the Bible had to say about prayer. Reece used the concordance in the back of his Bible to seek out a few verses. The list under the term "prayer" was long, citing passages almost too numerous to count. After studying the list, he decided to read Proverbs 15:8, since he knew that book contained wise sayings. *The LORD detests the sacrifice of the wicked, but the prayer of the upright pleases him.*

Reece read and reread the verse. Setting his Bible down in his lap, he closed his eyes. Reading the Bible had given him unimaginable insight. While he still had a lifetime of learning before him, he had already gained wisdom. He felt ashamed of how clueless he had been when he met Enid. But she had been patient with him.

For the first time in recent memory, Reece recounted the events in his life. He remembered the things he had done that he wished he hadn't, an exercise that brought back pain he had long suppressed. With even more remorse, he brought to mind the deeds he had left undone that he wished he had taken time to do. Wistfully, he wished he could go back and relive a few of life's precious moments so he could make a few alterations. Then he realized, what if he could? He wouldn't be the person he was today. Maybe he wouldn't have even met Enid. And if he hadn't met her, perhaps he might have gone his whole life giving the barest lip service to Christianity, but not truly accepting Jesus as his personal Savior.

Had his prayers not been pleasing to the Lord before he truly accepted Christ? The thought sent an unpleasant shiver throughout his being.

At that moment, Reece felt compelled to bend to his knees, an act of worship he hadn't felt led to do since he was about Connie's age. He closed his eyes and prayed that the Lord would forgive his previous sinfulness. He prayed that his reception of Jesus into his heart would lead to a true, lasting faith. A deep, unshakable faith.

Reece's eyes flew open. He didn't see a bolt of lightning or experience an angelic vision. Rather, he felt a sense that his prayer of contrition was just another baby step toward the journey of a lifetime. Somehow, the emotion left him comforted.

The peace that showered him brought with it a feeling of drowsiness. Heading to his bed, Reece slid in and pulled the white sheets over his shoulders, seeking security in their cover. Moments later, he drifted into a sound sleep.

In a house across town, Enid was coming to terms with the transformation in Reece's relationship with the Lord and consequently, how that might change her own friendship with him. Never had she expected to gain the victory of Reece's emergence from doubtful hesitation to full acceptance of the Lord. Enid knew she couldn't take any credit. The Holy Spirit was at work. Without Him, Reece's change of heart would have been impossible.

Since they parted, Enid had been praying throughout the day about what had transpired at the picnic.

She had lingered over her quiet time, meditating on Reece. Where she had been doubtful about him in the past, she was beginning to feel at peace. Questions about Connie remained unanswered, but her prayers revealed that they would be resolved when the Lord saw fit. In the meantime, she had come to the awareness that Connie's parentage and Reece's relationship to Connie's mother didn't matter. Enid had no idea why she should feel this way after being skeptical for so long. This was not the first time she didn't understand the Lord's response to her questions right away. She knew from experience she could trust Him all the same. To her immense gratitude and relief, the Lord had sent her assurance. At this point in time, she wasn't certain whether she and Reece could eventually become romantically involved or if they would simply remain friends. But she did know she would not be unequally yoked with her life partner, the man to whom she was to be a helpmeet. Selfishly, she wanted to pray that the Lord would allow Reece to see her as someone he could love as a wife. Since the Lord knew the desire of her heart, He sent her an answer from Romans 8:25: "But if we hope for that we see not, then do we with patience wait for it."

"Lord, grant me the patience I need," she murmured as she drifted off to sleep.

Chapter 10

"Guess what! I found the next clue!"

The familiar voice was a welcome sound. Enid swiveled her office chair away from the computer so she could face Reece. No matter how many times she saw him, her heart always seemed to jump as soon as she caught a glimpse of his handsome face. Today, as he victoriously held up a piece of white paper, the smile that engulfed his face made him even more attractive than usual.

"Isn't that great?" he prodded.

She could tell from his rushed speech that Reece was too excited to bother with pleasantries. She didn't mind. Seeing such ebullience in a grown man was refreshing. Perhaps Agnes saw this boyish quality in Reece, and she knew a puzzle would be just the way to bring those emotions and gestures to the surface. No matter what Agnes had been thinking, Enid was glad that Agnes had made the best of the idea.

"Congratulations! So what was the evil box?"

"You'll never guess." He shook his head. "The television."

"The television? You've got to be kidding."

"Nope." He headed for the extra chair and sat down. "I went over to her house today between dropping Connie off and going to work. Just as I suspected, the clue was taped to the back of the television set."

"So how did you figure it out?"

"I didn't, really. Well, I sort of did. But Connie helped me." Reece related how his discussion with Connie during dinner had led him to put together the clues to solve the puzzle.

"Oh, I see. That makes perfect sense once you explain it," Enid observed.

"Aunt Agnes would probably be surprised it took me so long to figure it out. She knew how I try to keep Connie from watching too much TV."

"Don't be so hard on yourself. I didn't figure it out right away either." She rose from her seat. "Why don't you let me pour you a cup of coffee while you read me the next clue?"

"Sounds like a win/win proposal to me. The best one I've gotten all day."

"Just all day, huh?"

"Considering that I'm the one who's supposed to be making proposals. . ."

Enid's heart lurched at the insinuation. But, of course, Reece didn't mean a marriage proposal. "Indeed?" Enid launched into her most upper-crust Victorian accent. "My good sir, I beg your pardon. I shall not be so forward in the future. Mama would be extremely vexed to learn I haven't acted like a proper lady should. My confidence is safe with you, I hope?"

"Indeed," he mimicked in an equally affected accent. "As a matter of fact, I find your forwardness quite charming. I would go so far as to say enchanting."

As Enid's eyes met his, she forgot she was supposed to be handing him the cup of coffee. Instead, she froze, not wanting the moment to end. Reece returned her expression, studying her eyes with concentration. His face tilted closer, as though he wanted to kiss her. Suddenly, seeming to think better of it, he stopped short, returning his attention to the coffee.

"A proper lady would be most embarrassed if she spilled coffee on her gentleman caller's lap," Reece let her know.

"So your visit is a social call? In the capacity of a gentleman caller?" She handed him the coffee, her heart racing at the prospect of his answer.

"Do you want it to be?"

Unsure how best to respond, Enid broke her Victorian veneer. "Ah, the ball's in my court. How smooth."

"When you take care of a preschooler, you become quite adept at eva-siveness." His grin was teasing, meaning his expression revealed nothing of importance.

Enid straightened herself, hoping the motion would hide her disappoint-ment. "I suppose that goes along with the territory." She took a sip of her own coffee, although she didn't taste it. "Speaking of Connie, I guess we should get back to the present. What does the next clue say?"

Reece unfolded the paper and read aloud:

> *But a certain man named Ananias, with Sapphira his wife, sold a possession (Acts 5:1).*
>
> *Jewels may of value be*
> *But they are not the world to me.*

Concentrating on the new mystery, Enid almost forgot how closely she had just come to confessing her developing feelings for Reece.

He looked up from the paper. "Got any ideas for this one?"

"I think so. The next clue must be on the bottom of the globe in her study."

Reece read the clue once more, though silently this time. "World." He nodded. "I see. Makes perfect sense." His brown eyes met hers. "You're brilliant, Enid."

"I wouldn't say that."

"I would. In fact, your quick detective work deserves another lunch. How about it?" He flashed her a disarming smile. "This is becoming a habit. A habit I don't have any desire to break."

His words caused Enid's heart to race. She had no desire for him to break the habit either. "I have to say, the offer is very tempting. But I really can't today." She grimaced and tilted her head toward the computer. "I've got to print out this bulletin and run off copies for Sunday."

"Oh. That's okay. I understand." He didn't sound as though he did.

"I really wish I could join you." She cast him a look filled with regret. "Let me know what the next clue says, will you?"

"I will. As Connie would say, 'Pwomise.'"

As she watched Reece exit, Enid let out an audible sigh. For the first time since she had taken her job, she resented the computer and its ability to chain her to the desk. She longed to go with Reece, not only for the excitement of discovering the clues together, but to enjoy his company. She made a mental note not to turn down one of his lunch invitations again. The next time, she'd take off for lunch and stay in the office running the copier until late at night if need be. In the meantime, she consoled herself with the notion that maybe playing a little bit hard-to-get wasn't such a bad idea.

Less than an hour later, Enid was proofing the bulletin and munching on celery boats filled with low-fat peanut butter. The telephone rang. Enid was certain the call was from the minister, checking in to be sure the bulletin production was running on schedule. She quickly swallowed her celery, picked up the receiver, and enunciated an unenthusiastic "Prince of Peace Church" into the telephone.

"Don't sound so happy." The voice belonged to Reece.

"Reece!" She knew her voice gave away her zeal, but at the moment she didn't care. "I didn't expect to hear from you until the end of the week."

"The end of the week? How do you expect me to wait that long when I'm getting so close?"

She chuckled. "So what does the next clue say?"

His responding laugh held no mirth. "The truth is, I don't know. I didn't have any luck."

"You mean you've already been to Agnes's house? What about lunch?"

"What about it? I have enough fat around my waistline to take me through to dinner." He paused. "And I grabbed a candy bar at the convenience store on my way to work this morning."

Enid took all of her willpower to suppress a groan. "Reece, didn't you learn anything from our picnic lunch together? You really need to pay better attention to your diet."

"I know. Spare me the lecture. I only have a minute or two before I have to hang up. I'm on the pharmacy phone and I can't keep the line busy. At least, not for a personal conversation." He hurried to share his story. "As soon as I left you at the church, I drove over to the house. I searched the whole globe, front ways, backwards, and sideways. Every which way. Nothing."

"I'm so sorry."

"I even looked through her atlas, hoping she'd tucked a note in the pages. Still nothing."

"Oh, Reece. I feel so bad. Look, why don't you read me the clue again? I'll write it down and see if I can think of anything else."

"That would be great." Reece read the clue to her once more.

"Sorry I'm not as brilliant as you thought."

"Don't worry." He let out a chuckle. "Your reputation's safe with me."

◈◈◈

"I'm sure glad you thought of another angle," Reece told Enid that afternoon. He unlocked the door to Agnes's house and then stepped aside for her to enter.

"Me, too. I just hope I'm right this time."

"What's an angle?" Connie asked. "Is that kinda like an angel?"

Enid and Reece laughed together.

"What's so funny?" Connie wanted to know. A roll of her eyes told them she suspected she was the source of their entertainment.

Reece patted the top of her head. "We just think you're cute, that's all." He turned to Enid. "Let me go get the jewelry box out of my aunt's room. I'll be right back."

"Sure." Enid hadn't forgotten the original question. She sat on the floral couch and patted the place beside her as a sign for Connie to join her. The little girl rushed to comply. "You know about angels, don't you?" Enid asked.

"Sure! I have a guardian angel all my own."

"That's wonderful." Enid held Connie's hand. She could hardly believe how small and soft it felt. "An angel isn't the same thing as an angle. An angle can be the corner of a triangle or a square or, in the case we were using it, another way of looking at things."

"Oh." She nodded blankly.

Since Connie clearly had lost interest, Enid decided to ask the question that had been burning in her mind for some time. "You know what, Connie? I forgot to ask how you liked the supper I sent over the other day."

Connie didn't answer right away and sent her gaze to the tennis shoes she wore on her feet. "Oh. Yeah." She looked up and tried to smile. "It was nice of you to send it. Thank you."

"You're welcome." Enid tried not to let her own smile waver. She could see that Reece had coached Connie on what to say should she be asked about the meal. The child's unenthusiastic tone of voice and averted eyes told the truth behind the polite façade.

"I'm afraid she's not used to so much green food," Reece apologized, obviously having heard the tail end of their conversation as he returned from Agnes's room, box in hand.

Enid wasn't surprised by Connie's disappointment in the meal but kept her observation to herself. "That's quite all right, Connie. New foods are hard to get used to. And you were very polite to thank me."

A relieved look spread over Connie's face. "I did kinda like the cookies. Even if they weren't my favorite."

"Connie!" Reece corrected.

Enid laughed. "That's all right. What kind is your favorite, Connie?"

"Chocolate chip." Connie tugged on Enid's sleeve. "If you could be a cookie, what kind would you be?"

Enid didn't miss a beat. "Coconut macaroon."

"Coconut macawoon?" Connie's nose wrinkled. "What kind is that?"

"Very sweet." Enid smiled with equal sweetness at the little girl. "Let me tell you something that hardly anybody else knows. Not even Reece." She sent him a conspiratorial look.

"What?" He feigned disappointment and shock. "Not even I know about this deep, dark secret?"

"Nope."

"Whisper it!" With a swipe, Connie placed her hair behind her right ear. She cupped her hand to her ear and leaned closer to Enid.

Enid did as she was told. "When I was a little older than you, I dressed up like a cookie for a play."

Connie leaned back and squealed. "You did? How come?"

"Did what?" Reece looked as eager as Connie to be let in on the secret.

"Should I tell him?" Enid asked Connie, teasing Reece.

"I don't know. He is a boy," the little girl pointed out.

"He's not too yucky," Enid observed. "Maybe it would be okay to let him in on our secret." She gave Reece an earnest look. "I dressed up like a cookie for a school play once. We were showing what a well-rounded meal looks like. I was dessert."

"If you dressed as a cookie, at least we know that dessert was well-rounded."

"You and your jokes." Enid let out a groan that was nevertheless followed by an irrepressible snicker.

Oblivious to the adults' observations, Connie intervened. "Can I dwess up like a cookie some time, Weece?"

"Maybe." He chuckled.

Reece? Why did she call him that?

Enid studied Reece. He didn't seem the least bit embarrassed that Connie had just called—or at least attempted to call him—by his name. Not "Father." Not "Daddy." But "Reece."

Still unruffled, Reece sat on the couch beside Connie. He placed a wooden box on his knee. "Here's her big jewelry box. She has tons of ceramic boxes all over the dresser. How in the world did she manage to keep up with them all?"

Enid barely heard Reece's comment and, at the moment, wasn't interested in speculating. She had a more pressing question on her mind. "Connie?" she asked. "You brought your coloring book with you, didn't you?"

She nodded.

"Why don't you take your book and crayons and color on the kitchen table for a while?" Enid knew her voice betrayed her tension.

"Can I see what's on TV fiwst?" Connie asked Reece.

Reece checked his wristwatch. "I suppose so. There should be something good on channel six. You remember how to turn on the television, right?"

"I'll twy!" Eagerly she ran out of the room. Enid suspected one of the reasons she answered so quickly was to give Reece no time to change his mind.

Reece didn't seem happy with Enid. "Why did you do that?"

"Sorry. I couldn't think of any other distraction."

"I see." He set the box on the coffee table. "So why were you trying to get rid of Connie?"

Enid didn't hesitate. "I noticed something strange. Although you don't seem to think it's strange."

"What's that?"

"She called you 'Reece.' "

He grinned. "At least she tried to. You notice how it comes out 'Weece.' I think it's the funniest thing. I'm afraid I might have shown my amusement and hurt her feelings, though. She tries not to say my name much."

"She'll master how to say the R soon," Enid commented offhandedly, anxious to move on to the topic she wanted to pursue.

At that moment, Connie ran back into the living room. "I can't. I can't make the television go."

Reece rose from his seat. "I'll be right back."

While she waited for Reece to return, Enid viewed the outdoors through the picture window. The street where Agnes had spent all of her adult life was never busy. A car would pass by every few minutes, but otherwise, there was little activity. She thought about how quiet and serene the neighborhood was, especially in comparison to the busy thoroughfare on which her rented house stood.

Maybe one day I can live somewhere like this, she mused, staring at several antiquated oaks that shaded the ground. The wooden porch swing, its green paint peeling, nonetheless looked inviting. She wondered what it would be like to relax for an afternoon, just watching the world go by. An unbidden, though pleasant, picture of Reece sitting in the swing beside her as they watched Connie jump rope on the curved sidewalk entered her mind. *This is a place where a family can feel safe. This house is a good house, a home where anybody can waste a long Saturday afternoon and be thankful for it.*

A feeling of sadness came over her. Once the mystery was solved and Reece collected his inheritance, the house would have to be cleared of all Agnes had possessed in life, then sold. Enid sent up a silent prayer that the house would go to a nice young couple, or an established family—someone who could enjoy the house and make it a home, a place where children's laughter would echo through the rooms and fond memories would be made.

"I'm back. Sorry I took so long," Reece said.

Enid jumped, her hand involuntarily touching her chest.

"Oh, no. I always seem to scare you. I'm sorry."

"That's all right. I'll recover." She sent him a reassuring smile.

He walked to her side and stared out the window. "What's so interesting out there?"

"Nothing. And everything. I was just thinking, that's all."

"I'm not sure I like this pensive Enid. I like the one who shared the picnic with me better." Enid knew he was jesting, but seriousness bubbled just below the surface. "Does this have anything to do with what you wanted to talk to me about?"

She turned from him and sat on the sofa. "Not really."

"What is it, then?" He took the seat beside her.

Since she could never tell how long Connie might be kept amused, Enid didn't take time to soft pedal her concerns. "Your name. Connie called you by your name."

"Okay." He said the word gingerly. With his fingers, he made a circling motion, indicating he wanted her to explain herself. "I hope you're not telling me that my aunt said I have to change my name on top of everything else." He patted her on the knee jokingly.

Enid shook her head in answer to his rhetorical question. "I just expected Connie to call you. . ."

"To call me what?" He seemed genuinely perplexed.

"Well, I expected her to call you—Daddy."

Reece's mouth dropped open. "Daddy?" He paused for a moment. Enid could visualize cartoonish cogs rolling around and around in his head. "Oh, because I'm raising her." He nodded, but he didn't look at her. "I can see how some people might think that, but really, nobody can replace her dad. And I really miss him too. Nobody can replace Dad. Nobody."

Enid tried to absorb what he was telling her. "Do you mean to say, Connie and you have the same dad?"

"Sure," Reece confirmed. "But not the same mother, of course."

"Wait a minute. You have the same father, but not the same mother."

"That's right."

"So you're her half brother." Enid was stating the obvious so she could absorb this new information for herself.

Reece widened his eyes. "You mean, Aunt Agnes never told you?"

"No. It's not exactly like we talked about you all the time." She playfully patted him on the knee.

"I'm so disappointed. I thought everyone talked about me all the time." He rolled his eyes in mock derision before turning serious again. "So after you met Connie and me, what did you decide about us—other than that I was Connie's dad?"

Enid vacillated, but decided this was no time for duplicity. "At first I thought you were divorced or a widower. But then, you never mentioned any wife."

"I didn't mourn a departed saint or complain about my ex, huh?" He rubbed his chin. "Which would you have liked better?"

"Neither," she admitted. "But if I had to pick, I'd probably say I'd rather you complain about an ex. It's easier to compete with a live person than a cherished memory."

"Compete, huh?" His eyes softened. "Do you really think there could be any competition for you?"

Suddenly shy, Enid didn't answer, but pretended to become entranced once again with the view of the outdoors.

"I think I know what happened," he continued, his voice still tender. "When I didn't mention anyone, you finally decided I'd never been married, but I had fathered this little girl anyway. Isn't that right?"

Enid felt a hot flush rise to her cheeks. She was still unable to look Reece in the face. "I wasn't sure."

"No wonder you thought I was the biggest heathen you'd ever met." She could hear the hurt in his tone.

Her head snapped in his direction. "Now, that's not true at all," she protested, not caring whether or not Reece realized she was offended. "I don't judge other people. At least, I try not to."

Reece thought for a moment. "You know, I have to say, from the time we met, I never saw your kindness to Connie and me waver. I had no idea you were going through all this turmoil, wondering about me." He placed his hand on hers. Enid felt protected by its warmth. "Maybe you're not like some of the other Christians I know. I don't think a lot of them would have wanted anything to do with me if I'd fathered Connie before I was married. They would have left me all alone, floundering, hoping I'd solve this mystery on my own. Or maybe they would secretly be glad to see me fail."

"Don't be so hard on them. You might be surprised by the acceptance you and Connie would find in the Christian community, whatever your circumstances." She flipped her hand over, never letting go of his. She gave his fingers a squeeze. "I'm just glad Connie finally called you by your name."

His steady gaze met hers. "Does knowing she's my half sister make a difference?"

"If you had asked me that when we first met, I would have said 'definitely.' I might have gone full steam ahead in showing you how much I care for you." Realizing she'd just blurted too much, Enid hastened to continue. "I think this

314

was the Lord's way of encouraging me not to come on too strong."

"I somehow can't imagine you as coming on too strong."

"Oh, really?" She arched an eyebrow. "I can't believe you don't think I have strong opinions."

He thought for a moment, a twinkle lighting his eyes all the while. "Do you? What a shock! I never would have guessed you had any opinions about diet or anything else."

"Then you get the picture." She studied his face, letting her eyes take in each feature. She could imagine herself looking at Reece every day. Not wanting to become too distracted, she continued. "I've been praying about us, and the Lord had already given me a sense of peace. I can honestly say that your blood relationship to Connie isn't important in my eyes. Your emotional bonds to her and to the Lord are what's important."

"But you're glad I'm her brother."

Chagrined that she was so transparent, Enid stared at the top of the coffee table. In the sunlight, an increasingly thick layer of dust was evident. "I really should come in here and spruce up sometime. When is everything supposed to be moved out?"

Reece's hesitation in responding indicated he wasn't enthusiastic about the abrupt change in subject. Nevertheless, he complied. "Her lawyer says that Aunt Agnes left provisions in her will for everything. He told me not to worry about it, that it would happen in good time."

She returned her gaze to his face. "Wonder if he knows more than he's letting on? Sure sounds like it."

"I have a feeling he does, too. But he's not talking."

Reece let go of Enid's hand and retrieved the box from the top of the table. Opening it revealed a wide array of costume jewelry. Gold chains with assorted pendants, one strand of pearls, and several strands of glass beads hung from necklace hooks. Agnes favored one pair of button style clip-on earrings, so only a few other pairs were present among her collection. Rings seemed to be her favorite jewelry, if the contents of the box were any indication. Eyeing rubies, emeralds, sapphires, diamond chips, opals, and onyx, Enid remembered that Agnes changed rings to suit her mood and outfit. Though lovely, all of the pieces appeared to be costume, of little monetary value.

Giving up on finding anything in the first section, Reece opened a drawer and pulled out a small blue ring box inside. He flipped it open. Inside was a sapphire ring with a note rolled inside. "The next clue!"

Reece unrolled the paper and read aloud:

> *And she gave the king an hundred and twenty talents of gold, and of spices great abundance, and precious stones: neither was there any such spice as the queen of Sheba gave king Solomon (2 Chronicles 9:9).*

They say these give variety to life
Instead live simply, without strife.

"You don't think this has anything to do with television variety shows, do you?" Enid wondered.

"No. Aunt Agnes only had one television, and there's nothing else taped to that one. I already checked."

"Radio, then?"

"I doubt it." He thought for a moment. "I do remember an old saying, though. 'Variety is the spice of life.'"

Enid snapped her fingers. "The spice rack!"

Without another word, both of them headed for the kitchen. Surprisingly, Connie had turned off the set and was busy coloring a book on the sturdy wooden table. She looked up. "Whatcha doin'?"

"We think we may know where the next clue is," Reece explained while Enid looked behind the spice rack.

"Here it is!" She carefully tore the taped message off the back of the rack. After unfolding it, she read aloud:

And he that sat was to look upon like a jasper and a sardine stone: and there was a rainbow round about the throne, in sight like unto an emerald (Revelation 4:3).

Just look around and you
Will see in sight an emerald, too.

"She knows we were just looking in her jewelry box. Maybe there's an emerald ring or necklace in there," Reece suggested.

They hurried back to the jewelry box, still half open on the coffee table in the living room. After a quick look revealed no green stones in the top section, they inspected the inside of each drawer. No emeralds were to be found anywhere.

"What could she possibly mean?" Enid wondered.

"Beats me. Let's look around." From their perch on the couch, they eyed everything in the living room. There was nothing green among the creams and mauves in the room.

"Maybe it has something to do with money. Money is green," Enid pointed out. "Did she have a safe deposit box by any chance, Reece?"

"How am I supposed to know?" His irritation and exasperation with the continuing puzzle were evident in his voice. Immediately he looked contrite. "Sorry. You've been a lot of help. I didn't mean to snap."

"That's all right. Most people don't have to work this hard to realize an inheritance."

"Maybe at least this is the last clue. If the inheritance is in a safe deposit box, it must be the money."

"That would stand to reason. What time is it?"

"Yikes!" Reece said as he looked at his wristwatch. "It's already after noon. The bank lobbies are closed."

"We'll just have to wait until Monday."

"What will I do until then?" Reece groaned.

"You don't have plans for tomorrow?"

"Sure don't," he admitted.

"Why don't you come with me to church?"

Reece hesitated. "I usually sleep in on Sundays, but after what happened between us and the Lord the other day, I know I really should start going. And I especially need to start getting Connie there."

"I'm glad to hear you say that," said Enid. "The service I go to starts at nine forty-five. I'll see you at your house at nine."

Reece smiled, the emotion reaching his brown eyes. "It's a deal."

Chapter 11

"We're ready!" Reece greeted Enid at the door of his apartment the next morning.

Enid let out an appreciative whistle when she saw Reece wearing a dark suit and deep red tie that looked sharp against a fresh white shirt.

"You didn't think I owned a suit, huh?" Reece tried to keep his tone teasing. In reality, when he'd hunted for his old suit, he had let out an audible sigh. It was still reasonably in style and not too snug.

"I figured you were hiding one or two somewhere in your closet. Don't be surprised if you're one of the few men dressed in a suit today, but you look marvelous."

Surprised by this new information, Reece wondered aloud, "My grandpa used to dress up for church. When did men stop wearing suits to church?"

"The ones who want to wear them still do. But the dress code is more relaxed now."

"Are you sure? Look at you," Reece noted. Enid was dressed beautifully in a cream-colored suit with black trim that set off her silken skin and blond hair.

"You know me."

Reece liked the way that sounded. The fact she could make such an off-the-cuff remark and know he would understand her spoke volumes about their relationship. A satisfied smile tickled his lips.

Enid knelt in front of Connie, her eyes alight with friendly approval as she inspected Connie's attire. "And you look beautiful, too!"

"Thank you!" Connie was pleased. "I never had a dwess this fancy. We just got it—"

Reece interrupted. "That's enough, Connie." He saw no need for Enid to know that Connie hadn't owned a dressy outfit before the previous afternoon. Since she spent most of her time at home, in day care, or at tumbling lessons, lace dresses were hardly necessary.

Her eyes wide, Connie looked up at him. "But why can't I tell her we got a new dwess?"

Enid laughed. "She's proud of her new clothes, Reece. And I don't blame her." She stroked Connie's brown locks. "I'm pleased that you went to all that trouble, Connie. You look very pretty. Very pretty indeed."

Reece noticed the woman standing before him, not for the first time. "And so do you."

"And so do you," Connie repeated.

"Thanks." Enid studied her black patent leather purse and fidgeted with its gold-tone chain handle. "Enough of this mutual fan club meeting. We'd better be going." She took Connie's hand and turned to make her way to the car.

So casual and nonchalant, Enid obviously had no idea how nervous Reece was about going to church. He remembered the few times, on Christmas and Easter, that his dad allowed his grandfather to take him to church. He also remembered his childhood church experiences as boring, with a minister droning on and on and the congregation singing songs he didn't know. He welcomed noon as the time to leave the confines of the sanctuary, to strip off his tie, and relish the freedom of the outdoors.

As late as that morning, he wasn't sure he wanted to go. Even at this very moment, he still wasn't sure. But his motives weren't exactly pure. He wanted to be with Enid. If that meant listening to a tedious sermon and reading passages of liturgy from a book, so be it. Seeing her standing before him, in her ravishing way, he decided putting up with the hour-long service would be worth the trouble.

After a short hop across town, they arrived at Enid's church fifteen minutes before the service was to begin. Reece felt a fresh attack of nerves as they made their way to the foyer. He recognized the minister from Aunt Agnes's funeral.

"Why isn't he wearing a robe?" Reece whispered to Enid.

"This service isn't that formal."

Reece observed the other parishioners. Most were dressed in clothing more appropriate to a casual atmosphere or the office instead of how he remembered Sundays. In spite of Enid's kind warning, he felt overdressed. He regretted going to the expense of buying Connie a fancy dress, even though he had managed to find it on sale at a discounter. Finally, when Enid greeted a teenage boy wearing earrings and an unconventional hairstyle, Reece knew for certain that church had changed since he was a boy.

"Connie," Enid asked, "would you rather go into the big service with us or to Sunday school with other little girls and boys your age?"

Connie didn't hesitate. "Sunday school."

"Is that all right with you, Reece?" Enid asked.

Remembering his unfavorable impressions of past worship services, he nodded his assent. Moments later, as he met the teacher and saw the other kids in the class, Reece was glad Connie could be with a group of people who seemed so kind.

During the service, Reece was in for more surprises. Rather than an organ or piano, a band complete with drums, horns, and electric guitars provided the music. The songs they played weren't the slow, traditional ones he remembered, but modern and upbeat. "They can rival any rock group," Reece whispered in Enid's ear.

"We think so." She smiled and clapped in time to the beat.

From the corner of his eye, Reece watched Enid throughout the service.

During the songs, she seemed to glow with happiness and joy, even lifting her arms in praise at particularly emotional points. Reece felt too inhibited to participate so fully, but he could understand why worshippers could get caught up in the lively spirit.

As the congregation prepared to hear the sermon, Reece expected the service to hit a low point. The pastor hadn't been too long-winded at his aunt's funeral service, but what was he like behind the pulpit? Did he love the sound of his own voice, relish the idea of his own wisdom, so much that he preached on and on every Sunday? Sighing, Reece folded his arms and sat back in the pew, hoping he wouldn't embarrass Enid by falling asleep.

When he instructed them to open their Bibles to Malachi 2:15, Reece remembered his Bible sitting beside his chair at home and resolved to bring it next week. In the meantime, he was grateful that Enid had brought her Bible. Quickly she thumbed to the correct passage, a feat Reece wouldn't have accomplished so expertly. The minister read:

> *Has not the LORD made them one? In flesh and spirit they are his. And why one? Because he was seeking godly offspring. So guard yourself in your spirit, and do not break faith with the wife of your youth.*

Reece stole a glance at Enid to see if he could discern from her expression what she was thinking about the sermon on a godly marriage. She leaned forward, rapt as she listened to the minister's knowledge. Reece couldn't remember ever before seeing anyone truly delighted to hear a sermon. As he settled in to listen, though, even Reece had to admit that the message was riveting. Perhaps the sermons he had failed to hear in the past were, too. Only now, timeless topics the Bible addressed were more relevant to his life and current situation than they were during his childhood. When the opportunity availed itself, Reece placed his hand on Enid's and to his delight, she grasped his hand and gave it a gentle squeeze. He envisioned sitting beside her every Sunday from then on.

Before he knew what had happened, the last song was sung and Reece followed Enid to the Sunday school classroom to pick up Connie. The little girl put the finishing touches on her crayon drawing before running into Reece's arms. She handed her picture, drawn on pink construction paper, to Reece. "Look! It's Noah's awk!"

"Beautiful, Connie," he remarked as he studied the artwork.

"Can I come back next week, huh? Can I? Can I?"

"We'd love to have Connie back again," the teacher assured him. She seemed as though her invitation was sincere. "Connie is such a sweet girl."

His eyes widened in admiration of the teacher's ability to call Connie by name after only one class session, and Reece nodded his thanks. He grabbed Connie's hand and walked beside her and Enid to the exit.

"So you had a lot of fun?" Reece asked after they had cleared the crowd.

Connie nodded. A slight breeze touched her brown hair. With the locks away from her face, Connie's chubby cheeks seemed more cherubic than ever.

"What did you do?" Enid wanted to know.

"We sang songs about Jesus. And the teachah read a stowy." Connie returned her gaze to Reece. "Can I come back?"

"Of course you'll be coming back," Enid assured Connie. She sent a compassionate look Reece's way.

"Of course we will." Reece opened the car door for her. "Let's say we take Miss Enid out to lunch?"

"You don't have to do that," Enid protested.

"I know I don't. But I want to."

"Me, too!" Connie agreed.

"You don't want to disappoint her, do you?"

"I suppose not," Enid admitted, sliding into the passenger seat of Reece's car.

After he secured Connie in her seat, Reece took his place behind the wheel. He observed Enid one last time before starting the engine. He couldn't think of a better way to spend the afternoon.

The following afternoon, Enid gathered her belongings in preparation to end another day of work. The previous day had stayed on her mind. Lunch had proven to be a time of warm fellowship. Enid imagined herself as part of their little family. She had a feeling Reece's emotions followed the same path.

"Good," a voice said from behind her. "You're still here."

She turned to see Reece. Her heart never failed to skip a beat when he surprised her with a visit. "Reece! You surprised me! And that's a good thing." She sent him a winning smile.

"You'll never guess what."

Enid made an optimistic guess despite Reece's disappointed tone. "You found the inheritance."

"No. But I did go to the bank. I found out that Aunt Agnes didn't have a safe deposit box."

Enid's body slumped. "Oh, no. I was sure that would be the answer."

"Me, too. I have no idea where this leaves us. What do you think?" He handed her the paper on which the clue was written:

And he that sat was to look upon like a jasper and a sardine stone: and there was a rainbow round about the throne, in sight like unto an emerald (Revelation 4:3).

Just look around and you
Will see in sight an emerald, too.

Contemplating the clue, Enid didn't answer right away. "Wait. It says 'you will see in sight.' Wonder where she thought you'd be when you read this clue?"

"Where I'd be?" He shrugged. "I don't know. In her house, maybe?"

"That's it. There must be something green in her house. We'll just have to go back and look around again."

"You willing?"

"Of course I'm willing. Why don't I follow you to the house right now?"

"Sure. But I have to pick Connie up from day care first. Why don't you let me give you the key, and you can start without me?"

As Enid drove to Agnes's house, she thought again about church the previous day. Reece had seemed pleasantly surprised by everything about the service. He had even complimented the minister on how the sermon related to everyday life. Initially she feared Reece would think Enid looked upon him primarily as a prospect for church membership. But the way he set his hand on hers during the service told her otherwise. A secret smile touched her lips.

A few moments later, Enid entered Agnes's house. Time had passed since she had been there alone. Though the weather was pleasantly warm, the brick structure had maintained winter's chill, leaving the house feeling less than hospitable. Enid was glad when she heard footsteps behind her.

"Hi, Miss Enid!" Connie ran up to her for a hug. "Can I help you look for somethin' gween?"

"So Reece told you about the clue?"

She nodded.

"Of course you can. Although the proper way to ask is to say 'may I help you look for something green.'"

"That's what Weece always says." Connie rolled her eyes. "May I?"

Enid chuckled. "Of course."

"You'll have her set straight before all this is said and done," Reece commented.

"I hope you don't mind. I don't mean to interfere."

"Are you kidding? I need all the help I can get."

Enid smiled to herself. Reece's humility and willingness to admit he didn't know everything left her respecting him all the more.

"I don't see nothin' gween so faw," Connie said, her eyes surveying the room.

"Don't look a gift horse in the mouth," Reece commented.

Connie's mouth twisted. "Huh?"

"That's an old saying that means not to criticize a gift," Reece explained.

"What's cwi, cwi, what's that word?"

"Criticize. It means to say something bad."

"Oh."

"He just means that we're just glad there aren't a lot of green things in the house, sweetie," Enid elaborated. "That means we might not have to look so long for the next clue."

"Oh." She nodded. "Okay." Without further ado, Connie took off running into the living room. Reece and Enid followed. In an instant, Connie began pointing at the draperies and jumping up and down. "Look! Look!"

"You're right. They're green," Reece noticed.

"Emerald green, at that," said Enid. "I don't see how they could hold a clue, but it's worth looking into."

"Help yourself," Reece scoffed. "I'll go look in the kitchen."

Enid searched every inch of the draperies in the front, but could find nothing resembling a clue. "Maybe she pinned a clue to the back," she mused aloud. Lifting one side of the draperies slightly, she peered underneath. She was just about to give up when she noticed something white near the top, too far up to be observed from the outside. With her heart racing, she reached up and touched the paper. A sharp prick greeted her finger. "Ouch!" After inspecting the wound to be sure she wasn't bleeding, Enid approached the paper a second time, exercising more caution. She extracted the pin from the curtain and loosened the paper. It was the next clue!

"Reece!" she called. "I found it!"

He and Connie bounded into the room. "You're kidding!"

"Nope."

"Where was it?"

"Pinned to the top of the curtain, underneath." She tilted her head in the direction of the window.

"I never would have guessed. I'm glad you were persistent!"

"Me, too!" After opening the paper, she read the clue aloud:

> *Thou preparest a table before me in the presence of mine enemies: thou anointest my head with oil; my cup runneth over (Psalm 23:5).*

> *To the table I have come*
> *Dust gathers on my place to run.*

"Table. . .gathers. . .run. . ." Enid snapped her fingers. "I know. Family gathers at the table, and her table has a runner. The next clue must be in the dining room!"

Reece and Enid rushed into the dining room, with Connie following fast on their heels. A careful inspection of the embroidered runner revealed no clue.

Reece looked at the paper again. "Look." He pointed to the last part of the Scripture. "It says 'my cup runneth over.' Maybe the next clue is hidden in a coffee cup."

"It's possible."

Connie pulled on Reece's pants leg. "This is no fun any mo'. May I go watch TV?"

"Oh, Reece, you can't turn down such a polite request," Enid pointed out. "Congratulations on remembering to say 'May I', Connie!"

"I agree." Reece clapped his hands. "All right, you can go."

As Connie scurried into the next room, together Enid and Reece searched every place in the house where a coffee cup might be hiding. The kitchen cabinets, the china hutch, even the display case in the living room revealed nothing. "There must be a clue somewhere. Is there anywhere else a coffee cup might be?"

"Wonder if there's one somewhere in the den?" Reece guessed. "On a shelf, maybe."

"That's the one place we haven't looked." Enid led Reece to the den, although, since they were discouraged, neither moved with haste.

"I don't see any shelves anywhere." Reece let out a tired sigh. "Now what?"

Enid extended her hand. "Here. Let me see the clue again."

Reece relinquished it with no argument.

"You know what? The Scripture says 'runneth' and the clue mentions 'run.' Maybe it means not a table runner, but something to do with the sport of running."

"Did she belong to a gym?" Reece wondered aloud.

"Not that I know of." At that moment, Enid's gaze landed upon a treadmill in the corner. The machine was being used as a clothes closet instead of a mode of exercise. Several garments hung off the handles. A pair of shoes was still placed on the tread. "Reece! The clue says 'Dust gathers on my place to run.'"

"So?"

"Let's look through this mess on the treadmill. I'll bet the clue is somewhere in this pile."

"Something valuable must be," Reece observed. "I can't imagine Aunt Agnes leaving a mess around without a good reason."

Digging through the clothes unearthed nothing, but when Reece shook one of the shoes, a piece of paper fell out.

"You did it!" Enid applauded.

"I couldn't have without you." He unfolded the paper. "Let's see what it says."

And God called the light Day, and the darkness he called Night. And the evening and the morning were the first day (Genesis 1:5).

Tick-tocking the time away
Whether it is night or day.

"This one's easy," Reece said. "Obviously, the next clue is on one of the clocks."

"The question is, which one?"

"Let's find out."

As if they could read each other's minds, Reece and Enid immediately separated and began going through the house. They inspected each clock, hoping to find a clue taped to or hidden in a clock crevice.

"Found it!" Reece called from the living room a few minutes later.

Enid rushed to join him. "Where?"

Reece was holding up the clue victoriously. "Taped on the back of the grandfather clock."

"We are really on a roll!" Enid shook her head in amazement. "At this rate, we might be able to solve the whole mystery tonight."

"You just might be right."

Enid and Reece read the next clue together:

I am the rose of Sharon, and the lily of the valleys (Song of Solomon 2:1).

Close to God's creation you'll be
When you smell the flowers with me.

"This suggests the next clue is in the garden," Reece said.

"But how can that be? Nothing has been planted this season." Enid thought for a moment. "You don't suppose she wants us to plant a garden and see what happens, do you?"

"I sure hope not. No, there must be another answer."

"Hmm. Wonder if it has something to do with growth."

"Spiritual or physical?"

Enid was glad to see Reece even contemplating the prospect of spiritual growth. "Speaking of spiritual growth—"

"Uh-oh. I knew I shouldn't have gone there." Despite his words, Reece's face wore a smile.

"Well, since we have," Enid said with a sly grin, "what about church? You never did share your thoughts."

"I would have, but Connie spent the whole lunch time telling us about Sunday school."

Enid giggled. "She sure did. I don't think I've seen her as happy since the day we flew her kite."

"Me neither." With a pensive motion, he took both of her hands in his. "Thank you, Enid." He leaned closer and placed a light kiss on her forehead.

Enid wasn't sure whether she was more surprised by the kiss or by his thanks. Affected by his friendly kiss, she thought it best to stay on safer turf lest she pull him close to her for a more romantic gesture. "Thanks for what?"

"Everything." He gave her hands a squeeze. Enid could see in his eyes that he wanted more.

To Enid's disappointment, Connie chose that moment to interrupt. "I'm hungwy. And sleepy." As if to punctuate her exhaustion, she stuck her thumb in her mouth.

Reece broke his grasp on Enid's hands. "You're actually admitting that you're tired? Whoa, you must be about ready to fall down."

"I didn't sleep at nap time."

"Why not?"

"I wasn't sleepy then."

Chuckling, Reece swept Connie up into his arms. Her sleepy little head rested on his shoulder. Connie kept her thumb in her mouth as she closed her eyes. Enid couldn't imagine a more serene picture.

Enid's wristwatch revealed the time was almost seven o'clock. "Wow, I had no idea it was getting so late."

"And I didn't even see to it that you got supper." A sheepish look covered his face. "I'm sorry, Enid. I feel I've really taken advantage of you this evening. I guess I got carried away and forgot all about eating."

"I got carried away right along with you. To tell you the truth, I didn't think a thing about dinner either."

"Why don't you let me at least get you some fast food? If you think you can stomach a couple of drops of grease, that is," he teased.

"You've seen me put away a big burger and a bag of French fries loaded with ketchup before," she pointed out. "But that's okay. Really. There's no need to keep Connie out a minute longer." She patted her slim stomach. "Believe me, I'll live."

"I don't know. You're mighty scrawny," Reece said in his best imitation of his aunt.

"Not too scrawny, I hope."

"Not at all." Reece looked at her appreciatively. "Not at all."

Chapter 12

Almost a week passed before Enid saw Reece again. Friday, when the workday was complete, she pressed the "shut down" switch on her computer. As she waited for the process to finish, Enid prayed, "Lord, thank You for this week. You have used these days to show me how much I miss Reece when I don't see him. And Connie, too, Father. I know I'm being selfish, but I pray it is Your will for Reece to feel the same. In Jesus' precious name. Amen."

"What are you muttering?"

Enid turned toward the familiar male voice. "Reece!"

"I think I've finally gotten to the point where my surprise entrances have stopped scaring you."

"And that's a good thing."

Reece chuckled. "Speaking of good things, I have good news. I found the next clue."

Enid let out a gasp of pleasure. "You did? Where was it?"

"In the shed with the garden supplies."

Enid slapped her palm to her forehead. "Why didn't I think of that?"

"Because I have to think up a few of the answers on my own every once in awhile. The old ego can't take me being wrong all the time."

"I don't think there's any danger in that." She leaned closer. "So let me hear the next clue."

Reece took a familiar piece of white paper out of his shirt pocket, unfolded it, and read:

> *The vine is dried up, and the fig tree languisheth; the pomegranate tree, the palm tree also, and the apple tree, even all the trees of the field, are withered: because joy is withered away from the sons of men (Joel 1:12).*

> *An old granny with a wrinkled face*
> *You will find the next clue in this place.*

"Hmm. The next clue must be taped to the back of one of her photographs. There are scads of those around her house. I'm sure at least one of them must be of her in her later years." Enid chuckled. "You know, Agnes always talked about the wrinkles she'd earned through her faith walk. I think she was torn between pride in earning them and sorrow in losing the smooth skin of her youth."

"Then she's like most people. Who wants to get old? Unless you consider the alternative." Reece visibly shuddered.

"The alternative isn't as bad as you think, if you have the faith to know where you're headed after you leave the earth."

"You mean, heaven and all that."

"You believe in heaven, don't you? If not, I'm sure you know that most people don't believe in hell. Although I do. I don't see how you can believe in one without believing in the other."

"Me either." Reece planted his hands in his jeans pockets. "I admit, I believe in heaven and hell. I sure don't want to spend all of eternity in hell."

"Aren't you glad that, thanks to the Lord, you know where you're going once you leave the earth?"

"You better believe it!" He let out a sigh. "I know it won't be easy, though. I enjoyed church last Sunday, but I know there's more to membership than sitting in the pew every week. They'll make me give ten percent of my income, even if I need it for something else, won't they? Enid, I just don't know if I can do that." Reece's eyes widened with distress.

"Reece, do you believe you're the first person to ask these questions? Do you think you're the first person who's been scared to take that step? I was afraid at first, too."

"You were? I don't believe it."

"Believe it. I remember when I first accepted Christ. I was just as afraid as anyone else. I thought if I accepted Him, I wouldn't have any fun anymore. But now, I have more fun than I ever did. And you know something else? The more money I tithe to the church, the more money seems to come into my life. I never go without anything I need as long as I trust the Lord to provide."

"So since I've accepted Jesus as my Lord and Savior, if I start giving lots of money to church, I'll get a big raise at work?" Reece's teasing grin showed he wasn't entirely serious.

"Or maybe a big inheritance?" Enid twisted her mouth into a wry grin. "Just kidding. Seriously, the Lord won't necessarily give you a big windfall or a raise in pay. But in my experience, I've found He does provide. And if you remember the Lord's prayer, we ask Him to 'give us this day our daily bread.' When He taught this prayer to the disciples, He didn't say the Lord would give us an overabundance well into the future. We are to ask for our needs, not necessarily our wants. Although sometimes He gives us our wants, too."

"I suppose you're right. But it's so hard."

"Of course it is. You know, no one expects you to become a super-Christian overnight. You may not ever become as faithful as you would like throughout your life. But since you've accepted Him, He'll work on your growth. That's why He died for you. He wants you to live according to His plan. The free gift of salvation."

"Free? Nothing is free."

"The gift of salvation is free. But it will change your life."

"It's already changed my life. You got me to go to church. Wonder what else God has in mind for me?"

"It's hard to say exactly. God works with each person as an individual. But no matter what, the change will be for the better."

"How has it changed you?" he asked.

Enid didn't have to think long. "My priorities are different. Instead of competing with others in games no one ever wins, I walk in the light of His love."

"So you think I'm pretty awful to be chasing after this inheritance." The question was more of a statement. A look of sadness and doubt crossed Reece's face.

Enid placed a consoling hand over his. As always, she liked the way Reece's fingers radiated warmth. "I know you want the inheritance for Connie, not for yourself. And besides, we still don't know what it is yet."

He cast her a rueful grin. "You're right. It might be a trinket or a bunch of useless stock certificates."

"Somehow, I doubt Agnes would make you go to all this trouble for what she used to call a 'dustable.' Speaking of which, we'd better get moving if we ever hope to solve the mystery." She squeezed his hand.

"You're right." Reece glanced at the wall clock. "It's time for me to pick up Connie. Why don't you meet us at the diner for dinner? Then we can go to Aunt Agnes's house and start hunting."

"Sounds like a great plan to me."

❧

Two hours later, the hunters were stationed in Agnes's living room, ready to begin searching for the next clue.

"Why don't you investigate the photographs around the house," Enid suggested, "and I'll pull out her old photo albums."

"Sounds good to me." Reece exited into Agnes's bedroom, where a number of family photographs were displayed on the dresser.

Enid headed for the den, where she remembered Agnes kept her collection of picture albums. Once she got to the room and realized that several bookshelves were filled with memorabilia, she wondered how she would ever get through all of them. Sighing, she pulled a volume with a faded cover off the shelf and positioned herself comfortably on the well-worn sofa.

At that moment, Connie bounded into the room. "Whatcha doin'?"

"Looking at old pictures."

She scrunched her nose. "What fo'?"

"Oh, to see if your Aunt Agnes left us a clue somewhere."

Connie clapped her hands. "Oh, goodie! This is so much fun! Can I look at the books?"

"Fine with me, as long as you don't touch the pictures. They're very old and valuable. We don't want fingerprints on them."

"Do you get to touch them?"

"Oh, no. I wouldn't think of touching them either."

Satisfied, Connie investigated the book along with Enid. The black and white photographs were intriguing, many dating back to the early 1900s.

"How come they got on such funny clothes?" Connie asked.

"Because that's how they dressed back then, a long time ago."

"Did you used to dwess like that?"

"No. I wasn't born back then."

Connie's eyes widened. "Oh! That must a been a long, long time ago. You awe weally old."

Enid would have flinched had the remark been uttered by anyone but Connie. Instead, she laughed and put her arm around Connie, snuggling her close. "Yes, it was a long time ago."

Connie pointed to an image of a young, smiling girl. "Who's that?" Her finger touched the photograph.

Enid gently moved her hand away. "Remember, we don't touch the pictures."

"Sowwy. I fogot."

"To answer your question, I don't know who any of these people are. There aren't any labels anywhere. And that's too bad. We might not ever find out who a lot of them are."

"Did you find out who's who?" asked Reece, entering the den.

"You've looked at all the photos already?"

"Sure have. No luck." He tilted his head toward the album. "How about you?"

"No luck so far. I was telling Connie it's too bad there aren't any names under these photos. How will anyone know who they are?"

"Let me see if I can help." Reece sat beside Enid. "Oh, these are pictures of my grandmother when she was a girl." Reece flipped through several pages of the book, telling Enid and Connie the identities of most of the people pictured.

"Let's get anothah book!" Connie suggested after they'd viewed the first. Jumping up, she ran over to the bookcase to fetch another.

Reece ran up behind her. "These are too heavy for you, Connie. Better let me."

The latest book proved to be more recent. The pictures were taken in color and images of Agnes showed an older woman. "Maybe this is the book with the clue," Enid guessed.

Connie pointed to a cherubic infant. "Baby! Baby!"

"Sure is." Reece hurried to turn the page.

"Hey! Wait a minute!" Enid protested. "That baby wouldn't happen to be you, would it, Reece?"

Reece grimaced good-naturedly. "I'm afraid it is."

"Oh! Let me see!" Connie turned the page back.

"I want to see, too," Enid agreed. The chubby little boy looked lively and happy, full of energy. "Oh, Reece. You were so cute."

"And I still am!" He set his chest out in mock pride.

"Connie looks a lot like you. The same brown eyes."

"But I'm a giwl!" Connie objected.

"You certainly are." Enid giggled.

After flipping the page, Reece pointed to an attractive couple. "Look, Connie. Here's Daddy."

As Connie nodded with understanding, Enid leaned more closely toward the book to get a better view of the faded photograph. The man pictured looked like Reece, except his longish blond hair flared out into prominent sideburns. A flowered shirt and white bell-bottom pants placed him in the late 1960s. In the picture, he stood next to an apple-cheeked teenage girl with long, flowing brown hair. The girl pictured had to be Reece's mother.

"So that's your father," Enid remarked. "Handsome man."

"Thanks." Reece nodded before he slapped the book shut. "Connie," he told the little girl, "go get on your coat."

"Do I have to?" she argued. "We ain't done lookin' at the pictuahs."

"Not 'ain't,' " Reece corrected. "Aren't. We aren't done looking at the pictures."

Connie folded her arms. "Well, we ain't."

"That's enough, Connie. It's getting late. Go get your coat." Reece didn't raise his voice, but his tone contained enough of an edge that Connie could see he was serious. As she rushed out of the room to obey, Reece shook his head. "They pick up every kind of language at day care."

"I'm sure they do."

Reece placed the book back in its slot between two other albums. "I'm sorry if I seemed abrupt. It's still hard for me to look at pictures of Dad, even old ones."

She placed a comforting hand on his shoulder. "I understand."

"Thanks for putting up with us," Reece apologized.

"Not at all. But we still need to find the next clue."

"We will. Just not tonight. I'm not sure when. I'll call you."

❦

A few days later, Reece was still troubled. The photo albums had brought back so many memories. Even after all this time, he couldn't bear to talk about how his father and young stepmother were critically wounded in an automobile accident, with their toddler, Connie, miraculously sustaining only cuts and bruises. Reece had agonized over all of them, even praying that Connie's injuries wouldn't prove more serious than at first suspected and that her parents would survive. God chose not to answer, at least not with the outcome for which Reece had begged and pleaded. Connie came out of the ordeal without so much as a memory. Go took his father and stepmother. Reece was left to take care of Connie, a task fo which he knew he wasn't ready.

Why? Why was God permitting Connie to grow up with no parent If Reece couldn't trust God with the fate of his own father, how could he l expected to trust the Lord with his livelihood, as Enid had suggested?

Reece had to admit he never knew the Lord well. At the same time, he wa inexplicably drawn to Enid. Not just because she was a gorgeous woman, b because he could see that she possessed something Reece wanted for himsel Enid possessed a peace that he had never seen anyone else possess—except fo his Aunt Agnes. Since his father's death, Enid was the first person who ha convinced him to go to church. Though he enjoyed beginning the week with worship service, annoying questions persisted.

What would Enid do if she were faced with a tough question? Surely sh would find solace in the Bible. Since they had given up on finding the lates clue, Reece had made considerable progress in his Bible reading. Discouraged b tackling the historical books straight through, he had begun to go back and fort through the Old and New Testaments, often focusing on the passages he hear preached on in church. The words, particularly those in the New Testamen spoke to him as though they had been written the week before, not thousand of years in the past.

Reece flipped to the small concordance in the back of his Bible and looke for "trial." The entry led him to 1 Peter 4:12–13: "Dear friends, do not be sur prised at the painful trial you are suffering, as though something strange wer happening to you. But rejoice that you participate in the sufferings of Christ, s that you may be overjoyed when his glory is revealed."

As much as he loved his little sister, Reece couldn't imagine how havin premature fatherhood thrust upon him so dramatically could be God's plan fo him. Yet he was supposed to be joyful.

Somehow, he suspected Enid was part of the answer.

Chapter 13

A few days later, Reece called Enid's house just as she was finishing up the last of the dinner dishes.

"What's this?" she jested. "You've actually learned to use the telephone instead of dropping by my work? Not that I mind your visits, of course."

"I decided to go the formal route." His voice was flavored with mock seriousness. "This is a very formal question. I'd like you to go with me to a concert this Friday."

"A concert?" A gasp escaped her lips. "You don't mean the one they've been talking about on the radio for months!"

"I think that's the one. I have a list of the people who'll be there." He named one superstar and two up-and-coming Christian artists.

"That's the one!" With some chagrin, Enid realized she was squealing like a besotted fan.

"I'm glad to hear you're so excited," Reece said. "I had to call in a favor to get these tickets on such short notice."

"This is wonderful, Reece, but I didn't think you were in the least bit interested in Christian music."

"I have to admit, I wasn't before you suggested that radio station."

Enid remembered a shared car ride with Reece, when she had her car radio set on a local Christian station. She'd taken the opportunity to mention how the station had blessed her life with the music it played, but she figured he'd never go so far as to tune in for himself. The Lord had certainly surprised her yet again.

"Before I started listening," Reece continued, "I had no idea there were even stations devoted to Christian music. All the religious stations I knew about just broadcast preaching."

"I can recommend a couple of those, too," Enid teased.

"Uh, no, thanks," he quipped in return. "I started listening partially because Connie was so often in the car, and I knew none of the lyrics would be offensive for her. I didn't really think I'd like the songs myself. I have to say, I'm surprised by how talented the artists are. They're as good as the secular ones. Most are even better."

"I agree a hundred percent. You sound like the perfect spokesman for Christian music." She smiled into the phone. "I'm glad you enjoy it."

"What do you say? Are you willing to come along with me?"

"Sure! Who'd pass up the chance for such a wonderful concert? Connie should enjoy it, too."

He paused. "Um, I'm not taking her."

"You're not?"

"I want us to have an evening together where we don't talk about anything having to do with Aunt Agnes, the clues, or even Connie," Reece explained. "I've already arranged for her to go and play at a friend's house next Friday night. You don't mind that it's just me, do you?"

Enid was conscious of her rapidly beating heart. "Of course not."

"Good." Reece sounded more like an unsure adolescent than a grown man. Enid found his vulnerability endearing. "I'd better go. Connie's ready for her bedtime story, and I've got to set her clothes out for church tomorrow. And by the way, she doesn't know I've invited you to go to a concert without her. So don't mention it."

"Mum's the word."

❧

Almost as soon as Reece hung up, the telephone rang. Thinking the caller was Enid with a question about their date, Reece picked it up just after the first ring.

"Reece? You must have been right by the phone." The nasal voice hit a sour note when he was expecting the sweet melody of Enid's intonation.

"Yes?" Since he was unable to identify the caller, Reece's answer was tentative.

"Why, you sound like you don't remember me at all!"

Still unable to identify the woman's voice, Reece admitted he didn't.

"Oh, sure you do. We saw each other at the last family reunion. Remember?"

"The Parker reunion?" Reece was flummoxed. He wasn't able to attend the out-of-state reunion every year, although he had managed to put in an appearance the previous October. Over a hundred relatives, many whom he spoke to only in passing, attended the potluck dinner. He could spend all day on the telephone and never guess her name.

"I can tell you're totally lost. Well, I'm only the first grandchild." Her sarcasm was hard to miss.

Who had been the first grandchild of Grandma and Grandpa Parker? Reece had been the fifteenth of sixteen grandchildren. Since they were already in their twenties when he was a small boy, Reece had been too young to form a bond with his elder first cousins. A series of faces came to mind before he recalled a plain brunette. "Oh! Martie! How are you?"

"My branch of the family's just fine. I'm going to be a grandmother again in a couple of weeks. This will be number three."

"Congratulations."

"But your cousin Burt isn't doing so well," Martie informed him. "I suppose you heard he had a heart attack. And Aunt Madge just got out of the hospital—"

Reece politely listened, but he missed a good part of her account because he wondered all the while why she had called.

"Of course, I was sorry to hear that Aunt Agnes passed away," Martie eventually said, not a hue of regret in her voice. "But it's not like she didn't live a long time."

"She did live a very wonderful, full life. I only wish I had known her better." As soon as he uttered the words, Reece realized he wasn't just reciting a platitude. He meant what he said.

Why hadn't he spent more time with his elderly aunt? She had been the only Parker relative who lived close by. He should have gone to her house more often, maybe taken her out to the diner for a cup of tea. Talked to her a bit. She would have loved seeing more of Connie. He breathed a mental sigh. The time for visits with Aunt Agnes was past, but he wouldn't make that mistake again with anyone else.

Martie's voice broke into his regret-filled inner monologue. "I wanted to say something sooner, but Bill advised me against it. He said you needed time to yourself before all the vultures descended. But now I think more than enough time has passed, so I can speak up." Martie allowed a weighty silence to fill the phone line. Then she breathed inward. "I want you to know that years ago, Aunt Agnes promised me the dresser in her bedroom."

Reece could tell by the way she made her announcement that Martie expected an argument. "She did?"

"Yes, she did," Martie said, triumph and certainty filling her voice. "You know the one. It's tall and has five drawers. It's made out of mahogany. It was Grandmother Parker's, you know."

"Yes, I think she mentioned that."

"Well, being as I'm the oldest grandchild, and since Aunt Agnes didn't have any children of her own, I feel I'm entitled to some consideration. If Aunt Agnes had had her own daughter, she would have gotten the jewelry, but I'll let you have that. Maybe you have a girlfriend you can give it to?" Her voice was heavy with questions.

"Not exactly."

"Oh?" Martie's voice was dripping with curiosity. "So what happened to Lindsay, that girl your father mentioned several times? I thought surely you two would eventually get married."

"I have a lot of responsibility with Connie," he muttered.

"Oh. I get the picture." The briefest of pauses filled the telephone line. "How is little Connie, anyway? I'll bet I wouldn't even recognize her if I saw her. They grow so fast. How old is she now? Two?"

"Can you believe she's already four?"

"Is she really? Oh, my! How time flies. You'll have to send me a photo of her soon. You will, won't you?"

"Sure."

"I know it must be hard to keep in touch like you should when you don't have a wife to keep up with your social engagements. Speaking of which," she continued, "you know, one of Mom's college roommates lives somewhere around where you are. She has a daughter about your age. I've seen her picture. She's quite the beauty. Want me to see if I can fix the two of you up?"

"No, thanks." Reece realized the answer he had blurted was abrupt. "It's really nice of you to offer to go to all that trouble—"

"It wouldn't be any trouble."

"I can take care of myself in that department. Thanks anyway."

"All right." Doubt filled her voice. "But if you change your mind, let me know."

Why did everyone think just because he wasn't married yet that he couldn't take care of himself? Why did everyone want to play matchmaker? Reece decided to seize the chance to get back to the purpose of the call. "So what about the dresser? Are you planning to drive out here and pick it up?"

"No. It's too far. But I do have a niece that lives about five miles away. Her name is Savannah Hendley. You probably haven't met her." Martie waited for an answer.

"No, I haven't had the pleasure."

"She's on my husband's side of the family. Married with two children." Martie seemed to regret the lost opportunity to hook Reece up with someone. "She's already gotten a key from the executor of the will. I just didn't want to have it taken out of the house without letting you know."

"Thanks. I appreciate that."

"I suppose you'll be selling the house soon?" Martie guessed.

"Selling the house?"

"Sure. You aren't going to keep it, are you?"

"To be honest, I had no idea I was inheriting it."

"Why not? You're the only family member still living in the area. You mean, after all this time, you don't know yet who gets the house?"

"I don't know much of anything. Aunt Agnes left me a lot of clues I have to solve before I find out what my inheritance is."

Martie guffawed. "I see she still has her twisted sense of humor. She was always a funny old bird. Well, have fun solving your mystery. See you at the next reunion."

❧

The following Friday, Enid was ready at the appointed time for the concert. Running a brush through her blond curls, Enid inspected herself one last time in the mirror. She suddenly realized that Reece had never seen her in jeans. She hoped he would like her casual look, especially since the soft, lightweight pink sweater was her favorite.

The drive to the coliseum promised to be over an hour, more than enough time for them to have a good conversation. Suddenly, Enid felt nervous. Her talks with Reece had always focused on searching for clues, his Aunt Agnes, or Connie. He'd made clear that they weren't going to speak about any of those subjects on this night. Enid wondered what he wanted to talk about.

"Maybe that's just it," she thought. "Maybe he wants to see if we have anything in common." Enid knew one thing for certain. She was not going to talk to Reece about religion, unless he presented her with a burning question she needed to answer. The last thing she wanted was for him to think she looked upon him as a project or just as a new convert who needed to be nurtured. They would find something else to talk about.

Her thoughts were interrupted by his knock on the door. "Here I am!" he greeted her when she answered. To her delight, he handed her a bouquet of miniature pink and white carnations. Suddenly seeming reserved, he added, "These are for you."

"They're lovely! Thank you! Let me get these in a vase before we go." She motioned for him to enter the house and to follow her into the kitchen. "So is my house what you expected?"

"Yes. I imagined you living among fancy Victorian furniture, with lace pillows and everything all romantic, but still tidy as can be."

Enid laughed. "Everything you see looks Victorian, but each piece is a reproduction. And they're not especially good reproductions either. Most of it is pine with mahogany stain. One day, I might be able to get a few nice pieces. I figure this is good enough for now." Realizing she might have revealed too much, Enid pretended to be especially occupied with opening the kitchen cabinet door.

Thankfully, Reece didn't press the issue. "I can't believe I'm finally seeing you in jeans."

"Didn't think I owned a pair, did you?"

"Sort of like you didn't think I owned a suit."

"Good point." She arranged the flowers in the vase. "I think I'll leave these flowers right here on the counter where I can enjoy them all week. They're beautiful."

"Beautiful flowers for a beautiful lady."

Enid felt herself blush. "Thanks." Reece looked as striking as always. Instead of one of his denim work shirts, the one he wore was fashioned of an interesting purple material that shone various hues in the light as he moved. "You don't look so bad yourself," she said. "Cool shirt. Very cool."

"You think I'll pass muster?"

"You'll more than pass. Especially with me."

"I could listen to you talk like that all night, but I guess we'd better get going."

Soon they were settled in Reece's car. "So Connie doesn't suspect a thing, huh?" Enid slapped her forehead in a mock fashion. "Leave it to me to talk about one of our forbidden topics right from the start."

He laughed. "That's okay. No, she has no idea we're going out together. She's too excited about seeing her friend to pay much attention to my plans, anyway."

"When you're that age, the whole world revolves around you," Enid observed. "But really, that's the way it should be."

"As long as we outgrow that feeling by the proper time."

"I'll have to agree with that." A good topic popped into Enid's head. "Since we're going to a concert, it's made me think of how my musical tastes have changed over the years. Songs that used to speak to me often no longer do."

"Me, too." Reece launched into several examples, leading them into a conversation about music, art, and politics that lasted through the trip. Enid was pleased to discover they agreed on the issues that mattered. She knew that Reece felt likewise.

As they walked through the parking lot, Reece took Enid's hand as naturally as if they'd been a couple forever. Several years had passed since she felt like half of a couple. Reece's small gesture made her see how much she missed the feeling.

"Sure are a lot of church vans here," he noted.

"You're not surprised, are you? These concerts attract a lot of church youth groups."

"I hadn't thought about that. Makes sense. You know, it's good that they have these events now. When I was growing up, I don't remember a lot of concerts like this. I do remember concerts that no youth minister would think about going to, though."

"Modern Christian music has been around a long time, but back then you really had to know where to find out about concerts, and the outlets for the recordings weren't as numerous. I think it's easier now. And that's a good thing," Enid added.

A few moments later, they were waiting in line among a huge throng of people. Enid noticed that everyone around them was too involved in conversation to pay attention to her. "I have a confession to make."

"Uh-oh. This can't be good." His wry expression belied his serious words.

"It's not anything bad, silly." Suddenly self-conscious, she studied her athletic shoes as though she had never before seen them. "It's just that, before you picked me up, I was actually worried that I might not have anything to say to you tonight."

"I'm all that off-putting?"

"Oh, no. But we've been so involved in the hunt, we really haven't talked about much else. I was wondering if I could come up with anything to say that wouldn't bore you to death."

His mouth curled into a sheepish grin. "You know what? I was thinking the same thing about myself. I was afraid we would ride up here in silence, and then talk about the concert for five minutes on the way home, before we finally resorted to talking about the clues. I'm sure glad I was wrong."

"Me, too."

⚯

The heart-to-heart, though brief, left both them of them relaxed so they were able to enjoy the concert. As the three artists performed, the crowd burst into applause during the first notes of their most popular numbers. Reece enjoyed watching Enid singing along with several of the songs. To his surprise, he found himself humming along as well.

All too soon, the concert ended.

"Would you like a souvenir?" Reece asked after the concert. "Maybe a CD or a T-shirt?"

"I brought some money with me. Why don't you let me buy you one?"

"No way. This evening is my treat. I wouldn't have invited you if I didn't want you to come along." Reece studied the price list. "These shirts are surprisingly reasonable in cost. Most groups overprice their concert goods. Guess they want to make a killing on a captive audience."

"And the excitement and emotions that make you buy impulse items when you go to an event like this," Enid added. "Christian groups are usually pretty good about keeping their ticket prices reasonable, too."

"I noticed that when I bought ours," Reece agreed.

After they selected their shirts, Enid and Reece headed back to his car. "Normally I'd offer to take you out for a snack since it's still pretty early, but I promised I'd pick up Connie tonight."

"That's all right. The cotton candy was enough to blow my diet for the next month."

"As if you need to diet," he quipped. "I'll have to say, I was surprised that we didn't have to go through metal detectors or anything. And the crowd was so well-behaved and clean cut."

"What did you expect? A bunch of booze and tattoos?" She nudged him playfully. "Like we talked about before, I think there were a lot of church youth groups here."

"Yeah, but I hadn't really thought about what to expect. I sure didn't think the artists would actually bring a Bible out on stage with them and start talking about what the songs meant and the verses they were based on. I didn't expect them to tell their testimonies and what the Lord means to them."

"Why not?"

"I don't know. When I was growing up, my parents said they were Christians, and I guess they were. It's not like they were horrible people or anything. But we didn't talk about God or religion much. In fact, Dad always told me to watch what I said in public. He said to avoid the topic of religion altogether so I wouldn't offend the wrong person."

"I can't say that advice is totally wrong for a worldly person. I once heard a sermon about how God is sort of like a dad in that you can be ashamed of Him and His ways and His rules, sometimes. You're afraid of talking about Him, because some people think He's out of date. But he went on to quote from the first chapter of Romans, 'For I am not ashamed of the gospel of Christ: for it is the power of God unto salvation to every one that believeth.'"

Reece took a few moments to ponder her words. "That's a very good analogy. I felt like that about my dad a few times when I was a teenager. I didn't think he was cool enough. But now I know that Christians are to defend the faith no matter what."

"Exactly." Enid seemed led to be completely honest with Reece. "If you want to know the truth, I had vowed not to talk about religion tonight."

"Really? Don't worry. You can talk to me about religion—and about the Lord—any time you like. You're one of the few people I feel comfortable talking about God with."

"I hope that's a good thing." Enid laughed.

"Yes, it is a good thing." He turned serious. "I feel so much closer to God since I met you."

"As much as I'd like to take credit, it's really because you've been reading His Word. Your aunt has to take the credit for that."

"Yes, but if it hadn't been for you, I wouldn't have thought about coming to this concert. The people here seemed to be walking in the Light. Now that's a phrase I never thought I'd be using. It sounds so strange until you witness it for yourself."

Enid nodded. "I know what you mean."

"It seems like they don't have a worry in the world."

"Oh, I'm sure they do. God never promised the walk would be easy. I think you've seen that for yourself, in your questions about why Connie's parents died so young. You know, He didn't promise that His servants would live to an old age."

"I know," he admitted. "But it just isn't fair. Connie doesn't deserve to suffer."

"Sometimes the innocent do suffer. Didn't Jesus suffer?"

"Yes," he said.

"Jesus suffered even though He was innocent. Innocent Christians have suffered persecution since the early Church. Revelation 17:6 mentions them: 'And I saw the woman drunken with the blood of the saints, and with the blood of the martyrs of Jesus.' You can read all about the stoning of Stephen in the book of Acts."

"Now you're making me feel bad. I know Connie's suffering can't compare to that."

"Of course not," Enid hastened to assure him. "But she is a suffering innocent. Some might argue that it hardly looks like Connie is suffering. She couldn't ask for a better man to raise her."

Reece remained silent. Enid placed such trust and faith in him. He hardly deserved her confidence. He was so unworthy. Reece said a silent prayer. *Lord, I know I need to be closer to You if I'm ever to be worthy of Connie or Enid. Can You help me?*

He stole a glance at the woman sitting beside him. Enid was so good. The one woman he once thought he loved had been a nominal Christian at best. Her true colors showed when she discovered that Connie was to be a permanent fixture in Reece's life. She bolted faster than the Road Runner speeds away from Wile E. Coyote. Enid was the first woman he'd seen, other than Aunt Agnes, who really let her faith impact her life beyond occasional church attendance. Enid did more than wear a cross around her neck. She considered Christ in each decision.

He resumed his silent plea. *Lord, I want to be good enough for her. Please stay with me.*

Chapter 14

Weeks went by as Enid waited for Reece to mention hunting for more clues. The photo albums had stymied them, and neither had come up with any more ideas as to where the next clue could be. Could Agnes have tricked them so that Reece would never find his inheritance?

No. That couldn't be. Enid knew Agnes better than that. She wouldn't have gone to all the trouble to put together a mystery if she didn't think they could solve it. Perhaps her real reason was to give Reece time before he received his inheritance. Time to read the Bible. Time to accept the Lord, perhaps. What other reason could there be?

Reece's familiar voice brought her back into the present, where she was a passenger in Reece's car as it made its way from a local diner after an informal after-church brunch. "What are you thinking about, Enid?"

What could she say that wouldn't reveal too much or wouldn't be a lie? She thought fast. "Oh, I was thinking about all the questions life has to offer us."

"Like the sermon we heard today, 'How Do You Express Forgiveness?' "

Enid breathed an inward sigh of relief that Reece had so effortlessly diverted the subject into safe territory. "Yes, he had a lot of good ideas. It's not easy to show somebody forgiveness sometimes, even if you feel it."

"What is fo–give–ness?" Connie wanted to know from her perch in the back seat.

"It means you're nice to somebody even if they do something wrong to you," Reece elaborated.

"Oh." Her little eyebrows furrowed together as though she were contemplating the mysteries of the universe. "Yesta–day I fogave Michael for takin' my wed cwayon," Connie piped up. "Does that count?"

"Well, that wasn't yesterday, it was Friday," Reece told her. "Michael is one of her friends in day care," he explained to Enid.

"Oh. I figured as much."

Reece shot Connie a quick glance before turning his attention back to the road. "And yes, that does count."

"Good girl," Enid agreed, flashing the adorable urchin a big smile. "It's wonderful to see you doing what Jesus would want you to do."

Enid's reward was a beaming expression that made Connie appear quite the cherub. "I like chuwch. Can we go again next week? Huh? Can we?"

"I think you know the answer to that," said Reece. "We've been going every

Sunday for a few weeks now, haven't we?"

"Yay!"

Enid didn't say so, but in her heart, she wanted to shout for joy as well. The little girl's reaction—and Reece's willingness to keep taking her to church—was the answer to Enid's many prayers.

"Won't the two of you come in for dessert?"

"I can!" Connie piped up.

"Are you sure, Enid?" Reece asked. "I don't want to put you out."

"I wanna go! I like dessewt!"

Enid chuckled. "I'd be very disappointed if you didn't come in. I've tried a new recipe for pineapple upside-down cake, and I certainly can't eat the whole thing by myself!"

"I'll help!" Connie rubbed her tummy in a circular motion.

"I guess I can force myself," Reece teased, getting out of the car. "How did you know pineapple upside-down cake is one of my favorites?"

"I didn't! But I'm glad to find out."

"Yeah," he said, striding up beside Enid, "Mom used to make the best pineapple upside-down cake on Earth."

"Oh, no. I'll never be able to compete with that."

Reece didn't answer. He was looking a few steps ahead at the sidewalk. She could see by his clouded expression that his newly pensive mood was colored with sadness. She placed a hand lightly on his shoulder. "I'm sorry, Reece. I know you must miss her terribly."

"I know you probably think I'm silly, but yes, I still do, even though she died when I was only ten."

"Of course I don't think you're silly. There will always be a hole in your heart for her, no matter how many years pass," Enid observed. "Never be ashamed of that."

He nodded as he followed Enid through the front door.

Once they were in the living room, Enid knelt down so she could speak to Connie. "I have a surprise for you. If you'll go in the basket beside the couch, you'll find a coloring book and crayons, just for you!"

Connie's eyes lit up brighter than ever. She ran to the basket. Eagerly reaching in, she pulled out a large book with simple drawings plus the biggest box of crayons Enid was able to find.

"Ninety-six crayons! And a sharpener, too! That's really something!" Reece told her. "What do you say to Miss Enid?"

Connie looked up at Enid. "Thank you!"

"You're welcome! You can color on the table in here while I cut the cake, okay?"

Connie didn't have to be asked twice. She rushed to the table as Enid and Reece departed to the kitchen.

"You really didn't need to be so extravagant," Reece told Enid. "Eight crayons would have been more than enough. Now she'll be spoiled."

"Only when she comes to my house. The crayons stay here. I promise."

After washing her hands, Enid took the cake out of the refrigerator.

"Looks delicious," Reece assured her. "Just seeing it brings back memories. To tell you the truth," he said as Enid cut the cake, "I never thought I'd eat a pineapple upside-down cake again."

"If you'd rather not, it's all right."

"Oh, no. I don't mind." Leaning against the counter, Reece sighed. "Of course, things were never the same after Mom died. Dad remarried twelve years later. I couldn't fault him. He'd waited more than long enough. I just wasn't too thrilled that his new wife was younger than me. I guess I wasn't too pleasant to be around. Thankfully, I had my own place by then, and I didn't have to see them much."

"But that changed when Connie came along."

He smiled. "How did you guess?"

"You two seem to have a special bond."

"You're right. And that's probably why Hope—that's my stepmom—agreed I would be Connie's guardian if anything happened to both of them." Reece's expression became brooding. He seemed to forget the present, remembering, instead, the past. "When I signed the papers, I had no idea anything would ever happen. I thought they'd both live forever, especially Hope. The reality that I would actually have to be responsible for everything having to do with Connie's upbringing didn't dawn on me."

"So if you had to do it again, you wouldn't agree to be her guardian?"

"Yes, I would agree to it. I wouldn't take the world for Connie." His voice was strong, adamant. "But I really wasn't prepared to be a parent."

"Is anyone ever really prepared to be a parent?" Enid didn't wait for Reece to answer the rhetorical question. "I take it no one else was available. No other brothers or sisters. No other responsible, older adult."

"Yes and no. Hope's parents took me to court to gain custody."

"That must have been a nightmare."

He nodded. "Their health wasn't good enough for the court to justify taking Connie away from me, especially against the parents' expressly written wishes. Of course I would never keep Connie from seeing them, but that issue doesn't come up often. They live in an apartment complex in Florida that doesn't allow kids on overnight stays."

Connie chose that moment to zoom into the kitchen. She was holding up a sheet torn from the coloring book so that most of the picture was missing. Connie's attempts at artistry were typical for one her age—mostly scribbles in a mishmash of colors, without regard to the picture in question. "Look! Look what I colowed for you, Miss Enid!"

"Oh, thank you, Connie!" Enid let out an exaggerated gasp as she studied the artwork. "That's beautiful! Here. Let me hang it on a special place on my refrigerator." Enid chose a magnet in the shape of an apple and used it to anchor the picture in place. "See?" She pointed to a drawing of herself with green hair. "It's right beside the picture you drew of me." She stepped back and admired it. "Doesn't that look wonderful?"

She nodded vigorously. "I'll go make anothow one."

"You can color all you like," Reece cautioned, "but one picture for Miss Enid is enough for today. If you color too many all at once, she'll run out of room to put them on the refrigerator."

"I'll make one for you!" Undeterred, Connie ran back to her book and crayons.

"You know I wouldn't take the world for her," said Reece.

"I can see why."

"Like I said before, you two really do seem to hit it off, Enid. You have no idea how much that means to me. It's not every day a woman outside the family relates that well to Connie."

"I don't see why not," Enid protested. "Connie's adorable."

"I think so. But not many women my age want a ready-made family." Reece stopped himself. His look of chagrin made Enid think he regretted what he said. Perhaps he hadn't meant to reveal that part of himself.

Enid's heart jumped. Could Reece be thinking of her as someone he could look to for a lifelong commitment? She gave herself a swift mental kick in the pants. She was getting ahead of herself. Way ahead. "And not many women my age can make a great cake from scratch, no less." She deliberately kept her tone lighthearted.

"Can I sneak a piece?" With a winning grin that showed he was grateful for the change of topic, Reece began reaching for the cake.

Enid playfully swatted at the air near his hand. "Ah-ah-ah! No, you don't. It wouldn't be fair to Connie." She shook her head in mock derision. "Don't tell me you're a bigger kid than she is?"

"Okay. I won't tell you."

They were laughing together as they took the cake and a carton of milk into the dining room.

"What's so funny?" Connie paused from her coloring long enough to inquire.

"Nothing."

She made a face. "That's what gwown-ups always say when they don't want me to know somethin'"

Before they could dig into the treat, Connie stopped them. "I wanna say the blessin' Mrs. Jones taught us."

"Is she the one who runs Connie's day care?" Enid asked Reece.

He nodded and turned his head to Connie. "We're lucky to have Mrs. Jones to take care of you, aren't we, Connie?"

The little girl nodded, then prayed. "God is gweat. God is good. Let us thank Him fo' ouw food. By His hands we all are fed—"

Connie was saying the blessing so effortlessly, Enid wondered why she stopped. She opened her eyes and saw Connie, hands still together in front of her nose, concentrating. By this time, Reece had opened his eyes, too.

Seeing their questioning stares, Connie rested her gaze on her cake. "I forgot the west."

"Give us, Lord, our daily bread," Enid finished.

Connie beamed and nodded. "Give us, Lowd, our daily bwead. Amen."

After praising Connie's efforts, they began to enjoy the dessert. Enid was pleased that the cake was even better than she had imagined. Buttery cake was flavored generously with pineapple juice. A slice of pineapple and maraschino cherry made each square festive.

"Delicious, Enid," Reece complimented her.

"I'm glad you like it."

Connie touched her cherry with a fork tine. "What's this, Miss Enid?"

"A cherry. Isn't it pretty?"

She nodded. "Can you make a doll out of it?"

Enid was puzzled. She looked over at Reece. He furrowed his eyebrows together, equally mystified. "A doll?"

"Mrs. Jones says come this fall, we'll make dolls out of apples."

"Out of apples?" Reece questioned. "How would you do that?"

Connie shrugged. "She said they'll look all winkly, like an ol' gwamma. Will they look like Gwamma in Flowida, Weece? I hope not. I don't want an ol' doll that looks like Gwamma in Flowida. I want a pwetty baby doll." Connie stuck out her lips. "Can I have a pwetty baby doll? Do I havta make a doll that looks all winkly?"

"Yes, Connie," Reece answered. "If Mrs. Jones wants you to make a doll that looks wrinkled, you should do it."

"But I don't wanna—"

"I have an idea," Enid offered. "Maybe you can give the doll to Grandma. She'd like that, don't you think?"

As they talked, Enid's thoughts were spinning. Wrinkled! Suddenly, she remembered a granny doll whose face was made from a shriveled apple, just as Connie was describing.

"Reece!" she blurted. "That's it!"

Reece stopped his fork in midair, a piece of cake dangling from its end. "Huh? What's it?"

"That must be where the next clue is. On the granny apple doll Agnes has on the mantle!"

His mouth formed an astonished O. "You might be on to something there.

346

We've got to find out!" Reece set his fork on his plate and took it off the table. He was halfway to the kitchen before Connie interrupted.

"Can't we finish the cake?" Connie wondered aloud.

"Sure we can," Enid answered, patting her hand. "Reece, we may as well finish. The doll isn't going anywhere."

"Oh, all right." He returned to his seat. "Since you worked so hard and everything."

All the same, they polished off their cake quickly and were soon headed to Reece's car. What would the next clue say?

Chapter 15

Enid and Reece were delighted to discover that Enid's idea had been right. The next clue was underneath the granny doll.

"See, Connie? This is the kind of doll that Mrs. Jones is talking about. A granny doll."

Enid held the doll close to Connie for her to examine. The face was made of a shriveled apple. Cloves served for eyes and a nose. A miniature bandanna was wrapped around the head to resemble a scarf. The dress was made of similar but not matching cotton and covered the doll's cloth body so only painted-on black high-top boots peeked from underneath. A muslin collar that extended the width of Granny's shoulders served as decoration on the dress.

Connie reached for the doll.

"Be careful."

"Okay." She inspected the doll, looking at the prune-like face. "How come she doesn't have a mouth?"

"I don't know. Maybe you can give yours a mouth."

"I want mine to have a mouth." Connie fingered the gingham dress. "I guess the dwess is pwetty. Will my doll have a dwess like this one?"

"I don't know, honey. I guess you can ask."

Noticing that Reece was studying the clue, Enid turned to Reece. "What does it say?"

Jesus answered, Verily, verily, I say unto thee, Except a man be born of water and of the Spirit, he cannot enter into the kingdom of God (John 3:5).

Forty days was hardly bliss
Surely Noah tired of this.

"I guess he was tired of being on the ark," Reece guessed. "She doesn't have a little Noah's ark set anywhere, does she?"

Enid thought. "No, I don't think so. I've never seen one. But we can always look."

"I don't know. I think you would have seen something like that. It would have been on display."

"I'm sure he got tired of rain," Enid told him. She snapped her fingers. "I know! She used to collect rainwater in a bucket outside. The next clue must be near that." She motioned for him to follow her out the back door.

As they crossed the yard, Reece wondered aloud. "Why in the world did she collect rainwater? It's not like there was a water shortage here, even in the worst of times."

"You've never heard of that old beauty secret?" When a puzzled expression crossed Reece's features, Enid explained. "She washed her hair in it."

His mouth dropped open. "You're kidding."

"Nope. Agnes told me many a time that it was purer than any tap water. She swore by how soft it made her hair." Enid smiled. "She even tried to convince me to try it, but I never did."

"Interesting."

They had reached the bucket of saved rainwater. Both of them searched the area, but no white piece of paper was to be found. They tried lifting the bucket in case the clue was hidden underneath, careful not to spill the contents so that they wouldn't drench an important piece of white paper. Still no luck.

"I give up," Reece finally said.

"I have to agree, it looks like we've reached our stopping point, at least for a while. We need to think on this one. But we shouldn't get too discouraged. We had a lot of success today. Besides, there shouldn't be too many more clues."

"I wouldn't think so. We should be finished with this puzzle soon." He looked longingly at the house. "Wish we could go in and pour ourselves a nice tall glass of iced tea from the refrigerator."

"Me, too. The house sure isn't as hospitable without Agnes."

"Goes to show, a house is just a building. It's the people in it that make it a home." Reece allowed a moment of contemplation before he made an offer. "How about we go to the diner and have our tea there?"

"Sounds like a winner. I could use the break."

❧

An hour later, the threesome returned to the house, fresh from indulging in tea and pie—or in Connie's case, a kid-sized milkshake and four chicken nuggets.

"Ready to search every water-related object in the house?" Reece asked, referring to the ideas they had bandied about during the break.

"I sure am! Why don't I look around the kitchen sink and you take the bathrooms?"

"Good idea."

"Where do you want me to look?" Connie asked.

"Why don't you make sure all the plants have enough water?" Reece suggested.

"But the clue isn't in the plants!"

"You never know. After all, the plants do need water. Now, you know what to do because you've been such a big girl and helped me with this before. Just put your finger on top of the soil and make sure it isn't dry," Reece reminded her.

"I know!" Connie dashed off to investigate the numerous plants still living throughout the vacant house.

As Enid searched and found nothing, she heard Reece calling a few moments later.

"Found it!" He hurried into the kitchen, clue in hand.

"Wonderful! Where was it?"

"Underneath the foot of the old-fashioned bathtub."

"Figures. You know, I've never taken a bath in a claw-foot tub like that," Enid revealed. "Agnes always promised me I could bathe in there one day. I never did get around to it."

He swept his hand toward the bathroom. "The towels are still in the linen closet. Grab one and be my guest."

"That's okay. Thanks anyway," Enid said, waving her hand dismissively. "Maybe another time. We've got work to do now. Read me the next clue."

"Whatever you say, madame." He read:

> *Bring ye all the tithes into the storehouse, that there may be meat in mine house, and prove me now herewith, saith the LORD of hosts, if I will not open you the windows of heaven, and pour you out a blessing, that there shall not be room enough to receive it (Malachi 3:10).*

> *When you ask for daily bread*
> *Not excess, but this instead.*

"Hey, did you know about this?" he asked, screwing his mouth into a rueful line.

"What do you mean?"

"This is the same sermon you gave me some time ago, only this is the condensed version."

"So you think I go around preaching sermons, huh?" Enid jested.

"I don't mind hearing them from you," Reece hastened to say.

Laughing, Enid remembered their talk about the Lord's prayer. "You know, I'm not surprised your aunt and I came up with the same thought. I told you we were good friends. Guess we were on the same wavelength."

"Hmm. That could be dangerous," he joked. "Well, Miss Wavelength, where is the next clue?"

"It couldn't be in a loaf of bread. No food has come into this house for months." She motioned for him to follow her. "Come on. Let's go in the kitchen. I think there's a breadbox in there."

Enid's instincts turned out to be right. A clue was taped to the inside top of the breadbox:

THE THRILL OF THE HUNT

But God led the people about, through the way of the wilderness of the Red sea: and the children of Israel went up harnessed out of the land of Egypt (Exodus 13:18).

God dressed His favorites in jewels and He
Parted this Sea for them to flee.

" 'Parted this Sea for them to flee,' " Reece repeated. "I think I remember. It was the Red Sea, wasn't it? Maybe the next clue has something to do with the color red."

After reviewing the clue again, Enid had to agree. "There's nothing else tangible in this clue, unless the key word is 'flee' and it involves plane tickets."

"Plane tickets?" Reece's eyebrows rose. "Hmm, wouldn't that be nice? I could go for a trip to the Bahamas right about now. Or maybe Cancun."

"I have to admit, the idea of sunning on the beach all day sounds lovely. On second thought, I doubt Agnes would have splurged on plane tickets. She would have thought an exotic vacation was a terrible waste," Enid noted. "I think we should go with your idea first."

"All right. I'll go around the house looking for anything red. Why don't you take the jewelry box and see if she has any red stones, like garnets or rubies, that could give us a clue?"

Enid nodded. "What about Connie? Maybe we should call her. She can help you look for red things."

"Good idea."

As Reece tended to Connie, Enid headed for Agnes's jewelry box. Agnes's birthday had been in January, so she had a number of garnet items, reflecting the month's birthstone. However, none of the pieces offered any clue. Enid thought for a few moments. Why would Agnes lead them to her jewelry box over and over? Never one to covet fine things, the only jewelry she had owned of value was her mother's engagement ring that, as far as they knew, had been buried with her. Obviously, Reece's inheritance wasn't meant to be jewelry. So where was the next clue?

Enid studied her surroundings. Agnes had decorated her bedroom in blue. Not a trace of red was to be seen anywhere. Enid remembered that Agnes did enjoy wearing the color red, though. Maybe the clue was in her closet. Enid doubted that. Surely Agnes's clothes had been sorted and given away by this time. Then again, searching the clothes closet was worth a try.

Enid opened the closet door. To her surprised delight, she found Agnes's clothing still in its place, as though the garments' owner had merely stepped out of the house for a few minutes. Agnes's wardrobe wasn't extensive, but each item was well kept. Enid reached for a familiar red dress, one she had seen Agnes wear to church often. The conservative frock, a coat style, had two decorative front

351

pockets, one on each side. Enid reached in to the right pocket. Her heart began racing when her fingers touched a stiff piece of paper. Retrieving it, she saw the same paper on which Agnes had written the other clues. This was it!

"Reece!" she called, rushing into the living room. "I think I found the next clue!"

Connie was holding a red pillow. "Aw! I wanted to find it."

Reece and Enid chuckled together.

"You've been a big help," Enid assured her. "You might even help us find the next clue."

"I hope so."

Reece was tapping his foot impatiently. "Let's see it."

Enid unfolded the paper. "That's odd. There's no verse." She read:

> *Now that you know your Bible better*
> *From these clues take the first letter*
> *Of one word in each verse and you*
> *Will then be sure of what to do.*

"Oh, great." Reece groaned. "We'll never figure this one out."

"Sure we will. We'll just persevere, that's all."

"Is that the last one?" Connie asked.

"I'm afraid it is," Reece answered.

"But you said I could find the next clue. You pwomised!" Her lips were set into a pout.

"We still have a puzzle to solve. You can help us with that."

"A puzzle? Like the Sleeping Beauty puzzle I have?"

"No," Reece chuckled. "It's not a jigsaw puzzle. It's another kind of puzzle."

"Then I don't wanna help. Can I go outside now?"

"Not now. We've got to go back home."

"How come?"

"Miss Enid and I have to take all the clues and figure out what they mean." Reece turned to Enid. "Are you in the mood to tackle this tonight, or do you want to wait?"

"Are you kidding? We've come this far. There's no reason to stop now."

◈

"Can Miss Enid wead me a stowy?" Connie asked as they entered Reece's apartment a few moments later.

"Sure, if it's okay with her."

"Fine with me." Enid smiled at them both. Her heart was warmed by Connie's request. The prospect of reading her a story was appealing.

"I hate to tell you this, but it's bath night," Reece said.

"Bath night!" Connie groaned. "Do I haveta wash my hauh?"

"Yes, you have to wash your hair."

"Aww, Reece, can't it wait until another day?" Enid protested.

Reece sent his gaze skyward. "How can I possibly win with both of you ganging up on me?" he asked good-naturedly. "All right. I guess it can wait another day."

"Good!" Connie clapped her hands. "Come on, Miss Enid. Come see my bedwoom."

"All right!"

As he watched the young woman and little girl race to Connie's room, Reece felt a catch in his throat. What would life be like if he could watch that scene every night? As he considered the possibility, a feeling of warmth washed over him. He knew sharing his life with Enid would be beyond wonderful.

Nudging himself out of his dreaminess, Reece knew the task at hand took precedence. He gathered the clues and studied them, wishing he could even begin to decipher what Agnes meant by the wide variety of verses. How would he ever find out what they meant? Aunt Agnes said that the first letter of one word would reveal all. But which letter? Which word? He sent up a silent prayer to the Lord, thanking Him that Enid would be by his side to help.

Soon Enid entered the living room with Connie.

"Connie, I hope you aren't giving Miss Enid a hard time about going to bed."

"I'm not!" Connie protested.

"Connie and I have a surprise for you, Reece." Enid's excitement was almost palpable.

"You do? I could use a nice surprise right about now."

"All right, Connie." Enid bent down and whispered in Connie's ear.

Connie nodded and rushed up to Reece. She jumped into his lap. Without warning, she started giggling.

"What's so funny?" Reece asked. Connie's giggles were about to cause him to burst into laughter himself.

"I don't know if I can do it, Miss Enid," the little girl said.

"Sure you can!" Enid gave her a few quick nods. "Go on!"

Connie giggled some more and then finally composed herself. She looked up into her brother's eyes and said, "I love you, Reece!"

As she wrapped her small arms around his neck, Reece hugged her in return. "You said my name the right way! That's great, Connie!"

"Miss Enid told me how."

"She's wonderful, isn't she, Connie?"

Connie bobbed her head up and down in several big motions. She jumped out of Reece's lap and began running in circles around the room, shouting in a singsong voice, "Reece Reece Reece Reece Reece Reece Reece Reece."

"Okay, Connie. That's enough," Reece said, chuckling. "You'll have plenty more chances to say my name. You don't have to wear it out tonight."

"That's right, Connie," Enid agreed, unable to contain her own giggles. "Time to go to bed for real."

"Do I have to?"

"I'm afraid so," Reece and Enid said in unison. The coincidence caused them to break into fresh chuckles.

Connie could see clearly that she had lost. "Okay. I'll go." Enid escorted Connie to her room as she continued to say "Reece" intermittently.

Enid returned to the living room a few moments later.

"I think you made one little girl and one big guy happy today. How did you manage to teach her how to say my name, Enid?"

She shrugged. "Just a little persistence." Her green eyes twinkled. "And a lot of love."

Chapter 16

The next day was Memorial Day, a holiday for Enid and Reece. Since neither had any idea where the hunt would ultimately take them, they decided to begin the day fresh at Enid's house, where they could solve the puzzle in comfort and Connie could color and play to her heart's content. All three were glad they had made this decision as the day dragged on. Together they went through all sorts of possibilities—everything from trying to spell out the make of Agnes's car to local banks. Finally, through some trial and error plus a great deal of patience, they solved the puzzle:

1. "Deliver my soul from the sword; my darling from the power of the **dog**" (Psalm 22:20).

2. "Behold, I will stand before thee there upon the **rock** in Horeb; and thou shalt smite the rock, and there shall come water out of it, that the people may drink. And Moses did so in the sight of the elders of Israel" (Exodus 17:6).

3. "And unto man he said, Behold, the fear of the LORD, that is wisdom; and to depart from **evil** is understanding" (Job 28:28).

4. "But a certain man named Ananias, with **Sapphira** his wife, sold a possession" (Acts 5:1).

5. "And she gave the king an hundred and twenty talents of gold, and of **spices** great abundance, and precious stones: neither was there any such spice as the queen of Sheba gave king Solomon" (2 Chronicles 9:9).

6. "And he that sat was to look upon like a jasper and a sardine stone: and there was a rainbow round about the throne, in sight like unto an **emerald**" (Revelation 4:3).

7. "Thou preparest a table before me in the presence of mine enemies: thou anointest my head with oil; my cup **runneth** over" (Psalm 23:5).

8. "And God called the light **Day**, and the darkness he called Night. And the evening and the morning were the first day" (Genesis 1:5).

9. "I am the **rose** of Sharon, and the lily of the valleys" (Song of Solomon 2:1).

10. "The vine is dried up, and the fig tree languisheth; the pomegranate tree, the palm tree also, and the **apple** tree, even all the trees of the field, are withered: because joy is withered away from the sons of men" (Joel 1:12).

11. "Jesus answered, Verily, verily, I say unto thee, Except a man be born of **water** and of the Spirit, he cannot enter into the kingdom of God" (John 3:5).

12. "Bring ye all the tithes into the storehouse, that there may be meat in mine house, and prove me now herewith, saith the LORD of hosts, if I will not open you the windows of heaven, and pour you out a blessing, that there shall not be room **enough** to receive it" (Malachi 3:10).

13. "But God led the people about, through the way of the wilderness of the **Red** sea: and the children of Israel went up harnessed out of the land of Egypt" (Exodus 13:18).

"Look," Enid finally said. "I have an idea of the way your aunt's mind worked and I think I figured this out. The first letter of each of these words spells d-r-e-s-s-e-r d-r-a-w-e-r."

"That must be the solution!" Reece exclaimed. "The inheritance has to be in a dresser drawer."

"Oh, Reece, this is the day we've been waiting for!" A question came to Enid's mind. "But which dresser? And which drawer?"

Reece stood, eager to finish the puzzle now that they were so close to its final solution. "It's still not too late. Let's go to her house and see."

So much anticipation filled the air in Reece's car as they made their way across town that even Connie didn't chatter during the ride. As soon as Reece parked, the three of them leapt out of the vehicle and hastened into the bungalow. Enid and Connie followed Reece into Agnes's bedroom.

As soon as they crossed the threshold, Reece let out a groan.

"What's the matter?" Enid asked.

Reece pointed to a pile of clothes heaped upon the bed. "She's already taken it."

Enid was puzzled. "Who's already taken what?"

"The dresser. My cousin has already taken the dresser as her inheritance." He pointed to the empty spot in the room where the dresser once stood. "She said Aunt Agnes promised it to her years ago, and I had no reason not to believe her. So I said she could take it. I had no idea it would be part of the puzzle."

Enid spotted Agnes's clothing, apparently discarded from the dresser, on the bed.

"Maybe the clue is in the middle of this pile of clothes," she suggested.

"Let's hope so."

Reece and Enid searched through the clothing, but found nothing that could be considered an inheritance.

"You don't think the dresser itself is the inheritance, do you?" Enid asked Reece.

"I wouldn't think so. For one, the final clue was 'dresser drawer,' not 'dresser.' And she wouldn't have given me something she had already promised to somebody else."

"So apparently, we still need to see the dresser itself. I'm sure she won't mind us taking a look in it," Enid observed. "Where is your cousin's house?"

"It's not at her house. It's at her niece's."

"Huh?"

Reece shook his head and let out a sigh. "Don't ask. It's too complicated."

"Wait," Enid said. "Maybe that's not the dresser in question. Before we bother her about looking through that dresser, let's eliminate any other piece of furniture in the house first."

"I think that's the sensible thing to do," Reece agreed, "but I have a feeling that's the one. Not only was it in Aunt Agnes's bedroom and was the one she used all the time, but it belonged to Grandma Parker."

"You're probably right, then."

"But since there's only one other dresser in the house, we may as well search it."

As expected, the search turned up nothing.

"Who has the dresser now?" Enid asked.

"Why didn't I write down her name? I guess I was taken by surprise when Martie—that's my cousin—called. I just didn't have the presence of mind to take down her niece's name."

"Her niece. So you don't even know her?"

"Nope. She's not part of the Parker clan. Now let me think." Reece tried to remember. "Martie did mention that she lives somewhere around here. Let me think. Her first name is unusual. A city name that starts with an S."

"Saratoga?"

"No. It was Southern. I do remember that much."

"Oh, thank goodness. My next guess was going to be Schenectady. It wasn't

Scarlett, was it?" Enid joked. "How about Shenandoah?"

He shook his head.

Enid thought for a moment longer. "Savannah?"

Reece snapped his fingers. "That's it! Savannah!"

"You know what? Somebody in my stamp club is named Savannah. It wouldn't be Savannah Hendley, would it?"

"That's it! Savannah Hendley."

"Great! Let's call her now."

❦

The modest home they approached minutes later looked welcoming. Connie immediately spotted a tricycle on the porch.

"Does she have a little girl? Can I play with her?"

"I'm not sure if it's a boy or a girl, but I'm sure you can play," Reece told her.

Since she was expecting them, Savannah was waiting at the door. Two girls who appeared to be only slightly older than Connie introduced themselves and immediately disappeared into the basement with their new friend. Meanwhile, Enid introduced Reece to the petite brunette, who in turn proved hospitable in offering refreshments.

"Thanks anyway, but Connie needs to get to bed soon," Reece said.

"Well, all right. Sorry you have to miss out on a slice of my cherry cheesecake." Savannah shrugged. "The girls will be happy to have dessert tomorrow."

"I'm sure they will," Enid remarked.

Savannah tilted her head toward the recreation room. "The dresser is in here." As she began walking, she apologized. "Hope you didn't mind us leaving all of your aunt's clothes on the bed. I just didn't know what else to do with them." The three of them entered the room. Savannah stopped in front of the mahogany dresser, which looked out of place among a wet bar, billiard table, and high-tech stereo system. "I really didn't know what to do with this behemoth either, but you know how Aunt Martie is." She didn't wait for a response. "You know, I have to tell you something. I wasn't surprised when you called wanting to see this."

"You weren't?"

"When I got the key to your aunt's house from her lawyer, he kept asking if you would know where to find this dresser if you needed it. I have to say, he was making me a little nervous. I didn't want to get in the middle of a family feud."

"That's understandable," Enid sympathized. "So you didn't see anything unusual when you got the dresser? Nothing valuable among Agnes's belongings?"

"I didn't look through it. I figured nothing in there was mine." Savannah motioned to it. "Help yourselves. And good luck."

"We know the drawers are empty, so maybe a message is taped somewhere on the dresser," Reece offered.

"Right," Enid said. "Somewhere that wouldn't be readily visible."

As they inspected the dresser, Reece mused aloud, "I almost wish I'd told

Martie she couldn't have the dresser. If it contains my inheritance, wouldn't it be a great reminder to have around?"

Enid stopped abruptly. "No, Reece. Be glad you gave her the dresser. Everything on Earth belongs to God anyway. Even if there was no inheritance, think about all the wonderful things the Lord has given you. Considering how many blessings you have, a piece of furniture is a small token to give away."

Had anyone else but Enid made this point, Reece would have felt ashamed. But Enid understood him and his heart. At that moment, he loved her more than he ever had before.

"You're right. I hope Martie enjoys this dresser in good health."

After inspecting the bottoms of the drawers and other obscure hiding places, they found nothing.

Enid sighed in despair. "Maybe we'll just have to call Agnes's lawyer and admit we've just plain given up." When Reece didn't answer, she knew he agreed. Letting out yet another defeated sigh, Enid picked up a drawer with intent of placing it back in its proper position. To her astonishment, she felt a strange dent in its right-hand side. She turned over the drawer so she could inspect the wood.

"What are you looking at?" Reece asked.

Enid showed him.

"How about that? One side is thicker than the other."

Enid inspected the drawer. "It sure is."

"This drawer must have a secret compartment. Let me see if I can figure out how to open it."

After inspecting it briefly, Reece took a dime out of his pocket. Using the coin, he placed it in the dent and gave it a little shove. The small door that had been hidden sprang open!

Enid took in a breath with such force that she let out a whistle. "This must be it! Your inheritance!"

Reece's hands shook as he retrieved an envelope from the compartment. "Reece" was written in Agnes's familiar writing. The envelope contained a letter, which Reece read aloud to Enid:

Dear Reece:

If you are reading this, you have solved the mystery and have found your inheritance. Congratulations! I hope you will enjoy the material possessions I have bequeathed to you. However, it is my prayer that I have left you with an inheritance far more valuable. Because I instructed you to read your Bible, it is my hope that one of these valuable things is the beginning of a personal relationship with our Lord and Savior, Jesus Christ. If you are reading this as a saved soul whose sins have been forgiven, then I know He must be smiling down from heaven right at this moment.

To nourish that new relationship, I trust you will read your Bible every day. Enid was instructed not to let you have the first envelope until you had finished reading the whole book, but I suspect she disobeyed. As you might have discovered, she is compassionate to a fault and would not have wanted to see you suffer the wait. I'm counting on her compassion, for it is my guess she has been an untold help to you in finding your salvation and in solving the mystery. In fact, I hope she is standing by your side now as you read this.

"She got her wish." Reece cut his glance sideways and saw that Enid's eyes were growing moist. "Are you all right? Do you want me to stop reading?"

Enid shook her head.

Reece continued:

In this envelope is the deed to my house. May you live in it for many, many happy years.

"The house!" Reece extracted the deed from the envelope and held it up for Enid to see. "I can't believe it. My very own house."

"And a lovely one it is," Enid observed. "With a beautiful yard for Connie, too." She placed her hand on his shoulder. "Congratulations. Now you won't have to rent the apartment anymore!"

"I know. This really is a blessing. With what I can save in rent each month, I'm sure I can put Connie through school." He sent up a silent thanks to the Lord before he read more:

You'll find a second, smaller envelope as well. This is my second gift to you, one that I hope will help make you happy for the rest of your life.

Lovingly,
Aunt Agnes

Reece wondered what was in the second envelope. "Here. You take a look at the deed. See what you think."

As Enid complied, Reece turned away from her and opened the small envelope. Inside was a ring with a generous diamond set in gold filigree. Agnes had included a note:

This is the diamond engagement ring that my mother wore. If you have come to love Enid and believe that the Lord has willed that the two of you be together, you know what to do.

"Yes, I do know what to do," Reece said.

"What to do about what?" Enid asked.

Before she could protest, Reece took her in his arms and kissed her tenderly. She responded with a loving embrace.

"Wow!" Enid said as the kiss ended. "Did she tell you to do that?"

"She didn't have to. I've been wanting to do that for quite some time." He broke away and showed her the ring. "This is Grandma Parker's engagement ring."

Enid's eyes widened. "It's gorgeous!"

"Do you have any idea what she wants me to do with this ring?" Reece didn't give Enid time to respond. "Her note said that if I love you, I should give you this. And Enid Garson, I know I love you."

"Oh, Reece, you have no idea how long I've been waiting to hear you say that." Tears of joy streamed down her face, but she didn't care. "I know I love you, too!"

Wordlessly, Reece placed the ring on her finger. The fit was perfect.

A Letter to Our Readers

Dear Readers:

In order that we might better contribute to your reading enjoyment, we would appreciate your taking a few minutes to respond to the following questions. When completed, please return to the following: Fiction Editor, Barbour Publishing, Inc., P.O. Box 719, Uhrichsville, OH 44683.

1. Did you enjoy reading *Virginia Hearts*?
   - ❑ Very much—I would like to see more books like this.
   - ❑ Moderately—I would have enjoyed it more if _____

_____

_____

2. What influenced your decision to purchase this book?
   (Check those that apply.)
   - ❑ Cover ❑ Back cover copy ❑ Title ❑ Price
   - ❑ Friends ❑ Publicity ❑ Other

3. Which story was your favorite?
   - ❑ *The Elusive Mr. Perfect* ❑ *The Thrill of the Hunt*
   - ❑ *More Than Friends*

4. Please check your age range:
   - ❑ Under 18 ❑ 18–24 ❑ 25–34
   - ❑ 35–45 ❑ 46–55 ❑ Over 55

5. How many hours per week do you read? _____

Name _____

Occupation _____

Address _____

City_____ State _____ Zip _____

E-mail_____

If you enjoyed

VIRGINIA

Hearts

then read:

Kentucky
CHANCES

*Three Brothers Find Romance
Far From Home*

Last Chance by Cathy Marie Hake
Chance Adventure by Kelly Eileen Hake
Chance of a Lifetime by Kelly Eileen Hake

If you enjoyed

VIRGINIA

then read:

SAN DIEGO

Four Sun-Kissed Romances

Love Is Patient by Cathy Marie Hake
Love Is Kind by Joyce Livingston
Love Worth Finding by Cathy Marie Hake
Love Worth Keeping by Joyce Livingston